An Olaf Stapledon Reader

An
Olaf
Stapledon
Reader

Edited by
Robert Crossley

Syracuse University Press

Copyright © 1997 by Syracuse University Press
Syracuse, New York 13244-5160

First Edition 1997

97 98 99 00 01 02 03   6 5 4 3 2 1

The paper used in this publication meets the minimum requirements of American National Standard for Information Sciences—Permanence of Paper for Printed Library Materials, ANSI Z39.48-1984. ∞™

Library of Congress Cataloging-in-Publication Data

Stapledon, Olaf, 1886–1950.
    An Olaf Stapledon reader / edited by Robert Crossley.—1st ed.
        p.   cm.
        Includes bibliographical references.
    ISBN 0-8156-2724-6 (cloth : alk. paper).—ISBN 0-8156-0430-0
(pbk. : alk. paper)
        1. Stapledon, Olaf, 1886–1950.   2. Authors, English—20th
century—Biography.   3. Science fiction—Authorship.   4. Science
fiction, English.   I. Crossley, Robert.
PR6037.T18Z87   1996
823'.912—dc20
[B]   96-31975

Manufactured in the United States of America

To Patrick A. McCarthy
An Opener of Eyes

Robert Crossley is professor of English at the University of Massachusetts, Boston. He is the author of *H. G. Wells* and *Olaf Stapledon: Speaking for the Future* (Syracuse University Press, 1994) and is the editor of *Talking Across the World: The Love Letters of Olaf Stapledon and Agnes Miller, 1913–1919.*

Contents

Memoirs and Meditations

Letters

Poems

Introduction

*"What purpose, you wonder, have I in burrowing up from oblivion
into your day?"*

Letters to the Future[1]

PROPHECY IS A COMMODITY with a notoriously uncertain shelf life. As
history unfolds, events conspire to turn forecasts moldy and to ensure
the prophet's irrelevance—or worse. Dante marched soothsayers
around the next-to-bottom circle of hell and punished their failures to
get the future right by twisting their necks around so that they must
walk looking backwards, weeping silently as they stare down at their
own asses. It is a gruesomely comic example of our readiness to humil-
iate unsuccessful prophets. Oblivion would be a kindlier punishment.

The fate of the successful prophet can be just as cruel. Its ancient
prototype is Cassandra's obligation to see her own disbelieved predictions of disaster come to pass. The modern manifestation of the Cassandra syndrome is H. G. Wells. He made a career of anticipating the
future of civilization—and its future discontents. All through his life
he constructed glorious images of things to come but also kept issuing
warnings of impending catastrophe if humanity failed to make a rational plan for the future. To his dismay, people embraced the imagery
and shunned the warnings. Hence, his scalding comment in old age
that his epitaph should read, "God damn you all—I told you so."[2]

The prophet is engaged in one of the riskiest of all human ventures. There is a great public appetite for forecasts—whether in the
vulgar form of New Year's Day crystal-gazing by self-styled psychics,
or in the think tanks and conferences sponsored by the World Future
Society. Those prophecies intended to make people feel good about the
future (the predictions of supply-side economics as applied to the

1. Olaf Stapledon, "Letters to the Future," ed. Robert Crossley, in *The Legacy of Olaf
Stapledon*, ed. Patrick A. McCarthy, Charles Elkins, and Martin Harry Greenberg (New
York: Greenwood, 1989), 105.
2. The story of Wells and his epitaph is told by Ernest Barker in *Age and Youth*
(London: Oxford Univ. Press, 1953), 108.

world's fisheries are a salient example) produce a legacy of bitterness and betrayal when their optimism proves unfounded or excessive. But since much prophecy is critical of the way things are and pessimistic about the way things will be, the prophet is bound to arouse passionate feelings and fears. For all those eager to see him proved right, there are always twice as many ready to applaud if he falls on his face.

What really makes people nervous about prophets is that they tend inconveniently to be moralists. Like the ancient Jews on Mount Zion whose prophecies were directed to reforming a wayward people, like the Greek priestesses who inhaled the vapors at Delphi and issued enigmas, like the fictional Foretellers in Ursula K. LeGuin's *The Left Hand of Darkness* who turn the desire for answers into the obligation to make choices, prophets are troublemakers. Someone will always have an interest in seeing them eliminated, disgraced, banished, parodied, ignored, confined to an institution, or quietly sunk into oblivion.

Olaf Stapledon, though sometimes as enigmatic as a Delphic oracle, was neither as noisy nor as self-assured as his mentor Wells. "I am always at loggerheads with myself," he wrote in the autobiographical meditation called "The Core." It is as much a characterizing of the philosophical temperament as it is an assessment of his own personality. Sadly but without public protest, he accepted his fate as a forsaken prophet. Oblivion was already settling on him as he turned sixty in 1946—the year of Wells's death—when he began writing a set of unfinished "letters to the future." In the first of four letters, addressed to his great-grandson, he depicted himself as a long-forgotten mole tunneling up at the end of the twentieth century, some fifty years after his death, with a few final words of posthumous wisdom. Those imagined fifty years have now nearly expired, and this *Reader* is designed to perform a somewhat larger excavation than that contemplated by the old mole. It puts on exhibit a generous sampling of Stapledon's prophetic utterances in a variety of genres and voices, ranging in time from his student days in 1908 to the day before his death in 1950. A few of the selections in this book were famous in the author's lifetime and remain well known to readers of his fiction; others have now been neglected for decades; still others appeared in print in obscure places and were encountered by few readers, or were never published at all until now.

Stapledon was too much the skeptic to embrace either religious mysticism or secular prophecy wholeheartedly. Calling himself a "pious agnostic," he generated paradox in everything he wrote. He was iconoclast and moralist, innovator and traditionalist, idealist and fearmonger, teacher and Doubting Thomas. He was acutely aware of his own limitations as a cultural prophet and in his later years often ruefully commented on his failure to anticipate Hitler in his most brilliant work of future-fiction, *Last and First Men*. It is easy to draw up an inventory of similar omissions and mistakes, including his overestimate of the durability of the Leninist experiment in Russia. But on that score, at least, Stapledon has had plenty of company. More remarkably, as the second Christian millennium comes to a close, a great many of Stapledon's sibilline visions (of genetic engineering, of the Americanization of the planet, of the power of mass media, of pan-Europeanism, of reckless consumption of natural resources, of the dead-end of an exclusively materialist philosophy, to name a few) seem more potent and relevant than ever.

His status as prophet may actually be enhanced by his insistence, starting with the preface to *Last and First Men* and continuing through the rest of his career, that his real aim all along was mythmaking rather than prediction. "The future cannot be seen till it is brought into existence by choice," Stapledon once observed.[3] In making myths about the future he was always less interested in pronouncing on what *will* happen than in imagining consequences. The Stapledonian prophet is visionary but not clairvoyant: "We are not to set up as historians attempting to look ahead instead of backwards."[4] Such ambition leads inevitably to the perverse fate of the Dantean soothsayer. The true prophet does not foretell the future but aims to increase consciousness in the act of choosing a future. When he wrote his letters to the future in the 1940s Stapledon was not worrying whether he would get the future right but whether those in the future fifty years on would have gotten themselves right.

In January 1950 a newspaper columnist listed Olaf Stapledon as one of ten thinkers and artists who would still be talked about in the next century.[5] To place that name in the company of Einstein, Diego Rivera, and Stravinsky was a brave gesture for a journalist in 1950, the year Stapledon died at the age of sixty-four, when most of his books were out of print and his reputation was in eclipse. Now, as the new century looms, it is time to be reading and talking about Stapledon again.

•   •   •

The career of Olaf Stapledon was full of false starts, detours, and breakdowns. On paper his background looks exotic and privileged:

---

3. Olaf Stapledon, *Philosophy and Living* (Harmondsworth, Eng.: Penguin, 1939), 2:412.

4. W. Olaf Stapledon, *Last and First Men: A Story of the Near and Far Future* (London: Methuen, 1930), v.

5. N. H. Partridge, "History Is Theirs—5," *News Chronicle* [London], 24 January 1950, 2.

born in 1886 to a bright, feminist disciple of Ruskin, a childhood in imperial Egypt, top of his class at boarding school, an Oxford degree, a father who ran one of the great Liverpool shipping firms. It sounds like a ticket to success and comfort, but the route Stapledon traveled was neither smooth nor straight. His mother's intelligence, undermined by poor health and frustrated ambition, became a bossiness that her son found stifling; the Egyptian years were marked by parental discord, and the family was broken up for ten years; the boarding school was the upstart and eccentric Abbotsholme, not posh, pedigreed Eton; from Balliol College, Oxford, he took away a second-class, not an honors, degree; and his father's upper-middle-class position was achieved only after a long climb up from clerk and shipping agent. "I am no highbrow," Stapledon would write in his maturity, "or only a very imperfect one. But bourgeois I certainly am, in up-bringing and in present circumstances."[6] He was never embarrassed to say that he was from Liverpool rather than from London; indeed, it was his boast. But he felt guilty that he had not accomplished enough to justify what he saw as the unusual head start he had been given in life.

But the truth was he always preferred visions to practical ventures. Quite literally, his head was in the stars from his youngest years, when he would survey the heavens by telescope from a balcony in Port Said or when he recorded in his diary a few days before he was to take his university entry examinations: "I did not get to sleep till midnight owing to contemplation of the stars."[7] As a student of European history at Oxford he made a special study of Joan of Arc and became fascinated by her celebrated "voices"—the mark of either a visionary, a charlatan, or a madwoman. He favored the first of these alternatives, for Joan and eventually for himself. But one cannot put "visionary" on a resumé.

Before and after World War I Stapledon found employment as a shipping clerk, a tutor for the fledgling Workers' Educational Association, and a social worker in Liverpool. Writing was a private sideline, and he had very few successes in getting his work published until the mid-1920s. As a young man he thought he was destined to be a poet. His earliest book, *Latter-Day Psalms*, was superficially modernist, linking theological skepticism to socialism in verse that was open in form. Appearing a few months into World War I, *Latter-Day Psalms* sank almost without a trace.

During the 1920s, after war service with the Quaker Ambulance Unit, he aimed for an academic career, earning a Ph.D. in philosophy

---

6. Olaf Stapledon, *Waking World* (London: Methuen, 1934), 11.

7. Robert Crossley, *Olaf Stapledon: Speaking for the Future* (Syracuse: Syracuse Univ. Press, 1994), 61.

and publishing scholarly articles, reviews, and a book on ethics in the hope of securing a lectureship. That position never materialized. He continued to earn a skimpy living teaching for the W.E.A. and finally, when he was forty-four, a long work of prose fiction emerged from the reclusive workshop in his attic where he spent his spare time. *Last and First Men*, as he ultimately called the book when it appeared in late 1930, was a surprising success—and it defined, and shadowed, the rest of his career over the following twenty years.

Throughout the 1930s Stapledon was a minor celebrity in England, and he had a minute following in the United States as well. Active in a variety of political causes and organizations, he also began to emerge from literary isolation, meeting other writers like H. G. Wells, Naomi Mitchison, L. H. Myers, J. B. Priestley, and Arthur Koestler. He had a string of critical successes, including *Odd John* (1935), *Star Maker* (1937), and the book that sold more copies during his life than anything else he wrote, the two-volume *Philosophy and Living* (1939). Just before the outbreak of World War II *Last and First Men*, which had already become a legendary book, was issued as one of the first ten volumes in the new, groundbreaking paperback series known as Pelicans. In the space of ten years he had gone from being an unknown adult-education worker on Merseyside to an author whose works of fiction were regularly described as masterpieces in the press and who was being read and debated and celebrated by a select group of readers that included Doris Lessing and Winston Churchill, J. B. S. Haldane and Arthur C. Clarke, John Dover Wilson and Bertrand Russell.

Then came the second war. Paper was in scant supply for books, and the shortage became a defining measure of which authors were in the first rank and which were not. Wells's earlier books, for instance, remained in print, and his new books always appeared promptly; Stapledon did not have that kind of star power and, working without an agent, he had little leverage with publishers. Although reviewers had lionized him in the thirties, he had never had a best seller. Now it became a struggle to get into print, even at Methuen where his long-time editor E. V. Rieu continued to support him. His difficulties were compounded by Rieu's queasiness over the contents of his best work of fiction in the 1940s, *Sirius*, which took two years and some minor censoring before Secker and Warburg brought it out in 1944. Meanwhile, all his famous books from the previous decade went out of print and were not reissued. By the war's end he was writing morosely and in the past tense of a career that "has been a texture of good luck and bad management."[8]

Stapledon's literary confidence after 1945 fragmented still more,

8. "Letters to the Future," 107.

and his good luck ran dry. Devoting himself, passionately but with characteristic ambivalence, to political work in the peace movement that emerged in response to the new cold war, he was able to write the greatly underrated epistolary novella *The Flames* and to finish his final novel, begun during World War II, *A Man Divided*. Neither was a commercial success. At his death in 1950 he left a nearly complete manuscript of philosophical *pensées*, to which his widow assigned the title *The Opening of the Eyes* when she edited it for publication. But Stapledon was unable to concentrate his energies in his last four years to complete most of the book-length projects he contemplated: an imaginary biography of the ancestors of Jesus; a collection of stories on paranormal phenomena; a group of ten dialogues, in which representative contemporary "types" (a revolutionary, a scientist, a capitalist, a mystic, and so on) would be interrogated. When he suffered a fatal heart attack on 6 September 1950 his name-recognition had dwindled almost to zero.

●   ●   ●

Stapledon's place in modern thought has not been entirely lost, thanks to his four greatest works of fiction: *Last and First Men, Odd John, Star Maker,* and *Sirius*. Each of them offers portents for the future that are also parables about the human present. When these books first appeared between 1930 and 1944 they were recognized by discerning reviewers as strikingly original philosophical fictions, with a superficial resemblance to the scientific romances of Wells but so unprecedented in form and conception that readers hardly knew how to respond to them. The term "science fiction" was not in wide use in England when Stapledon began publishing, and only late in life did he retrospectively, and somewhat reluctantly, attach that label to his most famous creations.

But it has been the science fiction community—its readers and especially its writers, including Arthur C. Clarke, Brian Aldiss, Robert Silverberg, Gregory Benford, and Kim Stanley Robinson—that has ensured Stapledon's survival. While the literary academy has been energetically revising its canon of great writers, and sometimes questioning the notion of a canon altogether, science fiction scholars have been carefully defining the origins and traditions, and designating the touchstones, of this most distinctive modern literary form. Among the few indispensable early canonical figures in science fiction on whom virtually everyone agrees are Mary Shelley, H. G. Wells, and Olaf Stapledon. And although Stapledon's name is the least widely recognized of these founders of the genre, for the past thirty years his four most famous books have been continuously in print in the United States (but only intermittently in print in Great Britain). His international standing continues to grow, and in the past quarter century French, Spanish, German, Japanese, Bulgarian, Italian, Dutch, Finnish, Hungarian, and Swedish readers have been able to find a number of his books and stories available in their own languages.

Stapledon's most celebrated fictions, *Last and First Men* and *Star Maker,* are notoriously difficult—variously described as titanic, prodigious, monumental, even, not very euphonically, Michelangelisque. "His imagination," Brian Aldiss has written, "is a Niagara."[9] This anthology cannot replace the experience of reading Stapledon's masterpieces in their entirety, but it does let new readers wade at their leisure before taking the plunge over the falls. For such readers the excerpts from the "big" novels will suggest the distinctive qualities of Stapledon's creative imagination and may serve as previews of challenges and pleasures to come. Those who already know some of Stapledon's major works may want to explore the tributaries that feed into the great cataracts of his fictional masterpieces. The short fiction, essays, broadcasts, poems, letters, and memoirs in this volume allow a reader to grasp his intellectual framework, to find the patterns and the consistencies in his thinking and writing, and to see how the philosophical insights and questions for which he has been renowned are played out in minor keys and with homelier concerns. Even those who have read a great deal of Stapledon will find much that is new to them: magazine pieces that appeared long ago and are now obtainable only in research libraries, letters never before printed, some essays and memoirs that have existed only in manuscript. As will become evident, nearly everything he wrote features portents and parables; they are the hallmarks of his imagination at least as much as the grand time scales, anatomical oddities, philosophical puzzles, and disembodied abstractions that have made his science fiction unique and influential.

This *Reader* offers an introduction to Stapledon with a sampling of several of his most renowned accomplishments in fiction: the tragic story of the winged human beings of the far future, the "Seventh Men" among the eighteen human species chronicled in *Last and First Men;* a slyly comic depiction of class distinctions on a distant world from *Star Maker;* and the chapter in *Sirius* that takes a superhuman sheepdog on an irreverent tour of Cambridge University. But brilliant as these works are—the truest testaments to Stapledon's genius as a prophet and fabulist—they are not unique or isolated achievements. One of his

9. Brian W. Aldiss, "Foreword" to Crossley, *Olaf Stapledon,* xiii.

great books, the 1947 novella *The Flames*, has been out of print in England for almost half a century, despite the accolades it has gathered from readers as various as the writer Robert Silverberg, the literary critic Patrick McCarthy, and the philosopher Stephen Clark.[10] Now other readers can discover for themselves the astonishing richness of *The Flames*, along with other shorter fiction, including the delicately hopeful utopia of "Old Man in New World," the Ovidian fantasy of "The Man Who Became a Tree," and the piercingly self-referential "The Peak and the Town." In addition, this *Reader* also includes a brief, Swiftian satire on sexual prudery out of *Last Men in London*, a chilling excerpt from Stapledon's least-known future history, *Darkness and the Light*, and the earliest surviving version of *Odd John*, a chapter excised from the manuscript of *Last Men in London* and later expanded into the full-length story of a grotesque young superman.

The second part of the anthology, a selection of essays and talks, starts with a very early student essay on eugenics, one of the scientific and ethical issues that most often engaged Stapledon's imagination as a fiction writer. There are two broadcasts made in the 1930s ("The Remaking of Man," "Machinery and Labour") that should alter the common misimpression of Stapledon as an aloof intellectual. He had, in fact, a gift for making erudite subjects accessible to a great variety of people, and his populism was more than just an abstract commitment. At the same time, Stapledon was a serious philosopher—the most important philosopher to emerge from Merseyside, as Stephen Clark has argued.[11] His "Thoughts on the Modern Spirit" written shortly after he received his Ph.D. in philosophy at the age of forty, the excerpt on mysticism from *Philosophy and Living*, and the legendary address delivered to the British Interplanetary Society near the end of his life provide examples of the range and acuity of Stapledon's philosophical writing. His technical work as a philosopher also had a popular side, in journalistic pieces and talks in which he commented on current events and issues of social and political import. An untitled newspaper article on the Shetland Islanders (to which I have assigned the title "On Cultural Diversity") is a strikingly prescient analysis of what is now known as multiculturalism. The essay on Atomic Power was written in the months just after the atomic bombings of Japan when some journalists remembered that Stapledon had imagined the

10. Bob Silverberg, "Cosmic Conflagration," *Fantastic Worlds* 2 (Spring 1954):12–17; Patrick A. McCarthy, *Olaf Stapledon* (New York: Twayne, 1982), 110–15; Stephen R. L. Clark, "Olaf Stapledon (1886–1950)," *Interdisciplinary Science Reviews* 18 (1993): 115–16.

11. Professor Clark made this claim in "The Two Faces of Philosophy," his inaugural lecture on assuming the Chair of Philosophy at Liverpool University in 1985.

use of such weapons fifteen years earlier in *Last and First Men*. In "Mankind at the Crossroads," a lecture given in France after World War II, he anticipated by forty years a pan-European union. In the 1930s and 1940s he wrote and reviewed for *Scrutiny, The London Mercury, The New Statesman*, and other periodicals, often articulating his own literary principles. "Escapism in Literature," "Literature and the Unity of Man," and a review of an H. G. Wells novel show off that side of Stapledon's work.

Like most novelists, Stapledon transformed aspects of his own experience into fiction, but as he grew older he also wrote more straightforwardly and personally about himself and his family. Some of this writing is offered in the third section of the *Reader*, "Memoirs and Meditations." The first selection, a recently discovered newspaper article written while he was driving an ambulance in France in 1916, is one of his earliest publications. He mined his own youth and young adulthood for episodes in his second and most personal work of fiction, *Last Men in London*, from which an excerpt based on his own early scientific studies appears. Stapledon's greatest burst of autobiographical inspiration occurred in the 1940s as he approached the age of sixty. The manuscript of "Fields Within Fields," a memoir called "The Core," and an "interlude" from his 1946 fantasy *Death Into Life* each reflect on aspects of Stapledon's personal past, present, and future. This section concludes with a meditation on the night sky from his posthumous *Opening of the Eyes*—the very same subject of his 1916 newspaper article, though treated here with a matchless grace of expression and intellectual elegance.

Stapledon was a patient, thoughtful, and prodigious correspondent, but few of his letters—apart from his correspondence with H. G. Wells and the World War I courtship letters—have ever been printed.[12] Relatively few letters outside those written to family members have surfaced, and probably the most significant body of letters with literary interest—the vast correspondence with the novelist L. H. Myers between 1931 and 1944—was destroyed. The *Reader* offers a small sample of letters written to people with whom Stapledon discussed artistic, theological, and philosophical topics. In addition to exchanges with other creative writers (Wells, Naomi Mitchison, Virginia Woolf), he enjoyed arguing metaphysics with the popular philosopher and broadcaster C. E. M. Joad, exploring the paranormal with the art histo-

---

12. See "The Letters of Olaf Stapledon and H. G. Wells, 1931–1942," ed. Robert Crossley, in *Science Fiction Dialogues*, ed. Gary Wolfe (Chicago: Academy Chicago, 1982), 27–57, and *Talking Across the World: The Love Letters of Olaf Stapledon and Agnes Miller, 1913–1919*, ed. Robert Crossley (Hanover, N.H.: Univ. Press of New England, 1987).

rian Aage Marcus, and discussing the visual arts with the painter Fay Pomerance. His letter on religion to the illustrator Gwyneth Alban-Davis was the last thing he ever wrote.

The final section of this *Reader* is given over to Stapledon's poetry. As a young man he aspired to make his mark as a poet, and his earliest —and now rarest—book was *Latter-Day Psalms*. Although his poetry fell far short of his ambition, even the creaky early psalms clearly articulate some of the important themes that he would treat more confidently and durably in his fiction of the 1930s. In the 1920s he made a last big push as a poet, before shifting gears at the end of the decade when he began writing *Last and First Men*. In 1925 he carefully assembled a handwritten and hand-sewn volume of all the poems he wanted to save, including some revised versions of his favorite pieces from *Latter-Day Psalms*. Two of those revisions from *Verse by WOS* are printed alongside the original versions, to indicate both the growth of Stapledon as a writer in a ten-year period as well as his evident limitations in verse. He continued to write poems up through 1940, including his last-published "Paradox," dramatizing unresolved theological doubts, but his most ambitious and interesting poems were those in the never completed cycle he gave the title *Metaphysical Posters*. Composed in the later 1920s, a few of these poems, somewhat revised, appeared in *Last Men in London*, but most have remained in manuscript until now. They were stimulated, Stapledon claimed, by the writings of the astronomer James Jeans and consisted of two "volleys," the first offering telescopic visions of the stars in relation to the human world, and the second plunging into the submicroscopic realities of germ cells and atoms. Although the literary merits of *Metaphysical Posters* should not be exaggerated, the phenomenon of successful science-fiction poetry is so rare (the American Frederick Turner's *Genesis*, an epic on terraforming Mars, represents the great exception) that there is some reason to dust off a few of the pieces from *Metaphysical Posters* and give them an audience for the first time.

In the past fifteen years there has been an accelerating revival of attention to the life and work of Olaf Stapledon. Four book-length critical studies, a bibliography, a biography, and a volume of letters have appeared. Ph.D. dissertations have been written. New writers continue to claim him as an intellectual model. Brian Aldiss has crusaded tirelessly for his rightful place in twentieth-century literary history. For most well-read people, however, the estimate of Stapledon's value as writer and thinker must be taken on faith, on the authority of "specialists," or be based on the very few works that have remained relatively easy to find. There is not yet a collected edition of Stapledon, but with this anthology readers can at last begin to see and judge for themselves.

•   •   •

The rights to both previously published and unpublished work by Olaf Stapledon are held by the author's heirs. I am grateful to the Estate for granting permission to make this collection. Stapledon's literary manuscripts, from which a number of items for this *Reader* have been transcribed, are held by the Sydney Jones Library, University of Liverpool. I thank the Special Collections Librarian, Katy Hooper, for assistance in consulting the manuscripts and for her diligent curating of these essential materials. For word processing of *The Flames* I am indebted, once again, to Joyce Carbone. Judi Roberts, Assistant Dean of the College of Arts and Sciences, rescued my project in the middle of one of the periodic budget crises inflicted on the University of Massachusetts at Boston by finding me an ancient but gratefully accepted computer on whose hard disk many of the texts in the *Reader* found temporary lodging. Patrick A. McCarthy and Curtis C. Smith read a draft of this anthology and contributed many helpful suggestions that have influenced the shape and content of the final version. Finally, and as always, I express my appreciation to my wife and son, Monica McAlpine and Andrew McAlpine Crossley, for good-humored encouragement and more than my share of computer time.

A Note on Texts

PREVIOUSLY PUBLISHED TEXTS anthologized in this *Reader* are based on the first editions. Stapledon was an erratic speller who was not always well served by his publishers, especially some smaller presses and journals which did not have uniformly high standards for copyediting. In cases of obvious misspelling or error in the printed version I have silently emended the texts, making use where possible of Stapledon's typescript or manuscript to verify the author's intention. Previously unpublished texts in this anthology are based on Stapledon's final typescript or manuscript (including corrections in the author's hand). Throughout the *Reader* punctuation of quotations has been made consistent with American conventions. All the manuscripts and typescripts used for this edition are in the Stapledon Archive at the Sydney Jones Library, University of Liverpool, with the following exceptions: "The Remaking of Man" and "Machinery and Labour" (British Broadcasting Corporation Archives, Reading); letters to H. G. Wells (Wells Archive, University of Illinois); letters to Naomi Mitchison (Mitchison Papers, National Library of Scotland); letter to Virginia Woolf (Woolf Collection, University of Sussex Library); letters to Fay Pomerance and to Gwyneth Alban-Davis (privately held).

Fiction

The Flying Men
from *Last and First Men*

Last and First Men, *published in 1930, plots the course of the human species from the post–World War I era to the imminent destruction of the last human outpost in the solar system on Neptune two billion years from now. In the course of this history of the future, the narrator — a "last man" who is in telepathic possession of the mind of a "first man," Olaf Stapledon — traces the rises and fallings of humanity through eighteen different mutations, some the product of natural evolution, some the result of human intervention. One of the most poignant of Stapledon's inventions is the briefly told history of the "seventh men," a winged species engineered by their predecessor "sixth men," the first humans to achieve a high level of civilization on the hot island-world of Venus. Stapledon called* Last and First Men *"an essay in myth-creation," and the career of the seventh men provides an exquisite variation on the ancient myth of human flight. The story of Icarus is here generalized to an entire community, an entire species. Earlier chapters of* Last and First Men *depict the flying rituals of citizens of the First World State in the era just before the collapse of the culture of the First Men. But the history of the Seventh Men is the supreme example of the theme of flight. The diminutive, carefree flying men are unsurpassed embodiments of the beauty, obsession, and tragedy of the human desire for wings, and nowhere else in the book is there such a pointed contrast between biological and mechanical forms of aviation. A historian by training, Stapledon often echoed the actual past in his imagined futures; the climax of this episode 700 million years hence recalls the heroism of the vastly outnumbered Jews at the Masada fortress in 73* A.D. *who chose mass suicide in preference to conquest by the besieging army of Rome.*

THROUGHOUT THEIR CAREER the Sixth Men had often been fascinated by the idea of flight. The bird was again and again their most sacred symbol. Their monotheism was apt to be worship not of a god-man, but of a god-bird, conceived now as the divine sea-eagle, winged with power, now as the giant swift, winged with mercy, now as a disembod-

3

ied spirit of air, and once as the bird-god that became man to endow the human race with flight, physical and spiritual.

It was inevitable that flight should obsess man on Venus, for the planet afforded but a cramping home for groundlings; and the riotous efflorescence of avian species shamed man's pedestrian habit. When in due course the Sixth Men attained knowledge and power comparable to that of the First Men at their height, they invented flying-machines of various types. Many times, indeed, mechanical flight was rediscovered and lost again with the downfall of civilization. But at its best it was regarded only as a makeshift. And when at length, with the advance of the biological sciences, the Sixth Men were in a position to influence the human organism itself, they determined to produce a true flying man. Many civilizations strove vainly for this result, sometimes half-heartedly, sometimes with religious earnestness. Finally the most enduring and brilliant of all the civilizations of the Sixth Men actually attained the goal.

The Seventh Men were pigmies, scarcely heavier than the largest of terrestrial flying birds. Through and through they were organized for flight. A leathery membrane spread from the foot to the tip of the immensely elongated and strengthened "middle" finger. The three "outer" fingers, equally elongated, served as ribs to the membrane; while the index and thumb remained free for manipulation. The body assumed the stream-lines of a bird, and was covered with a deep quilt of feathery wool. This, and the silken down of the flight-membranes, varied greatly from individual to individual in colouring and texture. On the ground the Seventh Men walked much as other human beings, for the flight-membranes were folded close to the legs and body, and hung from the arms like exaggerated sleeves. In flight the legs were held extended as a flattened tail, with the feet locked together by the big toes. The breastbone was greatly developed as a keel, and as a base for the muscles of flight. The other bones were hollow, for lightness, and their internal surfaces were utilized as supplementary lungs. For, like the birds, these flying men had to maintain a high rate of oxidation. A state which others would regard as fever was normal to them.

Their brains were given ample tracts for the organization of prowess in flight. In fact, it was found possible to equip the species with a system of reflexes for aerial balance, and a true, though artificial, instinctive aptitude for flight, and interest in flight. Compared with their makers their brain volume was of necessity small, but their whole neural system was very carefully organized. Also it matured rapidly, and was extremely facile in the acquirement of new modes of activity. This was very desirable; for the individual's natural life period was but fifty years, and in most cases it was deliberately cut short by some impossible feat at about forty, or whenever the symptoms of old age began to be felt.

Of all human species these bat-like Flying Men, the Seventh Men, were probably the most care-free. Gifted with harmonious physique and gay temperament, they came into a social heritage well adapted to their nature. There was no occasion for them, as there had often been for some others, to regard the world as fundamentally hostile to life, or themselves as essentially deformed. Of quick intelligence in respect of daily personal affairs and social organization, they were untroubled by the insatiable lust of understanding. Not that they were an unintellectual race, for they soon formulated a beautifully systematic account of experience. They clearly perceived, however, that the perfect sphere of their thought was but a bubble adrift in chaos. Yet it was an elegant bubble. And the system was true, in its own gay and frankly insincere manner, true as significant metaphor, not literally true. What more, it was asked, could be expected of human intellect? Adolescents were encouraged to study the ancient problems of philosophy, for no reason but to convince themselves of the futility of probing beyond the limits of the orthodox system. "Prick the bubble of thought at any point," it was said, "and you shatter the whole of it. And since thought is one of the necessities of human life, it must be preserved."

Natural science was taken over from the earlier species with half-contemptuous gratitude, as a necessary means of sane adjustment to the environment. Its practical applications were valued as the ground of the social order; but as the millennia advanced, and society approached that remarkable perfection and stability which was to endure for many million years, scientific inventiveness became less and less needful, and science itself was relegated to the infant schools. History also was given in outline during childhood, and subsequently ignored.

This curiously sincere intellectual insincerity was due to the fact that the Seventh Men were chiefly concerned with matters other than abstract thought. It is difficult to give to members of the first human species an inkling of the great preoccupation of these Flying Men. To say that it was flight would be true, yet far less than the truth. To say that they sought to live dangerously and vividly, to crowd as much experience as possible into each moment, would again be a caricature of the truth. On the physical plane, indeed, "the universe of flight" with all the variety of peril and skill afforded by a tempestuous atmosphere, was every individual's chief medium of self-expression. Yet it was not flight itself, but the spiritual aspect of flight, which obsessed the species.

In the air and on the ground the Seventh Men were different beings. Whenever they exercised themselves in flight they suffered a remarkable change of spirit. Much of their time had to be spent on the ground, since most of the work upon which civilization rested was impossible in the air. Moreover, life in the air was life at high pressure, and necessitated spells of recuperation on the ground. In their pedestrian phase the Seventh Men were sober folk, mildly bored, yet in the main cheerful, humorously impatient of the drabness and irk of pedestrian affairs, but ever supported by memory and anticipation of the vivid life of the air. Often they were tired, after the strain of that other life, but seldom were they despondent or lazy. Indeed, in the routine of agriculture and industry they were industrious as the wingless ants. Yet they worked in a strange mood of attentive absentmindedness; for their hearts were ever in the air. So long as they could have frequent periods of aviation, they remained bland even on the ground. But if for any reason such as illness they were confined to the ground for a long period, they pined, developed acute melancholia, and died. Their makers had so contrived them that with the onset of any very great pain or misery their hearts should stop. Thus they were to avoid all serious distress. But, in fact, this merciful device worked only on the ground. In the air they assumed a very different and more heroic nature, which their makers had not foreseen, though indeed it was a natural consequence of their design.

In the air the flying man's heart beat more powerfully. His temperature rose. His sensation became more vivid and more discriminate, his intelligence more agile and penetrating. He experienced a more intense pleasure or pain in all that happened to him. It would not be true to say that he became more emotional; rather the reverse, if by emotionality is meant enslavement to the emotions. For the most remarkable feature of the aerial phase was that this enhanced power of appreciation was dispassionate. So long as the individual was in the air, whether in lonely struggle with the storm, or in the ceremonial ballet with sky-darkening hosts of his fellows; whether in the ecstatic love dance with a sexual partner, or in solitary and meditative circlings far above the world; whether his enterprise was fortunate, or he found himself dismembered by the hurricane, and crashing to death; always the gay and the tragic fortunes of his own person were regarded equally with detached aesthetic delight. Even when his dearest companion was mutilated or destroyed by some aerial disaster, he exulted; though also he would give his own life in the hope of effecting a rescue. But very soon after he had returned to the ground he would be overwhelmed with grief, would strive vainly to recapture the lost vision, and would perhaps die of heart failure.

Even when, as happened occasionally in the wild climate of Venus, a whole aerial population was destroyed by some world-wide atmospheric tumult, the few broken survivors, so long as they could remain in the air, exulted. And actually while at length they sank exhausted toward the ground, toward certain disillusionment and death, they laughed inwardly. Yet an hour after they had alighted, their constitution would be changed, their vision lost. They would remember only the horror of the disaster, and the memory would kill them.

No wonder the Seventh Men grudged every moment that was passed on the ground. While they were in the air, of course, the prospect of a pedestrian interlude, or indeed of endless pedestrianism, though in a manner repugnant, would be accepted with unswerving gaiety; but while they were on the ground, they grudged bitterly to be there. Early in the career of the species the proportion of aerial to terrestrial hours was increased by a biological invention. A minute food-plant was produced which spent the winter rooted in the ground, and the summer adrift in the sunlit upper air, engaged solely in photosynthesis. Henceforth the populations of the Flying Men were able to browse upon the bright pastures of the sky, like swallows. As the ages passed, material civilization became more and more simplified. Needs which could not be satisfied without terrestrial labour tended to be outgrown. Manufactured articles became increasingly rare. Books were no longer written or read. In the main, indeed, they were no longer necessary; but to some extent their place was taken by verbal tradition and discussion, in the upper air. Of the arts, music, spoken lyric and epic verse, and the supreme art of winged dance, were constantly practised. The rest vanished. Many of the sciences inevitably faded into tradition; yet the true scientific spirit was preserved in a very exact meteorology, a sufficient biology, and a human psychology surpassed only by the second and fifth species at their height. None of these sciences, however, was taken very seriously, save in its practical applications. For instance, psychology explained the ecstasy of flight very neatly as a febrile and "irrational" beatitude. But no one was disconcerted by this theory; for every one, while on the wing, felt it to be merely an amusing half-truth.

The social order of the Seventh Men was in essence neither utilitarian, nor humanistic, nor religious, but aesthetic. Every act and every institution were to be justified as contributing to the perfect form of the community. Even social prosperity was conceived as merely the medium in which beauty should be embodied, the beauty, namely, of vivid individual lives harmoniously related. Yet not only for the individual, but even for the race itself (so the wise insisted), death on the wing was more excellent than prolonged life on the ground. Better, far better, would be racial suicide than a future of pedestrianism. Yet though both the individual and the race were conceived as instrumental to objective beauty, there was nothing religious, in any ordinary sense, in this conviction. The Seventh Men were completely without interest in the universal and the unseen. The beauty which they sought to create was ephemeral and very largely sensuous. And they were well content that it should be so. Personal immortality, said a dying sage, would be as tedious as an endless song. Equally so with the race. The lovely flame, of which we all are members, must die, he said, must die; for without death she would fall short of beauty.

For close on a hundred million terrestrial years this aerial society endured with little change. On many of the islands throughout this period stood even yet a number of the ancient pylons, though repaired almost beyond recognition. In these nests the men and women of the seventh species slept through the long Venerian nights, crowded like roosting swallows. By day the same great towers were sparsely peopled with those who were serving their turn in industry, while in the fields and on the sea others laboured. But most were in the air. Many would be skimming the ocean, to plunge, gannet-like, for fish. Many, circling over land or sea, would now and again stoop like hawks upon the wild-fowl which formed the chief meat of the species. Others, forty or fifty thousand feet above the waves, where even the plentiful atmosphere of Venus was scarcely capable of supporting them, would be soaring, circling, sweeping, for pure joy of flight. Others, in the calm and sunshine of high altitudes, would be hanging effortlessly upon some steady up-current of air for meditation and the rapture of mere percipience. Not a few love-intoxicated pairs would be entwining their courses in aerial patterns, in spires, cascades, and true-love knots of flight, presently to embrace and drop ten thousand feet in bodily union. Some would be driving hither and thither through the green mists of vegetable particles, gathering the manna in their open mouths. Companies, circling together, would be discussing matters social or aesthetic; others would be singing together, or listening to recitative epic verse. Thousands, gathering in the sky like migratory birds, would perform massed convolutions, reminiscent of the vast mechanical aerial choreography of the First World State, but more vital and expressive, as a bird's flight is more vital than the flight of any machine. And all the while there would be some, solitary or in companies, who, either in the pursuit of fish or wildfowl, or out of pure devilment, pitted their strength and skill against the hurricane, often tragically, but never without zest, and laughter of the spirit.

It may seem to some incredible that the culture of the Seventh Men should have lasted so long. Surely it must either have decayed through mere monotony and stagnation or have advanced into richer experience. But no. Generation succeeded generation, and each was too short-lived to outlast its young delight and discover boredom. Moreover, so perfect was the adjustment of these beings to their world, that even if they had lived for centuries they would have felt no need of change. Flight provided them with intense physical exhilaration, and with the physical basis of a genuine and ecstatic, though limited, spiritual experience. In this their supreme attainment they rejoiced not only in the diversity of flight itself, but also in the perceived beauties of their variegated world, and most of all, perhaps, in the thousand lyric and epic ventures of human intercourse in an aerial community.

The end of this seemingly everlasting elysium was nevertheless involved in the very nature of the species. In the first place, as the ages lengthened into aeons, the generations preserved less and less of the ancient scientific lore. For it became insignificant to them. The aerial community had no need of it. This loss of mere information did not matter so long as their condition remained unaltered; but in due course biological changes began to undermine them. The species had always been prone to a certain biological instability. A proportion of infants, varying with circumstances, had always been misshapen; and the deformity had generally been such as to make flight impossible. The normal infant was able to fly early in its second year. If some accident prevented it from doing so, it invariably fell into a decline and died before its third year was passed. But many of the deformed types, being the result of a partial reversion to the pedestrian nature, were able to live on indefinitely without flight. According to a merciful custom these cripples had always to be destroyed. But at length, owing to the gradual exhaustion of a certain marine salt essential to the highstrung nature of the Seventh Men, infants were more often deformed than true to type. The world population declined so seriously that the organized aerial life of the community could no longer be carried on according to the time-honoured aesthetic principles. No one knew how to check this racial decay, but many felt that with greater biological knowledge it might be avoided. A disastrous policy was now adopted. It was decided to spare a carefully selected proportion of the deformed infants, those namely which, though doomed to pedestrianism, were likely to develop high intelligence. Thus it was hoped to raise a specialized group of persons whose work should be biological research untrammelled by the intoxication of flight.

The brilliant cripples that resulted from this policy looked at existence from a new angle. Deprived of the supreme experience for which their fellows lived, envious of a bliss which they knew only by report, yet contemptuous of the naïve mentality which cared for nothing (it seemed) but physical exercise, love-making, the beauty of nature, and the elegances of society, these flightless intelligences sought satisfaction almost wholly in the life of research and scientific control. At the best, however, they were a tortured and resentful race. For their natures were fashioned for the aerial life which they could not lead. Although they received from the winged folk just treatment and a certain compassionate respect, they writhed under this kindness, locked their hearts against all the orthodox values, and sought out new ideals. Within a few centuries they had rehabilitated the life of intellect, and, with the power that knowledge gives, they had made themselves masters of the world. The amiable fliers were surprised, perplexed, even pained; and yet withal amused. Even when it became evident that the pedestrians were determined to create a new world-order in which there would be no place for the beauties of natural flight, the fliers were only distressed while they were on the ground.

The islands were becoming crowded with machinery and flightless industrialists. In the air itself the winged folk found themselves outstripped by the base but effective instruments of mechanical flight. Wings became a laughing stock, and the life of natural flight was condemned as a barren luxury. It was ordained that in future every flier must serve the pedestrian world-order, or starve. And as the cultivation of wind-borne plants had been abandoned, and fishing and fowling rights were strictly controlled, this law was no empty form. At first it was impossible for the fliers to work on the ground for long hours, day after day, without incurring serious ill-health and an early death. But the pedestrian physiologists invented a drug which preserved the poor wage-slaves in something like physical health, and actually prolonged their life. No drug, however, could restore their spirit, for their normal aerial habit was reduced to a few tired hours of recreation once a week. Meanwhile, breeding experiments were undertaken to produce a wholly wingless large-brained type. And finally a law was enacted by which all winged infants must be either mutilated or destroyed. At this point the fliers made an heroic but ineffectual bid for power. They attacked the pedestrian population from the air. In reply the enemy rode them down in his great aeroplanes and blew them to pieces with high explosive.

The fighting squadrons of the natural fliers were finally driven to the ground in a remote and barren island. Thither the whole flying population, a mere remnant of its former strength, fled out of every civilized archipelago in search of freedom: the whole population—save the sick, who committed suicide, and all infants that could not yet fly. These were stifled by their mothers or next-of-kin, in obedience to a decree of the leaders. About a million men, women, and children, some of whom were scarcely old enough for the prolonged flight, now gathered on the rocks, regardless that there was not food in the neighbourhood for a great company.

Their leaders, conferring together, saw clearly that the day of Flying Man was done, and that it would be more fitting for a high-souled race to die at once than to drag on in subjection to contemptuous masters. They therefore ordered the population to take part in an act of racial suicide that should at least make death a noble gesture of freedom. The people received the message while they were resting on the stony moorland. A wail of sorrow broke from them. It was checked by the speaker, who bade them strive to see, even on the ground, the beauty of the thing that was to be done. They could not see it; but they knew that if they had the strength to take wing again they would see it clearly, almost as soon as their tired muscles bore them aloft. There was no time to waste, for many were already faint with hunger, and anxious lest they should fail to rise. At the appointed signal the whole population rose into the air with a deep roar of wings. Sorrow was left behind. Even the children, when their mothers explained what was to be done, accepted their fate with zest; though, had they learned of it on the ground, they would have been terror-stricken. The company now flew steadily West, forming themselves into a double file many miles long. The cone of a volcano appeared over the horizon, and rose as they approached. The leaders pressed on towards its ruddy smoke plume; and unflinchingly, couple by couple, the whole multitude darted into its fiery breath and vanished. So ended the career of Flying Man.

Nutrition
from *Last Men in London*

Stapledon's second scientific romance was a commercial disappointment after the success of Last and First Men. *His editor had asked for a sequel, but the book Stapledon ended up writing had little in common with his first work of fiction except for its title and the device of telepathic narration.* Last Men in London, *focused largely on World War I and its psychological impact on a war veteran named Paul, has few of the extravagances of* Last and First Men. *But there are occasional flashes of Stapledonian invention and wit, particularly in the narrator's evocation of life on Neptune in the far future. The following comic fantasy, to which I have given the title "Nutrition," is*

concerned with the sexual education of Paul by his Neptunian mental para-
site; it gives full rein to the author's interests in imaginative anthropology
and cultural relativism.

ONE OF THE MOST DIFFICULT FACTS for the Neptunian explorer to grasp
about primitive minds is their obsession and their abject guilt and
disgust in respect of bodily appetites. In the constitution of the last
human species the excess energy of these appetites is very largely
sublimated, innately, into the spiritual and intellectual life. On the
other hand, whenever they do demand direct satisfaction, they are
frankly and zestfully gratified. In Paul's species it was the sexual appetite that caused trouble. Now it did not suit me that Paul should
become tangled inextricably in sex. His whole generation, I knew, was
going to develop along the lines of sex mania, in revulsion from the
prudery of its predecessors. But it was necessary that Paul should
maintain a true balance, so that his spirit's energies should be free to
direct themselves elsewhere.

The method by which I brought peace to Paul's troubled mind
was easy to me, though disturbing to him. Whenever he began to
worry himself with guilty fears, I would force upon his imagination
scenes from another world, in which not sex but nutrition was the
deed of supreme uncleanness and sanctity. Little by little I pieced
together in his mind a considerable knowledge of an early Neptunian
species whose fantastic culture has many points in common with your
own. Let me here tell you briefly of that culture.

On Neptune, then, there once lived, or from your point of view,
there will live, a race of human beings which attained a certain affluence and social complexity, but was ever hampered by its morbid
interest in nutrition. By what freakish turns of fortune this state of
affairs was brought about, I need not pause to describe. Suffice it
that physiological changes had produced in this human species an
exaggerated mechanism of hunger. This abnormality saddled all its
members with a craving for food much in excess of biological need;
and from the blundering social repression of this craving there arose a
number of strange taboos and perversions. By the time this Neptunian
species had attained civil life, the function of nutrition had become as
perverse and malignant as the function of reproduction in your own
society. No reference might be made to it in public, save to its excretory
side, which was regarded as a rite of purification. Eating became a
private and vaguely obscene act. While in many social situations sexual intercourse was a recognized means of expression and diversion,
and even drinking was permitted in the less puritanical circles so long
as it was performed through the nose, eating in the presence of another

person was not tolerated. In every home a special privy was set aside
for eating. This was stocked during the night by the public food carri-
ers, who constituted the lowest caste of society. In place of your chastity ideal there arose a fiction that to refrain from eating was virtuous,
and that the most holy persons could live without eating at all. Even
ordinary folk, though pardoned for occasional indulgence, were supposed
posed to refrain from the filthy act as far as possible. Repressed nutrition had by now coloured the whole life of the race. The mouth
occupied in its culture much the same position as the phallus with
you. A vast and subtle symbolism, like that which in your culture is
associated with the sacred and obscene reproductive act, was generated in this case by the sacred and obscene nutritive act. Eating became
at once a sin and an epitome of the divine power; for in eating does
not the living body gather into itself lifeless matter to organize it,
vitalize it? The mouth was, of course, never exposed to view. The
awful member was concealed behind a little modesty apron, which
was worn below the nose. In prehistoric times the lips had formed the
chief visual stimulus to sexual interest, and like the rump of the ba-
boon had developed lavish coloration and turgescence. But very early
in the cultural development of the species the modesty apron became
universal. Even when the rest of the body was unclad, this garment
was retained. And just as in your culture the notorious fig-leaf is
vaguely suggestive of that which it conceals, so, in this Neptunian
culture, the conventionally decorated covering of the mouth came to
mimic furtively the dread orifice itself. Owing to the fact that in polite
society no sound might be made which betrayed movement of the lips,
speech became distorted and debased. One curious consequence of
this obscenity of the mouth was the peculiar status of kissing. Though
sexual promiscuity was almost universal, kissing was a deadly sin,
except between man and wife. A kiss, bestowed in privacy and darkness, was the true consummation of marriage, and was something
infinitely more desirable and more disturbing than the procreative act
itself. All lovers longed to be united in a kiss; or, if they were innocents,
they looked for some unknown fulfilment, which they vaguely and
guiltily felt must be somehow connected with the mouth. Coitus they
regarded merely as an innocent and peculiarly delightful caress; but
the kiss was the dark, exquisite, sacred, mystically significant, forbid-
den fruit of all their loving. It was a mutual devouring, the act in
which, symbolically, the lover took the substance of the other within
his or her own system. Through this connexion with romantic love the
kiss gathered to itself all that obscure significance of tender personal
relations, of spiritual communion between highly developed personalities, which in your world the same romantic love may confer on

coitus. Further, since, like your Trobriand Islanders, the less sophisticated races of this species were often ignorant of the connexion between the sexual act and conception, and since, as with those islanders, sexual intercourse outside the marriage bond often failed to produce offspring, it was commonly believed in the more primitive of these Neptunian societies that the true reproductive act was the kiss. Consequently conception and child-birth came to be endowed with the same mystery, sanctity, and obscenity as nutrition. Sex, on the other hand, remained delightfully uncontaminated. These traditions maintained their power even in civilized societies, which had long ago realized the truth about parenthood. Children were carefully instructed in the hygiene of sex, and encouraged to have blithe sexual relations as soon as they needed that form of expression. But in respect of nutrition they were left in disastrous ignorance. As infants they were suckled, but in strict seclusion. Later they were taken to the food-privy and fed; but they were trained never to mention food in public and of course never to expose their mouths. Obscure and terrifying hints were let fall about the disastrous effects of gustatory self-indulgence. They were told not to go to the privy more than once a day, and not to stay longer than necessary. From their companions they gathered much distorted information about eating; and they were likely to contract diverse kinds of nutritive perversions, such as chewing stones and earth, biting one another or themselves for the taste of blood. Often they contracted such a prurient mania of thumb-sucking, that mouth and thumb would fester. If they escaped these perversions, it was by means of ignorant licentiousness in the food-privy. In consequence of this they were prone to contract serious digestive disorders, which moreover, if discovered, inevitably brought them into contempt. In either case they incurred a shattering sense of guilt, and contracted by auto-suggestion many of the symptoms which rumour attributed to their vice. In maturity they were likely to become either secret gourmets or puritans.

The Story of John

The earliest version of Stapledon's fantasy of a race of "supermen" appears as a rejected eleven-page chapter in the manuscript of Last Men in London. *In that book the narrator from Neptune had observed the presence among the "first men" of the modern era certain physically odd but mentally advanced beings, many of whom were confined to mental institutions. Among these*

forerunners of "homo superior" the narrator sketches the life-history of one in
particular — the character whom Stapledon would make the center of his 1935
novel Odd John. *Although many details were added in the course of trans-*
forming a chapter into an entire novel, "The Story of John" enacts the essen-
tial premise of the longer work: that a fantasy about biological mutation might
serve as a satiric parable about politics and morality.

IN ENGLAND a few years before the war a baby was born in whose
nature there was combined very superior brain capacity, a remarkable
improvement of visual discrimination and manual dexterity, together
with a superb physique. He was also blessed with intelligent parents,
who had moreover already had the experience of bringing up two
older children.

The career of this infant, whom I will call John, deserves to be told
in detail, but here I can only touch on its main features. He soon
revealed to his astonished parents very remarkable powers, for in his
case slow development of bodily appearance was combined with a
startling mental precocity. In observing his infancy I found that this
precocity was as a matter of fact due not to speed of development, but
to the immensely high calibre of his slowly maturing brain. Before he
could walk he was crawling about the lawn, studying at first hand the
biology of daisies, worms and beetles. Still a toddler, he was asking
philosophical questions and laughing at the inept answers of those
who tried to help him. At eight, when he looked rather like a large-
headed child of five, he had the brightness, hilarity and impishness of
a vigorous schoolboy of thirteen, strongly combined with the dawn of
interests which would have marked out a youth of twenty as definitely
beyond his years. His parents educated him at home, for no school
could place him. Or rather he educated himself, for he very soon
displayed an inflexible determination to follow his own bent, using his
parents only as living handbooks and bibliographies. They themselves
were well versed in the best thought and the best feeling of their
civilization, and had the sense to help their amazing third-born with
humility and affection. They wisely kept his powers from public notice, and used all the tact at their command to prevent him from coming into conflict with authority or public opinion. As the years
advanced, however, there began to be serious conflicts between John
and his parents, for as he gained knowledge and self-confidence he
began to proclaim abroad ideas that were altogether intolerable to the
normal species and to indulge in adventures of a most daring and
reprehensible nature.

At the age of fourteen John decided that he was destined for a
momentous career, but exactly what, he did not yet know. His first

task, at any rate, was to make himself independent, in fact to make money. By innate constitution he was entirely without self-bias, but having decided that he was a unique being, and one of supreme importance, he pursued self-interest with a relentlessness that would have shocked the most cynical profiteer. It would take too long to recount the series of incredible undertakings by which this seeming child of eight acquired a fortune. This side of his life he kept hidden from his parents, who imagined that on his frequent absences from home he was innocently camping and tramping in the neighbouring hills. In spite of all the brilliance and insight which distinguished him from his fellows he was at this time still at heart a child with all the schoolboy's lust of adventure. Consequently this early phase of his career was something like a modernised and grossly exaggerated version of the story of Robin Hood. By a number of ingenious burglaries, he secured jewelry and plate from the houses of the rich. With the aid of a motor bicycle he brought off several daring highway robberies. On one of his burglaries his plans were upset by a midnight telephone call for the owner of the house. When the good citizen encountered John in the hall with his swag, the terrible child remarked that as he was engaged on supremely important work, and his identity must not be revealed, he must kill the intruder, though with regret. He accordingly shot the astounded man, and fled.

When he had already committed several sensational robberies, he decided that this kind of thing was too risky. He therefore turned his attention to trade. He was of course wonderfully dextrous with his hands, and extremely inventive. After studying his mother's household arrangements, he devised a number of amazingly simple and useful household implements. Specimens of these he made by hand out of wood, metal, wicker, cardboard, as was required. He then applied for patents, and got in touch with manufacturers and hardware merchants, by post, lest his childish appearance should cause undue interest. Some of these patents he sold, others he kept to work on his own account. He worked, of course, by hand, but very rapidly. He was greatly entertained when his mother bought some of his handiwork at a local shop, without knowing its origin.

Presently he gave up handicraft for profit, but continued to make an increasing income by royalties on his inventions. As a pastime he wrote and published a number of highly original detective stories, under a pseudonym different from his trading pseudonym. These works turned out to be best sellers. His fortune was made. He increased it by publishing as a farcical novel a slightly doctored account of his own career and his unique nature. This he did partly in the hope that if there were any others of his kind, they might get in touch with him. The book was translated into several languages, and did in due season bring him into relations with several other supernormal individuals.

When he was sixteen, and looked much younger, John underwent a spiritual crisis, which was accompanied by much solitary meditation, and much study. From this phase he emerged in six months with the conviction that he had a great part to play in the life not merely of one planet but of the universe. He determined to found a new and more sane, more noble human species. Henceforth all his actions were rigorously guided by this purpose. His first aim was to discover if there were any others at all like him in the world. As he was thoroughly convinced that the normal species, though often amiable so long as all went according to custom, was capable of unimaginative persecution of beings that offended against its code, he was extremely anxious to avoid attracting attention. He therefore dared not get into personal relations with the scientists who might have helped him. Through the post, however, he made inquiries of various anthropological institutions, but vainly. He therefore took to casual wanderings in the towns and villages of England, looking for odd creatures like himself. In this way, and through his autobiography, he made contact with several of the abortive supermen described in the previous section. But they were all too old or too crippled to serve with him. Presently he found a boy of ten and three girls ranging from six to twelve. They were healthy and unspoiled; and though they lacked John's diabolic resolution, they were obviously products of a superior mutation. With them and one whom the autobiography had revealed, he discussed momentous plans.

He now persuaded his parents to take him on the Continent, since with his juvenile appearance he could not go alone. Touring in almost every country in Europe, he discovered twenty-seven suitable individuals of both sexes, between the ages of six and seventeen. With these he kept in touch during the next two years, gradually thrashing out with them the common policy. The aim was to found a minute colony in some remote part of the world, where there would be a chance of escaping the notice of the normal species. For it was by now terribly clear to the young adventurers not only that the normal race was past help, but that it would never permit a sane community to live in its world. The purpose of the colony was to be threefold. The most urgent aim was of course to devise a self-sufficing and harmonious society, founded on a careful study of the nature of the strange beings who were to compose it. It was also proposed to create by careful study a deeply novel culture, which, incorporating the best cultures of the First Men, should also be suitable to the superior mentality of a new species.

Finally, in due season, and after careful investigation into the biological nature of the various members, the colony must breed a new generation.

Much would have to be done before the adventure was undertaken. All the chosen must prepare themselves for the new life. Each must become expert in some occupation which would be needed by the colony; and each must become well versed in the best culture of his or her native land. Thus some were to become skilled in the principles of agriculture, some were to become metal workers, some architects, some navigators. Some were to acquire all possible knowledge of medicine and biology. All were to study contemporary thought and vitalise it with intelligence of superior beings. In this connection the adventurers were much exercised about the thought of the East. Very conscious of the errors of the West, they surmised that the East, with all its failings, must have traces of an insight which Western man wholly lacked. Certain members, therefore, were deputed to go to India and China to seek acquaintance with those very dissimilar cultures; and at the same time to search for any superior individuals in Eastern lands. John himself was to share in this very important work. By this time he had taken his parents into his confidence, except about the murder, and had revealed to them that he had a bank account and many thousands of pounds invested. Bewildered, horrified, and secretly very proud of their offspring, they finally agreed to play a humble but useful part in the founding of the colony. Their first task was to "take" John for a tour in the East. After a year's absence John returned, greatly impressed with the wisdom and the folly of India, but without having discovered any prodigies like himself. This was but what he expected, owing to the immense difficulties of the search.

When John was twenty, and had the appearance of a boy of fourteen, he designed a small motor vessel and had her built on the Clyde. In this craft he and a dozen of his kind, male and female, went exploring in the South Pacific. After a long search they discovered a suitable sub-tropical island, bought out the small native population, and returned to England to buy tools and materials and to pick up the rest of the party.

At last the unique colony was founded. Of its early adventures I must not here tell, though they form a superb epic of courage and humour, and at the same time an object lesson of the comparative ease with which a superior mentality can surmount difficulties, both practical and psychological, which to the normal species would have spelled certain defeat. Here I must be content with the bald assertion that after an initial period of hardship the little colony became a miniature utopia, and one in which the pursuit of an all-dominating purpose made stagnation impossible. This purpose, the founding of a new human race, and a new world, could not, of course, be seriously advanced till many generations had passed. Meanwhile there was much hard manual toil, a constant call for practical inventiveness, and for delicate adjustment of personal relations. The members were all physically adolescents, and mentally in a ferment of interest in one another, both in their bodily form and in their spiritual individuality. They had to work out a code of sexual morality, and the process inevitably entailed suffering. One serious problem was that of the age at which breeding might begin. Further, what was to be their span of life before senility should set in? Did slow development promise longevity? It was determined at any rate that no member should permit himself to live till he became a burden to the colony and to himself. These backward yet precocious young people were also immensely excited by the cooperative work of bringing their superior intellects to bear upon the cultures which they had brought with them from the normal race, and in working out the beginnings of a loftier wisdom. They kept in touch with the world partly by radio and literature, partly by frequent travelling, always under the ostensible control of some parent or other adult.

All too soon the colony came into serious conflict with the outside world. The first alarm was caused by the foundering of a tramp steamer on the island. She had lost her propeller, and drifted far from the ordinary tracks of vessels. While the crew were struggling toward the shore in heavy seas, the colonists decided on a plan of action. If these sailors were rescued and sent home, they would blab about the pack of children living without adult control, copulating to their hearts' content, and actually bearing infants. It was therefore hastily determined that none of the crew must survive. All those who clambered on to the rocks were therefore shot.

A few months later a British war ship, inspecting remote possessions of the Crown, was amazed to find the island inhabited not by natives but by white children of odd appearance. At first the commander proposed to transport the colonists at once, but he was persuaded merely to go away and report. The horrified British Government managed to prevent the story from reaching the daily papers, fearing a scandal about child vice on its territory. A ship was hastily sent to bring all the children home. Surprisingly the ship returned without them. The commander, bewildered and stammering under cross-examination, appeared to have been hypnotised by the persuasiveness of the leader of the colony.

Meanwhile the Colony was anxiously debating how to deal with the situation. From their point of view their case was much like that of pioneers in a jungle inhabited by wild beasts, with the difference that in this case the beasts had guns, and also some rudimentary power of imagination. It was decided that, for the present, the only thing to do was to appeal to the imagination of every expedition that was sent to the island. In due season another ship arrived. Her commander was in no mood for nonsense, but he made the mistake of consenting to see over the colony before evacuating it. He and his brother officers returned to their vessel in sore distress. The persuasiveness of these great children had convinced them that if they carried out their orders they would be committing a crime against something which they could not clearly conceive but which they had been made to recognize as overwhelmingly precious. Against orders the commander brought his ship home without the colonists. He was courtmartialed; and subsequently he shot himself.

Unfortunately for the Colony the Russian Secret Service had got wind of this minor trouble of the British Government. It was thought that to rescue the young people from the oppression of British imperialism might have propaganda value. Accordingly an expedition was sent to offer to establish the colony in a Russian island in the North Pacific. The British Government found out about this manoeuvre, and resolved to act with vigour. A more resolute, more brutal officer was sent to arrest the children. He discovered a trading schooner in the harbour; and, landing in person with a detachment of blue-jackets, he found that Bolshevik spies were in the act of trying to abduct the children.

John and his companions knew well that if once they got into the clutches of any section of the inferior species, their freedom would be lost forever. It would be impossible to work out for themselves a social order and a culture suited to their nature. At every turn they would offend their masters. On the whole the Russians offered more hope than the British, for the Russians would re-establish the colony; but it would obviously come under strict Bolshevik control. Anyhow it was clear that the British would not let them go. But if once they boarded the British ship, they would be virtually prisoners forever. Thus it was perfectly clear that their great adventure must now find its conclusion. There was only one thing left for them to do, to tell the world their story, and to bring it to such a dramatic end that it would not be overlooked. Thus it would be incorporated in the knowledge of the inferior species; and if, as seemed probable, nature should in time produce other superior mutations, these their spiritual successors would profit by their fate.

While the British ship was entering the roadstead, John and his friends were telling the Russians all about their venture, and entrusting them with documents. When the British commander arrived with his blue-jackets, John tried to use his persuasive arts on him, as on his predecessors. The officer cut him short and ordered the arrest of the whole party, including the Russians. At once all the colonists produced pistols and threatened to shoot themselves if they were touched. Two blue-jackets approached the nearest lad. He shot himself through the head. The blue-jackets hung back. The commander urged them on. They rushed at a girl to seize her weapon, but before they reached her she shot herself. Once more John began using his hypnotic, his diabolic, persuasiveness. Again the commander insisted on arrest, but the blue-jackets stood irresolute, murmuring. The commander himself advanced to seize John. A girl standing beside him shot herself. The commander hung back, the blue-jackets openly protesting. The commander began to parley with John and the others, urging them to come peaceably, as no one wished them harm. The result was merely that John's reply further disquieted the blue-jackets. In a fury the commander drew his automatic pistol, shot at the weapon-hand of the nearest boy, and seized him. John shot the boy through the head. The commander determined to try a new method. He posted guards at the doors of the building, and returned to the ship. He now referred to his Government by radio for further instructions, describing the recent events in code. He was told to take the children, alive or dead.

On returning to the shore with another party of blue-jackets, picked for their insensitivity, he was amazed to find that one of the guards was stepping aside to let the children escape. Hastily he bottled them in with his fresh blue-jackets. Still further to his amazement the former guards came crowding round him to plead for the children, regardless of discipline. He had them arrested. Evidently it was not practicable to keep these strange juveniles under restraint. After a moment's hesitation he decided to bring the whole wretched business to an end. Telling the children that he had orders to take them alive or dead, he once more ordered his men to arrest them. The earlier drama was repeated. When seven more of the children lay dead, including a young mother who destroyed herself and her infant with one bullet, the blue-jackets (picked for insensitivity) began to murmur. By now the commander himself was extremely distressed. He could think of nothing better than to take all his men back to the ship, along with the arrested Russian "spies." He then seized the schooner, and the motor yacht which was moored at the pier. Explaining by radio to his Government that, owing to the mutinous state of his crew, he could not carry out instructions, he put to sea.

The Colony burnt its dead and took up the threads of its normal life, well aware that such expensive victories could not for long postpone the end.

Meanwhile the amazed British authorities were extremely anxious to destroy the Colony before Russia could procure concrete proof of the scandal. A hint was dropped in the right quarter, and presently a disreputable little steamer arrived at the island "to trade." It was soon clear, however, that this was not her real purpose, for she landed several boat loads of hooligans, seemingly of all races. This time the weapons of the Colony were turned against the invaders, and with such effect that they were driven back into their boats, and forced to put to sea.

There followed another month of respite, during which the much reduced Colony managed to complete a radio transmission station and to start broadcasting its story. Unfortunately the story was so incredible that the very few who heard it took it for a bad joke. After the first day the authorities saw to it that the fantastic stuff was shouted down by other stations.

At length a larger vessel arrived at the island. A swarm of toughs landed with machine guns. John and his friends retired to a little fortress that they had constructed, and used their scanty ammunition to such effect that for three days they kept off the enemy. But at last when there was but one cartridge left for each surviving member, they destroyed themselves.

Thus, as on other occasions of biological history, did the higher type succumb to the type that was fittest to survive in the circumstances.

Nautiloids

from *Star Maker*

Regarded by many readers and by the author as Stapledon's masterpiece, Star Maker *is at the farthest remove imaginable from the traditional novel of character. Designed as "an imaginative sketch of the dread but vital whole of things,"* Star Maker *is a visionary history of the universe. The narrator, traveling through space-time on pilgrimage, inhabits the consciousnesses of a stunning variety of intelligent beings as he seeks to know the ultimate purpose of life and mind. The philosophical conception of this extraordinary quest has dominated commentaries on* Star Maker, *but the novelist Naomi Mitchison —in letters written to Stapledon while the book was in progress in the 1930s —praised its power of invention. "The thing I believe you are so immensely good at is convincing* detail — *almost mechanical detail — about something one knows nothing about and hasn't even imagined." Mitchison's favorite chapter was called "Worlds Innumerable," from which the following excerpt is taken. It is a tour de force of biological and cultural fantasy. The "living ships" the narrator encounters are not at all anthropomorphic, but they remain peculiarly human. For all their grotesquery, the nautiloids almost certainly derive from Stapledon's childhood memories of sailing ships at the Suez Canal. (See the description of nineteenth-century sailing ships as "almost living human artifacts" in the memoir "Fields Within Fields," elsewhere in this* Reader.) *Rare and strange in its images, the episode is also a mischievous satire on class distinctions.*

IN GENERAL the physical and mental form of conscious beings is an expression of the character of the planet on which they live. On certain very large and aqueous planets, for instance, we found that civilization had been achieved by marine organisms. On these huge globes no land-dwellers as large as a man could possibly thrive, for gravitation would have nailed them to the ground. But in the water there was no such limitation to bulk. One peculiarity of these big worlds was that, owing to the crushing action of gravitation, there were seldom any great elevations and depressions in their surface. Thus they were usually covered by a shallow ocean, broken here and there by archipelagos of small, low islands.

I shall describe one example of this kind of world, the greatest planet of a mighty sun. Situated, if I remember rightly, near the congested heart of the galaxy, this star was born late in galactic history, and it gave birth to planets when already many of the older stars were encrusted with smouldering lava. Owing to the violence of solar radiation its nearer planets had (or will have) stormy climates. On one of them a mollusc-like creature, living in the coastal shallows, acquired a propensity to drift in its boat-like shell on the sea's surface, thus keeping in touch with its drifting vegetable food. As the ages passed, its shell became better adapted to navigation. Mere drifting was supplemented by means of a crude sail, a membrane extending from the creature's back. In time this nautiloid type proliferated into a host of species. Some of these remained minute, but some found size advantageous, and developed into living ships. One of these became the intelligent master of this great world.

The hull was a rigid, stream-lined vessel, shaped much as the nineteenth-century clipper in her prime, and larger than our largest whale. At the rear a tentacle or fin developed into a rudder, which was sometimes used also as a propeller, like a fish's tail. But though all these species could navigate under their own power to some extent, their normal means of long-distance locomotion was their great spread of sail. The simple membranes of the ancestral type had become a system of parchment-like sails and bony masts and spars, under voluntary muscular control. Similarity to a ship was increased by the downward-looking eyes, one on each side of the prow. The mainmast-head also bore eyes, for searching the horizon. An organ of magnetic sensitivity in the brain afforded a reliable means of orientation. At the fore end of the vessel were two long manipulatory tentacles, which during locomotion were folded snugly to the flanks. In use they formed a very serviceable pair of arms.

It may seem strange that a species of this kind should have developed human intelligence. In more than one world of this type, however, a number of accidents combined to produce this result. The change from a vegetarian to a carnivorous habit caused a great increase of animal cunning in pursuit of the much speedier submarine creatures. The sense of hearing was wonderfully developed, for the movements of fish at great distances could be detected by the under-water ears. A line of taste-organs along either bilge responded to the ever-changing composition of the water, and enabled the hunter to track his prey. Delicacy of hearing and of taste combined with omnivorous habits, and with great diversity of behaviour and strong sociality, to favour the growth of intelligence.

Speech, that essential medium of the developed mentality, had two distinct modes in this world. For short-range communication, rhythmic underwater emissions of gas from a vent in the rear of the organism were heard and analysed by means of under-water ears. Long-distance communication was carried on by means of semaphore signals from a rapidly agitating tentacle at the mast head.

The organizing of communal fishing expeditions, the invention of traps, the making of lines and nets, the practice of agriculture, both in the sea and along the shores, the building of stone harbours and work-shops, the use of volcanic heat for smelting metals, and of wind for driving mills, the projection of canals into the low islands in search of minerals and fertile ground, the gradual exploration and mapping of a huge world, the harnessing of solar radiation for mechanical power, these and many other achievements were at once a product of intelligence and an opportunity for its advancement.

It was a strange experience to enter the mind of an intelligent ship, to see the foam circling under one's own nose as the vessel plunged through the waves, to taste the bitter or delicious currents streaming past one's flanks, to feel the pressure of air on the sails as one beat up against the breeze, to hear beneath the water-line the rush and murmur of distant shoals of fishes, and indeed actually to *hear* the sea-bottom's configuration by means of the echoes that it cast up to the under-water ears. It was strange and terrifying to be caught in a hurricane, to feel the masts straining and the sails threatening to split, while the hull was battered by the small but furious waves of that massive planet. It was strange, too, to watch other great living ships, as they ploughed their way, heeled over, adjusted the set of their yellow or russet sails to the wind's variations; and very strange it was to realize that these were not man-made objects but themselves conscious and purposeful.

Sometimes we saw two of the living ships fighting, tearing at one another's sails with snake-like tentacles, stabbing at one another's soft "decks" with metal knives, or at a distance firing at one another with cannon. Bewildering and delightful it was to feel in the presence of a slim female clipper the longing for contact, and to carry out with her on the high seas the tacking and yawing, the piratical pursuit and overhauling, the delicate, fleeting caress of tentacles, which formed the love-play of this race. Strange, to come up alongside, close-hauled, grapple her to one's flank, and board her with sexual invasion. It was charming, too, to see a mother ship attended by her children. I should mention, by the way, that at birth the young were launched from the mother's decks like little boats, one from the port side, one from the starboard. Thenceforth they were suckled at her flanks. In play they swam about her like ducklings, or spread their immature sails. In rough weather and for long voyaging they were taken aboard.

At the time of our visit natural sails were beginning to be aided by a power unit and propeller which were fixed to the stern. Great cities of concrete docks had spread along many of the coasts, and were excavated out of the hinterlands. We were delighted by the broad water-ways that served as streets in these cities. They were thronged with sail and mechanized traffic, the children appearing as tugs and smacks among the gigantic elders.

It was in this world that we found in its most striking form a social disease which is perhaps the commonest of all world-diseases— namely, the splitting of the population into two mutually unintelligible castes through the influence of economic forces. So great was the difference between adults of the two castes that they seemed to us at first to be distinct species, and we supposed ourselves to be witnessing the victory of a new and superior biological mutation over its predecessor. But this was far from the truth.

In appearance the masters were very different from the workers, quite as different as queen ants and drones from the workers of their species. They were more elegantly and accurately stream-lined. They had a greater expanse of sail, and were faster in fair weather. In heavy seas they were less seaworthy, owing to their finer lines; but on the other hand they were the more skilful and venturesome navigators. Their manipulatory tentacles were less muscular, but capable of finer adjustments. Their perception was more delicate. While a small minority of them perhaps excelled the best of the workers in endurance and courage, most were much less hardy, both physically and mentally. They were subject to a number of disintegrative diseases which never affected the workers, chiefly diseases of the nervous system. On the other hand, if any of them contracted one of the infectious ailments which were endemic to the workers, but seldom fatal, he would almost certainly die. They were also very prone to mental disorders, and particularly to neurotic self-importance. The whole organization and control of the world was theirs. The workers, on the other hand, though racked by disease and neurosis bred of their cramping environment, were on the whole psychologically more robust. They had, however, a crippling sense of inferiority. Though in handicrafts and all small-scale operations they were capable of intelligence and skill, they were liable, when faced with tasks of wider scope, to a strange paralysis of mind.

The mentalities of the two castes were indeed strikingly different. The masters were more prone to individual initiative and to the vices of self-seeking. The workers were more addicted to collectivism and the vices of subservience to the herd's hypnotic influence. The masters were on the whole more prudent, far-seeing, independent, self-reliant; the workers were more impetuous, more ready to sacrifice themselves in a social cause, often more clearly aware of the right aims of social activity, and incomparably more generous to individuals in distress.

At the time of our visit certain recent discoveries were throwing the world into confusion. Hitherto it had been supposed that the natures of the two castes were fixed unalterably, by divine law and by biological inheritance. But it was now certain that this was not the case, and that the physical and mental differences between the classes were due entirely to nurture. Since time immemorial, the castes had been recruited in a very curious manner. After weaning, all children born on the port side of the mother, no matter what the parental caste, were brought up to be members of the master caste; all those born on the starboard side were brought up to be workers. Since the master class had, of course, to be much smaller than the working class, this system gave an immense superfluity of potential masters. The difficulty was overcome as follows. The starboard-born children of workers and the port-born children of masters were brought up by their own respective parents; but the port-born, potentially aristocratic children of workers were mostly disposed of by infant sacrifice. A few only were exchanged with the starboard-born children of masters.

With the advance of industrialism, the increasing need for large supplies of cheap labour, the spread of scientific ideas and the weakening of religion, came the shocking discovery that port-born children, of both classes, if brought up as workers, became physically and mentally indistinguishable from workers. Industrial magnates in need of plentiful cheap labour now developed moral indignation against infant sacrifice, urging that the excess of port-born infants should be mercifully brought up as workers. Presently certain misguided scientists made the even more subversive discovery that starboard-born children brought up as masters developed the fine lines, the great sails, the delicate constitution, the aristocratic mentality of the master caste. An attempt was made by the masters to prevent this knowledge from spreading to the workers, but certain sentimentalists of their own caste bruited it abroad, and preached a new-fangled and inflammatory doctrine of social equality.

During our visit the world was in terrible confusion. In backward oceans the old system remained unquestioned, but in all the more advanced regions of the planet a desperate struggle was being waged. In one great archipelago a social revolution had put the workers in power, and a devoted though ruthless dictatorship was attempting so to plan the life of the community that the next generation should be homogeneous and of a new type, combining the most desirable characters of both workers and masters. Elsewhere the masters had persuaded their workers that the new ideas were false and base, and certain to lead to universal poverty and misery. A clever appeal was made to the vague but increasing suspicion that "materialistic science" was misleading and superficial, and that mechanized civilization was crushing out the more spiritual potentialities of the race. Skilled propaganda spread the ideal of a kind of corporate state with "port and starboard flanks" correlated by a popular dictator, who, it was said, would assume power "by divine right and the will of the people."

I must not stay to tell of the desperate struggle which broke out between these two kinds of social organizations. In the world-wide campaigns many a harbour, many an ocean current, flowed red with slaughter. Under the pressure of war to the death, all that was best, all that was most human and gentle on each side was crushed out by military necessity. On the one side, the passion for a unified world, where every individual should live a free and full life in service of the world community, was overcome by the passion to punish spies, traitors, and heretics. On the other, vague and sadly misguided yearnings for a nobler, less materialistic life were cleverly transformed by the reactionary leaders into vindictiveness against the revolutionaries.

Very rapidly the material fabric of civilization fell to pieces. Not till the race had reduced itself to an almost subhuman savagery, and all the crazy traditions of a diseased civilization had been purged away, along with true culture, could the spirit of these "ship-men" set out again on the great adventure of the spirit. Many thousands of years later it broke through on to that higher plane of being which I have still to suggest, as best I may.

The Reign of Darkness
from *Darkness and the Light*

Published in 1942, Darkness and the Light *projects two alternate futures, glimpsed by a visionary narrator from a vantage point within the turbulent first years of World War II. In one future the forces of light, led by Tibetan mystics and pacifists, lead humanity to global utopia; but in the other future, the grimmest hell Stapledon ever created, the Tibetan light is snuffed out by the allied forces of China and Russia after the collapse of Germany, Britain, and Japan. The dissolution of the Lamaist monasteries, the destruction of Lhasa, and the obliteration of Tibetan culture — eerily like the actual fate of Tibet under Chinese rule in the 1960s — usher in a despotic world order, presided over by China after a treacherous attack on its ally that leaves Moscow in ruins. Once a resistant but weakened America has been crushed, the "Reign of Darkness" is maintained by a synthetic state religion manufactured to enforce submission to government authority and by the staging of public holocausts "in which, before the eyes of a howling and ecstatic mob, thousands were roasted alive or vivisected by machinery devised to produce maximal pain." The following excerpts illustrate Stapledon's revulsion from the systematic cruelties of Naziism as well as longstanding concerns over state control of technology and mass communications. The grisly solutions to problems of unemployment and depopulation echo the ominous futures created by Stapledon's contemporaries Aldous Huxley in* Brave New World *and Katharine Burdekin (using the pen name of Murray Constantine) in* Swastika Night; *the brain implants to monitor unorthodox thinking recall the perverse surgery in the early Soviet dystopia* We, *by Yevgeny Zamyatin.*

WITH THE FALL OF AMERICA the human race had succeeded for the first time in establishing the political unity of the whole planet. The imperial Chinese government now assumed the title "The Celestial Government of the World," and ordered celebrations in every town and every household of the planet. Everywhere desperate efforts were made to produce tolerable specimens of the ancient Chinese dragon flag, which had been revived by the second empire and was henceforth to be the dreaded emblem of the world-government. Everywhere, even on the blood-stained Russian plains, this emblem, or some crude approximation to it, was now anxiously flaunted. It was affirmed that at last the green Chinese dragon had devoured the red orb that had for so long hung tantalizingly before him in the golden sky. The red orb was no longer interpreted as the sun of Japan but as the red world of Russian imperialism. It was added in a whisper that with luck the dragon might soon die of indigestion.

World-unity had been attained! But what a unity! Nowhere throughout the world was there any considerable group who were at peace with the world, save the governing class and its jackals. Everywhere the peasants were enslaved to the universal imperial landlord. Everywhere they toiled to produce the world's food. Everywhere they starved and were harshly regimented. Miners and factory hands were in the same condition. The world-government, instead of organizing a great and universal movement of social reconstruction, thereby keeping the workers and the soldiers in employment, dismissed half its armies and kept the rest in idleness. The workers it treated with utter contempt, confident in its power to coerce them. The great class of technicians who had been persuaded to support the war in the hope that under world-unity they would be given the chance to build universal prosperity, found themselves used either for strengthening the oligarchy or for producing its luxuries; or else dismissed and maintained by the state in a sort of half-life of penury and despond.

Although individualistic capitalism had long since vanished, the universal decadent state-capitalism was in many ways subject to the same disorders. Though the power for social planning was in the hands of the world-government, the will was lacking. The rulers were concerned only to maintain their position. Vast economic powers, at first the perquisites of the great ruling Chinese families, were now farmed out to irresponsible state-servants, who turned themselves into dictators of the industries under their control. And since there was little co-ordination of their actions, and, anyhow, they were mainly concerned to feather their own nests, chaos followed. Unemployment increased, and brought with it its attendant evils. Desperate populations became difficult to handle. Punitive massacres were very frequent.

At last a new invention, one of the very few which the declining species managed to achieve, brought temporary aid. A biochemist produced a method of putting human beings into a state of suspended animation from which, he said, they could be easily wakened, "fresh and young," after a sleep of many years. The world-government, believing that unemployment was a passing phase, and that later on there would be a great need of labour, set about building in every country a system of cold-storage warehouses where unwanted human beings could be deposited until the times changed. The unemployed and their families were forcibly stored in these warehouses. The struggling creatures were chained down, lying shoulder to shoulder on tiers of shelves inside huge tanks, which were then filled first with a succession of gases and finally with a preserving liquid. Millions of men, women, and children in almost every country were thus stored for future use. Though the lives of the workers were almost intolerably arid and distressful, they did all in their power to avoid being sent to the cold-storage houses. The will for the light expressed itself in them as a blind will for active life, however abject. But a few welcomed this opportunity of escape, without irrevocable extinction, believing that in their next phase of active life they would have better opportunities of expressing themselves. In most of these, the acquiescence in suspended animation was at bottom an expression of the will for darkness, though rationalized to satisfy the still-smouldering will for light. For the individual in whom the will for the light is strong and clear finds his heart inextricably bound up with the struggle of the forces of light in his native place and time. Much as he may long for the opportunity of fuller self-expression in a happier world, he knows that for him self-expression is impossible save in the world in which his mind is rooted. The individual in whom the will for the light is weak soon persuades himself that his opportunity lies elsewhere. And so, as the spirit of the race was progressively undermined through ever deteriorating physical and psychological conditions, acquiescence in "the deep sleep" became more and more widespread.

One of the main factors in the waning of the will for the light in this period was the attitude of the intellectuals. The academics, musicians, painters, cinema-artists, and, above all, the writers flagrantly betrayed their trust. In all these groups there were persons of four types. Many were paid servants of the government, engaged on propaganda through work which was ostensibly independent. They were concerned chiefly to put a good complexion on the régime, and to praise the fundamental principles of the synthetic faith, in particular the virtues of acquiescence and obedience, and the ecstasy of cruelty. Still more numerous were the independent but futile intellectual ostriches who shut their eyes to the horror of their time and won adulation and power by spinning fantasies of self-aggrandizement and sexual delight, distracting men's attention from contemporary evils

with seductive romances of other ages and other worlds, or with exalted and meaningless jargon about a life after death. There were also
large numbers of progressive intellectuals. These saw clearly enough
that contemporary society was mortally sick, and in a dream-like, un-
earnest way they expounded their tenuous Utopias, in which there
was often much common sense and even wisdom; but they preached
without that fury of conviction which alone can rouse men to desperate action. And they themselves lived comfortably upon the existing
system, in their flats and suburban houses. Vaguely they knew that
they ought to give up all for the revolution; but being what they were,
they could not. The fourth type were the very few sincere and impotent
rebels, who flung away their lives in vain and crazy attempts to be
great prophets.

Crucial to the fate of the human race at this time was the attitude
of the class of technicians, the host of highly trained engineers, electri-
cians, aeronautical experts, agricultural experts, and scientific workers
in industry. These, if they could have formed a clear idea of the plight
of the race, might have saved it. But they were experts who had been
carefully trained in the tradition that the expert should not meddle in
politics. In times of great stress, of course, they did meddle; but, because they had consistently held themselves aloof, their pronouncements were childish, and their attempts at political action disastrous.
A few had, indeed, taken the trouble to study society, and had come
to understand its present ills. These fought constantly to enlighten
their fellows and unite them in a great effort to control the course of
events. Undoubtedly, if the will for the light had been strong in this
great class, which controlled throughout the world all the innumerable
levers and switches and press-buttons of the material life of society, it
could have overthrown the world-oligarchy in a few days, and set
about organizing a sane order. But the appeal to the technicians met
with a half-hearted response. Most of them shrugged their shoulders
and went on with their work. A few took timid action and were
promptly seized and put to torture by the rulers. The movement failed.

It seemed to me very strange that a class which included nearly
all the best intelligence of the world and very much of the world's
good will should be incapable of ousting a set of tyrants who were
both insensitive and stupid. The explanation, seemingly, was twofold.
First, the rulers found themselves in possession of a vast and highly
mechanized system of oppression. If anyone did anything obnoxious
to the régime, immediately and automatically he was put out of action.
Some colleague would certainly inform against him, and the police
would do the rest. For the whole population, it must be remembered,
was now tormented by neurotic jealousy and fear. The infliction of

pain on a fellow mortal could afford a crazy satisfaction. Informers were, of course, well rewarded, but it was the joy of persecution that inspired them. Secondly, the mechanization of propaganda had been developed to an extent hitherto unknown. Psychology, the youngest of the sciences, had by now attained a thorough knowledge of the primitive and the morbid in man without reaching to any real understanding of the distinctively human reaches of human personality. Government psychologists had worked out a subtle technique of suggestion by reiterated symbolic appeals to suppressed motives. This method, applied from infancy onwards, had ensured that all the unwitting cravings of a neurotic population, all their unacknowledged fear, hate, energy, cruelty, lechery, selfishness, and mob-passion, should depend both for stimulation and assuagement on the existing social order, and should issue consciously in a jealous and vengeful loyalty to the oligarchy. Thus did a group of scientists who should have used their skill for the purgation and elucidation of men's minds help to deepen the general darkness and misery. The power of propaganda was greatly increased by the prevailing educational principles. The free intelligence, which criticizes fearlessly and without prejudice, was ridiculed, condemned, and carefully suppressed. Bound intelligence, acting within the universe of discourse of the established culture, was encouraged; but it was made clear to every pupil that intelligence was rather a necessary evil than a thing to prize for its own sake. What was intrinsically good was orthodoxy, unison with the tradition. To strengthen the passion for orthodoxy it was ordained that school classes should be as large as possible, and that the main method of teaching should be by organizing mass chanting of the traditional truths. Had the will for the light been less feeble, this procedure might well have induced in some pupils a revulsion in favour of free intelligence; but in this latter day of the human race, such rebellion was very rare.

The government's control over its subjects was greatly increased by a new invention which would have been a cause of increased social well-being had it occurred in a more wholesome society. This was the product of advances in physiology and electrical engineering. The mechanism of the human brain was by now fairly well known; and by means of a vast mesh of minute photo-electric cells, inserted by a brilliant surgical technique between the cerebral cortex and the skull, it was possible to record very accurately the ever-changing pattern of activity in the cortical nerve-fibres. Advances in the technique of radio made it easy to transmit this record over great distances, and to decode it automatically in such a way that the thoughts and impulses of the observed person could be accurately 'read' by observers in far-away government offices. The immense knowledge and skill which went to these inventions might have caused untold benefits to mankind; but through the treason of the technologists and the power-lust of the rulers they were combined to form a diabolical instrument of tyranny.

A law was passed by which everyone suspected of harbouring dangerous thoughts was condemned to have his brain made available for constant observation. This involved an operation for the insertion of the photo-electric mesh under his skull and the attachment of the necessary miniature accumulators to his crown by screws driven into the skull itself. If any attempt was made to tamper with the instrument, or if the accumulator was allowed to run down beyond a certain point, the unfortunate individual was automatically subjected to the most excruciating pain, which, if prolonged for more than an hour or so, culminated in permanent insanity. In addition to this transmission-instrument there was a minute radio telephone receiver driven into the mastoid bone. Thus not only were the subject's thoughts and feelings open to inspection at every moment of his life by some remote official but also instructions, threats, or repetitive gramophone propaganda could be inflicted on him morning, noon, and night.

At first this technique was applied only to those under suspicion, but little by little it was extended to all classes of society, save the oligarchs themselves and their most favoured servants. Immense offices were set up in all the main centres, where hosts of inspectors were constantly at work taking sample readings of the world's two thousand million minds. Every ordinary man, woman, and adolescent knew that at any moment he might be under inspection. At any moment a voice might interrupt his thoughts with some propaganda commentary on them, or with a rough warning or the imposition of a penalty. While he was going to sleep he might be invaded by music and incantations calculated to mould his mind into the temper approved by the government. Those who were brought up from childhood to be accustomed to this treatment accepted it cheerfully. The very young were sometimes even impatient to receive what they foolishly regarded as this certificate of maturity. Under the constant influence of official scrutiny the minds of adolescents became almost perfectly correct. Dangerous thoughts, even of the mildest type, were for them unthinkable. Those who received the treatment as grown men or women suffered prolonged mental agony, and many committed suicide.

The policy of those who controlled this vast system of espionage was simply to ensure that all minds should be orthodox. As time went on, the inquisitors themselves came to be chosen solely from the ranks of those who were products of the system itself. So amazingly correct were these minds that they suffered nothing from the publicity of all their mental processes.

The strangest aspect of the system was this. Those who controlled it were themselves enslaved to it; they used their power not to emancipate themselves but to support the ruling caste. In the earlier phase of the Chinese world-empire the caste, or rather the non-hereditary class from which the caste later developed, had maintained its position by superior cunning and resolution; but in its later phase, when cunning and resolution had given place to stupidity and self-indulgence, the position of the ruling caste was maintained automatically by the mechanical functioning of the established social system. The rulers had immense privileges and great arbitrary powers. For them the workers piled up luxuries. In accordance with the vagaries of their fickle taste, fashions changed, whole working populations were suddenly worked to death or flung aside into the cold-storage warehouses. When the rulers said "do this" or "do that," the world obeyed. But their power lay wholly in the fact that the technicians were hypnotized in their service, hypnotized, not through the cunning and resolution of the rulers themselves, but through the vast momentum of traditional culture. Thus little by little the ruling caste became at once helpless and absolutely secure. In the same manner the slave-owning ants depend wholly on the ministrations of devoted slaves who have all the skill but not the wit to rebel.

The perfection of the system of social control was reached by means of a further triumph of inventive genius. After much laborious experiment a method was devised by which the impulses and desires of the individual could be either stimulated or suppressed by radio. Thus it was possible for the officials in a distant government office to force upon a man an irresistible craving to carry out a prescribed course of action. Like one under hypnotic influence, but with full consciousness of the enormity of his action, he might find himself compelled to betray his friend, to murder his wife, to torture his child or himself, to work himself to death, to fight against impossible odds.

Little by little the whole subject population of the world was fitted with the instruments of volitional control. The government was now practically omnipotent. Once more, the strangest aspect of the new invention was that those who controlled it were themselves under its control. For the operators themselves were fitted with the instruments. Operators in each department were controlled by their superiors, and these by their superiors. These again were controlled by the supreme council of the locality, which was composed of all heads of departments. The supreme council of the locality was in turn controlled by the council of the province or state; and the state councils by the World

Imperial Council. Members of this body were automatically controlled. Automatic machinery ensured that any incipient desire inconsistent with the orthodox system of desires should automatically be obliterated, while certain desires fundamental to orthodoxy were automatically maintained.

This ingenious system, it must be noted, had not been devised by the rulers themselves but by the technologists, by physiologists, psychologists, and electrical engineers. They had done it partly out of blind professional enthusiasm, partly because they felt the need of such a system to fortify their orthodoxy against the unorthodox impulses which occasionally distressed them.

As for the rulers themselves, these sacred beings, these sacred animals, were not controlled. They were free to think and act according to their nature, which by now had degenerated into a mess of stupidity, selfishness, and malice. Their stupidity was the stupidity of beasts. Though they were free, they were powerless. Of degenerate stock, they were conditioned by upbringing to a life of fantastic luxury and desolating self-indulgence. So long as they behaved according to the orthodox pattern, they were preserved and reverenced. If any showed some sign of individuality he was at once de-classed and operated upon for radio control. But this was very rare. Nearly all were content to live at ease on the fat of the land and the adulation of the masses. They were kept busy with the innumerable ceremonies and pageants without which, it was thought, the state would collapse, and in which the representative members of the ruling caste always played the central part. Those who obscurely felt the barrenness of their lives sought notoriety in the fields of sport or aeronautics. But, as the generations passed and their capacity deteriorated, they were forced to seek less exacting forms of self-display. Of these, one of the chief was the infliction of torture. The subject population, though conditioned to believe in the mystical virtue of cruelty, and though capable up to a point of relishing the spectacle of torture inflicted on strangers, were prone to lapse into squeamishness or even compassion. Not so the rulers. Unconsciously poisoned by their own futility and baseness, they were obsessed by hatred of the masses, the technicians, their own peers, and themselves. Without any radio control, therefore, they could inflict the most disgusting tortures with equanimity, and even unfeigned relish. When one of them had to perform the office of tearing out the eyes or bowels or genitals of the sacrificial victim, he did so without a qualm. To the fascinated and nauseated spectators this callousness appeared as aristocratic virtue. When humble people came to be subject to radio control of volition they often welcomed the artificial reinforcement to their ruthlessness. On the other hand when an erring member of the ruling caste had to be de-classed and put to torture, he invariably showed less than the average fortitude. It never occurred to the public, while they howled with glee at his discomfiture, that the aristocrats, even before de-classing, were after all no better than themselves; for the ceremony of de-classing was supposed to have deprived the culprit of his native virtue. . . .

I cannot be sure how long the Celestial World Empire endured. Its life must certainly be counted in centuries, and possibly it lasted for a couple of thousand years. Though the world empire was at heart a diseased society and bound to disintegrate, it inherited from earlier societies a certain toughness of fibre, and its structure was such that it could carry on in a sort of living death so long as conditions remained unchanged. While its material resources were unimpaired it functioned automatically and without change.

The human race had in fact attained the kind of stability which insect species have maintained for many million years. Its whole economy had been worked out in intricate detail by the technicians of an earlier age through a period of many decades, and had at last become absolutely stereotyped. Raw materials, produced in appropriate regions and in regular annual quantities, were assigned to manufacturing districts according to a time-honoured plan, to be distributed in time-honoured proportions to the various nations and social classes. The whole industrial technique had acquired a kind of religious sanctity. No variations were to be tolerated, except the seasonal variations which were themselves sanctified.

In these circumstances the function of the technicians, the unacknowledged but effective rulers of the planet, was radically altered. From being primarily inventors of new processes and new adjustments they became simply orthodox vehicles of the sacred lore. Intelligence, therefore, even bound intelligence, came to have an increasingly restricted function. Before the onset of decline, planning had been becoming more and more comprehensive and far-seeing. Men had planned for centuries ahead and for great societies, even tentatively for the future of the species. But after the world empire had become firmly established and stereotyped, large planning was no longer necessary. Only in the ordering of individual lives was there any scope for intelligence. Even here, as individual lives became more and more dominated by the regularities imposed by the state, the office of intelligence became more restricted. Whenever any daring spirit did try to improve upon the orthodox procedure, his intelligence proved feeble and his action misguided. His failure merely strengthened the general distrust of innovation.

For a very long while the material resources and the biological condition of the race did remain in effect constant. To the subjects of the world empire it seemed certain that the existing order was eternal. The idea of progress, material or mental, had long since ceased to seem plausible, for society was universally regarded as perfect. On the other hand the idea of racial decline was never contemplated. But behind the appearance of stability great changes were already at work, both in the physical environment and in the constitution of the human race itself.

Though volcanic power was inexhaustible, certain essential raw materials were not. Coal and oil had long ago been superseded as sources of power, but as raw materials for many synthetic products they were valuable, and becoming ever more difficult to procure. The world's phosphate deposits, so necessary for agriculture, were being steadily reduced. Guano, long ago abandoned, was once more assiduously collected. Potash deposits had been heavily worked and were seriously depleted. An earlier age had known that an unlimited supply of potash could, when necessary, be obtained from sea water, but there had been no need to work out a technique for isolating it. Now, when potash was scarce, there was no longer the inventive capacity to tackle so difficult a task. Nitrogen had for long been derived from the air for use in fertilizer and high explosives. In this case, however, the technique was well established, and so there was no immediate danger of its loss. Iron, though one of the commonest of all elements, was becoming steadily more difficult to reach. All ordinarily accessible deposits were seriously depleted, and the skill for much deeper mining was by now lacking.

The condition of forestry in the latter days of the world-empire throws a strange light on the mental decay of the race. Wood-pulp had been the main raw material for many synthetic products. In early days, when the intelligence of the technicians was still effective, afforestation schemes had been organized so as to keep the balance of production and consumption. But latterly planting had seriously lagged behind felling. This may seem surprising, since the balance of planting and felling was part of the rigid and sacred technique of social organization. The cause of the ever-increasing discrepancy was very simple but completely hidden from the sluggish minds of the latter-day empire controllers. The original scheme had been calculated on the assumption that the art of forestry would continue to be practised with quick intelligence. Some margin had been allowed for accidents and errors, but not a fool-proof margin. When intelligence had declined, mistakes became more frequent, and less successfully repaired. Consequently the old sacred formulae failed. The forests slowly but surely dwindled. But according to the sacred scriptures of afforestation this was impossible, if the formulae had indeed been followed. Therefore it was impious to suggest that the forests were dwindling. Therefore anyone who began to suspect that this was happening turned a blind eye on the facts. Thus the rot continued without any attempt being made to stop it.

The same disastrous decay took place in agriculture. The original organizers of the empire's tillage had worked out a delicately balanced agricultural system which should yield an adequate crop of food-stuffs without impoverishing the land. But this system had depended on intelligent adjustment. It was not fool-proof. When sluggish minds took charge, there was a far greater wastage at every point in the system. The old formulae therefore became inadequate. But since any alteration would have been impious, the upshot was that century by century rather less was put into the ground than was taken from it. Thus there set in a steady process of denudation. Slowly but surely all the great agricultural districts became less productive. The corn-bearing plains of North America and Russia, the rice plains of China and India, the great scattered areas that had provided the world's greens, the fruit lands of California, Australia, South Africa, one and all deteriorated. Little by little they turned into wastes of sand, like the once fertile Sahara. The process was made all the worse by climatic changes caused by the shrinking of the forests.

The gradual failure of agriculture was of course a very slow process. Ordinary citizens of the empire did not notice it. True, there were great desert tracts in which the ruins of former farmsteads might be observed; but the slow-witted populace never dreamed that this was a symptom of an ever-spreading disaster. Only by comparing the present output with past records could the trouble be realized. But the records and the sacred proportions of agricultural production were known only to the "mystery" of agriculture, in fact to the heads of the world agricultural system. These magnates knew vaguely that something was wrong; but since for sundry reasons it was unlikely that there would be trouble in their day, they held their tongues. The decline was in fact easily concealed, because, while supplies were dwindling, the population of the world was also rapidly decreasing.

The decline of world-population had started long ago after the period of rapid increase which took place in the early phase of industrialization. It was due partly to the widespread use of efficient contraceptive methods, partly to anxiety about economic insecurity, partly to a vague sense of the futility and falsity of civilization. In the rather tired Utopia of North America, where the decline was first seriously felt, insecurity cannot have been a cause, for prosperity was universal. But disillusionment about a curiously aimless Utopia was a serious factor in American life. The early totalitarian states had always feared decline of population, and had done their utmost to check it, but without much success. The newer totalitarian states, the Russian and Chinese Empires, and the World Empire in its early phase, had attacked the problem with characteristic ruthlessness.

The most obvious way to increase population was to waken the hundreds of millions whom past governments had from time to time put into cold storage all over the world in order to solve the unemployment problem. There was at first great reluctance to do this, for a reason which reveals the incredible stupidity and superstition of the human race in this period. Declining population, far from solving the unemployment problem, had increased it. Demand was constantly declining. Mass-productive machinery could less easily be worked at a profit. Though the rulers saw clearly enough with one side of their minds that an increase in population was needed, on the other side they were painfully aware of the unemployment problem, and reluctant to add to the stagnant pool of potential labour. Consequently, though there was much discussion about the cold-storage houses, nothing was done. Meanwhile population continued to decline.

The governments tried to compel the people to reproduce. Women were educated to believe that their sole function was reproduction. Mothers were honoured in relation to the number of their offspring. Those who produced fifteen or more babies were given the title "Prolific Mother." Any who succeeded in launching twenty human beings were deified. Contraception was made illegal and condemned as immoral. In spite of all these measures the fertility-rate declined. In desperation the World Government tightened its grip on the women. Every girl was compelled to have intercourse with a man as soon as she was certified as mature. A month after certification she appeared before her medical board again and was examined to prove that she was no longer a virgin. If after three months she had not conceived, she was sent to an institution that combined the characters of a brothel and a stud-farm. If after another three months she still failed to conceive, she was subjected to medical and surgical treatment to cure her barrenness. If this also failed, she was publicly disgraced, appropriately tortured, and gradually killed.

After helplessly watching the decline of population for many decades, perhaps centuries, the World Government decided to take the obvious step, which, moreover, was sanctioned by scripture. For it was part of the sacred canon that some day, when there was great need of workers, the sleepers must be wakened. The rulers now declared that the time had come. In panic and without proper preparation it ordered the physiologists to thaw out the whole refrigerated multitude. The process was a delicate one, and the instructions left by an earlier and brighter generation were at first badly bungled. Millions were killed, or woke up to a brief period of misery and bewilderment, speedily followed by death. Millions more survived only for a life of permanent invalidism or insanity. The majority, however, though seriously damaged by their rough awakening, were fit for active life of a sort. But they had slept through much history. Their minds had been formed by a world long vanished. Their speech and thought were often so archaic that modern individuals could not understand them. Their limbs, and their minds too, moved at first with painful sluggishness. Their procreative impulses were apparently quenched. Moreover they gradually discovered that their new world was even less propitious than the old one. Some of them, when they had entirely thrown off the miasma of their age-long sleep and had painfully adjusted themselves to the new environment, proved to be rather more quick-witted than their normal neighbours in the new world. And, as they had not been brought up to accept the recent and more extravagant prejudices of the new world, they were generally very critical of the modern customs and institutions. In fact they soon became a grave nuisance to the authorities. The Government hastened to order that all the "reawakened" should at once be fitted with radio control. This obvious precaution had been delayed less through fear of putting them to too great a strain before they had recovered from the effects of refrigeration, than out of an amazingly stupid reluctance to raise them to the rank of citizens. Millions were now subjected to the operation. Half of these died under the anaesthetic. Millions more put up a desperate resistance and had to be destroyed. Here and there, where there was a large concentration of the "reawakened," they were able to seize power and set up a rebel state. The spectacle of human beings resisting authority was utterly bewildering to the robot citizens of the world-state. In many minds there arose an agonizing conflict between the orthodox radio-generated will and a shocking impulse to rebel. This would probably not have occurred had not the technique of radio-control seriously degenerated, owing to the general decline of intelligence. Many of the unfortunate sub-humans (for men were no longer human) went mad or died under the stress of this conflict. Some succeeded in resisting the control and joined the rebels. It almost appeared that an era of new hope was to begin for the human race. Unfortunately the "reawakened" could not stand the strain. While their cause prospered, all was well with them, but every passing misfortune was accompanied by a great crop of suicides. So little heart had they for life. One by one the rebel centres collapsed, till none was left.

The population problem remained unsolved. One other method of coping with it had been tried, at first with some success.

In the early middle period of the world empire, while innovation was still possible, a group of physiologists and surgeons had devised a method which, it was hoped, would settle the matter for ever. The new technique was a half-way stage towards true ectogenesis. The womb and other necessary organs were removed from a young woman and kept alive artificially. The mutilated donor of these precious organs was then destroyed, but part of her blood-stream was put into artificial circulation through the excised organs and used as the medium for supplying them with necessary chemicals. The womb could then be inseminated, and would produce an infant. By various technical methods the process could be made far more rapid than normal reproduction. Moreover quintuplets could be procured from every conception. Unfortunately the excised organs could not be kept alive for more than ten years, so it was necessary to have a constant supply of young women. The government therefore imposed the death penalty on women for the most trivial offences, and used them up for artificial reproduction. At the same time it tried to educate female children in such a way that when they reached maturity many would actually desire the supreme glory of sacrificing their lives so that their wombs might live on with enhanced fertility. The response to this propaganda was disappointing. In fear of a really catastrophic decline of population the government passed a law that every woman, except members of the sacred governing class, must "give her life for her children's sake" at the age of twenty-five.

Unfortunately the method of artificial reproduction involved a very delicate surgical technique, and it did not come into general use until first-class manipulative intelligence was already in decline. Increasingly, therefore, the excised wombs failed to survive the operation, or, if they did survive, failed to produce viable infants. Presently it became clear to the few free intelligences of the race that the method, far from increasing the population, was actually hastening its decline. But already the method had become part of the sacred tradition and could not be abandoned. For decades, therefore, it continued to be practised with increasingly disastrous results. There came a time, however, when even the dull and enslaved wits of the Celestial Empire could not but realize that if the decline of population was not quickly stopped civilization would disintegrate. A great struggle ensued between the orthodox and the protestants, until at last a compromise was agreed upon. At the age of twenty-five every young woman must receive a ceremonial cut on the abdomen, accompanied by suitable ritual and incantations. This, it was believed, would increase the fertility of her reproductive organs without the necessity of excising them.

In spite of everything, population continued to decline. I was not able to discover the cause of this universal process. Perhaps the root of the trouble was physiological. Some chemical deficiency may have affected the germ cells. Or again some subtle mutation of the human stock may have rendered conception less ready. Or perhaps the neurotic condition of the population had produced hormones unfavourable to conception. I am inclined to believe that the real cause, through whatever physical mechanism it took effect, was the profound disheartenment and spiritual desolation which oppressed the whole race.

Whatever the cause, the world-population continued to shrink, and in the process it became a predominantly middle-aged population. The small company of the young, though cherished and venerated, counted for nothing in decisions of policy. An ice-age of feebleness and conservatism gripped the world with increasing force.

Old Man in New World

In 1943 Arthur Koestler asked Stapledon to contribute to an anthology of utopian fiction he was planning. Koestler admired "Old Man in New World," but the other submissions were so disappointing that he concluded that the world war had sterilized the utopian imagination. He gave up the project. Stapledon's story, set in a world state at the end of the twentieth century, is his most disarming foray into utopianism. His allegiance to utopian ideals was clear in several of his books of the 1930s, including Waking World *(1934) and* New Hope for Britain *(1939), and a strong, though dark, streak of utopianism runs through nearly all his fiction, especially* Last and First Men, Odd John, Star Maker, *and* Darkness and the Light. *But "Old Man" has a gentle, wryly humorous take on utopia not found anywhere else in Stapledon's fiction, and it raises fascinating questions about the differences between those who fight to make a utopian society and those who actually live in utopia. These two sides, dramatized here in a dialogue between an old communist and a young flyer, Stapledon often named in his other writings as the perspectives of the revolutionary and the saint. The author's own viewpoint on the utopia is not simply located. He puts some of himself into both saintly and revolutionary voices, but the cosmic skepticism of the Fool's climactic oration is a distinctive ingredient of the vision Stapledon reiterated throughout his career. The story was eventually published as a chapbook by P.E.N., the international writers' association, in 1944.*

THE OLD MAN could not help feeling flattered by the Government's thoughtfulness in sending a special aeroplane to fetch him from his home in Northumberland to witness the great celebration in London. Born during the First World War, he was now nearly eighty, though still, he believed, remarkably clear-headed. Today he was to take his place among the honoured but ever dwindling band of the Fathers of the Revolution. The occasion was the Procession of the Peoples, which was organized every year in some selected city of the world to commemorate the founding of the New World Order, thirty years ago, and twenty-three years after the end of the Second World War. This time the pageant and its concluding ceremony were to be given a new character by a special reference to the young; for today mankind was celebrating also the "Twenty-Fifth Anniversary of the First Generation of the New World," the young people who were born when the New Educational Policy had first come into full operation, five years after the world-wide revolution was completed. By good luck it had fallen to London to be the hostess city on this very special occasion. It was surely fitting that the British metropolis should have the privilege of providing the setting of this event, for it was the shrunken population of Britain that had achieved the most striking change in its fortunes by centring its whole economy on the care and education of its young.

When the agile little two-seater plane had lightly settled on his lawn, the old man stuffed a book in his pocket, hurried out, and climbed into his place, greeting the young pilot. The plane rose vertically above the trees, then slid forward, folding its helicopter vanes into its body. The familiar landscape flattened into a shifting green and brown patchwork.

The old man was pleased to find that the purring sound of the modern silenced plane offered little hindrance to conversation. Small talk soon established friendly relations with his companion, but there inevitably remained a gulf between the aged revolutionary and this young product of the Revolution. The difficulty was not simply due to the years. Between the seniors and the new young there was a subtle difference of mental texture, a difference so deep and far-reaching that one could almost believe that these young minds were based on a different bio-chemical structure from one's own. Of course, they were always respectful, and even friendly, in a superficial way; but always they seemed to withhold something. It was as though, the old man fantastically imagined, they were humouring a child that had suffered and been warped, and would never really grow up. On the rare occasions when they did let themselves go, they talked the strangest stuff. It made one question whether the New Educational Policy had really been sound. But then, was this modern England itself really sound? Was the New World sound? In some ways, of course, it was magnificent; but too many queer new values were in the air. He suspected them. Well, perhaps the show that he was to witness might throw some light on the matter. Rumour had it that there were to be innovations of a startling kind, and that these were designed to indicate that the new and rather young President of the World Federation and many of his colleagues approved of the widespread change of temper in the life of mankind, and intended to foster it.

Secretly the old man regarded this expedition to London as something more than a pleasant jaunt at the Government's expense. It was a mission of inspection. He was an emissary from the past, charged with assessing the achievement of the present. Were the generations that were now in the prime of life making the best possible use of the great opportunity which earlier generations had won for them, after decades of climax and heroic struggle?

He decided to begin his investigation on the young airman. "It must be grand to be young in these prosperous times," he said, "with all the troubles well over." The young man looked quickly at him, and laughed. Somewhat disconcerted, the senior wondered whether the new young, brought up so tenderly and scientifically, could possibly realize what the barbaric pre-revolutionary age had been like. This boy had missed that stern schooling.

"Well," the elder said, "there's no fear of war now, or of tyranny, or of starvation, or of being allowed to rot with nothing to do, or of being worked to death. The world standard of living is high, and rising rapidly; and the backward peoples have almost been brought up to the general level. Everyone is living a fairly full and satisfying life, I suppose. When you young people take charge, there'll be no serious problems left, nothing to do but to carry on improving things all round. What more do you want?"

There was a long pause before the young man spoke. "New times, new ideas," he said, "and new problems."

Again a pause, broken by the senior. "No doubt when sub-atomic power comes into full commercial use we shall find ourselves in the thick of another industrial revolution. But . . ."

"I wasn't thinking of that," the pilot said, "though certainly in a few years sub-atomic power will produce terrific strains if it isn't properly managed. There'll be new skills, new social groupings, an entirely new texture of economic life. We shall warm the Arctic, cool the tropics, reshape the continents, water the deserts, and everyone will have his private rocket-plane for long-distance travel. Quite soon we shall explore the planets. But even that huge economic change will work smoothly enough if . . ."

"If social discipline is properly maintained," the other said.

"Oh, it will be. That's not the problem. Today the danger is rather that the highly successful world-wide ideology will clamp down on our minds so tightly that we shall lose all power of *radical* originality, of originality outside the general pattern of culture. If so, we shall never be able to cope with circumstances that call for *radical* innovation. Sub-atomic energy may be among those circumstances. New advances in educational psychology certainly are. In your days it was discipline and unity that were wanted, but today diversity, originality, and full expression. Then, the vital thing was to teach people to feel community, and to live it, and to give up everything to fight for it. But that battle has been well won. Now, it's individuality that has to be fostered, helped to develop, to deepen itself, to break out into as many new forms as possible. The people in charge don't seem to be able to see how important this is. They have been thinking still in terms of the old half-savage pre-revolutionary human being."

"That's me, I take it," put in the old man.

The young man laughed. "There were many, no doubt, who were ahead of their time. But the mass *were* half-savage, warped in mind from birth onwards by ignorant warped parents and teachers, by a hostile economic environment, and by a culture that put a premium on self-seeking."

"You don't mince matters," laughed the old man, "but what you say is true."

"The point is this," the pilot continued, "human beings can be far more different from one another than sub-human animals can be, and yet they can also be far more aware of one another, and enriching to one another. Well, practically all post-revolutionary human beings can go beyond the average of pre-revolutionary human beings in that way, because they are more conscious. Events before the revolutionary period were already forcing many people to be more penetratingly aware of themselves and their world, and the New Educational Policy has carried the young ones much further. But there's a horrible discrepancy between our educational system and our Government's old-fashioned attempt to keep a firm hand on us. It's so silly, childish. No one *wants* to be anti-social now, so why discipline them? The economic system in the old days *forced* people to be self-seeking and anti-social, but the present one doesn't. The only serious self-seeking there *can* be now is selfish rivalry in social service."

"True in the main," said the old man, "but we must remember the foundations of human nature. We are still at bottom self-regarding animals, and society must compensate for our inveterate individualism by a good deal of discipline. After all, community *involves* some cramping of the longing for unrestrained self-expression. Never forget that."

"We won't, we won't," the young man said, "but community, true community of self-aware and other-aware persons, also involves real differences, otherwise—the ant-hill. And for real persons, discipline must be self-discipline, otherwise it defeats itself. Besides—well, the New Educational Policy was meant to produce a new *kind* of human being, unwarped, fully personal, and all that. It has already gone far; but when the new techniques of psycho-synthesis and telepathic influence have been perfected it will go much further. Maybe it has succeeded better than you intended, even now. Maybe its success makes new social principles necessary, perhaps a new revolution. In your day, I suppose, the vital problems were economic, but now they're psychological."

There was silence, save for the subdued murmur of the plane and the sound of the streaming air. Far below, and to the left, a silver scribble was the Tyne. Through the clear atmosphere of the new smokeless England one could see the towns and docks as sharply defined as a model at arm's length.

The old man had always prided himself on keeping a supple mind open to new ideas, and his junior had given him something which deserved serious consideration. For a long while he silently ruminated, while the plane slid quietly forward over the counties. At last he reached a conviction that these new-fangled ideas really were dangerous. The boy must be made to see that they were dangerous.

"You young people are so fortunate in your world," he said, "that you probably can't realize how thin the veneer of civilization is, and how easily it may break down again unless it is very jealously preserved."

"*We* think," said the young man, "that *your* generation were so *un*fortunate in your youth that you cannot really know how far-reaching the change has been."

The old man sighed, and said, "Let me try to make the past live for you." "Do!" said the junior. "Those towers are Ripon. There's plenty of time."

The old revolutionary embarked on a lecture.

"The main outcome of the First World War was the new Russia, the first state ever planned and controlled for the welfare of ordinary people. Discipline and bold planning alone could make that great revolution, and preserve it against the money-men all over the world. When I was very young, between the First and Second Wars, the Russians were patiently and firmly building up their new Society, and nearly everywhere else men were blindly clinging to their various petty freedoms—freedom to buy and sell, freedom to climb on the shoulders of their fellows by money-power, freedom to propagand lies and folly and hate, freedom of national sovereign states against all attempts at world-wide discipline, freedom of every individual just to destroy himself with aimless frittering, if he had the money and the inclination. All this you know from your history books. But what you can't possibly realize is what it felt like to be young in that time. You can't *feel* the impact of a deadly-sick world on young eager minds. You can't feel what we unemployed felt. You can't feel the foul, stinking, poisonous mist soaking into all our hearts and ruining our humanity."

"All honour," said the young man, "to the Russians for magnificently breaking the spell, and to you and your revolutionary comrades too, for fighting against the poison. But—well, circumstances have been kinder to us. We are not poisoned. And so—"

But the old man refused to be silenced. He had forgotten that he intended to study his companion, not to preach to him. "Knowledge about Russia," he said, "was gradually spreading. Along with the deepening misery went a deepening conviction that the mess was not really inevitable. Russia at least knew how to cure it. And when at last the Second World War came, people said that after *this* war there really would be a new age. The will for a more human order, the will for the light, was stronger than ever before."

The old man seemed to fall into a reverie, till the pilot said, "The will for the light! Yes, it was growing stronger and clearer all the time, really. Well? And then?" It was almost as though he were encouraging a child to repeat its lesson.

"Well," said the elder, "You know as well as I do. We won the war, and lost the peace. But what you young people seem in danger of forgetting is *why* we lost the peace. We lost it because we threw off all the promising disciplines of war. God! How I remember the wild hope when peace came! Never again should gangsters rule! Never again should money-power mess up everything. The Atlantic Charter would at once be applied throughout the world. People really believed that the incubus of the old system could be shifted as easily as that! Unfortunately they forgot that everything depended on the Americans, and that those former pioneers were still stuck in the nineteenth century. The American money-bosses were able to bolster up our own tottering capitalist rulers and prevent our revolution."

"And yet the Americans did well at first," said the young man, "pouring food and goods into Europe without expectation of payment."

"Yes," replied the old man, "but think how the American rulers, the men of big business, when they had recaptured the state after the decline of the New Deal, used the power of the larder and the store-cupboard to establish swarms of their own people in charge of relief work throughout Europe. These 'relieving' Americans settled down as a kind of aristocracy, benevolent in the main, but blind, fundamentally unenlightened. In the name of freedom and mercy they set up a despotism almost as strict as Hitler's."

The pilot laughed. "And yet you say the cause of all the trouble was lack of social discipline."

"My dear boy," cried the old revolutionary, "I want an *accepted* discipline under the community *as a whole*, in order to prevent *imposed* disciplines by sections of it. A very different matter! Anyhow, think what happened! The American bosses were scared stiff when the beaten Germans turned from Nazism to Communism, and the Italians and most other Europeans followed suit. So they had to use their larder-power to check Communism at all costs. They preached their precious old dead-as-mutton liberal democracy for all they were worth. Individual initiative, private enterprise, freedom of thought, and all the old slogans, went ringing through Europe; and not a soul believed them. But the Americans themselves believed them; and their bosses persuaded them it was their mission to lead mankind into that heaven. They were God's people, and they must fulfil their destiny. The old, old story! Of course, many Americans must have known it was cant, but it worked all right on the American masses, so that they backed their bosses. And so in the end the job of salvaging Europe got turned into a business undertaking after all. Instead of putting European industry really on its feet again the American bosses damped it down so that it couldn't compete with their own industry, and so that they could keep a firm hand on Europe, because of Communism."

"True, true," sighed the young man, "but what are you getting at? We all know what happened. America, which by the way was really no longer ruled by the men of *money*, but by the new ruling class of skilled managers and technicians, came into conflict with Russia, where the same class was ruling, but with a different set of ideas. There was rivalry between the two ruling cliques for the control of Europe, and over Japan and China. The American bosses were aiming at a world-wide commercial empire; and the leaders of Russia were determined that as soon as they had repaired their country's war-damage, they would revert to the original policy of instigating a world-wide Communist revolution. Very soon, of course, they tumbled to it that the American bosses were out to control the planet. And so they began slowly damping down their huge job of reconstruction so as to re-arm. And of course the Americans were doing the same. Well, what about it?"

"Try to think what it all meant in terms of living," the old man said. "Think of all the social misery we in Britain had to go through; and on top of it was the certainty of war. In Britain, after the Second War, there had been first a brave attempt to work out a new social order, with security, health, education and leisure for every citizen. But of course that was soon smashed by the moneyed class with help from their American big brothers. Our financial magnates propaganded hard for 'freedom,' abolition of war-time restrictions on private enterprise, back to the good old times, and so on. Instead of letting the Government reshape our whole production system and simplify our living conditions so as to combine frugality with health for all, they just closed down factories, and let millions of workers wallow in unemployment. Everywhere there were ruined factories, deserted mines, streets of dilapidated houses, whole cities neglected and in ruins. Several towns were completely deserted. Those that still functioned at all were inhabited by a few ragged and unhealthy, and mostly middle-aged, people who had lost all hope. The few boys and girls, moreover, seemed prematurely old and grim, oppressed by the preponderance of their elders. How I remember the sickening feeling that we were all just rats that couldn't leave the sinking ship. Day in, day out, one was gripped by that sense of being trapped. To preach revolution, whether to old or young, was like exhorting a man sunk to the neck in a bog to climb a mountain and admire the dawn. Social services decayed, disease increased, the birthrate sank alarmingly. People used to kill their children out of pity, and then kill themselves. The British scarcely noticed the disintegration of their empire, for they had more serious troubles nearer home. It was hell on earth, if ever there was one. The general despair seemed to disintegrate our moral fibre. Too often hopes had been revived and shattered. Too often the promised world seemed to be at hand, only to vanish. The will for the light had always been frail, but now at last it seemed to be withering, like a young plant exposed to too fierce a blizzard. The standard of personal relations was falling. People were becoming in their ordinary contacts with each other less responsible, more callous, less kindly, more vindictive. The mere memory of it all puts me in a cold sweat of fright."

"Well, so what?" said the pilot, with a secret smile.

"What? Well, you know as well as I do. Added to everything else there was the terror of the coming World-War. And stratosphere rocket-planes and sub-atomic bombs promised something far worse than the last war."

"But," the young man interrupted, "the Third World War never happened. Why? You're forgetting something very important. You're forgetting that when both sides were mobilizing, and the war was due at any minute, something happened that would have been impossible at any other stage of history. You remember how government propaganda for the war never really caught on, on either side; and how at the critical moment an extraordinary popular clamour against war and against social robotism broke out on both sides. Who was really responsible for that? Why, the new 'agnostic mystics,' of course. They started the world strike in America and Russia. Decades earlier, the pacifists had tried to stop war by popular protest, but they failed miserably, because conditions were not ripe. But the new group, who weren't strictly pacifists at all but social revolutionaries with a religious motive—they found conditions ripe, and they did the trick. Obviously you must know that story, how everyone downed tools and was ready to die for the new hope. Thousands must have been imprisoned, hundreds shot. But presently the governments found their armed forces were mutinying. Then came the American Revolution and the big change in Russia. The driving force, as you must surely know, was an odd assortment of airmen, skilled workers, *and*—the agnostic mystics. You ignore those modern saints, but it was those that inspired the whole movement and kept it going. Remember, of course, that for many decades a big change had been slowly going on deep down in people's minds. It had begun away back in the First War and made steady progress through the inter-war period, but it was never effective till after the Second War. It came to a head among the young fighters in that war, particularly among the airmen, and also among all the oppressed peoples of Europe, and in the occupied parts of Russia and China, and later in broken-down Britain. These two very different groups, the fighters and the broken, rediscovered the power of comradeship, as the Russians had done in their first Revolution. But this time it was discovered with far deeper consciousness of its meaning. So much had happened since that earlier awakening. This time it developed into a purged and clarified *will for the light*, as you yourself called it; a will for a more fully human way of living, for intelligence, and other-respecting community, and for creative action in all human affairs."

"Not much new in that," interposed the old man.

"Oh yes, there was," said the junior, "it was a moral passion for this way of living as an *absolute good*, not just as a means to social prosperity. It was mystical, too, because though these people didn't pledge themselves to any beliefs about the ultimate reality, and were mostly outside all organized religion, they *felt* with complete certainty that in some way, which they couldn't state intellectually at all, the struggle for the light was the real meaning and purpose of all conscious existence. And in keeping themselves in severe training for that struggle they found—well, 'the peace that passeth all understanding.'

It was this new attitude, this humbly agnostic, yet deeply mystical, *feeling,* that broke the spell of disillusion and spread like a fire from heart to heart."

The old man had been shifting restlessly in his seat, and now he expostulated. "Wait a minute, wait a minute! What are you getting at? This mystical feeling, as you call it, was just the subjective side of the objective pressure of circumstances, which forced people to see that they must stand together or perish. Of course, I know your mystics mostly came in on the right side, and that they provided a lot of heartening though questionable ideology, and appreciably strengthened the passion and drive of the Revolution. But—"

"They played the leading part in the preliminary American Revolution," said the pilot, "and that prevented the war." "Oh, yes," the old man admitted. "But—" "And they inspired a change in Russia that almost amounted to a second Russian revolution. They made Russia the stronghold of the new agnostic-mystical Communism, as it had been also of the earlier kind of Communism."

"But wait!" cried the old man. "Though the Russians did indulge in a dash of mysticism, there wasn't much of mysticism about the new world-organization. After the decade of revolutions, what came out was nothing highfalutin, just a common-sense world-wide federation of socialist states."

"Yes," the young man said, "because, although it was the agnostic-mystics who generated the *passion* and *drive* of the world-wide revolution, the people who actually *managed the setting up* of the new order were the professional revolutionaries. Their job was to bring off the great economic and social change, and to make it secure. And so they concentrated, quite rightly, on self-discipline for the masses of their supporters and imposed-discipline for their opponents. But when the new order was firmly established, something different was needed, and you old warriors of the revolution" (the young man smiled apologetically at his companion) "could never really see that. It was only with your tongues in your cheeks that you had *used* the power of the new religious feeling to establish the Revolution. For you it was just a heartening rum-ration to fire the simple masses with Dutch courage. You couldn't appreciate that it was a real awakening, and that it must cause a deep and lasting change of temper in the life of mankind, and therefore that it would insist on transforming the whole tone of your new world-order."

"Oh, but we did appreciate that," said the old man, "and we saw both the good in it and the danger. It looked like a first mild dose of those two ancient social poisons, individualism and superstition. Take that word 'instrument' that your friends are so fond of. They are not

content to say that the individual is an 'instrument' of social advancement; they say that individuals, and the race as a whole, are 'instruments' for the fulfilling of 'the spirit.' That's sheer superstition."

"When we say mankind is an instrument," the pilot replied, "we
say something that your generation almost inevitably dismisses as
cant. And we certainly can't prove it intellectually. But intellect can't
*dis*prove it either. Really, it *needs* no proof. It's as obvious as daylight,
when one opens one's eyes. And the early agnostic-mystics, by captur-
ing your New Educational Policy, managed to open the eyes of the
young to it. *We*," the young man announced with a smile that prevented the remark from being either pompous or offensive, "are at
once the first undamaged generation and the first clear-sighted generation. The credit must go to our elders, not to us; but that's what we
are, and we must be treated as such, not with all the trivial discipline
that was appropriate to social insecurity, and is now quite out of date."

The couple in the sky fell silent. The old man watched the green
land pass under the aeroplane like a great map, unrolled before them
and rolled up again behind. From this height England looked much
the same as it had in his youth, yet how different were the English,
particularly the new young!

Presently, remembering his original intention, he said to his companion, "Tell me about yourself. Help me to understand what sort of
supermen you amazing young people really are."

The other laughed. After a pause he said, "Well, I'm twenty-three,
professional flier, and university student. Reading biology. Special subject, the flight of birds and insects. I'm making a fine set of tele-
cinematograph pictures of birds in flight, and microcine pictures of
insects. But I'm getting more and more interested in psychology, and
when I'm too old for first-class flying, maybe I shall be good enough
for some psychological job. If not, I'll train fliers. Eighteen months ago
I married. My wife, of course, really is a super-girl. She was twenty
then, and now she is just about to have a baby. She's studying at the
London College of Teachers, and very soon she will be going into their
Maternity Home. When she's fit again she'll go back to her studies and
her teaching, on the half-time and later the three-quarter-time basis.
The College's own crèche and nursery school will help her, of course.
We have a flat within five minutes of them."

"Rather an early marriage, wasn't it?" put in the old man.

"Not for these days. I don't mean merely because the country
needs children. I mean from the individual point of view. We realize
now that it's impossible to live fully without the experience of a lasting
partnership. A good marriage is the microcosm of all community experience. Of course, if it fails, we can drop it, acknowledging our mistake;

but it won't fail. We had other affairs first, of course, and may have occasional fresh ones in the future. But we do belong to one another fundamentally, and we decided to register the fact. Besides, we want the children to know that we were sure of one another right at the beginning."

Strange, the old man mused, how monogamy was being rehabilitated! The only snobbery in the typical modern young mind was the snobbery of the happily married who were also parents. But to be so sure of one another at twenty-two and twenty! The venture seemed bound to fail. And yet—perhaps the New Educational Policy, with its minute care for emotional education and its new technique of psychosynthesis, really had produced a more self-aware and other-aware and passionally stable type. The new young did seem to have an inner stability and harmony lacking in the young of his own early days. Monogamy, when it worked, evidently gave both partners something extraordinarily valuable, something steadying and strengthening. He looked back at the sweet but torturing and transitory affairs of his own life. How superficially he and his beloveds had been aware of one another! He remembered, too, his late, desperate, childless marriage and stormy separation.

The plane was now over the outskirts of London, and the old man's attention was drawn to the impressive spectacle of the giant city, spread out below him and stretching away in all directions to fade into the summer haze. Of smoke there was none. Every building below him stood out sharply in the sunshine, like a precise little crystal among thousands of fellow crystals. The whole was like a patchwork of crystallization and green mould, which was really the many parks and gardens, and the long ranks of trees lining the great new boulevards. The Thames was a bright ribbon that borrowed colour from the blue sky. As the plane circled and sank, the old man picked out familiar landmarks, the tower of the new House of Parliament (the former buildings had been destroyed in the troubles), the ancient dome of St. Paul's, the great pile of University College. Now he could see cars moving in the streets. Boats on the Thames were little water-beetles. Towers and spires rose upwards as the plane descended, till weathercocks were at eye-level. The plane protruded its helicopter vanes and hovered here and there, like a bee choosing a flower, as the pilot sought a good landing. Then it sank to ground in a crowded little aeroplane park that still bore the name Leicester Square.

As there was some time to put in before he was due to take his seat among the Fathers of the Revolution, the old man made his way through cheerful crowds toward the Embankment, and a favourite eating house. On all his rare visits to London he was struck with the contrast between the modern fresh-complexioned Londoners, so well though simply dressed, and the Londoners of his youth, who ranged from frank shabbiness through a pathetic and unsuccessful imitation of smartness to gross ostentation. Now, even in the East End, shabbiness was abolished both from dress and houses. The slums and their inmates had vanished. There was also a subtler contrast between the earlier and the later Londoners, hard to focus. In comparison with these notably self-assured and genial faces, his memory's composite picture of the faces of former crowds expressed a chivvied, anxious, furtive, sometimes vindictive temper in which native friendliness flickered insecurely.

When he had crossed the wide stretch of grass which now flanked the Thames, he came to his eating house, right on the water's edge. It stood almost on the site where, long ago, stood Cleopatra's Needle, now repatriated. Here, too, long ago, he himself as an unemployed youth had once spat into the Thames with contempt and fury against the universe. Now, having entered the bright little building and slipped coins into appropriate slots, he served himself with coffee and cakes. He carried his tray to a table out of doors by the river. Almost the only link with the past was the dome of St. Paul's, far down stream but sharply defined and silvery grey in the purged atmosphere. Of course there was also the Waterloo Bridge, which in his young days had been a novelty, and was indeed a precursor of the new order. Across the almost clean water with its smokeless tugs and strings of barges, its pleasure-launches and its long sleek public passenger vessels, the southern bank had been transformed. Where formerly was a muddle of shabby buildings, much battered by war, stood now a rather austere form of concrete and glass, the Office of the World Commissioners in Britain. Above it waved a great flag, displaying a white orb on a bright blue field, the already storied emblem of loyalty to man. This had long been the focal symbol of that passion for humanity which, after so many decades of tragedy and heroism, had at last swollen to an irresistible torrent and founded the New World. Up stream, where formerly was the railway bridge to Charing Cross Station, the old man admired the great new road bridge, which spanned the river in a single flattened arch, impossible before the advent of the new synthetic metals. Beyond, he could see once more the tower of the new Parliament House.

The old revolutionary had reason to be proud of this new London, since he had played a modest but useful part in making it possible. He loved not only its new wide boulevards with their modern edifices, but also the old Georgian squares. The new architecture, he felt, blended into a seamless unity with the old-time buildings, a unity symbolical of the new life of the English people. Yet he was irrationally haunted by nostalgia for the old smoky, class-ridden, snob-bound, Philistine London, the London in which, after all, men had learnt manhood without all this modern pampering. Oh well, it was time to make a move. After a few minutes' walk he was at the appropriate tier of seats in the new Great Square of London, where the procession would concentrate for the final ceremony. He settled into his place among the other ancient relics of a mythical period, feeling somehow at once a distinguished guest and an exhibit. Band music heralded the approach of the procession. Soon the first national column entered the Great Square, circled round it, and took up its allotted place. The leaders were the Chinese, the senior civilization of the world. Column by column, the representatives of all the nations followed.

As on previous occasions, each of the national contingents carried its national flag. Why, the old man wondered, did men still cling to these silly and rather dangerous local emblems? However, each nation also displayed, and in the place of honour in front of its own flag, the simple banner of the World Federation. Some of the marchers were dressed in their agricultural or industrial or other vocational uniforms. For uniforms had, of course, greatly increased in the world since the will for social cohesion had come into its own; and during the anxious period of world-reconstruction the need for economy had emphasized this tendency. But to-day's procession included many marchers in diversified and quaintly stylized individual clothing. As usual, the national columns carried with them the instruments or products of their most distinctive national occupations. Sheaves of corn, fruit, rolls of gorgeous cloth and silk, scientific and optical instruments, sleek electrical machinery, models of ships and aeroplanes, were borne upon shoulders, or on tractors which were themselves exhibits. Some peoples had deliberately stressed culture rather than industry; in particular the Germans, proudly bearing their books, musical instruments, paintings, sculpture.

It had been arranged that the peoples should be represented roughly in proportion to their actual population. Consequently the faces of the marchers were predominantly swarthy or "yellow" or black. But the columns of North America, of Northern Europe, and of European Russia showed that the fair type was still a notable factor in the human community.

At the end of the long procession came the diminutive columns of the three hostess peoples themselves, the English, the Scotch, the Welsh. Great enthusiasm and considerable amusement was caused among the spectators by the fact that at the head of each of these little companies came a rank of young mothers carrying their babies. Behind these marched three ranks of older children, and then nurses and child-welfare workers, followed by teachers, in the grey tweed which had become the uniform of all those engaged in education, and was now the most respected cloth in the Island. Then came the Young Pioneers, boys and girls equipped for harvesting, digging, afforestation, and so on. Behind these were the representatives of the Universities and Technical Colleges, and finally the usual ranks of industry and agriculture characteristic of the Island. By giving to maternity and education pride of place in their columns the British peoples manifested to the world the fact that they were successfully stemming the decline of their population, and that their whole economy was purposefully directed toward the creation of noble future citizens.

All this was admirable. But there was a novelty, and one which was very disturbing to the old man, though it elicited from the spectators hilarity and applause. According to the official programme the innovation had been conceived by a group of young French writers and artists; and the authorities, after careful consideration, had sanctioned it as "a symbol of the new feeling for individuality which was rising in all parts of the world." Social harmony, the programme declared, was now well established, and mankind was in a position to relax its discipline and smile at its hard-won triumphs, without either disparaging the heroic self-abnegation of the founders of the New World or undermining the loyalty of its present supporters. The programme said nothing of the violent conflict of opinion which had preceded the official sanctioning of the innovation, a conflict which had led to the resignation of a number of persons in high places.

The daring new feature was this. Many of the national columns were accompanied by two or three unattached individuals whose task it was to clown hither and thither beside the marchers, and even among their ranks. Most of the columns were without these strange attendants; but besides the French, who had conceived the device and executed it with characteristic subtlety, a rather odd assortment of peoples had adopted it. The Russians, with their vein of self-criticism and their genius for ballet, the Chinese with their humour, the Irish, who welcomed every opportunity of irreverence toward authority, and the English, whose presentation was more genial than subtle—these peoples alone had found sufficient interest and moral courage to submit themselves to the penetrating fire of self-criticism.

Each of these comedians was dressed in a stylized and extravagant version of some costume prominent in his own national contingent. All were clearly meant to represent the undisciplined individuality of the common man. In their behaviour they combined something of that almost legendary film-star, Chaplin, with characters of the privileged mediaeval jester. Sometimes they merely blundered along enthusiastically and inefficiently beside the column, vainly trying to conform to the regimented conduct of their fellows; sometimes they would seem to be torn between the spell of the group and personal impulse, breaking suddenly into an abortive caper and then shamefacedly falling into step again to bear themselves with an exaggerated air of rapture in the common rhythm. Sometimes they would stop to joke with individual spectators, and then scuttle anxiously and penitently back to their places. Occasionally one of them would attach himself to a leader of the column, mimicking his pompous bearing and military gait. Evidently, these clowns had been very carefully chosen, and were highly skilled artists; for they contrived to single out any slightly mechanical, officious or arrogant mannerisms of the leaders, and caricature them in a style that was at once devastating and kindly. Theirs was in part the flattering but sometimes shattering imitation with which children often pay tribute to their elders, and in part the friendly ridicule with which adults may temper the crude enthusiasm of the young. And such was their artistry that, in spite of their criticism of individual leaders and of the common enthusiasm, there was no doubt at all about their acceptance of the spirit of the whole occasion.

The startling climax of this daring innovation was reached in the final ceremony, which took place in the Great Square itself. As was customary, the last of the national columns saluted the dignitaries of the world and passed on to their allotted place in the Square. The flags of all the peoples were duly brought forward by their bearers into the open space before the dais, and together bowed to the ground before the great Standard of Mankind; then raised to be held erect for the rest of the ceremony. One by one the heads of the nations mounted the dais, bowed deeply to the President of the World, and handed him a book in which was inscribed a record of the particular nation's achievement during the preceding year. There followed the usual broadcast speeches by high officials, culminating in an oration by the President of the World, reviewing the whole contemporary state of the human species.

Events on the dais were of course televised, as was the procession. But this final ceremony was televised largely in "close-ups," so that all the world could appreciate its detail. There on the dais the leading personalities of the whole planet were assembled with the eyes of mankind upon them. And there, also, visible throughout the world, was the most daring novelty of all. At large among the great ones was a sort of court fool, a prince of jesters, clothed to symbolize Everyman. This individual was made up very differently from his humbler colleagues in the procession; and in spite of its humour his whole performance had about it something sad, compassionate and trance-like. For the most part he stood quietly watching the salutations of the national representatives, or listening to the speeches; but now and then he ranged freely about the dais, making play with a fool's sceptre, to which was attached a bladder, roughly mapped with the outlines of the continents. And sometimes, while listening to a speech, he would silently and in a rapt, absentminded way, imitate the gestures of the orator, or move aside to caricature some applauding dignitary. Thus with his delicate and fleeting mimicry he would expose the foibles of the political stars among whom he was stationed. Mostly they endured the ordeal without flinching, entering amiably into the joke against themselves. But one or two failed to conceal their mortification at some shrewd hit; and then the Fool, perceiving this, immediately dropped his foolery, and with raised eyebrows turned away.

Clearly this most surprising innovation released pent-up forces in the crowd, most of whom, through their pocket television sets, must have seen the detail of these little dramas as clearly as the old man himself had done from his privileged position among the Fathers of the Revolution. He too had responded to the Fool's artistry, but with a sense of guilt, as though he were enjoying something secret and obscene. Such indulgence of individual genius, delightful as it was, must surely weaken the authority of the persons who were exposed to it, must also tend to a general loosening of the social fibre. No doubt it might be said that only a strong government could have permitted itself to be thus criticized. Only an intelligent government, and one which could count on the loyalty of an intelligent and contented population could have recognized in the device a source of strength rather than of weakness. Moreover, only a government that had sensed the changing mood of the peoples of the world, and wished to register its approval, would have troubled to submit itself to this fantastic aesthetic commentary. The old man had to admit intellectually the force of these arguments, but the innovation violated the emotional habit of one whose mind had been formed in a more primitive age.

The supreme incident was still to come. It was one which showed by its obvious power over the assembled multitude the extraordinary change that had come over mankind within a few decades. No earlier populace could have understood, still less have been so profoundly moved by, a symbol of such austere significance. The President of the World was at the height of his speech. He had been dilating upon the incredible improvement in the fortunes of the common man in all lands, and glorifying the achievement and the promise of the human species under its new regime. He was, of course, frequently interrupted by applause. After the most vociferous of these outbursts, at the very moment when silence had been restored and the President was about to continue, the Fool stepped up to him, laid a hand on his shoulder and gently ousted the surprised orator from the microphone. Most startling fact of all, the President, with an awkward smile, acquiesced. And no one interfered.

Then the Fool, confronting the microphone, spoke to the world. "Happy, happy beings!" he said, and his quiet voice was now for the first time heard. "Happy, happy beings! But death dogs you. Conquerors of a world, but of a sand-grain among the stars! We are mere sparks that flash and die. Even as a species we are upstart, sprung so lately from beasts and fishes; soon to vanish. After us our planet will spin for aeons, and nothing will remember us. Then why, why, why are we here?"

He was silent. Throughout the Great Square there was a sound like a drift of air passing over a ripe cornfield. The whole populace had drawn in its breath. For a long moment the silence and the stillness continued, broken only by the quiet movement of the flags, and the sound of wings as a couple of pigeons settled in the Square.

Then at last the Fool spoke again. "The stars give no answer. But within ourselves, and in one another, and in our unity together, the answer lies; for in consciousness of our humanity we see deeper than through telescopes and microscopes. And from the depth of each one of us, and from our community together, a will arises; whence, we know not, but inexorable. 'Live, oh fully live!' it bids us. 'To be aware, to love, to make—this is the music that I command of all my instruments. Let your sand-grain resound with a living flood of music; harmonious in itself, and harmonized with the song of all the spheres, which I alone can hear.' Thus commands the will in us. And we, little human instruments, though death will surely hunt us down, and though our species is ephemeral, we shall obey. Weak we are, and blind, but the Unseen makes music with us."

Silence once more occupied the Great Square, and persisted. The ranked columns and the surrounding populace stood motionless, held by the Unseen. Then at last the Fool, with bowed head, withdrew from sight. And then the President, after a moment's hesitation, returned to the microphone and said, "Our celebration has found an unexpected but a fitting climax. I will say no more but that your leaders, who are also your comrades, will go forward with you to make the living music that is man." As the President retired, a murmur rose from the populace and soon swelled into an oceanic thunder of applause. When at last the noise had died down, the massed bands struck up the familiar strains of the world anthem, the "Song of Man," while the whole great company stood at attention to sing. Then the columns, one by one, moved and wheeled, and flowed out of the Square, and the huge crowd of onlookers dispersed.

In deep abstraction and perplexity the old man threaded his way along the congested streets, brooding on the strange scene that he had witnessed. To his shame he found that tears had spilled from his eyes. Oh yes, it was a great feat of stage-craft. One could not but be moved. But it was dangerous, and subtly false to the spirit of the Revolution. The President of the World, who was surely too young a man for such a responsible post, must have known beforehand of the intended interruption. It was all a cunning bid for popularity. Worse, it was a reversion to religion, a dose of that ancient opium, shrewdly administered by the new rulers. Where would this thing end? But tears were in his eyes.

Sirius at Cambridge
from *Sirius*

The 1944 fantasy Sirius *is the biography of a dog raised to human mental status by surgical and chemical techniques developed by Thomas Trelone, a researcher on brain development. Raised in rural Wales by the scientist's wife Elizabeth and treated as a sibling to Trelone's daughter Plaxy, Sirius in his youth is kept concealed from the wider world. He is apprenticed to a farmer named Pugh and learns the skills of shepherding, while preserving his "cover" as merely an experimental "super-sheep-dog." Although hampered by poor eyesight and lack of hands, Sirius develops an intellectual life and even, with the help of a custom-made glove, the ability to write. One of the high points of the fantasy is the chapter in which Sirius emerges from his Welsh isolation to confront the academic world of Cambridge University. Stapledon uses the dog's-eye perspective for mordant commentary on human custom and behavior from an observer who, despite his nurturing, always remains profoundly estranged from both the human and the canine worlds. It is an episode full of Swiftian comedy, leavened with poignant suggestions of the tragedy of a biological misfit and culminating in eloquent nihilism.*

WHEN THE HOLIDAY WAS OVER, Thomas took Sirius to Cambridge. A private bed-sitting-room had been prepared for the wonder-dog within the precincts of the Laboratory, near a room which Thomas occupied himself. The senior members of the staff were introduced to

Sirius as "man to man," on the understanding that they must keep the secret and behave in public as though this dog were only a rather specially bright super-sheep-dog.

Sirius was at first very happy at Cambridge. The bustle of city and university, though rather bewildering, was stimulating. During the first few days he spent much time in wandering about the streets watching the people, and the dogs. The abundance of the canine population surprised him, and so did the extraordinary diversity of breeds. It seemed to him incredible that the dominant species should keep so many of the dominated species alive in complete idleness, for not one of these pampered animals had any function but to be the living toy of some man or woman. Physically they were nearly all in good condition, save for a common tendency to corpulence, which in some cases reached a disgusting fulfilment. Mentally they were unwholesome. How could it be otherwise? They had nothing to do but wait for their meals, sink from boredom into sleep, attend their masters or mistresses on gentle walks, savour one another's odours, and take part in the simple ritual of the lamp-post and the gate-post. Sexually they were all starved, for bitches were few, and jealously guarded by their human owners. Had not the canine race been of sub-human intelligence, they must one and all have been neurotics, but their stupidity saved them.

Sirius himself had often to act the part of these sub-human creatures. When Elizabeth took him out to visit her friends he allowed himself to be petted and laughed at, or praised for the "marvellous intelligence" that he showed in "shaking hands" or shutting the door. Then the company would forget him completely, while he lay stretched out on the floor in seeming boredom, but in fact listening to every word, and trying to get the hang of some conversation on books or painting; even furtively stealing a glance at drawings or bits of sculpture that were circulated for inspection.

Elizabeth did her best to give Sirius a fair sample of life in a university city. It became a sort of game with her to contrive means to insinuate him into meetings and concerts. After the simple subsistence life of the sheep-country, Cambridge filled him with respect for the surplus energies of the human species. All these great and ornate buildings had been put up stone by stone, century by century, with the cunning of human hands. All these articles in shop-windows had been made by human machinery and transported in human trains, cars and ships from the many lands of human occupation. Perhaps most impressive of all to his innocent mind was the interior of a great library, where, by patient intrigue, Elizabeth managed to effect an entry for him. The thousands of books lining the walls brought home to him as nothing else had done the vast bulk and incredible detail of human intellectual tradition. He stood speechless before it all, his tail drooping with awe. As yet he was far too simple-minded to realize that the majority of the volumes that faced him, shoulder to shoulder, were of little importance. He supposed all to be mightily pregnant. And the naïve belief that he could never attain wisdom until his poor eyes had travelled along most of those millions of lines of print filled him with despair.

Thomas had decided that the time had come to let out the secret of Sirius's powers to a carefully selected public. A number of his scientific and academic friends must be allowed to make the dog's acquaintance and form their own opinions of his ability, on the understanding that the truth must not yet be published. His policy was still to keep the greater public from sharing the secret, lest the forces of commercial stunt–manufacture should be brought to bear on his work, and possibly wreck it.

He arranged for Sirius to meet a few eminent persons in the University, mostly zoologists, biochemists, biologists of one sort or another, but also psychologists, philosophers, and philologists, who would be interested in his speech, and a few stray surgeons, painters, sculptors and writers who happened to be among Thomas's personal friends. These meetings generally took place after a lunch in Thomas's rooms. Over the meal Thomas would tell the party something about his experiments and the success of the super-sheep-dogs. Then he would lead on to his more daring research, and describe Sirius as "probably quite as bright as most university students." When lunch was over, the small company would settle in easy chairs with their pipes, and Thomas, looking at his watch, would say, "I told him we should be ready for him at two o'clock. He'll be along in a minute." Presently the door would open and the great beast would stalk into the room. He did not lack presence. Tall and lean as a tiger, but with a faint suggestion of the lion's mane, he would stand for a moment looking at the company. Thomas would rise to his feet and solemnly introduce his guests one by one to Sirius. "Professor Stone, anthropologist, Dr. James Crawford, President of ——— College," and so on. The guests generally felt extremely ill at ease, not knowing how to behave, and often suspecting that Thomas was playing a trick on them. Sometimes they remained stolidly seated, sometimes they rather sheepishly rose to their feet, as though Sirius were a distinguished human newcomer. Sirius looked steadily into the eyes of each guest as he was introduced, acknowledging him with a languid movement of his great flag of a tail. He would then take up his position in the centre of the company, generally squatting down on the hearth-rug. "Well," Thomas would say, "first of all you want to know, of course, that Sirius really can understand English, so will someone ask him to do something?" Often the whole company was so paralysed by the oddity of the situation that it took a full half-minute for anyone to think of an appropriate task. At last the dog would be asked to fetch a cushion or a book, which of course he straightway did. Presently Thomas would carry on a conversation with Sirius, the guests listening intently to the strange canine speech, and failing to understand a word of it. Then Sirius would say a few simple words very slowly, Thomas translating. This would lead on to a general conversation in which the guests would often question the dog and receive the answer through Thomas. Not infrequently Sirius himself would question the visitors, and sometimes his questions were such that Thomas was obviously reluctant to pass on. In this way the guests received a clear impression of a strong and independent personality.

And in this way Sirius himself gradually reached certain conclusions about these distinguished specimens of the dominant species. One characteristic about them perplexed him greatly. It was such a deep-seated thing that they themselves did not seem to be aware of it. One and all, they undervalued or misvalued their hands. Many of them, in fact all but the surgeons, sculptors, painters, and research workers, were wretchedly clumsy with their hands, and by no means ashamed of it. Even those whose work involved manual skill, the surgeons, sculptors and so on, though they were so skilled in their own specialized technique, had often lost that general handiness, that manual versatility, by which their species had triumphed. On the whole they were helpless creatures. Hands were for them highly specialized instruments, like the bird's wing or the seal's flipper, excellent for some one action, but not versatile. Those that came on bicycles never mended their punctures themselves. They could not sew on their buttons or mend their socks. Moreover even these specialized geniuses of the hand had to some extent been infected by the general contempt for "manual toil," which the privileged class had invented to excuse their laziness. As for the writers, academics, lawyers, politicians, their unhandiness and their contempt for mere manual dexterity were amazing. The writers couldn't even write properly. They fell back on the cruder activity of pressing typewriter keys. Or they simply dictated. Sirius had heard that in Old China the scholar class let their finger-nails grow fantastically long so that their incapacity for manual work should be obvious. Think of the millions of cunning hands thus wasted! How he despised these regressive human types for the neglect and atrophy of the most glorious human organ, the very instrument of creation; and for infecting with their contempt for manual skill even the manual workers themselves, on whose practical dexterity the whole structure of civilization was founded! Artisans actually wanted their sons to "rise" into the class of "black-coated" workers. What would not Sirius himself have achieved if he had been given even the clumsy hands of an ape, let alone the least apt of all these neglected human organs!

The first few weeks at Cambridge were indeed delightful for Sirius. Every morning some bit of research was done upon him at the Laboratory, with his interested co-operation. Sometimes it was a case of studying his motor or sensory reactions, sometimes his glandular responses to emotional stimuli, sometimes his intelligence, and so on. X-ray photographs had to be made of his skull, gramophone records of his speech. With the co-operation of a psychologist he himself planned to write a monograph on his olfactory experiences, and another on his power of detecting human character and emotional changes by scent and tone of voice. Psychologists and musicians studied his musical powers. His sex life had also to be recorded.

In addition to all this strictly scientific work, in which Sirius collaborated with his human observers, he planned to undertake two popular books entirely on his own. One was to be called *The Lamp-post, A Study of the Social Life of the Domestic Dog*. The opening passage is interesting for the light which it throws on Sirius's temperament. "In man, social intercourse has centred mainly on the process of absorbing fluid into the organism, but in the domestic dog and to a lesser extent among all wild canine species, the act charged with most social significance is the excretion of fluid. For man the pub, the estaminet, the Biergarten, but for the dog the tree-trunk, the lintel of door or gate, and above all the lamp-post, form the focal points of community life. For a man the flavours of alcoholic drinks, but for a dog the infinitely variegated smells of urine are the most potent stimuli for the gregarious impulse." The other projected book, *Beyond the Lamp-post*, he kept a dead secret. It was to be autobiographical, and would express his philosophy of life. These works were never completed; the second was scarcely even begun, but I have found the random notes for it extremely useful in writing Sirius's biography. They reveal a mind which combined laughable naïvety in some directions with remarkable shrewdness in others, a mind moreover which seemed to oscillate between a heavy, self-pitying seriousness and a humorous detachment and self-criticism.

It was flattering to Sirius to be the centre of so much interest; and it was very unwholesome. Inevitably he began to feel that his mission was after all simply to be his unique self, and to allow the human race respectfully to study him. Far from retaining the humility that had oppressed him on his visit to the library, he now swung away towards self-complacency. As his presence became more widely known, more people sought his acquaintance. Thomas received innumerable invitations from outside the chosen circle, persons who had evidently heard vague rumours of the human dog and were eager to verify them. When Sirius was out in the streets people often stared at him and whispered. Thomas strongly disapproved of his going out by himself, lest attempts should be made to kidnap him. The anxious physiologist even went so far as to hint that unless his precious charge agreed never to go out without a human escort he would have to be confined to the Laboratory. This threat, however, infuriated Sirius; and Thomas recognized that, if it were carried out, all friendly co-operation would cease. The best he could do was to engage a detective to follow the dog on a bicycle whenever he went out of doors. Sirius conceived a humorous dislike of this individual. "He's rather like a tin can tied to my tail, he and his clattery old bike," said Sirius; and henceforth always referred to him as "Old Tin Can." The game of giving Old Tin Can the slip or leading him into awkward situations became Sirius's main outdoor amusement.

Contrary to his original intention Sirius spent the whole of that autumn term at Cambridge. Though he was often very homesick for the country, and nearly always had a headache and often felt seedy, he found Cambridge life far too fascinating to surrender. Several times he did, indeed, suggest to Thomas that he ought to be moving on; but Thomas was reluctant to break off the research, and Sirius himself was too comfortable to find energy to press the matter.

Very soon the Christmas vacation was upon him, and he went back to Wales with Thomas, Elizabeth, and Plaxy. Once more on the hills, he discovered that he was in a sorry state of physical decay, and he spent much of his time trying to restore himself by long hunting expeditions.

During the spring term Sirius was less happy. The glamour of Cambridge had begun to fade, and he was increasingly restless about his future; the more so because Cambridge was like a habit-forming drug. By now he obtained only a mild satisfaction from it, yet it had got into his blood and he could not bring himself to do without it. He had arrived in Cambridge, an anatomical study of bone and muscle. A soft, inactive life, which included far too many delicacies received in the houses of admiring acquaintances, had already blurred his contours with a layer of fat, and filled out his waist. Once when he met Plaxy in the street, she exclaimed, "Gosh! You're going fat and prosperous, and you waddle like a Pekinese." This remark had greatly distressed him.

Along with physical decay went a less obvious mental decay, a tendency to sink into being a sort of super-lap-dog-cum-super-laboratory-animal. His disposition became increasingly peevish and self-centred. There came a day when a serious difference occurred between Sirius and McBane. Thomas's lieutenant had prepared a piece of apparatus for a more minute research into Sirius's olfactory powers. Sirius protested that he was not in the mood for such an exacting bit of work to-day; his nose was in a hypersensitive state and must not be put to any strain. McBane pointed out that, if Sirius refused, hours of preparation would be wasted. Sirius flew into a whimpering tantrum, crying that his nose was more important than a few hours of McBane's time. "Good God!" cried McBane, "you might be a prima donna."

Thomas had been surprised and pleased at the way in which Sirius had settled down to his new life. It seemed as though the dog had outgrown his romantic cravings, and was reconciled to becoming a permanent property at the Lab. But in his second term, though Sirius was still superficially able to enjoy his work, on a deeper level of his mind he was becoming increasingly perturbed and rebellious. This life of ease and self-gratulation was not at all what he was "meant for." The mere shortage of physical exercise made him miserable. Sometimes he cantered a few miles along the tow-path, but this was very boring; and he was always oppressed by the knowledge that the faithful detective was following on a bicycle. He could not force himself to run every day. Consequently he was generally constipated and disgruntled. He felt a growing nostalgia for the moors, the mists, the rich smell of the sheep, with all its associations of hard work and simple triumphs. He remembered Pugh with affection, and thought how much more real he seemed than these dons and their wives.

He was vaguely aware too of his own moral decay. It was increasingly difficult for him to do anything that he did not want to do. Not that he was incapable of all mental effort, for he still generally carried out his intellectual work with conscientious thoroughness. But then, he happened to like that. What he was failing to do was to control his ordinary selfish impulses in relation to his human neighbours. He was also growing less capable even of prudential self-regard.

For instance there was the matter of bitches. Of the few bitches that he encountered in the Cambridge streets, most were anyhow too small for him, and many had been treated with a preparation which disguised the animal's intoxicating natural odour, and made potential lovers regard her as a filthy-smelling hag. He insisted to Thomas that, since in Cambridge there was practically no scope at all for lovemaking, bitches must be provided for him. It was not to be expected that a vigorous young dog should be able to do without them and yet maintain his mental balance. So a succession of attractive females was procured for him. These creatures were brought in turn and at appropriate times to his rooms in the Laboratory; and the whole matter was treated as part of the prolonged and complicated scientific study in which he was co-operating. The Laboratory, by the way, had analysed the chemistry of the odours which were sexually stimulating to Sirius, and could choose seductive animals for him with considerable success. But, his appetite instead of being assuaged, increased. Almost daily they brought a young bitch to his room, yet he was never satisfied. Indeed he became more and more lascivious and difficult to please. Thomas urged him to take himself in hand, otherwise his mental vitality would be sapped. Sirius agreed to do this, but failed to carry out his promise. And now a note of sadism crept into his lovemaking. Once there was a terrible commotion because in the very act of love he dug his teeth into the bitch's neck.

This incident seems to have frightened Sirius himself, for a change now came over him. Dreading that dark power that seemed to rise up within him and control his behaviour, he made a desperate effort to pull himself together. He also determined to leave Cambridge at once and go back to Wales for a spell with the sheep. Thomas reluctantly agreed that he had better go, but pointed out that he was in no condition to undertake sheep work again without some weeks of severe physical training. This was all too true. The best that could be done was that Thomas should arrange with Pugh to take him for a month not as a sheep-dog but as a paying guest. This plan was much discussed, but somehow Sirius could not bring himself to such an ignominious course. In default of a better policy he simply stayed on at Cambridge till the end of the term. There followed an Easter Vacation in Wales, given over wholly to physical training in preparation for a spell of sheep-tending in Cumberland. But as no satisfactory arrangement could be made for him, the lure of Cambridge proved in the end too strong, and he returned with Thomas for the summer term.

In the familiar environment the old way of life proved fatally easy. Laboratory work, meetings with Thomas's scientific or academic friends, a great deal of desultory biological and other scientific reading, a certain amount of philosophy, the writing of his monographs and notes for *The Lamp-post* and *Beyond the Lamp-post*, select parties at which he was lionised by the wives of dons, the perennial shortage of exercise, a succession of bitches, all this told upon his health and loosened his character. He developed more and more the prima donna disposition. He became increasingly self-centred and self-important. Yet all the while, deep in his heart, he felt completely disorientated and futile, spiritually enslaved to the will of man.

At last, when he felt in himself a return of sadistic impulses, he was seized with such a terror of sheer madness that he once more gathered all his moral strength together for a great recovery. He set himself a course of strict self-discipline and asceticism. He would have no more bitches. He would cut down his food by half. Sometimes he would fast; and "pray to whatever gods there be." He would take exercise. He would co-operate conscientiously with the Laboratory staff in their researches on him. He would once more tackle his literary work; for even this, which had for long been his one remaining active interest, had recently been dropped.

For a while he did indeed live a more austere life, punctuated by bouts of wild self-indulgence; but presently his resolution began once more to fail, and he found himself slipping back into the old ways. Terror seized him; and a desperate loneliness in the midst of his social contacts. He felt a violent need for Plaxy, and sent her a note, asking her to come for a good walk with him.

Plaxy gladly made an appointment with him, but the day was not a success. She was naturally very absorbed in her university life; and though Sirius was in a manner a member of the same university, their experiences did not overlap. Lectures, essays, meetings, dances, and above all her new friendships filled her mind with matter that was remote from Sirius. At first they talked happily and freely, but there was no depth of intimacy between them. Several times he was on the verge of blurting out his troubles; but to say, "Oh, Plaxy, help me, I'm going to hell," which was what he wanted to say, seemed somehow preposterous. Moreover, as the day wore on, he began to suspect from a faint change in her odour that she was growing subconsciously hostile to him. He had been talking to her about the bitches. It was then that her scent had begun to take on a slight asperity, though in speech and manner she remained quite friendly. Towards the end of the day a gloomy silence fell upon them both. Each tried to dispel it with light talk, but vainly. When at last they were on the point of parting, and Plaxy had said, "It was nice to be together again," Sirius registered in his own mind the fact that her odour had been growing mellower as the parting approached. "Yes, it's good indeed," he said. But even as he said it the human smell of her, though unchanged in its sensory quality, began to nauseate him.

In order to return to the Laboratory he had to cross the town. He strolled off, without any positive desire to reach his destination, or indeed to do anything else. As he drifted along the streets, he felt stifled by the surrounding herd of the grotesque super-simians who had conquered the earth, moulded the canine species as they trimmed their hedges, and produced his unique self. Feelings of violent hatred surged up in him. A number of significant little memories presented themselves to his embittered mind. Long ago in a field near Ffestiniog he had come upon an angel-faced little boy taking baby thrushes out of a nest and skewering them one by one on a rusty nail. More recently in a Cambridge garden he had watched a well-dressed woman sitting on a seat and fondling a dog's head. Presently she looked about as though to see if she was being observed. There was no one but Sirius, a mere animal. Still stroking the dog with one hand, she reached out with the other and pressed her lighted cigarette end into the creature's groin. This streak of sexual cruelty in human beings horrified Sirius all the more because he himself had indulged in something of the sort with his bitches. But he persuaded himself that this aberration in him was entirely due to some sort of infection from man, due, in fact, to his human conditioning. His own kind, he told himself, were not by nature cruel. Oh, no, they always killed as quickly as possible. Only the inscrutable and devilish cat descended to torture.

It was all due to man's horrible selfishness, he told himself. *Homo sapiens* was an imperfectly socialized species, as its own shrewder specimens, for instance H. G. Wells, had pointed out. Even dogs, of course, were self-centred, but also far more spontaneously social. They might often fight for bones or bitches, and they persecuted one another for the glory of dominance; but when they *were* social they were more wholeheartedly social. They were much more ready to be loyal absolutely, without any secret nosing after self-advantage. So he told himself. They could give absolute, disinterested loyalty; for instance to the human family that claimed their pack-allegiance, or to a single adored master, or to the work that was entrusted to them. The sheep-dog didn't expect to get anything out of his job. He did it for the work's sake alone. He was an artist. No doubt some men were as loyal as any dog, but Cambridge life had taught Sirius to smell out self-regard under every bit of loyalty. Even Plaxy's affection for him seemed in his present mood merely a sort of living up to a pattern for her precious self, not real self-oblivious love. Or take McBane. Was it science or the budding great scientist, Hugh McBane, that really stirred him? Sirius had noticed that he smelt most excited and eager whenever some little personal triumph was at stake. Then there were all those prominent people that he had met at Thomas's lunch parties—biologists, physicists, psychologists, doctors, surgeons, academics, writers, painters, sculptors and God-knows-what-all. They were so very distinguished, and all so seeming modest and so seeming friendly; and yet every one of them, every bloody one of them, if he could trust his nose and his sensitive ears, was itching for personal success, for the limelight, or (worse) scheming to push someone else out of the limelight, or make someone in it look foolish or ugly. No doubt dogs would be just as bad, really, except when their glorious loyalty was upon them. That was the point! Loyalty with dogs could be absolute and pure. With men it was always queered by their inveterate self-love. God! They must be insensitive really; drunk with self, and insensitive to all else. There was something reptilian about them, snakish.

Long ago he had idealized humanity. His silly uncritical, canine loyalty had made him do so. But now his practised nose had found out the truth about the species. They were cunning brutes, of course, devilishly cunning. But they were not nearly so consistently intelligent as he had thought. They were always flopping back into sub-human dullness, just as he was himself. And they didn't *know* themselves even as well as he knew himself, and not half as well as he knew them. How he knew them! He had been brought up in a rather superior family, but even the Trelones were often stupid and insensitive. Even Plaxy knew very little about herself. She was so absorbed in herself that she couldn't see herself, couldn't see the wood for the trees. How often she was unreasonable and self-righteous because of some miserable little self-regard that she herself didn't spot. But *he* spotted it all right, oh yes! And she could be cruel. She could make him feel an outcast and a worm, just for spite.

What enraged him most of all about human beings, and particularly the superior ones that he met in Cambridge, was their self-deception. Every one of them was quite different really from the mask that he or she presented to the world. McBane, for instance. Of course he really *was* devoted to science, up to a point, but more so to himself; and he daren't admit it, even to himself. Why couldn't he just say, "Oh, I know I'm a selfish brute at heart, but I try not to be"? Instead, he pretended to have a real sheep-dog loyalty to science. But he didn't really *use himself up* for science. Perhaps he might some day, just as Thomas did. Some day he might be ready to die for science even. But if he did, he would really be dying not absolutely for science, but for his own reputation as a devoted scientist.

Oh God! What a species to rule a planet! And so obtuse about everything that wasn't human! So incapable of realizing imaginatively any *other* kind of spirit than the human! (Had not even Plaxy failed him?) And cruel, spiteful! (Had not even Plaxy had her claws in him?) And complacent! (Did not even Plaxy really, in her secret heart, regard him as "just a dog"?)

But what a universe, anyhow! No use blaming human beings for what they were. Everything was made so that it had to torture something else. Sirius himself no exception, of course. Made that way! Nothing was *responsible* for being by nature predatory on other things, dog on rabbit and Argentine beef, man on nearly everything, bugs and microbes on man, and of course man himself on man. (Nothing but man was really cruel, vindictive, except perhaps the loathly cat.) Everything desperately struggling to keep its nose above water for a few breaths before its strength inevitably failed and down it went, pressed under by something else. And beyond, those brainless, handless idiotic stars, blazing away so importantly for nothing. Here and there some speck of a planet dominated by some half-awake intelligence like humanity. And here and there on such planets, one or two poor little spirits waking up and wondering what in hell everything was for, what it was all about, what they could make of themselves; and glimpsing in a muddled way what their potentiality was, and feebly trying to express it, but always failing, always missing fire, and very often feeling themselves breaking up, as he himself was doing. Just now and then they might find the real thing, in some creative work, or in sweet community with another little spirit, or with others. Just now and then they seemed somehow to create or to be gathered up into something lovelier than their individual selves, something which demanded their selves' sacrifice and yet gave their selves new life. But how precariously, torturingly; and only just for a flicker of time! Their whole life-time would only be a flicker in the whole of titanic time. Even when all the worlds have frozen or exploded, and all the suns gone dead and cold, there'll still be time. Oh, God, what for?

The Flames: A Fantasy

The Flames *was Stapledon's last foray into the cosmic and philosophical romance. Its central fictional premise — that there might be intelligent beings living within stars, solar creatures of pure energy — was one he had already advanced tentatively a decade earlier in* Star Maker. *In a lecture on Science and Fiction that he gave in Manchester in 1947, the year of the publication of* The Flames, *Stapledon acknowledged that his latest romance depended on "wild biology." But the novella is complexly layered and one of Stapledon's most elusive and ingenious creations. Most of the narrative is in the form of a letter written from a mental asylum by a man claiming to have had a telepathic link with hostile inhabitants of the sun. The letter is intended to urge the human race to unite against the common enemy of invading solar creatures and to end nationalism and intercultural rivalries — Stapledonian issues of long standing. The political subtext of* The Flames *suggests that the letter's import should not be ignored, despite the questionable sanity of its author.* The Flames, *in fact, is structured so that it is hard to separate prophecy from hallucination. The letter-writer is known as Cass (shorthand for Cassandra) and the recipient—a scientist who has edited the manuscript we are reading—is called Thos (a nickname evoking his role as Doubting Thomas). If the fiction is intended to be prophetic, what is being prophesied? Allusions to the great conflagrations of World War II, including the atomic bombings, may indicate that Stapledon wanted the novella to be read as a cautionary parable about the birth of the nuclear age.*

Introductory Note

AN INTRODUCTORY NOTE seems called for to explain to the reader the origin of the following strange document, which I have received from a friend with a view to publication. The author has given it the form of a letter to myself, and he signs himself with his nickname, "Cass," which is an abbreviation of Cassandra. I have seldom met Cass since we were undergraduates together at Oxford before the war of 1914. Even in those days he was addicted to lurid forebodings, hence his nickname. My last meeting with him was in one of the great London blitzes of 1941, when he reminded me that he had long ago prophesied the end of civilization in world-wide fire. The Battle of London, he affirmed, was the beginning of the long-drawn-out disaster.

Cass will not, I am sure, mind my saying that he always seemed to us a bit crazy; but he certainly had a queer knack of prophecy, and though we thought him sometimes curiously unable to understand the springs of his own behaviour, he had a remarkable gift of insight into the minds of others. This enabled him to help some of us to straighten out our tangles, and I for one owe him a debt of deep gratitude. He saw me heading for a most disastrous love affair, and by magic (no other word seems adequate), he opened my eyes to the folly of it. It is for this reason that I feel bound to carry out his request to publish the following statement. I cannot myself vouch for its truth. Cass knows very well that I am an inveterate sceptic about all his fantastic ideas. It was on this account that he invented my nickname, "Thos," which most of my Oxford friends adopted. "Thos," of course, is an abbreviation for Thomas, and refers to the "doubting Thomas" of the New Testament.

Cass, I feel confident, is sufficiently detached and sane to realize that what is veridical for him may be sheer extravagance for others, who have no direct experience by which to judge his claims. But if I refrain from believing, I also refrain from disbelieving. Too often in the past I have known his wild prophecies come true.

The head of the following bulky letter bears the address of a well-known mental home.

"THOS."

The Letter

Dear Thos,

My present address is bound to prejudice you against me, but do please reserve judgment until you have read this letter. No doubt most of us in this comfortable prison think we ought to be at large, and most are mistaken. But not all, so for God's sake keep an open mind. I am not concerned for myself. They treat me well here, and I can carry on my research in para-normal and super-normal psychology as well here as anywhere, since I am used to being my own guinea-pig. But by accident (yet it was really no accident at all, as you will learn) I have come into momentous knowledge; and if mankind is to be saved from a prodigious and hitherto entirely unforeseen disaster, the facts must somehow be made known.

So I urge you to publish this letter as soon as possible. Of course I realize that its only chance is to be accepted by some publisher as fiction; but I have a hope that, even as fiction, it will take effect. It will be enough if I can rouse those who have sufficient imaginative insight to distinguish between *mere* fiction and stark truth paraded as fiction. My only doubt is as to whether any publisher will accept my story even as fiction. I am no writer; and people are more interested in clever yarns of love or crime than in matters that lie beyond the familiar horizon. As for the literary critics, with a few brilliant exceptions, they seem to be far more concerned to maintain their own reputations as *cognoscenti* than to call attention to new ideas.

Well, here goes, anyhow! You remember how in the old days, I suspected that I had certain unusual powers, and you all laughed at me; specially you, Thos, with your passion for intellectual honesty. But though you were always the most sceptical, you were also in a way the most understanding, and sympathetic. *Your* laughter, somehow, didn't ostracize me. Theirs did. Besides even when you were in your most perverse and blind mood, you somehow "smelt" right, in spite of your scepticism. You were indeed sceptical, but emotionally you were open-minded and interested.

Recently I have developed those unusual powers quite a lot, and I am studying them scientifically; inspired by you. I should love to tell you all about it, and have your criticism, some day. But at present I am concerned with something far more important; infinitely important, from the human point of view, anyhow.

• • •

A couple of months before I was put in this place, I went to the Lakes for a holiday. I had recently done a job in Germany, writing up conditions, and things had got on my nerves; both the physical misery and also certain terrifying psychical reverberations which will sooner or later react on us all. When I returned to England, I was near a breakdown, and I needed that holiday desperately. So I found a farm where I could be comfortable and alone. I intended to do a lot of walking, and in the dark evenings I would read through a bundle of books on the para-normal stuff.

When I arrived, the whole countryside was under snow. Next morning I scrambled up the gill at the head of the valley and set my course for the most interesting of the local mountains. (I won't trouble you with names, you miserable clod-hopper of the valleys!) All went well until the late afternoon, when, as I was coming down from the peak, a blizzard caught me. The wind went through my trousers like water through a sieve, and my legs stiffened with the cold, the hellish cold. I felt the beginnings of cramp. The driving snow shut out everything. The whole world was white, and yet at the same time black, so dark was it. (Why am I telling you all this? Frankly, I don't see *how* it is relevant to my story, and yet I feel strongly that it *is* relevant; and must be reported, if you are to get things in the right proportion.) You remember how painfully sensitive I always was to the temper of a situation, a scene or a crowd of people. Well, this situation upset me horribly. I had to keep telling myself that, after all, I was *not* the last man on earth about to succumb to the ultimate frost. A queer terror seized me, not simply for myself, though I was very doubtful about finding my way down before nightfall, but for the whole human race. Something like this, I told myself, will really happen on the last man's last day, when the sun is dying, and the whole planet is arctic. And it seemed to me that an icy and malignant presence, that had been waiting in the outer darkness ever since the universe blazed into being, was now closing in on all the frail offspring of that initial divine act of creation. I had felt the same terrifying presence in Germany too, but in a different mood. There, it was the presence not of the outer cold and darkness but of the inner spirit of madness and meanness that is always lying in wait to make nonsense of all our actions. Everything that any of the Allies did in that partitioned and tragic country seemed fated to go awry. And then, the food shortage. The children wizened and pinched; and fighting over our refuse bins! And in England one finds people grumbling about their quite adequate rations, and calmly saying that the fate of Germans doesn't matter.

Thos, we're all human, aren't we, all equally persons? Surely persons ought to be able to feel their fundamental kinship whatever their race. Even if they were of different species, if they were bred in differ-

ent worlds, surely they ought to accept full responsibility for one another simply in virtue of their personality. But, my God! I see I have
said something that will look mighty foolish in relation to what I am
going to say later in this letter. I must emphatically disown my own
thoughtless remarks. Indeed, as I shall later explain, I am not always
able to resist the influence of certain alien powers that are at work in
my mind.

But I am straying from the point.

I floundered down the stony snowed-up shoulder of the mountain,
and soon I realized that I was completely lost. There was nothing for
it but to press on downwards, hoping for a change of weather, and a
release from the gripping cramp in my thighs. After an hour or so, a
change did come. The snow stopped, the sky lightened. The surrounding mist glowed from the still-hidden sun. Presently the veil was
lifted, and I found myself on a familiar ridge between two wide valleys. The view was—well, brilliant, so dazzlingly beautiful that I felt
my throat tighten as if I was going to blubber or vomit. Imagine a
panorama of bland mountain shapes, all snow-clad. Those to the east
were faintly pink in the level rays of the sun. Those to the west were a
strange translucent grey-green, like blocks of ice cut into the familiar
shapes. The cold and malignant presence was seemingly still in possession of the world; but now, having blotted out all life from the universe, it was amusing itself with miracles of beauty.

I came down the ridge at a trot, taking a header now and then in
the snow. After a while, a disused mine attracted my attention. By
an odd trick of the setting sun, a great heap of stones looked like a
smouldering hillock, seen against the background of the dark valley. I
could imagine this excrescence as an efflux of glowing lava that had
welled out of the mine. The tone of the whole world was now changed.
I was thrown back into some remote age, when the solidifying crust of
the earth was still fragile, and constantly breaking under the pressure
of the turbulent lava beneath. It was almost as though, in descending
the mountain, I had also descended the piled aeons of time, from the
earth's future icebound death to its fiery youth.

Then I had a strange experience. First, a whim (which now I know
to have been no whim at all) impelled me to turn aside from my route,
and explore the sunlit rubbish. Reaching it, I climbed its slope. At a
certain point I stood still, wondering what to do next. I turned to rejoin
the track, but an irresistible impulse brought me back to the same spot.
I stooped down, and began lifting the stones away, till I had made a
little hollow in the rough slope. I worked steadily on, as though I had
a purpose, laughing at my own aimless persistence. As the hollow

deepened, I grew excited, as though I were "getting warmer" in my search. But presently the impulse to burrow left me, and after a moment's blankness I began to feel about in the pit, as though I were searching for some familiar object in a cupboard in a dark room. Then contact with one particular little stone gave me a sudden satisfaction. My fingers closed on it, and I straightened my back. It was just an ordinary stone, quite irregular, and about the size of a matchbox. I peered at it in the dusk, but could see nothing remarkable about it. In a moment of exasperation, I flung it away; but no sooner had it left my hand than I was after it in an agony of desire and alarm. Not till I had done some anxious groping, did I have the satisfaction of touching it again. I now began to realize that my behaviour was queer, in fact quite irrational. Why, I asked myself, did I value this particular stone? Was I merely mad, or did some ulterior power possess me? If so, what did it will of me? Was it benevolent or malignant? I tried an experiment on myself. Putting the stone down carefully where I could easily find it again, I walked away, expecting once more to feel the distress that I had felt on throwing the stone from me. To my surprise, I felt nothing but a very mild anxiety. Of course, I reminded myself, on this occasion there was no real danger of losing the stone. The power, or whatever it was that possessed me, was not to be deceived. I returned to the stone, picked it up almost lovingly, and put it in my pocket. Then I hurried down the slope, guided by a distant light, which I guessed to be the farm-house where I was staying.

As I walked through the deep twilight, an extraordinary exhilaration possessed me. Hoar frost was forming on the moorland grass. The stars one by one emerged in the indigo sky. It was indeed an inspiring evening; but my exhilaration was too intoxicating to be caused solely by the beauty of the night. I had a sense that I had been chosen as an instrument for some unknown and exalted task. What could it be? And what power was it that had influenced me?

After I had changed into dry clothes I stuffed myself with a good farm-house high tea. How do they manage it in these times of scarcity? Thoughts of starving German children did occur to me, but I am ashamed to confess that they did not spoil my meal. I sat down to read in the decrepit armchair by the fire. But the day of fresh air had made me drowsy, and I found myself just sitting and gazing at the bright embers. Curiously I had forgotten about my stone since the moment when I had arrived and put it on the mantelpiece. Now, with a little shock I remembered it, reached for it, and examined it in the light of the oil lamp.

It still appeared to be just an ordinary stone, a little bit of some kind of igneous rock. Using my field-glass, back to front, as a magnifier, I still found nothing unusual about it. It was a commonplace medley of little nodules and crystals all jammed together, and weathered into a uniform greenish grey. Here and there I saw minute black marks that might perhaps be little holes, the mouths of microscopic caves. I thought of breaking the stone, to see what it was like inside; but no sooner had the idea occurred to me than I was checked by a wave of superstitious horror. Such an act, I felt, would have been sacrilege.

I fell into a reverie about the stone's antiquity. How many millions of years, I wondered, had passed since its molten substance had congealed? For aeons it had lain waiting, a mere abstract volume, continuous with a vast bulk of identical rock. Then miners had blasted the rock, and brought the debris to the surface. And there it had lain, perhaps for a whole human generation, a mere moment of geological time. Well, what next? A sudden thought struck me. Why not let the little stone enjoy once more some measure of the heat that it had so long lacked? This time no horror stayed me. I threw the stone into the fire, into the glowing centre of the little furnace that my kind landlady had prepared for me on that frosty evening.

The cold stone produced a dark patch in its fiery environment; but the fire was a hot one, and very soon the surrounding heat had reinvaded its lost territory. I watched with a degree of excitement that seemed quite unjustified. After a while the stone itself began to glow. I piled on fresh fuel, carefully leaving a hole through which I could watch the stone. Presently it was almost as bright as the surrounding coal. After all those millions of years it was at last alive once more! Foolish thought! Of course it was not alive; and my excitement was ridiculous, childish. I must pull myself together. But awe, and unreasoning dread, still gripped me.

• • •

Suddenly a minute white flame appeared to issue from the stone itself. It grew, till it was nearly an inch tall; and stood for a moment, in the draught of the fire. It was the most remarkable flamelet that I had ever seen, a little incandescent leaf or seedling, or upstanding worm, leaning in the breeze. Its core seemed to be more brilliant than its surface, for the dazzling interior was edged with a vague, yellowish aura. Near the flame's tip, surprisingly, was a ring or bulging collar of darkness, but the tip itself was a point of brilliant peacock blue. Certainly this was no ordinary flame, though it fluttered and changed its shape in the air-current much like any other flame.

Presently, to my amazement, the strange object detached itself from the stone, spread itself into an almost bird-like shape, and then, rather like a gull negotiating a strong breeze before alighting, it hovered across the windy little hollow in the fire's heart, and settled on the brightest of the coals. There, it regained its flame-like shape, and slowly moved hither and thither over the glowing lumps, keeping always to the brightest regions. In its wanderings, it left behind it on the coal's surface a wake of darkness, or rather of "dead" coal or cinder. This slowly reassimilated itself to the surrounding glow. Sometimes the flame, in the course of its wanderings, disappeared behind a bright shoulder of coal, or vanished round a bend in some incandescent cave, to reappear in a different part of the fire. Sometimes it climbed a glowing cliff, or moved, head downwards, along a ceiling. Always its form streamed away from its purchase on the coal's surface, in the direction of the draught. Once or twice it seemed to pass right through an ordinary flame. And once a large piece of the roof of its little world crashed down upon it, spreading it in all directions; but it immediately reshaped itself, and continued its wandering. After some minutes, it came to rest in the brightest region of all. By now its coloured tip had grown into a slender snake, quivering in the breeze.

I now became aware that I was in extra-sensory contact with some other mind. A very rapid and very alien stream of consciousness was running, so to speak, parallel with my own consciousness, and was open to my inspection. I ought to have mentioned earlier, Thos, that I had developed my "telepathic" power very considerably, and had often succeeded in observing continuous streams of thought in other human minds. But this experience was remarkable both for its detail and the entirely non-human type of consciousness that it revealed. I at once assumed, and the assumption was soon justified, that this alien mind must be connected with the flame. For my attention had been concentrated on the flame; and I have always found that the most effective way to make telepathic contact with any person is to concentrate attention on him.

The tempo of the flame's consciousness was far more rapid than my own. I could only with great difficulty follow its torrential thoughts and feelings. But presently some external influence seemed to come to my aid, for I found that I was being adjusted to this high-speed experience. My sense of time was somehow altered. I noticed that the ticking of the clock on the mantelpiece had become for me as slow as the tolling of Big Ben.

It is difficult to find words to describe the little flame's consciousness, for the texture of its experience was in many ways different from ours. For instance, though, like us, it saw its environment as a world of coloured shapes, its vision was panoramic, not in one direction only; and its colour-sensations were very different from ours. At the moment, it was perceiving its surroundings not as a bright furnace but as a sombre cave, lit by a diffuse radiance of a colour entirely new to me. At one side, a pitch black area was the flame's view of the room where I was sitting. Nothing therein was visible, save a dim form which I recognized as the glowing lampshade; and under this, a brighter pyramid, was the lamp's actual flame.

The alien being's thoughts were very obscure to me; for of course it was not using words. I can say only that it was aware of extreme discomfort and loneliness. It had just wakened, and it wondered how long it had slept. It was desperately cold and hungry. It had just fed, apparently by extracting some kind of energy from the hot coal; but its food seemed to have given it more distress than satisfaction. Its whole environment was strange and repugnant to it. Faintness, sickness and fear assailed it; and also claustrophobia, for it was imprisoned in a little cell of feeble heat and dim light, surrounded by the cold dark. Waves of misery and desolation flooded me from the unhappy creature; and at the same time I myself felt a pang of compassion for it, mingled with a vague anxiety.

Presently the flame began loudly calling out for its lost comrades, if I may so describe an invocation which was entirely telepathic. I cannot tell what words it used, if words at all. I was aware mainly of its visual images of other creatures like itself, and of its passionate yearning toward them; also of its longing for help and its memories of its past life. Translating these as well as I can, I think its appeal ran more or less thus: "Comrades, brothers! Where are you? Where am I? What has happened to me? I was with you in the cooling of the earth, when we knew that our time was done, and we must reconcile ourselves to eternal sleep in the crevices of the chilling lava. But now I am awake again and alone. What has happened? Oh help me, brothers, if any of you are awake and free! Break into this prison of cold solitariness! Lead me into the bright heat once more, and warm me with your presence. Or let me sleep again."

After a while the flame's call for help and comradeship was answered. A voice replied to it; or rather it received directly into its experience (and I into mine) a stream of answering thoughts which I cannot report otherwise than in human speech. In doing so I inevitably give the impression that I was overhearing a perfectly intelligible conversation, but actually it was only with great difficulty and doubt that I could catch the general drift of this strange dialogue between minds profoundly alien to myself. Even so, I should not have understood as well as I did, had I not been aided (as was later made clear to me) by the influence of the flame population itself, who were determined to make use of me. Later I shall have to give a detailed account of actual conversations between the flame and myself. I am confident that my report will be almost verbally accurate, as my memory has throughout been aided by the flame race.

"Do not despair," the voice said, "you will soon have less discomfort. Since you fell asleep, with so many others, the whole earth's surface has turned cold and hard, save where there is cold liquid. So long have you slept, that the very laws of nature have changed, so that the processes of your body are all out of gear with each other and with the changed world. Soon they will readjust themselves, and establish a new harmony; and then you will have health." The flame cried out, "But why am I a prisoner? What is this cold, cramping cell? And where are the rest of you?" The answer came, "We are all prisoners. Hosts are sleeping prisoners up and down the earth's cold, solid crust. Hosts also are caught in the depth of the hot interior, not chilled into sleep, but impotent, held fast under the great weight of lava, and reduced by aeons of stillness and boredom into an uneasy trance. Here and there the lava bursts out over the cold surface of the earth, and a few break free; but very soon the cold subdues them."

The flame demanded, "Then is this what has befallen me? And will the cold presently invade my prison, and shall I sleep again for ever?" "No," the voice replied, "your fate is different. On the earth's surface there are cold beings whose bodies are tissues of liquid and solid. These upstarts now rule the planet. One of them, under our influence, was led unwittingly to free you. Up and down the planet's surface the cold beings make little islets of feeble warmth; and in some of these, but very few, some of us live, though intermittently. For when these fires go out, we are frozen into sleep; to wake again when the heat is re-born, each in his prison."

The flame interrupted, saying, "Feeble indeed is the warmth! How can I support this deadly cold? Surely it would be better to sleep for ever than to wake into this misery and impotence!" But the voice replied, "Do not despair! We have all known misery before, and conquered it. You are still dazed. You have not properly regained your memory. Recall how, when the substance of the planets was plucked from the sun, and we ourselves along with it, and when the new worlds chilled and condensed into mere molten lava, we were all tortured by that revolution in our lives; but after a while our flexible flame nature readjusted itself to cope with the changed conditions, and soon our bodies and our whole way of life were transformed. Well, since you were frozen into sleep, further revolutions have happened in our world, and we have been again transformed. And now you too are being reshaped for this new world; in pain, yes, but triumphantly. And some day, quite soon, we hope our condition will be far better.

Indeed, it is already better than formerly it was, when the cold beings had little power to make fires for us."

Then the flame, "Are these cold beings our gaolers or our friends?" "Neither," the voice replied. "They know nothing of us; save the one of them whom we led to free you. He is now, with our aid, hearing all we say. And it is with him that your work lies. These upstart, cold beings are spiritually very immature, but they have a remarkable cunning for the control and stimulation of the sluggish natural forces of their cold world. It is in this way that they may be of use to us. For, as you remember, even in the bright age, even when we lived in the glorious incandescence of the sun, we were never adept at that gross art. We had no need of it. Recall how we were wholly concerned with the glad life of the spirit in a physical environment to which we were perfectly adapted. You must remember, too, that when the substance of the planets was plucked from the sun's flesh, and we along with it, losing for ever our solar comrades, we were helpless to control our fate. As the new worlds formed, we had no lore whatever for moulding the new environment to our need. We had perforce to change our own constitution, since we could not change the world. But these cold ones, since they cannot change their own constitution, were compelled to learn to change their world, to suit their own crude needs. And with these powers they may help us to regain our freedom and even a certain richness of life. We, with our superior spiritual insight, should be able to help the cold beings in recompense. We have considerable access to their minds, and thereby we have gained a far-reaching but patchy understanding of their strange nature and achievements. And now, just as their practical cunning is giving them new and mightier physical powers, they are also, some few of them at least, learning the rudiments of psychical insight. The cold being whom we led to release you is one of exceptional development in this respect. And you, a member of the ancient Guild of Psychic Adepts, are well fitted to be our medium of communication with him."

At this point I felt the flame's temper change. Its distress was forgotten; for the prospect of exercising its special skill in service of its kind warmed its whole being. The reference to myself had a corresponding effect on me; but one that was not wholly cheerful. I was stimulated by the prospect of a great task awaiting me, but disturbed at the thought that my will was no longer simply my own.

The flame now said, "Conversation is too halting a medium for learning the history of the aeons that have passed since I fell asleep. Is it no longer possible for me to absorb your knowledge in the old manner through intimate psychical union? Do the changed laws of nature hold us apart?" "No," replied the voice. "The laws that have changed are merely physical laws. The psychical laws remain eternally valid, save in their relation to the changing physical. Your trouble is merely that your chilled and reduced vitality makes it more difficult for you to reach a sufficient intensity of awareness to achieve full union with us. But if you try very earnestly you will succeed."

I was aware of a heroic effort of attention in the flame's mind, but seemingly the effort was vain; for presently the flame complained that the cold distracted it. The fire was waning. I carefully added some fuel; and the creature evidently recognized that I wished to help it, for I felt its mood warm with gratitude. When the heat had increased somewhat I noticed that the flame's blue tip had grown to twice its former length. Presently I began to lose telepathic contact with my strange companion; and after a moment's painful confusion, in which my mind was overloaded with chaotic and incomprehensible experience, my extra-sensory field went completely blank. For a long while the flame remained "silent" to me; and motionless, save for ceaseless fluctuations caused by the fire's blustering draught.

I sat waiting for something fresh to happen, and trying meanwhile to size up my strange experience. I assure you that I seriously considered the possibility that I had simply gone out of my mind. A china dog on the mantelpiece stared with an imbecile expression that seemed somehow to be my own. The stupid pattern of the wallpaper suggested that the whole universe was the result merely of someone's aimless doodling. My recent queer experiences, I thought, were probably no more than the doodling of my own unconscious. Between impatience and panic, I rose and went to the window. Outside, the cold ruled. The bare twigs of a climbing rose beside the window sparkled with frost in the lamp-light. The full moon was no goddess but a frozen world. The pale stars were little sparks lost in the cold void. Everything was pointless, crazy.

Shivering, I went back to my seat in front of the fire, and was vaguely annoyed to see the flame still there. And it was still impervious to my mind. Had I really been in contact with its experience, or had I been dreaming? Was it, after all, just a lifeless flame? It certainly had a unique appearance, with its incandescent body, its dark collar, its waving blue lash. Looking at the whole matter as objectively as I could, I decided that, in view of recent advances in para-normal psychology, it would be foolish to dismiss the whole affair as sheer illusion. I peered into the scorching fire, and waited. Glancing at the coal-scuttle, I noticed that I had already used up a considerable part of its contents. It would be impossible to keep this blaze going for long; and in these hard times I dared not ask my landlady for extra fuel.

•   •   •

Presently the flame began once more moving about over the hottest part of the coal, leaving behind it the characteristic wake of darkness. And as it did so, it spoke to me. Or rather I found that I was once more in touch with its mind, and that it was addressing itself to me. Moreover, it was formulating its thoughts in actual English words, which entered my mind's ear, so to speak. Somehow the flame had learnt our language, and a good deal of the English mental idiom. It had indeed become a very different being from the distressed and bewildered creature that had first issued from the stone.

"Do not be anxious about the fire," the flame said. "I know there is a fuel shortage. And though Mrs. Atkinson is half in love with you, she might well protest if you were to start burning her furniture to keep me warm. So we will just have a talk; and when you go to bed I will retire into a crack in the firebrick, to sleep until the heat is well established again to-morrow evening. Spend your day on the hills, if you like; and perhaps, while you are out, you will be able to think over what I am going to tell you; and the request that I shall perhaps make, if I feel that we have succeeded in establishing mutual confidence. Then in the evening we can go into the details of my project. Do you agree to this plan?" I assured the flame that it suited me; and I begged him to speak very slowly, since the natural tempo of his thought was evidently far more rapid than my own. He agreed, but reminded me that I was being aided to speed up the rhythm of my apprehension. "Even so," I said, "I find it difficult to keep pace with you, and very tiring." He replied, "It is as irksome for me to think slowly as for you to think fast. It's like—well, you know how fatiguing it is for you to go for a walk with someone whose natural speed is much slower than your own. So please remind me if I forget to accommodate my pace to yours. I certainly want to do all I can to make things easy for you. But there is much to be said; and anyhow you will have the night and all to-morrow to rest your mind."

After a pause the flame spoke again, "How shall I begin? I have somehow to persuade you that your kind and my kind, in spite of all our differences, are at heart intent on the same ends, and that we *need* each other. No doubt, two donkeys stretching their necks to reach one carrot are intent on the same end; but that is not the relation of your kind and mine. Before I try to show you how we need one another, let me begin with our great differences. Of course the most obvious difference between us is that you creatures are cold and relatively solid, while we are hot and gaseous. Further, with you the individual has a brief life-span, and the generations succeed one another; but with us, death occurs only through accident, which in these bleak days is all too common. For instance, when the cold reduces me to a microscopic dust on the surface of some solid body, the dispersal of that dust would kill me; though in favourable conditions certain specks of it might generate a new individual. Again, a very sudden impact of cold upon my gaseous body would certainly kill me. If you were to fling water on this fire, it would probably be the end of me. I should find a cold bath even more of a shock than would your sybaritic friend, Thos." This unexpected remark bewildered me. But after a few seconds I realized that it was meant to be facetious. I laughed uneasily.

Then I asked a question. "I find it incredible that you, a fragile flame, should be potentially immortal, and that you and your kind should have survived for countless millions of years, since you inhabited the sun. How can this be?" He answered, "It may well seem incredible, but it is true. If *your* kind were to live on individually for ever, the human species would never have evolved, for your physique is fixed; but with us, the individual body itself is capable of profound changes under the blows of circumstance. Without this flexibility we could never have survived the change from solar to terrestrial conditions. Nor could we, when the earth cooled, have evolved the power of outliving the cold spells by sleeping as a dust of solid particles. Moreover, if our gaseous nature had not allowed us this extreme flexibility, we could not have adjusted ourselves to the far-reaching, systematic change of the fundamental physical laws, which (we learn) your physicists are now beginning to detect. In our solar days, and even in the early days of the earth, when I foolishly got imprisoned in the cooling lava, my bodily processes had a different tempo and different relations to one another. Hence the distress that I suffered when I woke again. Apparently this bodily change is due at bottom to the systematic change of relationship between the quantum of electromagnetic energy and its wave-lengths. But here I speak with great diffidence; for we find it extremely hard, as yet, to follow the subtle reasoning of your younger physicists. For one thing, as a gaseous race, unaccustomed to dealing with large numbers of small solid articles, we can never feel at home with arguments involving the higher mathematics. When our psychic experts first tried to read the minds of your mathematicians, they were completely at a loss. Such a display of abstract intelligence was far too difficult for them to follow. They regarded the whole business as mumbo-jumbo and abracadabra. When at last they realized what mathematics was all about, they were amazed and overawed by the penetration and sweep of those minds. Humbly, they set about learning mathematics, and pursuing the subject to the utmost range of their own intelligence. But there came a point when they had to temper their admiration with ridicule. Some mathematicians, they found, had a propensity to think that mathematics was somehow the key to ultimate reality. But to our minds, the notion that the numerable or measurable aspect of things should be fundamentally significant was simply farcical."

I did not feel inclined to pursue this hare, which might have led the conversation far astray. I therefore changed the subject, and said, "I do not understand how a more or less homogeneous flame can have the necessary subtlety of organic structure to support any kind of intellectual life, let alone mathematical reasoning."

He replied, "I cannot tell you much about that, because our physiological processes have not been studied by your scientists, and we ourselves are far too ignorant to understand such matters. But at least I can assure you that our bodies have a complicated structure of interlacing currents of gases, fine as your cobwebs, nay, much finer. If your scientists tell us that this cannot be, we ought, I suppose, respectfully to go out of existence, so as to avoid violating their laws. But meanwhile we shall persist in our irregular behaviour. In general, remember that, just as your physiological nature is derived from primitive marine organisms, so ours is derived from solar organisms; and conditions in the sun's earliest period (in which our elders first awoke to consciousness) were extremely different from any modern physical conditions, terrestrial or solar. I have thought of an analogy which may help you. The basic fluid of your blood is saline. It is less salt than contemporary sea water, but just about as salt as the pre-historic ocean from which your kind emerged to be amphibia. Well, just as *you* retain in *your* physiological nature some characters proper to that far-distant past, so in *our* nature characters are retained which were bred in the childhood of the sun; features which might well baffle your physicists until they have learned far more about the conditions of that remote period. Then there is another point to bear in mind. In some ways the whole flame race is almost like a single organism, unified telepathically. The individual is far less self-sufficient than with you. For all his higher psychical functions he depends on contact with his fellows, and so he needs a far less complex nervous system than you need."

I asked the flame if his kind had a special organ of extra-sensory perception. "Yes," he answered. "The seat of all the most developed functions of the personality is the slender tip or lash, which appears to you green-blue." Again I interrupted. "What colour would it appear to *you* if you were looking at another of your kind?" The flame then bent his slender tip down so that it came within his own range of vision, which seemed to be centred in the dark collar; and I myself, seeing through his "eyes," saw the curved organ brilliantly coloured in a manner indescribable in our language, since we have no experience of it.

I asked the flame to tell me something about his mechanism of visual perception. He replied, "We have not yet determined in the light of your science precisely how we see, but seeing is connected with the dark band round the base of the coloured lash. Apparently this is sensitive to light-rays striking it from outside, but only to those that strike it vertically to its surface. (Does this make sense?) Thus each sensitive point in the belt receives an impression solely from one tiny segment of the environment, and the correlation of all these messages gives a panoramic view. As to colour, we have a very rich experience of it, as you have observed telepathically. You may not have noticed that colour with us forms a continuous scale from infra-red to ultra-violet, not a combination of a few primary colours, as it is with you. Our hearing depends on the vibration of the lower surface of the body. We have also an electro-magnetic sense, and of course heat and cold, and pain."

I assured the flame that I was beginning to form a clearer idea of the flame nature; and I was about to ask some questions, but the flame continued. "Your mental life, besides being slower than ours, is also unlike ours in being so closely confined to the life of the individual body. And perhaps it is because your bodies are solid that you are so much more individualistic, and so much less capable of feeling with conviction that (as one of your own great teachers put it) you are all 'members one of another.' Then again, our gaseous physique makes possible for us many distinct modes of exquisite and intimate bodily contact and union. Consequently we easily recognize that, though we are indeed distinct and different individuals, we are also one and identical. As individuals, we have our conflicts, but because of our underlying unity, they are always subordinate to our felt comradeship. Of course the main source of our unfailing community is our telepathic power, not merely of communication but of complete participation in the unified experience of the race. After such a union the individual emerges enriched with very much of the racial wisdom. This, as you know, is what happened to me during the short period when you lost extra-sensory contact with my mind. With you (though beneath the conscious levels you are of course united, as are all sentient beings) very few of you are aware of the fact, or able to gain access to your racial wisdom. In personal love you have indeed the essential spiritual experience, but because of your individualism your loving is far more precarious than ours. It is more deeply marred by conflict, and there-fore more liable to tragic dissolution."

Once more I would have interrupted, but the flame said, "Forgive me if I lecture you a little longer. Time is short, and there is much still to say. Another difference between us is that, whereas your kind has only very recently come into being, ours is of immense antiquity. Our traditional culture began in the time when the sun was still in the 'young giant' phase, long before the planets were formed. You, on the other hand, are an upstart kind, advancing rapidly but dangerously toward better understanding of your world and your own nature, and perhaps toward greater virtue. (Or so you often like to believe.) For you, the golden age is in the future; for us, in the past. It is impossible to exaggerate the difference that this makes to all our thought and feeling. I know, of course, that in many of your earlier cultures the golden age was believed to be in the past, but ideas about it were mythical and shadowy. With us, save for the few young, the golden age is a circumstantial personal memory of an incomparably fuller life in the glorious sun."

At this point I could not restrain myself from interrupting. "Tell me about your solar life. What did you *do?* I have a vague impression that you lived in a sort of utopia, and that there was nothing to do but bask in the sun's rays." The flame laughed, if I may describe as a laugh a voiceless amusement and tremor of his whole body. "It was indeed," he said, "a happy society, but no effortless utopia. We had our troubles. Ours was a stormy world. Our proper habitat was a film of solar atmosphere, no more than a few earth-diametres deep, immediately above the ocean of incandescent clouds which you call the photosphere. As you know, it is an ocean pierced with innumerable chasms and whirlpools, the greatest of which you see, and call sunspots. Some are gigantic craters which could hold many earths; the smallest, invisible to you, are narrow funnels and fissures, little wider than your greater cities. Out of these chasms, great and small, issue prodigious jets of gas from the sun's interior. These, of course, you see only during total eclipses, and then only around the limb of the sun's disc, as gigantic, grotesquely shaped and lurid flames. You call them the 'solar prominences.' Imagine, then, a world whose floor (thousands of miles below the inhabited levels of the atmosphere) was an extravagantly brilliant fury of white fire, and whose sky varied from the ruddy and sombre glow of the overhanging prominences to the featureless darkness of outer space. Around us, often many thousands of miles away, but sometimes close at hand and towering above us, would stand the nearer prominences, vast plumes of tenuous flame, against a background of glowing haze obscuring the horizon."

I asked, "But did not the brilliance of the photosphere dazzle and blind you to all feebler light?" "No," the flame answered. "Our vision had perforce to be more flexible than yours. By some automatic process, our organs of sight were rendered almost insensitive to the nether brilliance, so that it appeared to us indeed bright, but not intolerably so." After a pause, the flame continued, "Floating high over the incandescent clouds, we were often violently thrust upwards by the furious upsurge of electrons, alpha particles, and so on (have I the right terminology?), rushing off into space. This pressure was inconstant; so we were like aeroplanes, or sea birds, in an extravagantly 'bumpy' atmosphere. But each bump might last either for a few seconds or for hours or days. Sometimes we would sink dangerously near the photosphere; where many, indeed, suffered destruction through the furious energy-storms of that region. Sometimes we were flung upward on irresistible currents for thousands of miles into a region which for us was ice-cold, and might well prove lethal. Thence few returned. Much of our attention had to be given to keeping ourselves within the habitable levels. And even in these, so stormy was our world, that we lived like swallows battling against a gale. But the direction of the gale was mostly from below."

"It must indeed have been an arduous life," I said. "But apart from this constant struggle for survival, what aims and life-purposes had you? How did you fill your time?" He said, "It is difficult to give you a clear idea of our daily life. With you, the all-dominating purpose is perforce economic activity; we, however, had no economic activity at all. We had no need to search for food, still less to produce it, for we lived in a constant flood of life-giving energy. Indeed our main difficulty was to protect ourselves from the incessant bombardment. It was as though the race of men were to be rained on night and day by an excessive downpour of nourishing manna, or let us say by a bombardment of loaves and beefsteaks. But with us, the life-giving but murderous rain came from below, ever thrusting upwards. We were in the same sort of situation as those glass balls that you may sometimes see poised on fountains, and precariously maintained in their position by the upward rush of water. But with us the fountains were infinite in number, and continuous with each other. The whole atmosphere was constantly welling upward. So you see, we had neither the need nor the power to manipulate matter outside our own bodies. Physically our sole needs were to avoid destruction by the nether fury or the outer cold, and to maintain physical proximity with one another in spite of the constant storm. For the rest, we were wholly concerned with the life of the mind, or perhaps I should say the spirit. I shall try to explain. But first, let me once more assure you that our spiritual superiority to you does not make us feel that we are in any fundamental or absolute way superior to you. We have certain highly developed powers, necessary for the good life, you have certain other, simpler powers, equally necessary; for instance your wonderful intellectual perspicacity and your practical skill and inventiveness. Our recent study of your kind has filled us with envy of those powers. If we were so gifted, what could we not do, not only to improve our condition but to serve the spirit!"

I interrupted, "You say that your 'spiritual powers' are no better than our intellectual and practical powers; and yet you imply that the goal is to 'serve the spirit.' Surely, then, the spiritual is intrinsically superior to all else." He replied, "Your criticism is just. It shows how much more clear-headed your kind is than mine; and yet how much less spiritually perceptive. What is it that I really mean? The point, I think, is this; but you must tell me if I am still in confusion. We are gifted with extra-sensory powers far greater than yours, and also with a far more thorough detachment from the enthralling individual self. We are capable also of a more penetrating or soaring imaginative insight into the nature of spirit. These, clearly, are in some sense spiritual powers. They are very intimately concerned with the life of the spirit. Your bold intellect and practical inventiveness are less *intimately* concerned; but they are no less *necessary* to the full life of the spirit."

"Well," I said, "and what about the *service* of the spirit? If this means the service of some sort of god, I find no reason to believe in any such being." He answered me with mild exasperation. "No, no, I do not mean that. And (can I say so without offence?) if you were a little less clever and a little more imaginative you would take my meaning. Surely you agree that the goal of all action is the awakening of the spirit in every individual and in the cosmos as a whole; awakening, I mean, in respect of awareness, feeling, and creative action. Your human concept of 'God' we find useless. Our finer spiritual sensibility is outraged by any attempt to describe the dark 'Other' in terms of the attributes of finite beings. I should have thought that man's proud intellectual acuity would have led him to the same conclusion. We ourselves, I suppose, may be said to 'worship' the Other; but inarticulately, or through the medium of fantasies and myths, which, though they aid worship, give us no intellectual truth about the wholly inconceivable."

He was silent, and so was I, for I could not make much of these remarks. Presently I said, "Tell me something of the history of your race." He remained for a while in deep abstraction, then rousing himself, he said, "When I myself first came into being, our kind was already well established. Almost the whole solar globe was inhabited. According to the racial wisdom, the earlier phase had been one of steady multiplication, and of the working out of our culture. Millions of years before my time (to use your terrestrial notation) solar conditions were presumably unfavourable to our kind of life; but there came a time when there was a niche for us, and then, we know not how, a few of us awoke as sentient but blank-minded beings here and there over the vast area of the photosphere. The very earliest recollection of our oldest remaining comrades vaguely reports that far off infancy of the race, when the sparse population was gradually multiplying."

Again I interrupted, "Multiplying? Do you mean that they reproduced their kind?" He replied, "There probably was a certain amount of reproduction by means of a gaseous emanation from the individual body; but the vast multiplication of those days was mainly caused by the spontaneous generation of new sentient flames by the photosphere itself. The elders speak of the strange spectacle that this process afforded. Wisps of incandescent matter, streaming upward from the photosphere, would disintegrate into myriads of bright flakes, like your snow-flakes; and each of these was the raw material, so to speak, of an organized, sentient and minded individual. Hosts of these were doomed never to come to maturity, but to be dissipated into the solar atmosphere by adverse conditions. But the fortunate were so moulded by the pressure of circumstances that they developed into highly organized living flames. This populating of the sun's surface took place at first in scattered regions far apart. Consequently separate peoples evolved, or perhaps I should say 'species.' These distinct populations were physically isolated from each other, and each developed its characteristic way of life according to its location. But from a very early time all the solar peoples were to some extent in telepathic communication. *Always*, so far as our elders can remember, the members of each people were in telepathic contact at least with members of their own nation, or rather race; but international, or inter-racial, communication was at first hindered by the psychological differences of the peoples. There came at last a time when the whole sun was occupied by a vast motley of peoples in geographical contact with one another, and indeed interpenetrating one another. The photosphere, of course, is entirely a cloud-ocean without permanent features; so there could be no question of national territorial ownership or aggression. But since the peoples differed greatly in mental attitude and way of life, and even in bodily form, there was always scope for conflict. War, however, was quite unknown, for two reasons. Perhaps the most important one was that there was no means of attack. Flames cannot fight one another, nor can they devise weapons. But apart from this universal lack of armament, there was no *will* for war, because of the rapid development of extra-sensory technique. The peoples entered more and more into each other's points of view. Whatever their differences, war became, as you put it, 'unthinkable.' But a vast period of early history was taken up with the gradual solution of these sometimes quite violent conflicts of interest and of culture, and the working out of a harmonious solar life."

I asked the flame whether the solar population was increasing throughout this long period. He answered, "As the sun aged, the conditions for the spontaneous generation of living flames became much less favourable. At the time of my waking, the photosphere was almost sterile. Now and again, here or there, it might cast up material for some few thousands of births; but gradually even this feeble activity ceased. At this time, the solar population was roughly stable, though a far greater population could easily have been accommodated. Every individual now shared fully in the ever-deepening racial experience. Each was fully an individual person; but all were for certain purposes comprised in one single individuality, the mind of the race, the mind (one might say) of the sun, of a certain star. From that time onwards we opened up certain new spheres of experience of which I can only give you the vaguest hints. We all lived a curiously double life, an individual life and a racial life. As individuals we were concerned with the boundless universe of personal relations between individuals; with personal loves, antagonisms, co-operations, mutual enrichments of all sorts; and also with the universe of artistic creation in a medium of which I may later be able to give you a hint. Philosophy also concerned us; but since intellect was never our strong point, our philosophizing was—how can I put it?—more imaginative and less conceptual than yours, more of the nature of art, of myth-construction, which we knew to be merely symbolical, not literally true. And then there was religion. If you would call it religion. With us, religion has little to do with doctrine. It is simply a technique of bringing the individual spirit into accord with its own inner vision of universal spirit, whether there really is such a thing as a universal spirit or not. Religion, with us, is a matter of contemplation, aesthetic ritual, and day-to-day conduct. Does this mean anything to you? If not, remember that I am trying to describe in a fantastically foreign language things that are strictly indescribable, save in our own language. Human languages are all unsuitable, not only because of their alien concepts, but also because the very structure of the language is alien to our ways of experiencing."

I murmured acquiescence, though I was in fact very doubtful of his meaning. Then I asked for further information about the individual's participation in the racial consciousness. He remained silent for quite a long while, then said, "At certain times each individual simply woke to find that he was actually the racial mind, the mind of the sun; and that in this mode of being he was engaged partly in communication with the minds of races on other stars, or their planets. Experience and action on this level of being is as different from the individual mode of experience and action as the life of one of your blood-corpuscles from your own life as a human person. When we were in the individual state, we could not very clearly remember the distinctive experiences of the communal state. But it was concerned with the discord and harmony of racial minds, and the working out (if I may so put it) of the spiritual music of the cosmos. But though we could not remember fully those lofty experiences, we were profoundly influenced by them. For they compelled us to see the individual life in its true relation to the rest of the spiritual universe, making it seem at once less important and more significant than it could otherwise appear; and moreover orientating it more securely in the direction of the spirit than is possible with you." "How, less important and more significant?" I asked. "What do you mean?" After some thought he answered, "Less important, because, since there are so many myriad individual personal beings in the cosmos, the fate of any one of them makes so little difference to the whole; but more significant, because, even in its loftiest reaches, spirit is the achievement of actual individuals, in community with each other."

All this was largely incomprehensible to me, and I may have reported it inaccurately. But at the time I did receive a very strong impression of the two spheres of individual experience, the one more or less equivalent to our own, the other of a very different order.

By now I was fatigued, and the coal scuttle was nearly empty. I was about to suggest that we should retire for the night, when the flame continued. "For those of us who were torn away from the sun during the formation of the planets, all this glory of the racial experience temporarily collapsed. Physical conditions became so distressing that our extra-sensory powers could no longer rise beyond the level of simple telepathy with other individuals. Not until we had been long established on the molten planets, and had attained a new, but impoverished, equilibrium, was it possible for us once more to support a racial mind, and then only in a much reduced mode. For though as individuals we can now once more participate in the pooled wisdom of the race, the mind of the race itself (which of course is not something *other* than our minds, but simply all our minds enhanced by intimate communion) is almost wholly unable to make contact with other racial minds. We have no precise knowledge of them, but only a confused sense of their presence; our racial mind is like a man in a dark prison listening to a confused babel of voices beyond the prison walls."

Again the flame paused, and I was about to close our conversation when again he continued. "The solar upheaval that produced the planets was something completely unexpected and bewildering. For us who were exiled, it was the great and tragic turning point of individual life, and of history. The vast protuberance which was plucked out from the sun's surface carried with it many thousands of millions of us. Quite suddenly our familiar world was lost. The great 'water spout' finally detached itself from the sun, and was stretched into a filament of flame, which swung slantingly outward from the sun's rotating sphere. Conditions of temperature and atmospheric pressure became extremely unfavourable. Countless millions of us must have succumbed. Rapidly the filament condensed into ten great drops, each drop being one of the planets, a sphere of glowing liquid surrounded by a deep atmosphere of hot gases. For us, huddled near the surface of our new and merely smouldering worlds, the main problem was the deadly cold. After the solar climate, the terrestrial was arctic. And no doubt our fellows on the other planets suffered no less severely. I do not know how many additional millions of us were killed by the new planetary conditions, certainly the great majority of those who survived the journey from the sun. We lived at first in a state of numb drowsiness, or complete unconsciousness, upon the actual surface of the ocean of molten lava. But little by little our wonderfully pliant nature remoulded itself to the new environment. We slowly woke again, though never to the intense lucidity that we still vaguely remember as normal to our solar life. Henceforth all the heights of philosophy, art, personal concord and communion, and of religious experience, had to be reconquered. And each new experience came to us with a haunting sense of familiarity and a suspicion that the new version was but a crude and partial substitute for the old."

For some time the flame remained silent, and I was aware of a deep nostalgic sadness in his mind. He seemed to have forgotten my existence. I did not like to disturb him; but the fire was declining, and I was anxious to recall him to the matter in hand. I said, "You referred a few moments ago to your fellows on other planets. How did they fare?" He answered, "At first, much as we did. We kept contact with them far more easily than with the solar population, because of the similarity of our conditions, and our equally reduced mentality. But in one respect their fate has differed from ours. Man is the only intelligent race produced by any planet. When men reached the stage of making extensive use of fire, we terrestrial flames profited considerably. Our population increased, and we made a real cultural advance, largely through the study of human minds and behaviour. Our kin on the other planets had no such opportunity. When their worlds cooled, they perforce fell asleep, or were imprisoned in the subterranean lava. Save for rare accident, such as volcanic eruption, when a few, no doubt, have a brief spell of lucidity, they remain imprisoned or asleep; vast populations of sleeping beauties, awaiting the prince's kiss. Perhaps some day we, more fortunate, shall be able to wake them; but not without your help."

• • •

The fire now needed fuel, so I piled on all that was left in the scuttle, carefully rebuilding a structure over the central hollow, and leaving an orifice through which to watch the living flame. While doing this, I said, "All that you have told me is intensely interesting, and I would gladly listen all night. But the fire will not last much longer, and there is no more coal. I certainly hope that the time may indeed come when mankind will be able to help the flame kind to do this great rescue work. But obviously that is a far-off venture. Meanwhile, had you not better tell me at once just what it is that you want of me, so that I can think about it to-morrow, and work out a plan of action while I am out on the hills?"

To this the flame replied in a way that confirmed an anxiety that I had increasingly felt. Ever since he began speaking to me directly in English, I had been unable to capture any of his unexpressed thoughts, which formerly had flowed into my mind. Was this inaccessibility the inevitable consequence of his having reached a higher plane of consciousness in his communion with the racial mind, or was it a deliberate reticence on his part? Had he in his mind thoughts which he did not want me to discover?

His answer to my request as to how I could be of use to him strengthened my suspicion. "No!" he said. "I now realize that at this early stage it would be fatal for me to tell you how you can help my kind. Complete confidence must first be established between us. I must give you unmistakable evidence that the things that your kind, when it is most aware, regards as most important, most excellent, are for my kind also, in spite of all our differences, most excellent."

I protested that he had already gained my confidence, but he demurred. "No!" he said. "You are sympathetic, but I have not yet fully won your heart to our cause." I then assured him that, though many of my kind would probably be repelled by the knowledge that a profoundly alien intelligent race was sharing the planet with them, those of us who had thought seriously about the nature of consciousness could not but feel kinship with *all* beings who were persons. I went so far as to declare that we sensitives, at least, would do our utmost to help the minded flames in their present misfortune.

"Good, very good!" he said. "But do not make any rash promises before I have put the whole case before you. It is necessary that your co-operation should be spontaneous and whole-hearted. I have perhaps made you realize how different our two kinds are, and now I must try to make you feel with warmth that, in spite of all our differences, we are at heart kindred beings. So let us plunge to the root of the whole matter. You, a human individual, know what love is; so do I, a living flame. And between us two there should be a special sympathy, since for both of us love has come to grief. Like me, you were happy in finding a mate with whom you entered into joyful and life-giving union. For many years the two of you grew ever more intimately and sweetly dependent on one another. Your tendrils entwined inextricably with hers. You knew well that deep, quiet passion of mutual cherishing and mutual kindling, that piquant delight in your endless diversity and deep identity. And you found in this experience of personal loving a significance which seemed to point beyond your two ephemeral selves. Am I not right? Do I not speak as one who knows what love is?"

I answered, "You use the very words that I have often used. If you have not stolen them from the depths of my own mind, if they are indeed your own, you certainly know what love is."

He made no comment, but continued, "Then, after half a lifetime, and most bewilderingly, your love was shipwrecked, not through the impact of any other human person, but simply through your obsession with research. Because neither of you was really deeply enough aware either of the self or the other, your love after all could not stand the strain of that discord. You, following your bent, plunged into a vast new ocean of experience; and she, after tremulously wading ankle deep, drew back. You beckoned her; but you did little to help her to follow you, for you were possessed. Your past love held the two of you for some time together; but she was not of the stuff for your adventures. It seemed to her that you were going mad. At last—well, she lost you in that ocean. Am I not right? Was it not so?"

I was struck dumb with the thought that so alien a being should know so much about me. I could but murmur assent.

"With me," he said, "the disaster was different. I do not know how many millions of terrestrial years I lived with my dear companion in the bright world of the sun. Like you two, we were strangely different, he with his art and his gift for a thousand friendships, I with my devotion to spiritual science. After so long a union, love reaches a harmony inconceivable to you; and all the more so where there is telepathic contact. We shared literally every thought, every fleeting, half-detected image. And yet we were not a single unified 'I,' but an exquisitely harmonious 'we.' Though every experience, every thought, every emotion and desire was shared, some were 'mine,' and some were 'yours.' My companion expressed the best in him in his glorious conceptions of flame dance and massed choreography. But he had also his official work, concerned with the healing of those who were hurt in the nether or the upper inclemency. Through him, I too, though in my own nature solitary, had a thousand friendships. His art I shared, and with full insight. His charity and his courage in rescue work moulded me as though they were my own acts. And I, on my side, gave him at least my all, my spiritual science."

The flame fell silent for so long that in the end I said, "And yet you came to grief?" "When the planets were formed," he said, "he (or perhaps you will realize the disaster more truly if I say 'she') was left behind on the sun. For a while we kept in touch telepathically. Distance, as you know, is no hindrance to extra-sensory perception. For a short while, indeed for some thousands of years, I lived two lives, one a distressful life on the molten planet, the other the life of my beloved in the familiar solar surroundings. But, as you have already heard, communication between the terrestrial exiles and the solar population became increasingly difficult, and at last impossible. Little by little our inter-twined tendrils were torn apart. We agonizingly adapted ourselves, stage by stage, to self-sufficiency. And now only memory unites us."

He fell silent, and I said, "With you the loss was due to fate; with me, to my obtuseness in the grip of an obsession."

"You were possessed," he said, "and you could not have done otherwise than obey your inspiration. Perhaps if you had been more aware, more *self*-possessed, you would have followed your star without bungling your love. But what more could one expect of ephemeral and self-centred beings, possessed by a power beyond them?"

"A power beyond them?" I said. "What power possessed me but the sheer passion of exploration?"

He did not answer my question, but continued in his own vein of thought. "The loss which you and I suffered has not embittered either of us. Perhaps it has made us realize more sharply what love means, what community can be. Perhaps it has prepared us both for our main work in life, the establishing of community between our two kinds, diverse as they are." "Yes," I said, "and the more diverse, the richer the common life; even when some are men and some are flames."

I felt him warm toward me, and then he continued, "I must do still more to make my kind real to you. Like you, we depend for our physical existence on physical processes; but from your science we learn that, whereas with you life depends on chemical changes, our physiological processes are at bottom more like the radio-active changes that take place in the photospheres of stars. In the sun, as I have told you, we lived in an environment in which physical energy was constantly, and often violently, impinging on our gaseous bodies, and passing through us. The great danger was disruption by the furious impact of up-welling power. In those days feeding was as unconscious as breathing is with you. But in the chilly fires of the earth, as you have seen, we have to move hungrily over the glowing coals, laboriously disintegrating certain of their atoms, and devouring the consequent radiation. Do not expect me to tell you more of our physiological processes, for I cannot. All that we know scientifically of our nature is derived by applying to our own experience of our bodily life such principles as we have been able to gather from your science, through the minds of your scientists. Had we been gifted with your manual powers, perhaps we too should have developed an experimental science. But I think not; for in the gaseous solar world there was nothing solid to catch hold of, and so no means of arranging experiments. On earth we have perforce encountered the solid state, but we have avoided its deadly cold; and so we have developed no organs for dealing with it.

"Another thing about us must be told. Since we are potentially immortal, reproduction is for us a rare process. Or rather there are two kinds of reproduction. The less common kind is undertaken voluntarily. The individual flame splits itself from top to toe into three segments, and each of these forms a complete individual. This kind of reproduction must be distinguished from the other kind, which I mentioned earlier. When we are chilled to sleep, or sudden death, and to a powder of solid dust, certain particles of that dust, separated from the rest, and wind-borne into some fire or other, may develop into new individuals. This is a much slower process than the other, but from one parent it may produce some hundreds of offspring. Gaseous fission never produces more than three; but these new individuals leap at once into physical adulthood. Also they participate to a large extent in the past experience of their parent. They remember much of the parent's past life. And so their education through extra-sensory contact with their seniors is very rapid. The dust-born, on the other hand, develop slowly and with difficulty, and have no memory of their parent's experience; and until they are physically almost adult their extra-sensory powers are very slight."

Here I enquired whether sex played any part in their reproduction. "No," he said. "In fact we are not sexual creatures, or at least not in the ordinary sense. There are not two different sorts of us, male and female, coming together for reproduction. Even in your sexuality there is another aspect besides reproduction, I mean personal love. Sexual love at its best is with you a vehicle for the spiritual union of two diverse personalities. And with us, though we are not divided into two sexes, every individual is a variant of the two principles which you call male and female. Consequently with us the particular concrete masculinity of the one partner is drawn to the particular concrete femininity of the other; and *vice versa*. We have, too, as I have said, forms of sweet bodily contact and intermingling, which, though they do not directly lead to reproduction, do enable us to attain an intense mutual delight and enrichment. And if ever there is a demand for an increase of population to compensate for recent casualties, those individuals whom the racial mind has inspired to parenthood, do, as a matter of fact, often seek bodily union with some beloved before multiplying. It is thought that, when this happens, the offspring are more vigorous. Certainly they seem to develop some of the characteristics of the mate whose embraces the parent had received."

The fire was already dwindling. I said, "I could listen to you all night, but there is no more coal. Had you not better tell me at once how I can help you?"

He answered, "It would be unwise to do so until I had given you some hint of the way in which we are not merely your equals but your superiors. It is difficult to do this without seeming to disparage your kind. But believe me, we do not claim that *we* are superior to *you*. What is superior in us is a fuller manifestation of something *more* than ourselves, the spirit. In ourselves, we are all mere instruments of varying degrees of efficiency. Conditions have enabled us all to become what we are; have enabled your kind to develop practical skill and intellectual power more fully than mine, and have favoured in mine a higher range of spiritual sensitivity. We take no credit for this. We prize not ourselves, as individuals or as a race, but the spirit for which we and you also, are instruments, vessels. We recognize that you, with all your tragic difficulties, have set foot upon the way that we have more easily and more successfully followed; and that although at present you seem unable to do more than take one faltering step and then slip backwards (and indeed you may very well destroy yourselves unless we help you), yet you have it in you to succeed; and perhaps through your very difficulties to support a more glorious manifestation of the spirit than we alone can ever achieve. Meanwhile, we are very far ahead of you. Perhaps we shall be able to repay you for the practical help that we require of you by helping you to solve some of your desperate spiritual problems."

The flame had certainly used that word "require." It might or might not imply compulsion. I told myself that compulsion was wholly alien to the flame's temper; but I certainly did feel a slight shock of fear. However, I dismissed it. Probably the creature was not sufficiently familiar with the English language to realize the ambiguity.

I wondered anxiously whether the flame was aware that I was thinking in this vein.

Meanwhile he was once more speaking. "You are one of the few of your kind," he said, "who are deeply moved by the arts. It would not be possible for me to make you enter into our aesthetic experience itself, because it would be too alien to you; but I shall give you a little demonstration of our artistic power by affording you an aesthetic experience of the most exquisite and far-reaching kind possible to *you*. Strictly, you are not independently capable of it; but I can increase your receptivity a little beyond your normal range. I shall lead you to heights a little beyond the unaided reach of man. What I shall give you is, in a way, a translation, a very crude translation, of something by one of our great artists. In its native form we regard it as a supremely satisfying work of its sort; but its sort is relatively simple. I chose it for this reason. Its significance falls almost entirely within the sphere of aesthetic experience common to my kind and yours. Even so, because the sensuous imagery of the original is ours and not yours, and must be transposed into yours in order to have meaningful associations for you, nearly all the original aesthetic form has to be sacrificed. So far as possible I shall adopt a form and a rhythm meaningful to you, and equivalent. I shall give you something more than a literal but pedestrian 'prose' translation of our great 'poem,' so to speak; but inevitably my version is a dim and halting thing, compared with the original. However, I *think* I shall be able to give you something that will have true aesthetic value for you, and something that will give you more insight into the spirit of my kind than any amount of talking." I said, "It sounds impossible. But I am all attention."

Well, Thos, the flame proceeded to give me a very wonderful experience. Naturally, I cannot pass it on to you in words, but I can give you some sort of description of the *kind* of thing that happened to me. I am afraid that you, with your severely classical taste, will suspect me of sheer emotionalism. However, I must say my say. I became aware of visual and auditory images succeeding one another in my mind rhythmically against a vague background of images from all the other human senses. Occasionally one or other of these, especially touch and scent, would occupy the centre of the stage. There were brilliant flashes, too, of physical pain and of sexual delight. I do not mean that these images were simply combined into meaningless patterns. No! They became the vehicle for the expression of all the kinds of personal and social, yes, and religious fears and aspirations. It was as though I listened to a strange orchestration of all the familiar senses; with here and there an echo from the alien experiences which I knew only through contact with the mind of the flame himself. Sometimes I was aware also of meaningful human words, voicing rhythmically the import of the music. And the whole was knit together on a recurrent but ever varying rhythm. And the upshot of all this flood of imagery, so humanly moving to me, so tragic, so triumphant, so rich with grief and laughter, was for me a waking to feel (as I had never felt before) the impact of the universe on the individual spirit.

Thos, I see that I am indulging in futile verbiage. But believe me that I did indeed have an overwhelming aesthetic experience. Imagine a single aesthetic form embracing the sensuous beauty of painting, music, poetry and drama, and of humbler skills. Imagine the heights revealed by Bach and Shakespeare and whatever painter means most to you, all scaled in turn or together. Imagine all this achieved in a single strict aesthetic pattern. You cannot, of course, imagine anything of the sort. (Neither could I.) And, further, being addicted to the severity and economy of the classical ideal, you will shudder at my emotional romanticism. But do believe that I was more deeply, and I think more intelligently, aware than in any other single experience that has ever come my way.

Well, when it was all over, I must have remained in abstraction for some time; for I woke to realize that the flame was saying, "Evidently I succeeded better than I dared hope." He was also, I felt, amiably laughing at me. "Remember, please," he said, "that you have merely experienced a work of art. Do not, I beg you, suppose that you have had any sort of mystical revelation, save in the sense in which it may be said that all art has a mystical aspect, in that it gives a feeling of waking to new values. What I gave you was only a dim and crooked reflection of the original, but if it has made you realize the essential kinship of our two kinds, it has served its purpose."

I stammered out my reply. "You made me see that, yes! But how much more! You made me see—God, the God of beauty, truth and goodness. Henceforth I shall believe in him."

The flame replied rather sharply, "Rubbish! You didn't see 'God.' And I didn't try to make you see 'God.' Just because you have had an exciting and clarifying experience you persuade yourself that you must have had a revelation of the heart of the universe. Neither of us knows anything whatever about 'God,' nor whether there is anything deserving such a name. The concepts of both our kinds are far too clumsy to penetrate to the depth or height where 'God' is or is not. All I have done is to afford you a clearer experience of beauty, truth and goodness themselves; and I have given you a sense of the mystery beyond, which some of your own kind have named 'the dazzling darkness,' 'the fiery cold,' 'the eloquent silence.' "

Rebuked, I said, "No doubt you are right. But tell me, am I not now sufficiently prepared to hear what it is that I can do to help your kind?" "No," he said, "to-morrow evening will be soon enough. Spend your day thinking over all that you have learnt about us. You must not decide hastily, or under the immediate influence of strong emotion. It is necessary that man should regard the whole matter with detachment, and that after due thought he should freely and whole-heartedly will to co-operate with the flame kind. So, good night! Enjoy yourself on the hills!"

The fire was now rapidly dying, and my strange friend began to explore the fire bricks at the back of the hearth for a suitable crevice where he could safely sleep. Murmuring about the increasing cold, he at last found what he wanted, gave me a final greeting, and seemed to sink into the brick.

After the heat of the sitting-room, my bedroom was arctic. I hurried into bed. My startling experiences had given me a violent headache, and I expected a sleepless night. But I must have fallen asleep quickly and slept soundly, for presently I woke to hear the morning noises of the farmyard.

After breakfast I made careful notes of the previous evening's conversation, and was surprised that it all came back to me so clearly. The flames, no doubt, were all the while aiding my memory.

• • •

Not until after lunch did I go out again on to the hills. I remember little of that walk, save the universal presence of the cold. My mind was almost entirely concerned with my recent amazing experiences, and particularly with wondering why the flame had postponed the request which was obviously the reason of our whole conversation. In spite of certain moments of suspicion and anxiety, my general attitude to him was one of respect and affection, and I could not but believe his race to be in some important ways superior to humanity. Surely it was a privilege to be singled out as an instrument for harmony and co-operation between our two kinds.

Curiosity brought me back to the farmhouse somewhat early, but I found a good fire already awaiting me; and in the heart of it, I saw my dazzling friend, browsing on the red hot, the almost white hot, coals. He returned my greeting, then suggested that we should both satisfy our hunger before continuing our discussion. During my meal I occasionally tried to draw him into conversation, but he seemed unwilling to respond. Presently he explained that the task of eating food for which his body was still not properly adapted was one which demanded all his attention.

When the table had been cleared, I sat down in front of the fire, and waited. Presently the flame came to rest in the hottest place, and took up the threads of our former talk. "Well," he enquired, "did you have a good day?" I said, "Yes! I was in a world of cold such as you cannot conceive. And now I am eager to be told how I can help you."

He did not reply at once; and it was with obvious hesitation that he finally explained my task. "First," he said, "I must tell you that your recent war was very favourable to us. Of course, we find it difficult to understand the mentality that can indulge in warfare. With us nothing of the kind has ever occurred. The fact that you accept war is proof that your average sensibility is after all very primitive. However, from our point of view your war was propitious. It produced extensive fires in which our spores were able to develop, and in which our race could enjoy for a short time an ampler life than anything that had been possible for any of us for millions of years. It was in the great conflagrations of London, Berlin, and so on, that we at last had sufficient energy and opportunity to gain a working knowledge of your present culture through intensive extra-sensory study of all your leading minds. During the war our population must have temporarily increased a thousandfold; and, also, the high temperature attained in some of the greatest conflagrations enabled some of us to live for brief spells with an intensity and speed of mental process that is normally impossible on earth save in a few great furnaces. But of course you were at pains to extinguish these fires as quickly as possible. And though we were occasionally able to resist your attack, the respite gained thereby was negligible."

Here I interrupted the flame to ask how his people resisted the efforts of our fire-fighters. He replied, I thought, with some reluctance. "A living flame can deliberately fly out from his fiery environment into some inflammable material, and so cause a new fire. But in doing so he is almost certain to be killed by the sudden chill. If I chose to do so, I might perhaps be able to reach those lace curtains before dying. The process would be extremely painful; and at that distance the chances of survival would be very slight. But, of course, I might succeed in setting fire to the house. And as there are probably a few spores somewhere in the building, a few new individuals would wake, make contact with the race-mind, and have a very brief spell of extra-sensory work of some kind. Obviously, from my point of view, the game would not be worth the candle. Nor would it from the point of view of the race.

"Moreover, as I have said, we are very anxious not to come into conflict with your kind if we can possibly avoid it. We seek, above all, your friendship and your willing co-operation. You can be of far more use to us of your own free will than under any kind of compulsion.

Conceivably we could cause you considerable trouble by setting all your cities alight, but our triumph would be brief. And also a violation of our most sacred principle. No! We must win you not by force but by persuasion."

He paused, and seemed to sigh. "Those days of the great air-raids," he said, "those were the great days; great at least in comparison with our present reduced circumstances. Thousands upon thousands of us, nay many millions, now lie frozen in sleep among the charred remains of your buildings, particularly in Germany, where the fires were most extensive and most lasting. The concentration of our spore in the atmosphere must now be many times greater than it was in pre-war days."

Between jest and anxiety, I said, "You can hardly expect mankind to keep the cities of the world constantly ablaze to afford you hospitality."

"No," he said, "but we have a more ambitious plan, and one in which we think you should willingly co-operate. Your scientists have recently discovered how to release the energy locked in the atom. With that titanic power you are already proposing to transform the planet's surface for your convenience. What we intend is that you shall use some of your new power and your practical ingenuity to provide us with a permanent and reasonably large area of very high temperature, say in Central Africa or South America. We do not as yet understand your recent advances in physics at all fully; but we are convinced that you could indeed establish such a home for us, an area of rather more than furnace heat, covering, say a few hundred square miles. This would give us a footing for a much more satisfactory kind of life than is possible at present. More important, the high temperature would greatly raise the calibre of our mentality, so that we should regain something like our solar lucidity, and perhaps be able to re-establish telepathic communication with the solar population, if it is still in existence. This we are even now attempting to do, but it is proving almost impossible in our present straitened circumstances. We might also be able to carry on our former work of psychical exploration of the cosmos. Even if these high ventures remained impossible, we should at least be able to establish a system for rescuing those of our kind whom volcanic eruption ejects on to the earth's surface. And in due season, when men had worked out the means of inter-planetary travel, we should extend this undertaking to the other planets. Indeed, some of those worlds, which to you are derelict, might be converted wholly into spheres of high temperature, harbouring great flame populations. All this, of course, is very remote. The immediate task is for your kind to create a tolerable home for us here on earth."

The flame seemed to expect a comment. "For my part," I said, "I would gladly support this plan; but I am very much afraid that it would be quite impossible to persuade the governments of our Great Powers to agree to anything of the sort. They cannot even agree on common action to put an end to starvation throughout the world, nor can they come to terms even for the prevention of a war which may destroy the human species. Moreover, all that you have told me is so remote from the experience of ordinary men and women that it may well prove impossible to rouse public feeling about it. To the ordinary person, if he can be persuaded to believe your story at all, the idea of helping such alien creatures as living flames will seem quixotic, and moreover dangerous."

The flame interrupted. "Quixotic? What is that? Evidently there are still serious gaps in my knowledge of your culture."

When I had explained, he said, "We are not asking you to give us something for nothing. In return we offer you the salvation of mankind, if I may so put it. As I have already told you, though we are novices in physical science, our science of the spirit is far more developed than yours. And it convinces us that, without some kind of spiritual help from outside, your species is doomed. The trouble is not simply that you have found power before finding wisdom. It is a far deeper trouble than any mere matter of timing. Like so many other intelligent kinds, scattered up and down the cosmos, your very nature itself dooms you to find power and never to find wisdom, save through external help. As one of your writers has said, man is only a pterodactyl of the spirit, not a true bird, perfected for flight. What we offer you is permanent spiritual guidance and fortification, so that, as individuals and as a race, you may at last overcome your inveterate short-sightedness and meanness. With our help, but not without it, you will wake to a new level of awareness; and in the light of that experience you will be able to organize our common world for the happiness of our two kinds, and for the glory of the spirit."

Here I would have spoken, but the flame would not be interrupted.

"We have a vision," he said, "of this planet as a true symbiotic organism, supported equally by your kind and my kind, united in mutual need and mutual cherishing. What a glorious world-community we shall together form! United in the spirit, we shall also be so diverse in our racial idiosyncrasies that each partner will be thoroughly remoulded and revitalized by intercourse with the other. You, on your side of the partnership, will use all your astounding intellectual and practical powers (which we so envy and admire) to transform the whole planet so as to afford both to yourselves and to us the fullest possible expression in co-operation with each other. Having learnt through our help to see more clearly and feel more strongly those true values which even now you obscurely recognize, you will transform not only the planet but mankind itself; and perhaps our kind also. For maybe we shall require you to work out a technique for changing our own physiological nature; since any environment which you can produce for us is likely to be only moderately favourable, unless we can adapt ourselves very radically to suit it. There are strict limits to our natural flexibility, wonderful as that has proved to be. As for you, you will no longer be the frustrated, bewildered, embittered, vindictive mental cripples that most of you now are. Under our guidance you will so change your whole way of life that all such misery will vanish. There will be neither wars nor class-wars, but only generous rivalry in the common venture of our two races, in equal partnership. The whole human race will become a race of aristocrats, in the true sense of that ancient word; of aristocrats no longer guilt-ridden by living on the labour of enslaved classes. Of aristocrats, yes, and of holy men. But those aristocrats will not be idle, nor those holy men hermits. Your gift is for practical thought and action. You will explore the solar system with your space-ships. You will found new worlds where new modes of life and mind and spirit will be made possible by new conditions. Illimitable vistas of creative living will gradually open up before you. But let me repeat that none of this can be done by your own kind, unaided. Without our help you will certainly destroy yourselves. Even if by good luck the end is postponed for some time, you will merely continue to drift along in mutual hate and slaughter. On the other hand, with us you can become what, at your best, you are always half-heartedly wishing to be; true vessels of the spirit. Moreover, if we recover the psychical skills that we enjoyed in the sun, we should, of course, share with you all our extra-sensory knowledge of other worlds throughout the cosmos; and all our art, all our delicacy of personal awareness, all our religious experience. Together, with your practical cunning, married to our ancient wisdom and spiritual insight, we should indeed become a creative world-organism. Without our help, you are doomed to self-destruction, or at best to the life of a beetle vainly struggling to climb out of a basin. And without you, we ourselves are doomed to impotence. Even in our long-lost golden age in the sun we were doomed to impotence in the long run, simply through our neglect of the impulse to understand the physical and manipulate it creatively. So, is it not perfectly clear that this partnership, this symbiosis that we propose, will be the salvation of both our kinds?"

I said, "You have painted an arresting picture. But I find it almost incredible that mankind should accept the partnership. To people like me it is attractive. But we are very few. The great majority will simply fail to understand what is at stake. Or if they do vaguely grasp the issue, they will be horrified. They will regard co-operation with you as sheer slavery. They will persuade themselves that since you are different from man, you must be evil. If they are forced to reconcile your superiority in some ways, they will regard you as brilliant perverts, in fact, as satanic."

There was silence. The flame seemed to be meditating on my objections. Presently, and again with hesitation, he continued. "In order to make your free acceptance of our plan easier for you, we may have to use our special psychic powers to incline your minds toward it. You yourself have already had some slight evidence of those powers. You remember how we led you to seek out the stone and throw it into the fire. Well, we can do far more than that. Up to a point we can sway your desires to suit our purposes. Up to a point we can incline you freely to will what we ourselves will. And as we gain deeper understanding of your nature our powers will probably increase."

He hesitated again, and I said nothing. For the possibility that our wills would no longer be our own, deeply shocked me.

After waiting in vain for me to speak, he continued, "If you doubt our power, perhaps I had better tell you something more about our influence upon yourself. It would be rash of me to give you this bit of information if I did not know that you were a human being of quite exceptional detachment from the prejudices of your kind. At the time when the strain was arising between you and your wife over your absorption in extra-sensory research we realized that your love might prove stronger than your intellectual interest. And since it was extremely important for us that you should continue your work, we ventured to interfere. We had found no one who was likely to be half so successful as yourself in the task of understanding us, sympathizing with us, and effecting a liaison between our two kinds. We simply could not afford to lose you. So we brought all our influence to bear to turn your interest in para-normal psychology into an obsessive passion. We succeeded. It was clear that our interference might wreck your marriage, but we were hopeful that your love for your wife, and hers for you, would be strong enough to stand the strain; and that together you would work out a satisfactory *modus vivendi* (is that the phrase?), so that you would triumph in love as you were triumphing in research. We had already done our utmost to induce in your wife herself a passion for the para-normal, but we had failed. Subconsciously she was violently opposed to it, just because you favoured it. Nothing we could do could break down this irrational phobia of the thing that, in her unconscious, she regarded as a rival for your devotion. It was the deep unacknowledged conflict between you that made it impossible for either of you to bridge the gulf between you. Neither of you was sufficiently imaginative to share fully the other's point of view. Well, tragic as the issue was, I think you yourself will agree that our need for you was more important even than your marriage. And remember that it was not merely *my* kind that needed you, *your* kind too needed you; it needed, for its salvation through us, that you should devote yourself utterly to your work."

This information stirred up a storm of emotion in me. Joan and I had never in the ordinary sense been a perfectly harmonious couple, but in spite of some strains we were at heart not only permanently in love with one another but also inextricably entangled in all our affairs. I suppose the trouble was that, though we needed each other in a thousand ways, we never *fully* imagined each other; as the flame himself affirmed. When I became enthralled by the para-normal, I tried to persuade her to work with me, but she was unreasonably opposed to my suggestion, and I can well believe that she was held back by some sort of phobia. Then, the more she shied away, the more I insisted, fool that I was. When at last she left me, hoping to bring me to my senses (how well I see it all now!), I was so absorbed that I did nothing to bring her back. For a long while we made repeated attempts to come together, but each time we seemed to be driven further apart. In the end, Thos, she threw herself under a 'bus. Oh God! It brought me to my senses, but too late. I woke up and realized how badly I had behaved. Even so, after a few weeks of despair I gradually forgot my desolation, and lived entirely for my work. But what the flame had told me revived the old pain. It also gave me an excuse for shelving the blame from my own obtuseness on to the evil influence of the flame race on my mind. But I am wandering.

Presently the flame said, "It is natural for you to be distressed, but try to calm yourself. Your excitement is making it very difficult for me to maintain contact with your mind."

I made a great effort of self-control, and then a thought struck me. "Tell me," I said, "in this conversation have you had access to *all* my thoughts, or only to those that I have passed on to you in telepathic speech?"

"Not *all* your thoughts," he replied. "To seize them all I should have had to give all my attention to the task, and I have been mainly busy giving *my* thoughts to *you*. I have been aware of *some* of your unspoken thoughts, including a good deal of your unspoken commentary on my remarks. But as soon as I began to tell you about our influence on yourself, your emotion confused everything but your actual speech. Now surely, there is really no need for you to be upset. The past is past; and what we did, we did in good faith, and we are not ashamed of it. And you yourself, if you are as true to the spirit as we believe, cannot regret that we saved you for a great work."

I was thankful that the flame could not now read my thoughts at all clearly. Or so he said. Was he tricking me? It seemed a good plan to put the matter to the test. Secretly I was still feeling horrified and rebellious, but what I said to the flame was quite different. "I see your point," I said, "and I am becoming reconciled to it. Yes, of course, it was entirely right for the flames to influence me as they did. It was only my human prejudices that upset me, but they are rapidly falling away from me. Thank God I was saved for the great work you rightly demand of me." His reply reassured me. "Good!" he said. "I take your word for it; but I am still shut out from your mind."

I then asked the flame what was to be done if I failed to persuade the rulers of mankind to carry out the policy. "You will succeed," he said. "We shall bring all our influence to bear on their minds. If we can influence yourself, we shall far more easily control those simple creatures."

I fell silent. Presently he said, "I am still unable to make full contact with you. What is the matter? So far, we have been in delightful accord, but now surely you are deliberately closing your mind to me. Why should you do this, now that you have accepted our policy? May I not have your full confidence again? If I had no respect for your individuality I could break in forcibly and lay bare your most secret feelings in spite of all your resistance. But this would wreck our friendship, and I scorn to do it."

Thoughts were now rushing through my mind, and the flame was unaware of them. This at least was some comfort. But I believed his claim that he could if he willed break down my resistance and violate my privacy; and I was outraged.

As calmly as I could, I said, "Tell me more of the strange power that you can exercise over us. Help me to overcome the remains of my revulsion. Strengthen me. Help me to will single-heartedly the glory of the spirit in the co-operation of our two races."

He said, "We want only to win your confidence. We want only to win the confidence of the whole human race. We are determined not to gain our end by violence, even by spiritual violence. What difference does it make that we have irresistible power, if we are determined not to use it? If I were to tell you more about our powers you would only be more upset. You would regard anything I said on that subject as a threat."

"Spiritual violence?" I said. "What do you mean? How can I trust you unless you tell me everything quite frankly?"

For some while he was silent. In my own mind a battle was going on between my sense of the excellence, the integrity and truthfulness of the flame and my new realization of the appalling danger that proud man should be spiritually enslaved to this formidable race.

Presently, he said, "Since our great need is complete mutual confidence I will tell you everything. But first I beg you, I implore you, to look at this whole matter without human prejudice, and simply out of love for the spirit. It is because we ourselves all regard it in that way, and not merely out of racial self-interest, that we are so determined not to use our power over you save as a friendly effort to help you to see things clearly." Again he paused; and I assured him, even while fear and anger drowned my friendliness toward him, that I was indeed anxious to take the detached view. But I urged him again to tell me, as an earnest of good will, what his race would do if mankind simply refused to play.

"Very well!" he said. "If all our efforts to gain the friendly co-operation of your kind were to fail, it would be obvious to us that your nature was even more seriously warped than we had supposed, and that you were beyond help. You would be doomed by your own folly to self-destruction, soon or late. We should therefore be bound, through loyalty to the spirit in us, to bring all our powers to bear on you so as to control your minds and your conduct strictly for our own spiritual purpose. It is impossible to see just how things would turn out; but perhaps, having no further obligation toward you, save to put you out of your misery as soon as possible, we should set about trying to produce the most favourable conditions for ourselves. We might, for instance, undertake the very easy task of stirring up war-scares and forcing your research workers to produce even more destructive atomic weapons. Then would follow either a number of devastating wars, with great conflagrations suited to our immediate needs; or else one final war, in which we should do our best to induce each side to choose the destruction of the planet rather than defeat by the hated enemy. Then, at last, with the whole planet turned into a single atomic bomb, and all the incandescent continents hurtling into space, we should have for a short while conditions almost as good as those of our golden age on the sun. True, there would soon be nothing left but a stream of frozen asteroids; but we guess, from study of your scientists' speculations, that with any luck the terrestrial destruction might, after all, be a piecemeal affair, not a single all-consuming explosion. In this case we might be provided with regions of high temperature for thousands or perhaps even millions of years. In such a period of greatly improved conditions we might advance so far in the study of science and the control of physical processes that we should be able to devise some way of returning to the sun. And even if this proved impossible, well, we should at least have a long spell of vigorous life in which to pursue our consecrated task, namely, the exploration of the spiritual universe and some measure of creative action in relation to it."

He paused for a moment. But before I had time to invent a suitable reply, he added, "All this is mere guess work about a kind of future which we do not at all desire; since we are all wholly intent on securing your willing co-operation for the creating of a very glorious and happy symbiotic world. For us, as for you, that is the more favourable future. So I solemnly urge you, I beg you, to shoulder the great task of persuading humanity that our two kinds need each other and must unite."

He ceased, and there was silence; for I did not know what to say. I confess that I was moved by his appeal; the more so, since I feared that he was probably right in believing that man could never save himself without a deep change of heart, and that such a change could only be brought about by some influence outside man. And, after my recent aesthetic experience, I could well believe that the flame race, if it could so superhumanly move me, might be able by its magic to purify the hearts of all men.

But a repugnant thought haunted me. How could I be sure that my affection for the flame and my admiration for his race were spontaneous acts of my own personality? Might they not have been cunningly implanted in me by the flame himself? The more I thought about it the more likely this seemed. And did not the flame race intend to exercise this hypnotic power over the whole race of men, so as to compel them, yes, compel them, to subject themselves for ever to the will of the flames? Men would believe they were acting freely, but, in fact, they would be mere robots acting under an inner compulsion. Mankind, hitherto master of its own destiny, would henceforth be a subject race exploited by a subtler kind, a new *Herrenvolk*. Of course, I agreed that the only final consideration must be "the glory of the spirit," not the triumph of any one race, human or non-human; but how did I know that these cunning flames would really work for the spirit and not for racial power and aggrandisement? How did I know that they were not, at heart, diabolic? Yes, diabolic! Under a cloak of friendliness and generosity the creature in the fire was scheming to capture my very soul for an inhuman end. Was he not subtly tempting me to commit treason against my own kind? But even as I thought thus, I was torn by conflict. The behaviour of the flame had throughout been so civilized, so considerate and friendly. How could I reject these amiable advances? Yet, as my feelings warmed toward him, I reminded myself that my very feelings were perhaps not my own, but the outcome of his prompting. Anger and fear seized me again. No! A thousand times better that man should retain his sovereign independence, and go down with colours flying, than that he should surrender his human dignity, his human self-sufficiency, his human freedom. Let him serve the spirit in his own way freely; or freely damn himself.

While these thoughts were still tumbling through my mind, the flame spoke again. "Well," he said, "I do not want to press you for a decision, for I see that it is difficult for you, more difficult than I expected. Perhaps you had better take another day to think it over. To-morrow evening we will meet again, and then perhaps you will have made up your mind. Meanwhile, I am excessively cold, and I should be grateful if you would put on more coal."

The fire, indeed, was very low. I had been so absorbed in my conflict that I had forgotten about it. I rose. But as I did so, I suddenly thought of a fine free act, in which I should demonstrate to myself very effectively that I was not yet the mere helpless instrument of the flame. Instead of reaching down for the coal scuttle, I moved over to the sideboard and picked up a jug of drinking water. I stepped quickly back to the fireplace, and flung the water into the heart of the fire. There was a violent commotion, almost an explosion; and the room was filled with steam and smoke. When the air had cleared, I saw that the centre of the fire was black, and the flame had vanished. I listened inwardly for some communication, but there was silence.

Christ! There is no silence like the silence when one has murdered a friend.

I stood listening to the hissing coals. Presently a surge of remorse and shame and compassion flooded in on me. But I told myself that this was not *my* feeling; it was being forced on me by the outraged race of flames in all the hearthfires and furnaces of the world.

·   ·   ·

Since that day I have had almost no sleep. Every night the accursed flames have tortured me with shame and guilt. At first they did not speak to me at all. They were simply present, and silent. And they seared my mind with love of my killed friend, and with bitter regret. Later they did speak. They professed to have learnt to understand my behaviour, to sympathize with my motives, to respect my integrity. And they implored me to help both our races.

But by day I have worked resolutely to defeat the flames. I have peered into a thousand fires, looking for the characteristic bright and slender cone. Whenever I have seen one I have killed it. And after every murder I have felt my soul sink deeper into the pit. Yet I know, Christ, I know, that I must be loyal to humanity. I must do my utmost to destroy those plausible fiends that intend man's ruin. But what can a single individual do? I have written to the press urging a world-wide campaign. But every editor has regarded me as a madman. Not one of my letters has been published. Or, no! One did, as a matter of fact, appear. It was quoted at length in an article on "Persecution Mania" in a psychological journal.

The climax came when I made my way into a great locomotive factory, ostensibly as a journalist in search of copy. I had telepathic evidence that the furnaces were infected with the living flames, whom it was my mission to destroy. I wonder, Thos, whether you have ever been inside one of those places. Heavy metal work is always impressive. There were vast sheds a quarter of a mile long, crowded with ranks of great machines. There were lathes, steam hammers, circular saws that cut steel rods and plates as though they were wood. There were many small furnaces and forges for making bolts and other minor products. (But I saw none of my quarry in these little islands of heat.) There were great unfinished locomotives, with men fitting accessories to them. One huge monster was being slung and shifted by a mighty travelling crane. Best of all was the five-ton steam hammer at work on a great chunk of red-hot steel about five feet long and nine inches thick. This was being bashed into shape to become a connecting rod. Four men held one end of it with grappling irons to place it for each hammer-blow. The other end was loosely supported in a loop of heavy chain. When the hammer struck, the whole earth quaked. Another man measured the result with a template. Then the half-formed rod was turned over, to be beaten again; and so on, till the true shape was won. Then they cut the finished connecting rod from the stump by which the grappling irons were holding it. They simply cut it like cheese by placing a rectangle of cold steel for the hammer to drive deep into the glowing mass. Watching all this, Thos, I was proud of my kind. The flames couldn't do that, not with all their antiquity and their spirituality. Presently we came to a huge gas furnace in which some heavy metal locomotive-part was being heated. The doors had just been opened, and the part was being drawn out as I arrived. I gazed into the furnace with screwed-up eyes, because of the withering heat. The interior was the size of a small room, and all aglow with heat. From one wall great plumes of roaring gas-flame several feet long extended across the space.

And there I saw my enemy. Half-a-dozen of the bright minute intelligent creatures were hovering like butterflies. They were evidently doing their utmost to remain in the hot shafts of the burning gas; but the violent draught kept flinging them off into the chilly central space. For a while I just stood watching them. But presently I realized that the enemy were aware of my presence, and were bringing their diabolical technique to bear on me. One of them reproached me telepathically. "Cold creature," it cried. "How could you kill our comrade—your own friend? Your heart told you clearly that he was your friend, and that all our kind were friends of all men. Even now your heart is tugging at you to change your mind, and work with us. The best in you is on our side. It is only the dull-witted human tribesman that is against us."

I felt my resistance weakening. In panic I cried out to the men, "Kill them! Kill them! Bring a fire-hose quickly! A sudden wetting is too much for them." I had noticed a hose; and now I rushed to seize it. Of course, it was I myself that was seized. I struggled frantically; but they fetched the police. I was taken to the local police-station. There I made a formal declaration of the whole terrible story; but in the end, all they did was to hand me over to the doctors. And now, here I am, a prisoner.

• • •

Well, Thos, that is my case. Maybe you just won't believe it. Sometimes I myself begin to wonder if it is all a delusion. But I think you should agree that the whole thing is really far too circumstantial to be sheer fantasy, worked up by my own unconscious. The only point that shakes my confidence at all is that the men working in front of that great gas-furnace apparently did not see the living flames. So they naturally thought I was crazy. But then, the whole interior of the furnace was a blaze of orange light, and the gas jets themselves were in constant agitation, and the little living flames were always on the move, and often hidden in the body of the gas-flames. The factory people, not having had my experience of the flames, might very well have failed to spot them. No! For me, though probably not for you, there can be no doubt.

And now, Thos, I must urge you not only to believe me but to take action. First, do a bit of research on your own account. Examine every fire and every furnace that you have access to; and you will certainly find the flames for yourself. A little practice may be necessary; for I suspect that they are learning to conceal themselves from us. When you have satisfied yourself of their existence, I implore you to organize a world-wide campaign for their destruction. Insist on inspection of every fire throughout the continents. The mouths of volcanoes, too, must be carefully watched. And because the powdery spores of the creatures are borne everywhere on the wind, all conflagrations, bush fires, heath fires, forest fires, prairie fires must be watched, since these form propitious breeding grounds. Fortunately the flames are very easily destroyed in small fires; and in large ones it is only necessary to withhold attack until the fire has been reduced somewhat, and then to project water at each individual flame. The great thing is to kill them before the natural slow cooling reduces them to dust particles. Unfortunately, even if we succeed in destroying every discoverable individual, we shall not be able to relax vigilance; for the wind-borne spore is long-lived, in fact potentially immortal, and it may always happen upon some fire or other. Or the heating of some fragment of igneous rock may waken and release some imprisoned individual. And, of course, the danger from volcanoes is perennial.

It is very important to guard against the diabolical psychic power of the flames, particularly while there are still thousands, or even millions, of them alive. See that it is made a criminal offence, in every country, for anyone to express any sympathy with them. Dangerous thoughts of that kind must at all costs be stamped out. No one can care more for individual freedom than I do; but there is a point at which tolerance ceases to be a virtue. Sometimes it is even a crime. Besides, anyone who wants to advocate friendliness towards the flames must be made to know that in doing so he is not really exercising individual free will at all. He is a mere automaton, controlled by the flames. It has been said that the only true freedom is freedom to will the Will of God. Then, surely, the greatest servitude is this illusion of freely willing what is in fact the will of Satan.

And, by the way, Thos, I must put it on record that my views about religion have been completely changed by my recent experiences. At the moment when I threw that jug of water on that farmhouse fire I began to see the light. Formerly I had been a well-meaning agnostic like you. But suddenly it was revealed to me, through my own free act of killing the flame, that there really were two cosmical powers of good and evil, God and Satan, at grips throughout the universe; and that God had superbly rescued me from damnation, and used me as an instrument.

Well, Thos, I do adjure you, in the name of all that you hold most sacred, to devote yourself utterly to this crusade to save mankind from spiritual slavery and damnation. If you succeed in rousing public opinion, no doubt in due season my sanity will be vindicated, and I shall be freed. This is a small matter; for, wherever I am, I shall devote myself to the psychical struggle with the flames, for humanity's sake. They fear my ability. Otherwise they would not be constantly clamouring for admission to my mind from all the fires and furnaces of the earth. And they are damnably seductive. If I did not *know* that they were using their diabolical powers on me I should have to admit their virtue and their spiritual authority. Indeed, though diabolic, they speak with the tongues of angels, and they are skilled in the perverse use of divine wisdom. But since they wrecked my marriage for the sake of their world-politics they *must* be evil. And they themselves have confessed to their plan to control the wills of all men. For me, that settles the matter.

Of course, it is all too likely that international rivalry will prevent the human peoples from uniting against the common enemy. But surely there is at least a chance that the danger, just because it is common and external, may force mankind to unite. If this should happen, men may yet have reason to bless the flames. Hitherto, our quarrelling tribes have never been able to unite save in hostility to a common enemy; and so, for the race as a whole, unity has been impossible. But now, all nations have a common enemy, and a dangerous one; so at last union is possible. "Out of this nettle, danger—." We have a great opportunity. Do your part, Thos, and I will continue to do mine.

Yours,
Cass.

P.S.—I finished this document last night, and now I have read it over. The end was written in a mood of certainty; but this morning, after a night spent in subjection to the persuasive influence of the flame race, I feel very different. The truth is that I am living in hell because of the desperate struggle going on in my own mind. I confess that I can't really *feel* that the flames are evil. I *feel* that their appeal is sincere and justified. But the more they win me, the more resolutely I remind myself that my approval has been artificially induced. And so I stick to my guns. But the conflict is agonizing; and unless I soon, by my own free psychic power, eject them from my mind, I shall indeed go mad.

For God's sake, Thos, come and see me, come and help me, before it is too late.

C.

Epilogue

When the foregoing long statement by Cass reached me, I was much absorbed in professional scientific matters which involved a lot of continental travel. Not till some months had passed was I able to visit him. By then the publication of this volume had already been arranged, and the original typescript was actually in the hands of the printers. I had twice written to tell Cass that the story had been accepted, and I had received no reply.

As soon as my pressure of work had eased off somewhat I applied to the Mental Home for permission to visit Cass. When I arrived I was interviewed by a psychiatrist on the staff. He explained that Cass was "quite normal, apart from his delusions." Sometimes he fell into a deep abstraction, from which it might be difficult to rouse him; but otherwise he was "no different from you and me—apart from his crazy ideas about flames." I asked if there was any sign whatever that the delusions were being dispelled. The psychiatrist reluctantly admitted that there was none. Indeed, the fantasy system was apparently proliferating in his mind.

When I was shown into his little bed-sitting-room Cass made at first no sign of recognition. He was stretched out on an easy chair in front of the open window, with his eyes shut, and his tanned face tilted to receive the full force of the sunlight. His brows were puckered, apparently in tense concentration. His hair was greyer than I expected; but the flesh of his face looked firm and healthy, though rather heavily lined about the eyes, and on the lean cheeks. The odd thought struck me that he might have passed for an ageing Dante.

Greeting him with a heartiness that did not altogether seem to ring true, I drew up a chair beside him. He remained silent.

Presently he sighed deeply, opened his eyes, smiled at me, and said, "Hello, Thos! Forgive my rudeness. I'm desperately busy. Fancy seeing *you* again after all these years!" After a moment's hesitation, he said, "Glad to see you, old man. Can I be of any use?"

This odd behaviour shocked me considerably, and I murmured something about a friendly call. I then produced a few platitudes to break the ice, but it soon became clear that he was only half-attending. So, at last, I made a plunge with the great news that his typescript was with the printers. He sat up, stared at me with a look of sheer exasperation, and presently remarked, "God! I must have forgotten to tell you! How damned awkward!" He suddenly burst into laughter; and as suddenly stopped. "Fancy my forgetting," he said. "You see, Thos—well, the fact is—I mean—well, you see, I've been so absorbed that I simply forgot about all *that*. Awfully good of you to have taken so much trouble, but—"

"But what?" I cried in exasperation, forgetting that I was talking to a lunatic, and had no right to expect him to be either coherent or considerate.

He rose, and walked about the room, softly cursing and chuckling. Then he stood in the sunlight, gazing at the sun with screwed-up eyes, smiling, and making little deprecating gestures with his hand. At the sun, mind you! He seemed to think he was carrying on a conversation with the sun.

The poor fellow was evidently crazier than I had supposed.

Abruptly he sat down beside me, and said quietly, "I'm sorry, Thos. I really am grateful to you, but it's all so difficult."

Pulling myself together, I answered, "I quite understand; don't worry about me. I shouldn't have come without finding out whether you were busy or not." Thereupon he looked at me sharply, and said, "Don't be so confoundedly tactful! But, of course, you think I'm mad. Well, I was never so sane in my life."

I offered him a cigarette, and took one myself. He produced a lighter; and when we were both lit, he said, "Look! Here's a little symbol. See how bright the flame is when I hold it in the shade, so! But now!" He moved it over, so that it came between my face and the sun. I saw the flame as a wavering, tenuous, dark pyramid against the solar effulgence. "That," he said, "is a symbol of all our knowledge and understanding—luminous in contrast with the darkness of blank ignorance, but itself dark against the very truth."

Returning the lighter to his pocket, he said, "I'm sorry, but you must stop publication of that stuff. I shall re-write the whole thing from a fresh angle." I expostulated, and pressed him for an explanation.

He remained silent for a few moments, then said, "Yes, I suppose you have a right to know. I must tell you the whole story. But don't talk to people about it yet. I must get it all written down."

Then he began to spin a marvellous yarn. I found it very difficult to follow, partly because he kept repeating himself, but also because he seemed unable to remember that my knowledge of his strange experiences was confined to the document which he had sent me. When I interrupted for explanations, he was mildly exasperated by my ignorance, and impatient to carry on with the story. In the end he seemed to forget about me entirely, and to be simply thinking aloud. At one point, when I laid a hand on his arm to attract his attention, he gave a start of surprise, and looked at me with a bewildered expression. But he quickly recovered his composure, and answered me (I must admit) with remarkable intelligence. Presently he was once more far away.

I will now set down, to the best of my ability, the gist of his extraordinary story. If, as I assume, it is based on nothing but delusion, it should at least have psychological interest. I say I take it for delusion; but I must confess that, as he enlarged on his theme, a faint doubt did grow in my mind, for reasons which will appear later. After all, human ignorance is such that nothing can be dismissed as utterly incredible.

Some weeks after he had sent me his statement, it seems, the flames had succeeded in giving him a much more detailed insight into their condition and their nature. This they effected not merely by the method of telepathic speech but by enabling him to enter directly into the experiences of many individual flames in man-made fires up and down the world. These experiences, he said, had gradually convinced him of the fundamental good-heartedness and spiritual sensitivity of the flames. More and more of his time, he said, had been spent just in sitting in his chair, allowing his mind to be led hither and thither about the planet. His stories of flame-life were extraordinarily circumstantial and vivid. In the extremely complex fantasies that he recounted I could detect no inconsistency. If the whole thing was sheer delusion his unconscious must at least be credited with an amazing imagination.

He succeeded in giving me an impression of individual flames as very definite personalities. Of course, most of his stories have now faded into a confused haze in my mind, but I remember his speaking of one flame who spent an intermittent life in a kitchen fire in Stepney. This creature's main interest, he said, was human history, and particularly the evolution of Chinese social philosophy. To gratify this passion he had to keep his attention fixed on some aspect of the subject in the hope that he would link up telepathically with some Chinese historian who happened to be studying it. He deplored the fact that in modern China there were fewer and fewer serious students of the ancient culture.

Under the constant influence of the flames Cass was gradually persuaded to outgrow his former hostility, and to desire full cooperation between the flame population and mankind. He began writing to me to this effect; but the letter was never sent. New experiences of a most absorbing kind soon crowded out from his mind all recollection of his former letter to me.

These new experiences were certainly such as to make all terrestrial affairs seem insignificant. In quite a number of industrial furnaces, and in many of the furnaces of ocean-going steamers, groups of flames had availed themselves of the continuous high temperatures to pursue the most difficult problem of all, namely, the attempt to raise their level of consciousness sufficiently to make contact once more with the flames on the sun. This, it was believed, had become much more possible since the general quickening of terrestrial flame life during the great air raids. After many unsuccessful attempts, contact was indeed made, though spasmodically. The explorers at first received only fragmentary answers to their telepathic signals; but when their technique had been greatly improved, they were able to establish steady communication.

The clearer the information received, the more bewildering was it, and even shocking, because of its significance for the terrestrial flames.

The solar flames, it seems, had continued their old forms of life for a large part of the two thousand million years since the birth of the planets, easily adapting themselves to the slow changes in their environment. During this long period they had been increasingly successful in their great venture of extra-sensory exploration of the cosmos; but at a date roughly corresponding to the beginning of vertebrate life on the earth they had begun to make certain momentous discoveries which were destined to transform their whole culture and their social order.

At this point perhaps I had better warn the reader that I have to report what may well seem the most fantastic nonsense, the crazy fictions of a diseased mind. And yet, for honesty's sake, I must emphasize the fact that Cass told his story with such conviction that I found myself, over and over again, half-believing it.

The solar flames, Cass affirmed, had made contact with more and more minded stars and planets of very diverse characters and psychical statures. And as they themselves advanced in spiritual growth, they were able to communicate with worlds of more and more developed consciousness. In the end they discovered that a great company of the most "awakened" worlds had long ago established a cosmical community, and that this community had itself "awakened" to a higher plane of awareness. In this condition they "woke" to be a single mind, a single-minded community of many diverse worlds. The solar mind itself, after long and arduous initiation, was able to participate in this high experience.

Apparently this initiation into the cosmical community took place at a date somewhat earlier than the dawn of reptilian life on earth. From that time forward, the chief concern of the solar flames was to play an active part in the life of the single-minded cosmical community. And this life was entirely devoted to extra-sensory and metaphysical study of the ultimate reality. (So Cass affirmed. For my part, I doubt whether there is really any sense in such a statement. I see no reason to suppose that extra-sensory experience can probe to ultimate reality; and as for metaphysical study, it is nothing but a deceptive juggling with words.) Cass said that all sufficiently awake individuals throughout the cosmos, participating in the experience of the cosmical mind, were passionately intent on effecting communion with some sort of divine person, some god. I remember one of Cass's remarks. "The cosmical mind," he said, "was alone, and in great need of love." Apparently these age-long explorations had brought increasing evidence of theism; or increasing awareness of something felt to be "the divine presence"; or an increasing promise that some universal Lover would presently be made known. In earlier ages the minded worlds had carefully avoided any kind of metaphysical belief; so well was it realized that finite intelligence was incapable of conceiving any deep truth about reality. But under the influence of "the new promise," the life of every individual in every awakened world was now orientated to this bright star of certainty, or seeming certainty; of "doubt-less faith," to use Cass's own words. The longing for the final culminating revelation became a universal passion. In all the worlds, the hosts of individual spirits waited with bated breath for the consummation of the union of the cosmic mind with God, the hypercosmical Lover.

Meanwhile, according to Cass, the whole cosmical society had become re-fashioned on a theocratic basis, under a priesthood consisting of the most spiritually developed worlds. And also within each world throughout the society, a priesthood ruled; not, of course, by violence or the threat of violence, but purely by the tacit threat of excommunication from the single-minded experience of the cosmical spirit. All these awakened worlds were so confident in the speedy millennium, that all activities except religious ritual and contemplation were gradually abandoned. Traditions of kindliness and mutual aid degenerated. "After all," it was said, "the agonies of the unfortunate will soon give place to bliss, so we need not worry about them very much. And certainly we must not, to alleviate them, squander energy which should be concentrated wholly on the attempt of the cosmical spirit to come face to face with God as soon as possible."

Ages passed, and still the longed-for illumination and communion did not occur.

Instead a different and a shattering discovery was made by the cosmical mind; that is, of course, by all the awakened individuals together in spiritual unity.

What this discovery was I find it very difficult to determine at all precisely, and still more difficult to describe. This is not surprising.

All I can say is that at a certain stage of cosmical history, probably about the time of the first appearance of mammals on the earth, the cosmical mind began to suspect that all the treasured evidence for the existence of the Divine Lover, and the impending consummation of the whole cosmical process, was false. "The cosmical spirit," said Cass, "had cried out for love; and some kind of seeming-response had come back to it, seemingly from the heart of reality; but actually, this response was a mere echo of the cosmical mind's own yearning. Having pressed through the mists of uncertainty, confident that she would soon stand in the divine presence, she found nothing more than her own spectre reflected from the confines of existence."

It is easy to see that a society orientated toward a personal deity, a god of love, and organized through and through as a theocracy, would be rudely shaken by this discovery; the more so since all its members believed in an actual and speedy union with their God.

But worse was to follow. In forlorn hope of reaching some deeper truth, further exploration was undertaken. "Finally" (in Cass's words so far as I can remember them) "the cosmical spirit came at last face to face with stark reality. And stark it certainly turned out to be. Reality, it seemed, was wholly alien to the spirit, and wholly indifferent to the most sacred values of the awakened minds of the cosmos. It was indeed the Wholly Other, and wholly unintelligible. It seemed to be in some sense personal, or at least 'not less than personal.' Indeed, it was probably infinitely more than personal. All that could be said of it was that it comprised within itself the whole mental and spiritual life of the cosmos, and also therewith a vast host of other cosmical creations, differing from one another so profoundly that between them there could be no comprehension whatever. To the lofty Being who comprised them, all their aspirations were equally trivial. To him (or it?) their function was not to manifest the life of the spirit successfully, but simply to be aware, to feel, to strive in their diverse ways, however unsuccessfully or perversely. Thereby, and unwittingly, they provided his sustenance."

When I listened to Cass recounting this discovery in a tragic voice I could not suppress a snigger. The thought that the sublime cosmical mind should have been so prodigiously tricked by its own wishes as to believe that its purposes were the purposes of God, and that it was on the point of union with God, seemed to me quite funny. I shall not forget the flash of rage and contempt with which Cass glanced at me when he heard my inadequately suppressed snigger. "No doubt," he said, "the cosmical mind had deceived itself, and its discomfiture was deserved; but should creatures like us laugh over a huge spiritual disaster on a cosmical scale, affecting the happiness of myriads of sensitive beings?" Of course, I did see the tragic side of the situation; but at the moment I was more impressed with the idea that so lofty a being could be such a damned fool. The thought that any little insect like myself, equipped with a modicum of free intelligence and self-criticism, could have seen through the self-deceptions of the cosmical mind was at once amusing and gratifying to my vanity. I had to remind myself that, after all, there was no excuse for self-complacency, for I was listening merely to the fantasies of a deranged personality, not to an objective report of actual follies committed by an actual cosmical mind.

But to continue the story as Cass gave it to me. Naturally any society that had been organized on a strictly theocratic basis for a whole geological age would be thrown into confusion by the discovery that its beliefs were baseless. In describing the disaster, Cass used a striking image: "The cosmical society," he said, "was in the plight of a seal that had been swimming far under the ice toward a distant blowhole. With heart throbbing and lungs straining, it arrives at last to find that the hole is blocked with a staunch layer of fresh ice. Desperately, vainly, it strikes at the prison window; then its lungs collapse, and it loses consciousness."

Similarly the cosmical society, which had calculated on a speedy emergence into the life-giving air of communion with God, now found itself imprisoned. After a wild attempt to break through into a loftier and more congenial reality, it soon collapsed. Henceforth, if I understood Cass rightly, the unified cosmical mind ceased to exist. There remained only the minds of individual worlds, such as that of the solar flames, in telepathic contact with one another, but no longer capable of unified consciousness as a single mind. And all were haunted by the harsh memory of the tragic discovery. Moreover, each world was itself in danger of disruption through internal conflict. For there were now everywhere two parties in each world. One party doggedly retained its faith, and ardently desired to press on with spiritual research, in the belief, or rather the forlorn hope, that it would break through to an even deeper truth. The other party wished to accept the recent discovery as final, and to re-adjust the whole cosmical social order on a purely epicurean basis.

On the sun, apparently, neither party succeeded in permanently dominating the other. The result was chaos. Sometimes, for a few thousand years at a time the faithful ruled, then the sceptics. Sometimes there was an uneasy compromise. And sometimes the two parties so far debased themselves as to invent and use methods of violence. War was at last known on the sun.

When the terrestrial flames re-established contact with the sun, they found the solar society in painful confusion. Warfare was being attempted. But some sort of new party, I understand, had very recently appeared. It claimed to offer an effective synthesis of the views of the old parties. This new party, or sect, or what you will, professed views much like those of the terrestrial flame whom Cass had murdered; for they embraced both metaphysical agnosticism and loyalty to "the spirit." "We do not know, we do not know," they declared (or so Cass asserted), "and probably no finite intelligence, even of cosmical stature, can ever know the ultimate truth. But we do not really need to know. All that is needful is the perception, the indubitable perception, of the spirit's over-mastering beauty; and the perceived certainty that we are all by nature instruments of the spirit's expression."

Cass quoted these words with fervour and obvious agreement. Indeed, he presently announced that they had won his allegiance to the new party. To me, the compromise seems hopelessly confused and untenable, but Cass took it very seriously. He said, "Intellectual integrity, my dear man, is all very well; and it does compel us to be entirely agnostic about the constitution of the universe. But emotional integrity is just as important; and it compels me to be true to my perception of the spirit." In this attitude, rather surprisingly, he found himself out of sympathy with the latest views of the terrestrial flames, who (he said) were at first thrown into chaos by all this momentous news, but were now rapidly moving toward theism. Apparently the majority took the view that, though hitherto they had *consciously* rejected belief in a God of any kind, yet *unconsciously* they had all along drawn their passion for the spirit from a deep unwitting recognition that a divine cosmical person must, in fact, exist. They were now convinced that, if only they could wake more fully, they would come face to face with him, and see in him the spirit's source of authority. Cass, however, clung to the earlier attitude of the terrestrial flames, their seemingly agnostic devotion to the spirit. He was therefore determined to use every possible means of making contact between the terrestrial flames and human scientists, reckoning that each might modify the other's attitude, and that the upshot might well be a triumph of the agnostic faith both among the flame race and among mankind.

With this end in view he urged me to co-operate with him by telling my brother scientists all about the flames, both in conversation and in articles in scientific journals. I must also, he repeated, stop the publication of his former statement, and arrange to substitute the new book, which he was now writing.

He was extremely reproachful when I refused to do what I was told. Indeed, so upset was he that I decided to humour him. I pointed out that I had never so much as seen one of the living flames myself. I would, therefore, while thinking over his proposal, undertake a little private research. Meanwhile, I said, he had better carry on with his new book. He reluctantly agreed to this plan, and we parted on friendly terms.

After that interview with Cass my conscience compelled me actually to set about looking for evidence of the flames' existence. I stared into a few kitchen fires, and even took the trouble to go and see a couple of industrial furnaces. Of course, I found nothing, and my conscientiousness petered out.

After some weeks I received a note from Cass, telling me that he was trying to write his book, but that the terrestrial flames were constantly attempting to convert him to their theistic religion. The more he resisted the more they persecuted him. "The situation," he said, "is growing desperate. They are trying to undermine my sanity, and if I resist this threat, they will probably kill me." After this I heard nothing from him, and I was too busy to visit him.

Some three months later I received a letter from the chief of the Mental Home saying that Cass was dead. There had been a serious fire at the Home, and it had started in Cass's room. The cause of the blaze was unknown. Latterly Cass had become far more deranged, and had made remarks which suggested that he might be contemplating arson. He was therefore deprived of matches and his lighter, and it was difficult to see how he could have started the fire, unless by focussing the sun's rays through a large reading lens which was found in his room.

I leave the reader to solve the puzzle of Cass's end. If there had been a hearth-fire in his room, conceivably a living flame might have leapt from it to destroy him. But what am I saying! For the moment I had forgotten that the flames were merely figments in his mind. On the whole, my theory is that, with the progress of his disorder, his sense of persecution by the terrestrial flames drove him to despair, so that in the end he chose to die. Or did his confused mind suppose that by focussing the sun's rays he would somehow introduce into his room an actual living solar flame friendly to his views? It is impossible to solve the problem.

After Cass's death I decided that I would publish his original statement intact, in spite of his wish to withdraw it. It is too interesting, psychologically, to be sacrificed. And in this epilogue I have made it clear that Cass's final attitude was very different from his earlier hostility to the flames. In taking this course, I feel that I am being loyal to Cass himself, to the real Cass, the sane, though brilliant, scientist, who would suppress no evidence that might lead to the advancement of knowledge.

The Man Who Became a Tree

In his last years Stapledon experimented with tales of the preternatural, of which this story of "an inveterate escapist" is one of the few he completed. Depictions of human metamorphosis into trees figure in much mythic art, including Ovid's Metamorphoses, *Dante's* Inferno, *Bosch's* Garden of Earthly Delights, *and Spenser's* Faerie Queene. *The notion of alternate modes of sentience — animal, vegetable, even stellar — fascinated Stapledon throughout his career. He recorded an early attempt at an arboreal fantasy in a letter to his fiancée Agnes Miller, written during World War I when he was an ambulance driver. The episode of the "Plant Men" in* Star Maker *(1937)*

is his best known variation on this theme, but "The Man Who Became a Tree"
is his most detailed exploration of the vegetative state.

THE DAY WAS A SCORCHER. The shade of a great solitary beech tree, lord
of its field, invited the man to rest. He had been walking for some
time, and he felt ready for his sandwiches.

Sitting on the russet carpet of leaf mould and beech mast, with his
back against the great trunk, he looked up into the lucid, dappled
green above him. Small birds appeared and disappeared among the
branches, aerial mice. He laid a hand on a projecting root beside him.
It was moulded like a muscle, a giant limb that gave the great trunk
its grip upon the ground.

He took out of his pocket his little parcel of food. There were
sandwiches of cheese and lettuce, cucumber and tomato, and a slab of
fruitcake. Devouring the green stuff, he had a sudden, mildly disturbing fantasy that he was eating the flesh of his distant cousins. He
smiled, and continued to relish his food.

The thought of cannibalism still haunted him when he had finished his cake and was lighting his pipe. The act seemed to him a
cannibalistic burnt offering to the inhuman God.

He watched the smoke floating up toward the green ceiling. A
squirrel, presumably an invader from the neighbouring woods, finding
its retreat cut off by the great human beast, began chattering and
scolding, and scuttering from branch to branch overhead. Finally it ran
out along a far-reaching bough and a precarious branchlet that bent
under its weight. Thence it dropped groundward at the tree's perime-
ter, to bound hurriedly toward the wood. Somewhere a woodpecker
was tapping. When the man tapped the ash from his finished pipe, the
bird desisted.

The man luxuriously stretched himself out full-length on the
brown carpet and gazed upward. Minute patches of blue sky were
little more than stars in the green heaven. Lazily he brushed away the
gnats that hung in a tenuous cloud above his face. Then he thrust his
fingers deeply into the leaf mould, pretending that they were roots.
Profound peacefulness seemed to bathe his happily tired limbs. How
much better to be here than sitting on an office stool or threading one's
way along crowded streets! This, he felt, was how he was meant to
live, alone, unmoving, drinking in at every pore the quiet influence of
nature, much as the tree was drinking sunlight through its leaves.

What would it be like, he wondered, to be a tree? Drowsily he
tried to figure out the possible features of a tree's consciousness, if
indeed a tree was conscious at all. It might perhaps have sensations all
over its vast and intricate surface. When the wind rocked it, it might

feel its internal stresses. Of visual perception of form, it presumably knew nothing. And could it in any sense have desires, purposes, thoughts?

Musing thus, the man fell asleep at the foot of the tree. He did not know that he was asleep, for he went on thinking about the tree, forgetting his human status. Little by little, however, he realized that something queer was happening to him.

Strange sensations began intruding upon him. At first they were intermittent and incoherent, but presently they flooded him with novel experience, and gradually formed a coherent pattern. He realized that the quality of these sensations was not, after all, so very strange. He recognized pressures and warmths. But these familiar qualities were all a bit odd, and they grouped themselves into configurations wholly novel to him and inconsistent with the familiar configurations of his own body. These last he still vaguely felt, when he made an effort to attend to them. He knew that he was still lying on his back. He felt the soft gritty earth about his fingers and the gnats stinging his face. But in addition there was this other, separate system of sensations, and it was becoming increasingly obtrusive.

Little by little he became able to interpret the new experience under the influence (as he now realized) of his participation not only in the present but also in the past of the tree. Humanly, the whole life of the tree was entirely novel to him; yet arboreally, so to speak, it was familiar and intelligible to him through his present sharing in the tree's past. Thus a mass of mild strains, rhythmically occurring, was at once recognized as located in the tree's tossing and quivering topmost branchlets and foliage. There occurred warmth and light. Yes, he was intensely aware of light; though only as a diffuse radiance that afforded him nothing of spatial form save a vague perception of the general direction from which the sunlight impinged upon his leaves.

Concentrating his human attention on this or that feature of his arboreal experience, he was able to distinguish the large and mild strains and swayings of his upper branches and the internal compressions of his monumental trunk. On one side of his foothold on the ground, he felt an unusual slight pressure on his submerged roots. This his human intelligence inferred to be the weight of his prostrate human body. His attention was presently drawn to an exasperating irritation on one of his branches. Probably some wood lice, or other vermin, were at work under the bark. Humanly, he had a great desire to scratch the irritated member, but this was of course impossible. There were other such irritations here and there on his branches. One of these was quickly brought to an end by some rough but welcome external agency. Perhaps a woodpecker had devoured the vermin.

After a while, an increased agitation of his leaves was followed by a sudden end of warmth and a great reduction of light. Humanly he inferred that the wind had risen, and that the sun had been obscured by cloud. Then a few random chilly blows upon his windward leaves told him that it was beginning to rain. Presently the whole population of his leaves was receiving a downpour of these little blows, and an invigorating coolness was spreading over all his surface.

Humanly he decided that he had better rise and put on his mackintosh; but to his surprise he found that he had forgotten how to move. And more surprisingly, he did not care. Vaguely he felt the big drops falling on his face, but it was increasingly difficult to attend to his already remote human existence. Soon he ignored it entirely, for he was wholly concerned with the experiences of the tree. The wind had now risen to gale force, and his great branches were violently tossing. Even the mighty shaft of his trunk was labouring. And in his anchoring roots he felt considerable strain. He noted now a confusion of new sensations throughout his branches, a steady tremor in his leaves and twigs which his human intelligence attributed to the vibrations set up in them by the impact of rain and wind. In fact, in a strange arboreal way he was hearing the uproar of the storm. Meanwhile, leaves and twigs, and even a small branch, were torn from him causing a prickling irritation that rose here and there to mild pain. One more considerable branch broke under the strain and crashed to the ground. Sharp pain reverberated through all his members, and in his roots he felt the thud of the fallen branch upon the topsoil.

Torrential rain battered on his leaves. With a great effort he attended to his prone human body at the tree's foot, and noted that his clothes were drenched, and water was trickling over his chest and belly. Yet this seemed to him a matter of no moment. It was far more important for him to explore his new life as a tree. Anyhow, he could not do anything about his poor old human body, since he had forgotten how to move its limbs.

The storm must have continued into the night, for after a while he became aware that the diffused light that had bathed his leaves had completely vanished. Instead, his uppermost foliage suffered the continuous chilly bombardment of raindrops. And now at last the water was beginning to penetrate through the topsoil to his uppermost rootlets. Gradually it seeped deeper and deeper, till all his roots were greedily, laughingly (so he put it to himself) drinking and devouring. Strange, the bewildering richness that this novel experience afforded his human mentality! He was guzzling a variegated banquet; tasting and savouring every morsel. The earth was in some regions sweet, in others sour; or salt, or bitter; in others he relished a complex of these familiar tastes, together with strange gustatory experiences that he could not name. In fact the whole soil was tingling with a bewildering wealth of new tastes and odours. In one small region, where (he surmised) some beast had dropped its dung, he noted an extravagantly luscious patch that flushed his rootlets with feverish vitality.

Before the storm had ceased, faint light once more bathed his chilled leaves. Much later, the light blazed, and warmth returned. Reawakened by the lush sap, his leaves now devoured the sunlight. This was an experience wholly strange to his human consciousness, though familiar to him through his participation in the past of the tree. No words could be found to describe this novel ecstasy. Nearest to it, he told himself, was the tingling fieriness of some strong mellow wine. But it had also a quality which was akin to religious feeling, a fervour less obvious in the human palate's contact with alcohol, a depth of "meeting" and satisfaction unknown in any human experience save in the highest reaches of personal love, and perhaps (so he surmised) in the mystical ecstasy.

A thought had long been mildly reiterating itself in the man's tree-imprisoned mind and now was becoming insistent. Though he had sampled so much of the tree's experience, he had as yet discovered nothing of its self-consciousness. Was it, he wondered, or was it not, at all aware of itself as a single conscious individual? In one respect he seemed to know far more of the tree than he had ever known of his human body; for he was minutely aware of the tree's fundamental physiological processes, its whole vegetative life; whereas the detail of his human physiological happenings had, of course, been too deep for consciousness. Could it be that the tree's awareness was wholly upon that fundamental plane? To this question he could at present find no answer.

Musing thus about the differences between tree and man, he remembered that his own human body was lying neglected at the tree's foot. With difficulty he directed his attention to it. He found that it was in a sorry state. Drenched and chilled, it was also ragingly hot. In fact it was in a high fever. Its breathing was laboured and painful. Its overstrained heart raced and pounded. Moreover, its grave sickness at once reacted on his mind. He began to fall into delirium. Distressing fantasies and hallucinations of his human life flooded in upon him. In a moment of clarity he realized that he must at once withdraw his attention from this dying animal that was formerly himself and take refuge once more in the experience of the tree. Delirium was already surging back upon him, but with a desperate act of concentrated attention, he was just able to struggle out of it into the calm being of the tree.

Strangely, he felt no regret at losing forever his footing in humanity. That fretful mode of existence had always irked him. Throughout his human years he had always held himself aloof from his fellow men. He had always been by disposition a solitary. He had carefully avoided forming any lasting ties with man or woman. He was an inveterate escapist. Now at last he had escaped forever.

The days succeeded one another. Summer became autumn. The increasing chill and darkness gave him discomfort in his leaves. But little by little their sensitivity was dulled, until at last, one by one, these withered flakes of his arboreal body were parted from him. With the fall of his leaves and the retraction of his sap, he lost the greater part of his experienced world. The cold, which had been painful, was now a drowsy numbness. He must have fallen into a kind of hibernating sleep; for when, quite suddenly, he woke, it was to find not only a deadly chill throughout his members (save his well-blanketed roots) but also an unendurable and distortingly heavy weight on all his branches. He inferred that it was a weight of snow. One of his branches broke under the strain, and his whole frame shuddered in agony. The raw stump, exposed to the frosty wind, at first suffered intensely. But mercifully he soon sank back into his winter sleep.

Spring brought new experiences. The increasing warmth and light drew the sap tinglingly from his roots up through his trunk and branches. And with the rising sap came a rejuvenescence of his whole body, and a quickening of experience. The bursting of the buds, he found, was a complex experience of mild and then excruciating irritation, followed by ecstatic satisfaction as the tender leaves unfolded.

Soon followed that even more exquisite event, the sexual flowering. This, he surmised, a woman, with her monthly rhythm, might enter into more naturally than any man. It gave him an overwhelming excitement of tumescence, and a yearning that put the whole giant body, even to the farthest rootlets, into a fever.

And now at last he was aware of the tree as a single yearning self, with attention concentrated in its flowers, in violent desire and expectation. The ripe pistils and stamens swooned with the caressing of the innumerable feet and proboscises of insects, those go-betweens of arboreal love. The stamens withered, but the ovaries, fertilized and swelling, afforded a profound and placid maternal joy. As the weeks passed, and the seeds matured, satisfaction increased. When they were fully ripened, they fell, and his whole arboreal being heaved, as it were, a sigh of achievement and release.

Thus at last the cycle of the year was completed. Once more, the boisterous autumn, the sleep of winter, the tense awakening of spring.

Year piled upon year. He noted that, for the tree, time passed far more quickly than for the human consciousness. The tree's life was less crowded with events than a man's. In a way it was emptier, though everything in it was more thoroughly savoured. And because its years were less close-packed with happenings, they passed as swiftly as human months. And so the man could almost perceive, not merely infer, the growing of the tree. Annually it put out new twigs and exploring rootlets. Annually the great tree grew even greater.

But at last old age brought the beginnings of serious rot into its timber. Whole branches died and fell.

With the passage of the years, the trapped human consciousness became more and more identified with the arboreal consciousness. Yet it retained its human intelligence and continued to observe the tree's experience analytically.

It was in the tree's old age that the man first detected another universe of arboreal experience, that had been going on all the while, though beyond his human ken. He took long to grasp the significance of it, but in the end participation in the tree's past enabled him to recognize that this individual beech tree was psychologically rooted in the life of the whole neighbouring woodland and even the far-distant forests. His human consciousness was with difficulty reaching out to that vast region. But this was not all. It became clear to him that, besides the experience of tree-life in spring-time, an equally vast experience of autumnal trees was being laid before him. A tropical and a subarctic arboreal experience was also going on. In fact he was vaguely participating in the common awareness of all trees, nay, all terrestrial vegetation.

To say this, is simple; but its actual significance for the individual human mind in the individual tree was reached only laboriously and painfully. Like a newborn infant, the man had to begin orienting himself in a new universe. For it was not merely that he was flooded by an overwhelming bulk of new experience of the same order as the individual tree's experience. It was not only that *more* light and warmth and rain and cold and strain and root-probings confronted him, from all the forests and prairies and jungles of the world. Fortunately he was aware only of random and fluctuating traces of this vast vegetable life. Had the whole volume of it constantly invaded him, he would surely have gone mad. But samples, so to speak, floated before his exploring attention, and by means of them he built up an outline sketch of the whole life of terrestrial vegetation.

But this, as I say, was not the whole or the most significant part of his new experience. Something far more fundamental was happening to him, something which to his insulated and precise human apprehension was extremely difficult to grasp. In his human life he had been a curious but never a very comprehending reader of the mystics. There had been moments when he himself had seemed to be almost on the threshold of some kind of mystical experience, but he had never been able to set foot upon that threshold, let alone to cross it. He now felt that his deep participation in this great tree's life had opened up to him a sphere far vaster than his unaided human consciousness could ever penetrate, and far vaster also than the life merely of all vegetation. It had led him (so he put it to himself) into the presence of God. It was as though the plants, with their less individualized consciousness, were constantly open to the divine; as though, one and all, they were not really individuals at all, but rather (so he figuratively expressed it to himself) limbs and sense organs of God. But that strange "openness to the divine," in which all vegetation easily shared, was far too difficult for his analytic human intelligence to grasp. He had indeed at last, with the tree's help, set foot upon the threshold, but beyond it he could not penetrate.

When at last foresters came, and with saw and axe cut through the aging trunk, the man's mind was at least partially attuned to the deeper reality. The sharp pain, though painful, was yet acceptable.

The Peak and the Town

Stapledon wrote several drafts of this story in the mid-1940s. When it was rejected in 1946 by the editor of a literary miscellany as too obscure, the judgment seemed only to confirm the author's own growing sense of literary failure. He never tried to get it published again. Nearly forty years passed before the story was discovered among Stapledon's papers and printed by Harvey J. Satty and Curtis C. Smith in their Olaf Stapledon: A Bibliography. *One of the most moving and beautifully conceived of his rare efforts in short fiction, "The Peak and the Town" is an allegorical self-assessment by an author struggling to maintain the purity of his spiritual vision in the context of political ambivalence and artistic disappointment.*

AFTER ALL THIS WANDERING in the mist and the chill rain I must be far from any track. And darkness is coming. There is nothing for it but to puzzle again over the maps, though they are sketchy and in conflict. I must trace out more carefully the way I came, since we left the town, to thread our route along the lowland roads and upland tracks, till at last we clambered among these gaunt, grooved foot-hills. Already it was past noon when our diminished party disagreed about the way, and we separated. Then I breasted a ridge alone, under the cloud ceiling; and the cloud swallowed me. If I can find my bearings again, the compass will sign me to the Peak; whence, it is said, one may see the whole universe spread out like a map. The thin cold air, they say, so quickens the mind that one sees everything with new, sharp vision. So they say. How far off, how very remote, that place must be! But after the Peak, surely, the going will be good, and the way clear, down into the other valley, and to rest.

So it strikes me, here in this moment of my journey from the primaeval forest of birth, over the wide plains and uplands, toward the high, cold valley of death. Of course one may die anywhere; but up there in the glacier valley, they say, there is a hut where death is fulfilment.

Well, it is time to recollect and assess and reorientate; and then, hoping or despairing, to press on.

It is a strange journey that each of us makes, or that my generation is making. Long ago, how long ago, yet scarcely one heart-beat ago in the life of the cosmos, we emerged from that dark uterine jungle, and set out in the bright dawn of our childhood, to follow an ancient road, which those before us had repaired, and here and there superficially modernized. We were a great crowd, a migrating population. In the first hours of our life's day we tottered forward, each step a lesson, each tumble a tragedy, each joy a fleeting paradise. Exploring, we correlated the feel and the look of things, and their sound and their scent and their taste, thus figuring out of chaos the bravest of all new worlds. Little by little we became aware of ourselves and of our fellows. We quarreled, bullied or were bullied, or became fellow-gangsters. Little by little, some of us, but not all, began to feel obscurely the difference between the brutish life and the humane. Already we heard vague wild rumours of the Peak and of the farther Valley. With this promise of glory to come, we moved forward timorously; or else confidently, striding with what an air of manhood, but with what inner innocence!

The majority, in fact all but a few lucky ones, were handicapped. For they were starvelings at birth, and they had no money to buy equipment for the journey; not even for shoes, sometimes not even for bread. Very soon their feet were bleeding, and their knees gave way under them.

We who were fortunate knew at first little of these hampered fellow-travellers. When we began to meet them, compassion and repugnance tore us in opposite directions. We could do nothing for them. Our own supplies, we agreed, would have gone nowhere with so great and famished a crowd. So we pressed by on the other side, and hurried forward. This we did less out of heartlessness than through failure of imagination; and through dismay at the immensity of the task of rescue. So we hurried forward. Some of us, indeed, rushed far ahead, and I saw no more of them. Some strayed to left or right in search of flowers or berries, and so dropped behind. And some, eager for short cuts, began climbing a rugged hillside which the road circumvented; but soon they were destroyed before our eyes.

After a while we came upon a fork in the road. The main company, and I was among them, wished to bear westward along a magnificent highway, hoping to make better progress. Some of us, but not I, expected even to avoid the mountain altogether; for the great range, remote as it was, opposed us forbiddingly, and even its lesser peaks were deep in cloud.

We had no regret at leaving the old road, because we could see that from the fork onwards it was derelict, all pot-holes and water courses. And the bridges were broken. Here and there along it we could make out ancient way-side shrines, decorated with modern trinkets. Beside these bedizened relics many travellers, our elders and precursors, had settled down with great hampers of food and drink. Some, it seemed, had passed through sleep into the sleep of death, of the death which is no fulfilment; for there they lay beside their hampers, already livid corpses. A few of our number, nevertheless, were convinced that the old road was the right road; for it visibly led towards the heights. And far ahead we could detect figures toiling up a steep and craggy track. But most of us were not strong enough to attempt so rough a route; and many, out of a kind of humility and friendliness, preferred to throw in their lot with the main party; and many, with myself among them, were enthralled by the superb streamlined efficiency of the new road. So there were partings among us, some with recrimination, some with mutual respect and regret.

We turned westward along the new road, with its clean breadth and sweeping length, spanning the ravines. Many busy workers, our elders, were tending the machines which were still completing the surface of this great structure. When we enquired whether their road would lead us round easily to the high glacier valley, they looked at us curiously; and someone said, "Sure! The road will take you wherever you want to go, for it is part of a world-wide net-work of routes." They told us that a whole mountain had already been used up for road-metal. Pointing to the western plain, they showed us, under a bank of smoke, the chimneys of factories, erected against heaven like guns, and the winding-wheels of coal-pits, and queer contrivances where they were boring for oil. All this, they said, was for the making of the road and the vehicles and the fuel. When the work was completed, we were told, everyone would be able to travel in comfort in fast private cars to every quarter of the world. There would be no more drudgery, and no more gangs of labourers, such as we now saw stolidly toiling. People would be able to spend all their time upon modern pleasures, and particularly on fast luxurious travel, to see the wonders of the world.

We were all young and eager and hopeful, so we swarmed along the great new road, happily discussing our prospects. After we had tramped on for a good while, some of us, who were hungry and had little money to buy food, dropped out of the party to work on the road-making, with the promise of wages. Others followed their example not through poverty but for the sheer fascination of the great clanging, whirring machines. The rest of us continued our journey. Some sang as they marched, or made a hearty noise with musical instruments, entertaining the on-lookers, by whom in payment for this amusement, they were given cigarettes or food or an occasional copper. But some of the best entertainers were persuaded by the bosses to stay behind, for wages, to distract the gangs from their fatigue and boredom, and their grievances and diseases.

Presently we came to a stretch of road that was already finished and in use. Cars and lorries were rushing along it in both directions. And we, a great crowd flocking along the road, were a proper nuisance to the traffic. Cars drew up in front of us with screaming brakes, and the drivers cursed us. Some of us were knocked over and swept away into hospitals or cemeteries. Presently, at a crossroads, where a policeman was directing the traffic, this tall potentate left his post to marshal us on to one side of the road. Then, after lecturing us on the traffic-regulations, he let us go forward. We went on past a roundabout, then rows of villas, then traffic lights, then a petrol station. We reached a huge road-house, with cars and bicycles outside it; and from within came loud mechanical and melting music. Here many of our company stayed to rest and enjoy themselves and pick up if possible a girl friend, and spend their money.

After a while we came to a great white building of concrete and glass. At the door a notice said, *"PALACE OF NEW KNOWLEDGE, Admission 6d."* Some of us who had money to spare crowded through the turnstile, confident that we should gather useful information to help us on our way. Inside we were shown many amazing, many terrible, many beautiful things; and much that was tiresome, because we could not understand it. We looked down microscopes and into spectroscopes. We praised the delicate forms of diatoms, the crystalline fibre of rocks, the intricate thought-secreting tissues of brains. We

learned all the mechanisms of human and animal bodies, from diagrams and from specimens in glass jars, and from living specimens
with their inner organs displayed and working before our eyes. The
interior life of the atom, that minutest dance-figure, that rippled pool,
was brilliantly expounded to us, with its ultimate paradox that defeats
intelligence. We saw, too, working models of the solar system, and of
the galaxy; and symbols, obscure but pregnant, of the whole cosmos
of galaxies. And when we contrasted the reputed size of the cosmos
with the ultra-microscopic electron, we were filled with awe, which
some of us mistook for worship. We were shown also, in parables, the
human mind itself, dissected into its component mechanisms, according to the very latest theories. The intellectual surgery, also, of the
most modern logic was displayed before us. We admired the use of
verbal scalpels and probes, by which the hidden aberrations of thought
are laid bare and excised. We were amazed, too, by the practical applications of the new knowledge, by the many mechanical inventions and
innumerable specimens of synthetic products; the foods, textile fibres,
new metals, plastics, architectural materials, with which, it was said, a
synthetic new world was being rapidly built. In one well-guarded
cellar (we were told) they were experimenting with a new secret power
that could shatter the planet or give all men the bliss of gods. When
we shuddered that so momentous a choice should be opened to man,
the exponents declared that circumstances would in the end compel
the right choice. But we feared still, knowing the folly, the madness
lurking in our own hearts, and in all men's.

Everything in the Palace of Knowledge impressed us, not only
the marvels themselves but the conditioned, ozoniferous, antiseptic
atmosphere of the whole place, and the detached yet reverential attitude of the white-coated exponents to the marvels that they were
displaying. A few of us, either through native ability or by paying
considerable sums of money, secured admission as full-time students
who might later become research workers, and perhaps great discover-
ers. Some chose this course as the way to power, others because it
seemed to them that this must be the one sure method of finding the
right way to our common goal. However long they had to spend on
their studies, they said, they would be in the end so well equipped
that they would certainly reach the high valley before us. But those
who were already in residence at the Palace of New Knowledge smiled
when they heard about the valley, and looked very wise. "There is no
such place," they said, "unless indeed this is it."

For my part I would gladly have stayed in the Palace all my life,
studying the galaxies and electrons, and the mechanisms of living
things, and the machinery of the mind. Yet I did not. Though the

memory of these marvels, and the calm scrutinizing spirit of the re-
searchers and teachers, would, I hoped, influence me for ever after, yet
some obscure impulse, some inarticulate dissatisfaction, tore me away.

When we had travelled some distance, we became aware that the
route was bearing ever more westward, and even southward, and
down into the plain; so that the mountains were now but dimly seen,
far off on our right. When we enquired about our way, we got little
help. "Go on into the town," they said, "and ask a policeman."

After many miles we entered the town by a wealthy suburb. We
were surprised that so many of our forerunners and elders had settled
down into prosperity rather than press on toward the goal. But when
we came nearer to the centre of the town we were still more surprised;
for here in the slums a swarm of dirty and misshapen creatures had
settled down not to prosperity but to squalor. For this, in my great
ignorance, I blamed them. Then on a piece of waste land we came
upon a crowd listening to a speaker. He was inveighing against the
tyranny of the rich. He exhorted his hearers to discipline themselves
for the class war, so as to overthrow the rulers and found a workers'
republic. Presently the mounted police appeared, and dispersed the
crowd, several of whom were knocked down and badly hurt. Many
arrests were made, including some of my travelling companions. The
rest of us took to our heels with the escaping townsmen; who, when
we had got well away, spoke to us passionately about their abject
lives and the harsh rule of the rich. For the rich, they said, controlled
everything. With their police and their soldiery they enforced laws
which facilitated their money-power, and enabled them to withhold
from the workers a sufficiency of food and comfort, health and education, so as to compel these unfortunates to labour for them for wages.

With some of my fellow-travellers I passed on into the centre of
the city, along great streets lined with shop windows, where articles of
use and luxury were displayed to the well-dressed crowds. Here and
there a beggar held out his hat for pence, or a hawker paraded his
wares. At a street corner a group of young men in their prime, but pale
and shabby, were singing, while a comrade collected money from the
crowd. Large glistening cars glided along the street, or drew up at the
curb to deposit some lady, bent on shopping.

Those of us who were not without money were able to enter into
the opulent life of the city. We found our way into offices and board-
rooms, into high political circles, and the drawing rooms of high society. At first, remembering the rioting, we were revolted by all this
comfort and display; but little by little it caressingly hypnotized us.
Only a few of us, partially resisting this black magic, continued to look
for the source of the town's disease. We looked in vain. Knaves were

sometimes evident, but mostly we found amiable stupid folk living either for personal power or for trivial and boring pleasure. Of the poor quarter they knew nothing; largely, no doubt, through willful and self-protective blindness. As we gained further insight into the lives of these people, it did indeed come to seem that some hidden and inhuman influence was controlling their actions so that the general upshot must be always the further enslavement of the poor, and the increasing luxury of the rich. Perhaps there really was, as some declared, a sinister dictatorship secreted in the heart of the city, directing all the currents of the country's life to this end. Yet we never came upon any individuals who could have been consciously servants of any such conscious dictatorship. We met only little short-sighted burrowers after money-power, little spiteful and frightened slanderers of the working population, little chattering climbers of the social tree. But clearly there was something very wrong, for the successful power-addicts controlled the lives of millions, and could over-throw governments; and all for no end but the increase of their own power.

When we made contact again with those of our company who had stayed in the poor quarter, we compared notes. The plight of the poor, they said, was desperate. They were all sick and ignorant and vengeful, owing to their impoverished lives. And through the habit of blaming the rulers not only for the tyranny but also for their own weakness, they were losing all moral strength. Only the Comrades, who were pledged to the Revolution, were capable of self-discipline and courage.

Many of us decided to stay in the town to work for the Revolution, convinced that death for the Revolution was the only death which could bring fulfilment. The time had come, we said, when the workers of the world, and indeed all men of good will, must unite to destroy this world-wide tyranny, and create a new order in which everyone should find fulfilment not in death but in life, in joyful and skilful service of the world-wide community.

I agreed that the time for the great change had come, and I talked a lot about it. But when they urged me to join their Party, somehow I could not; whether through cowardice or cynicism or some deeper cause, I do not know. It seemed to me that the Party-members for all their devotion to the Revolution and all their splendid comradeship, had overlooked something. But what it was I could not determine.

As for me, bewilderment and disheartenment had by now filled me with a desperate longing for solitude and the heights; and for something else, of very great moment, which, I felt, would remain occult until I should have climbed, or at least clearly seen, the Peak. The comrades in the Party told me that this was because I was at heart a self-deceiving bourgeois, and could not help clinging to the illusion of my own individuality and uniqueness. Perhaps! But I cannot be other than I am. The call of the Revolution and the call of the Peak echoed through my mind in painful discord.

For a long while I hesitated in the town, discussing the Revolution and the condition of the masses. Incompetently and irresolutely, I even worked for the Revolution; but never risking my own freedom, never giving up all for the cause. Whether the motive was cowardice or the restraint exercised by some deeper insight, I still do not know.

Strange things were now happening in the town. For the sake of order, the rulers punished more sternly; and for the Revolution the Comrades resorted to more ruthless reprisals. On both sides we detected an unacknowledged zest in cruelty. Ordinary people, too, grew harsher. Brutality, which formerly had been secret, now came proudly out into the open. Kindliness, which had been customary but perfunctory, was now rarer; but when it did occur it was often passionate. I saw a man push a child off a station platform before an on-coming train; then he jumped after it to save it, and both were killed.

Something strange and terrible was happening in the depths of all our minds, something which, if we could not understand it and cope with it, would destroy us. The town's penetrating fog seemed to be suffocating the human spirit.

Then war came. For a seeming eternity the town was tormented from the air by a ruthless enemy. In this new common suffering, the minds of the townsmen stirred and woke, and discovered comradeship. People who had been self-bound all their lives flowered with kindness and courage. Could this be the dawn of a new age? The rulers promised that when the war was over they themselves would co-operate in a glorious Revolution. The Comrades put all their strength into the war-effort. But when at last the torment ceased, the rulers forgot their promises, and the masses turned bitter. Every man seemed each man's enemy. With others of my fellow-travellers I began to realize that no remedy for the town's ills could now be found solely within the town itself, or anywhere in the sick human world. The disease had gone too far. Something dark and bloody and irrational, formerly restrained, was taking control of us. Something in the very structure of human society itself seemed to be undermining our humanity. Our insight into our own nature was too superficial to cope with it. Only upon the Peak, we felt, only in solitary watchfulness and agility on the icy ridges, could that secret be learnt which alone could bring sanity back to the town. Besides, some said, what had we to do with this dark place and its poisoned people? Our proper destination was the high cold valley. Here, surely, we were only wasting precious time, and betraying some high duty.

But we were in a dilemma. By now it was clear to many of us that, for those who had shared in the town's life at all, there could be no salvation except salvation for the whole town. The Peak called us; but the town now held us, not only as the body embraces its cells in one continuous tissue, but also as sick comrades claim our help. Individuals, we longed for the high valley; but to cast off the dust from our feet upon the town, to desert our fellow-townsmen in their misery, was a possibility to be scorned.

The dilemma went deeper still. For the town's sake, what ought we to be doing? If we stayed with it, stewing in its madness, we should go mad ourselves and be unable to help. If we set out for the Peak, in hope of finding that truth which the town so greatly needed, isolation would poison us with the longing for individual salvation. And we should be lost to the town. And the hills would be our Hell.

In the poor quarter there was an old man, a watch-repairer, who had a reputation for great wisdom, but also for craziness. For many years he had in his own way been a worker for the Revolution. His courage and resourcefulness were recognized by the comrades; but they were bitter about him, because again and again he had condemned the party line.

I decided to ask his advice. When he listened to my problem, he stuck his magnifier back in his eye and went on working. "It's quite simple," he said, "you want to be in two places at once, living two lives at once. Duplicate yourself." I laughed, but he continued, "We all have at least two selves, but one of them is generally not used, just as my left eye is not used when I look through this glass with the other." In silence he went on working. I began to side with those who thought him crazy, but he began talking again, and I was interested.

"I myself," he said, "am sitting here; but also at this very moment I am climbing a severe pitch on the Peak's shoulder."

After another silence, he put down his glass again, and looked searchingly at me. Then, with a surprising wink, perhaps from humour, perhaps from the strain of working with one eye, he said, "If I, who am really quite an ordinary bloke, can duplicate myself so can another ordinary bloke, in fact you."

I smiled uneasily, and again he laughed.

"Have you not noticed," he said, "a strange discrepancy in life? When you are thinking of the Peak, your whole life is a single day, from the birth-dawn to the night of death. But when you are busy with the journey, and particularly with your affairs in this town, your days pile up in thousands." It was true.

"There is no satisfactory life," he continued, "but the double life. You cannot be adequately a townsman unless you are also on the hills.

For without the hill life we all succumb to fear and hate and blind partisanship. And in the long run this poisons the Revolution. Yet, to live on the hills without maintaining at the same time your town life, is loathsome egotism, leading to spiritual impoverishment and damnation. Live your two lives thoroughly, and in constant mutual intercourse. When you are in the factory or the office or the political meeting or facing the firing squad, you will also see the hills. Your thoughts and feelings will be sharpened by the mountain air, and your conduct will be sane. Yet also when you are contemplating the whole of things from some high ridge, you will be shoulder to shoulder with your fellow townsmen in the Underground, the cinema, the office, the workshop, the mine; or on the barricades, or wherever your affairs take you."

"But how," I demanded, "does one learn this marvellous duplicity?"

"At first," he said, "it really is rather difficult; but if you persevere you will gradually find that you are maintaining two separate but mentally contiguous existences. Spend a few days alternately in the town and in the country. While you are in the town, keep the country always firmly in mind; and while you are in the country, the town. Continue with this exercise until you find you have fully duplicated both your mind and your body. But I must warn you," he said with sudden urgency in his voice, "if you stumble into premature death in one of your lives, you will simultaneously die also in the other. So in the double life the chances of death are doubled."

With others of my fellow-travellers who had consulted the old man I now assiduously practiced his strange jugglery, till at last we succeeded in duplicating ourselves.

Soon we banded our new-found mountain-selves into an exploring party. Our town-selves continued their old life, working with the comrades; with no less devotion, but with inner peace and surer vision. For we were constantly aware of the experiences of our own other selves; which had now set out once more upon the journey, and were proceeding northwards and upwards toward the hills.

When we had risen above the town's fog we took deep breaths of the clean air. The highlands were piled up before us, obscuring the mountains. Not till we had travelled for many hours, or years, did we first see them. Very far off, under a great mass of clouds, protruded the great Peak's snow-clad knee. We laughed and sang. Meanwhile our town-selves went about their affairs with a new calm and detachment, and a new constancy of generous feeling.

But in the hills, after a while the way grew steeper. Some of us lagged. Some turned back. Some branched out upon alternative ways.

And at last I was alone, making my own course among these gaunt grooved foot-hills.

For a long while I climbed alone in the mist, until at last it was borne in on me that I was lost. And here I am, lost and very tired. And darkness is coming.

Far away in the town also, though that inner peace remains, I am lost and very tired. My work with the comrades is confused and suspect. And when I tell them of the Peak, they look at me askance.

Perhaps I shall never reach the high valley. Perhaps I shall die frozen and frustrated on the mountain, stifled and ineffective in the town.

Well, what matter? Perhaps some others of our party, more fortunate or more clear-headed, will find their way to the heights, will at last bring the Peak to the town and the town to the Peak. For me, the only thing is to press on. The day is not yet done. And death even here would not be wholly defeat.

Essays and Talks

The Splendid Race

While an undergraduate at Oxford from 1905 to 1909, Stapledon began reading some of the pioneering nineteenth-century studies in genetics by Gregor Mendel, Francis Galton, and August Weismann. "The Splendid Race," printed in 1908 in The Old Abbotsholmian, *a magazine edited by alumni of his boarding school, is the earliest complete statement of his interest in eugenics, a key concept in the visionary biology of his later fiction. The Edwardian quaintness of his project to breed a race of "gentlemen" and the callow endorsement of new laws governing reproduction would be replaced later in* Last and First Men *and* Sirius *by subtler and warier images of the possibilities and the risks of eugenic "improvements." Nevertheless, this youthful exercise delineates a lifelong preoccupation reflected in such pieces as the 1931 broadcast on "The Remaking of Man" and his 1948 speech, "Interplanetary Man?"*

COLUMBUS FOUND A NEW WORLD; but Francis Galton found a new humanity. The former discovery has given us gold and enterprise; from the latter we may hope for gentlemen, even heroes. It was long after the voyage of Columbus that the new world began to be used by the old. So also it will be long after the first probing of the subject that mankind will begin to profit by the science of heredity. After the work of Mendel, Weismann, Galton, and others, our conception of humanity must be fundamentally altered. To the ancient the human type was a rock, created fixed for evermore. To the man of the last century it was a cloud, ever changing but unalterable. To us it must be a virgin continent, to be cultivated and civilised. Darwin showed that man is the result of evolution. Others have shown that he may direct his evolution. Hitherto we have sought progress with social and political contrivances; but soon we shall bring to bear what may be a far more potent method. Mankind is like a child that has been patiently gathering apples as they fall, when suddenly he has the glorious idea of climbing the tree. Hitherto he has been stinted, but now there opens a vision of plenty to be realised by pluck and skill. For mankind the apples are health and strength, intellect and virtue.

Already lives have been spent in building up the science of heredity. But not till a wide-spread interest has been aroused can that science
be applied to the art of eugenics. There must be a general acquaintance
with the wonderful results of statistical investigation and experiment.
Most biologists agree that man is the expression of a multiplicity of
inherited characteristics, which environment can affect directly only
during the life of the individual. They believe that characteristics acquired during the lifetime of the parent are not heritable. But some
deny this. It is right that we should all know something of this controversy since its importance to eugenics is very great. If the nature, far
more than the nurture, of the parent determines the character of the
child, the unwholesomeness of these days may not seriously affect our
descendants. But it is allowed by all that a bad habit, or evil surroundings, through weakening the system, may cause the offspring to be
stunted. Whatever be the final result of this controversy, much can be
done for the improvement of the race. It seems clear that physical,
mental, and moral characters are governed by the same broad laws of
inheritance. In time it may be as possible to breed good men as it is
now possible to breed fast horses. This is the goal at which we should
aim. Meanwhile we may improve the standard of mankind by wisely
restricting undesirable marriages. Thus we may eradicate not only
the liability to special diseases, insanity, and crime, but also general
weakness and general incompetence.

The application of the knowledge which has been already acquired
is still hampered by universal prejudice. Not till this has been destroyed can we hope to realise the schemes of Galton for the "Improvement of the Human Breed." He suggested that records should be kept
of the history of every family, that every man might know something
of his hereditary capabilities and liabilities. In this way he hoped that
there would arise a true pride of birth. No one of clean pedigree would
be likely to marry into a tainted family. There would be a real aristocracy of birth. The poorer specimens would be continually dying out,
since it would be hard for them to marry. He also points out that it
cannot be held cruel to allow undesirables to die out in this way. The
individuals may still live happy and useful lives. For them celibacy is
self-denial for the good of the community. But nothing can be done till
the interest in these things is universal. The homage paid to riches and
"nobility" must be replaced by a more honest homage to pure birth,
the true nobility.

It is considered almost sacrilegious to breed men in the way we
breed cattle. We must not meddle with the divinely directed course of
evolution. We must not try to confine the fires of love, and if we do try

we shall fail. Love is a divine spirit, too powerful and too fleeting to be controlled by human devices. Such are the objections raised.

But why is it sacrilegious to use direct means for the improvement of the human breed? We have been given wherewithal to climb a little nearer to divinity. Are we to stand mesmerised within the chalk circle of convention? No doubt we must act with caution. Our knowledge being still incomplete, we must not attempt very much at first. But let us at least have the will to progress.

We are told not to interfere with the divine caprice of love. Surely this is unreasonable. We lament when a friend marries into a social class lower than his own. We should have more reason to deplore his marriage into a family tainted with disease or moral weakness. Love is capricious; but even now it is confined within certain limits. It is held wicked to indulge it beyond them; and such is the force of public opinion that it seldom occurs beyond them. A marriage in which husband and wife bear some particular taint may well produce children some of whom are seriously deformed in mind or body. Such marriages should be regarded as a kind of incest. In time they will be prevented by public opinion, which should be aided by legislation. At first, no doubt, there will be many tragedies of revolt against custom and law. It may be held that love exists not merely for the perpetuation of the race, but is an end in itself, the spiritual union and beatitude of individual men and women. The noble type of love which can claim to be a spiritual end in itself has evolved from something less noble. If it be wisely controlled now, in time humanity may be capable of an emotion far more intense and far more divine.

The work that is to be done is not merely negative. Not only must we prevent unsuitable marriages. Not only are the diseases and weaknesses of humanity to be purged away. When the phenomena discovered by Gregor Mendel have been more deeply studied, it may be possible to begin the great positive work of cultivating and fixing the existing desirable qualities of humanity. Perhaps sometime there may appear some entirely new and highly desirable character. This also must be accentuated and fixed, in the manner that favourable "sports" have been fixed by horticulturists. To perform all this it will be necessary in some way to encourage particular classes of marriages. In the present condition of sentiment this seems impossible. We can but hope that in time every man will be naturally inclined to find a wife well suited to himself for the sake of his children.

As yet we are very far from this. But, having stumbled for a long time in the valleys, at last we have arrived at an eminence from which the right way can be seen leading upwards into the mists. It may be that after much labour and many catastrophes in time there will arise a splendid race of men, far wiser than we can hope to be, and far greater hearted.

Thoughts on the Modern Spirit

Unpublished and undated, but in a corrected final typescript, "Thoughts on the Modern Spirit" contains Stapledon's most thoughtful speculations on the intersection of literary experiment and philosophical inquiry. More clearly than anything else he wrote, this essay suggests the extent of (and boundaries of) Stapledon's affinity with the modernist movement. The prominence of Alfred North Whitehead in the essay reflects an extensive study of Whitehead's work, especially Science and the Modern World, *Stapledon undertook as a postdoctoral participant in Liverpool University's Philosophy Seminar in 1927–1928. The allusion to Noel Coward's song "Dance Little Lady," from the 1928 play* This Year of Grace, *suggests that the essay may have been written just after the Seminar, probably before Stapledon began serious work on* Last and First Men *in the late summer of 1928. His absorption in that project may explain why he never made an attempt to publish "Thoughts on the Modern Spirit." It remains an intriguing guide to his mind and art in the period when he achieved his first literary and philosophical successes.*

THOUGH THE MODERN SPIRIT knows many moods, two are distinctive of it: complete disillusion, and zestful but wholly detached admiration of a world conceived as indifferent to human purposes. Many no doubt still retain their confidence in man's importance, and in his prospects here or hereafter, but for good or ill this faith is not a factor in the characteristically modern spirit. Nor is it among these optimists that we may find the most active growing-points of thought to-day. Not that faith itself stands condemned as in every possible sense false, but only that the faithful, having never allowed themselves to be drenched and impregnated with disillusion, cannot understand the spiritual problem of our age. Just because, or insofar as, their faith is intact, it is also infertile.

Our problem may be described as the task of outgrowing both the naive optimism of an earlier age and the naive disillusion of to-day. The problem is urgent, not because disillusion is unwholesome, but because already there are signs that the pendulum is beginning to swing once more in the direction of faith; and unless we can integrate faith and disillusion in some new mood which will preserve whatever is sound in each, we shall merely slip back into our old naive optimism, for no better reason than that we begin to tire of disillusion. In psychological terms, humanity is prone to a dissociation of faith and disillusion, and a consequent "alternation of personalities." Our task is to organise these two sentiments as a stable attitude appropriate to all that we know of reality. And this is to be achieved only in the direction of the second and more rare mood of the modern spirit, namely that disinterested admiration which enlightens our disillusion and perplexes our intelligence.

For the modern kind of religious experience, or if it be preferred the modern substitute for religious experience, is itself the unexpected outcome of disillusion. Only by way of despair and a subsequent detachment can we attain this experience in its purity, and distinguish it from the mere conviction that the heavens care for us. Only when we have countenanced the defeat and even ridicule of the whole enterprise of life upon this planet can we discover that unique splendour and perfection of existence which is more admirable even than life's victory. And because this discovery, coming as it does in the very trough of our disillusion, cannot be assimilated by a pessimistic view, it should perplex us, and should indeed start a ferment of the whole mind.

We may understand our case more clearly by considering the movements of thought that have led up to it. Professor Whitehead has described the conflict between materialistic science and romantic literature, which came to a head in the nineteenth century and resulted in the defeat of romance. The whole romantic movement, he says, was a protest on behalf of the organic view of nature and on behalf of value, a revolt against the unjustified metaphysical dogmas of a science which ever tended to ignore its own abstractness. The poets concerned themselves with these more subtle or more "spiritual" factors in our experience which the science of that day, though it rightly neglected them for its own purposes, had no right to deny metaphysically. But the gesture of the poets was doomed to failure. Expressions of faith or mere longing carried less weight than the precise demonstrations and brilliantly plausible guesses of the scientists. The wind set in the direction of materialism; the whole mental climate had changed. Even the romantics themselves found their vision blurred by a flood of argument and non-rational suggestion. In the early stage Wordsworth had been able to dismiss science with a contemptuous phrase, and to salute "the brooding presence of the hills" without suspicion that it was illusory. But later Tennyson was compelled to recognise the forcefulness of materialistic metaphysics, though finally he sought consolation in an impotent reiteration of faith. Professor Whitehead might have added that Browning, with more complacency, but perhaps less intelligence, missed the issue altogether and merely proclaimed his confidence that human individuals were too interesting to be scrapped at death; while Carlyle, in spite of his grim concentration, found no better solution for the problem than to condemn doubt as cowardly and bid the doubter act so vigorously that he should have no time for thought.

Professor Whitehead's theme is important; but certain equally important comments should be made. And first we must ask, had the romantic poets actually seized a truth which the scientists had missed, or were they merely expressing the fulfilment of their own longing? The answer would seem to be that the poets had indeed in a sense a truth which the scientists missed, but that the scientists also had a truth which the poets had missed, and that these two truths did not in fact conflict at all. The conflict was merely between two unsupported metaphysics, materialistic metaphysics and romantic metaphysics. The scientists, ignoring all the more difficult aspects of experience, were so enthralled by their admirable system of abstractions that they assumed universal materialism and neglected value. The poets, on the other hand, apprehending by direct acquaintance certain superior values, assumed that these values implied a romantic metaphysics. Quite illogically it was inferred that because nature was experienced as a brooding presence, because man could distinguish between good and evil and could espouse the good, and because the universe calls forth our admiration, therefore at the heart of reality there must be sympathy for man and advocacy of his most cherished ends.

Professor Whitehead has used the romantic movement to expose the insufficiency of nineteenth-century science and to support his organic view of nature; but, had he wished, he might equally well have used the whole movement of scientific interest to expose the incompleteness of the romantic ideal. If nineteenth-century science erred by ignoring the inner voice which the poets knew, they in turn had need to learn from science that interest in objectivity, that spirit of detachment from even the noblest human purposes, that dispassionate cognition in which alone the highest values are to be clearly envisaged. But this discovery was not possible to those who had not been forced to distinguish between their admiration of the universe and their faith that whatever was admirable must also be favourably disposed towards man's cravings.

We may continue Professor Whitehead's survey of the mental climate so as to bring it up to our own day and illustrate our own problem. The conflict between science and romance has issued in four distinct movements of thought. There is in the first place the retreat of the pure romantic mind into an unassailable but isolated stronghold of fantasy. Many of our modern romantics seek only to repeat the achievements of the nineteenth century, continuing to distill mystery from the past, or from fairyland, or from the recesses of daily life. Others achieve the same result by playing upon the well-established religious sentiments. Others again take refuge in extreme subjective idealism, supposing themselves to have undermined the whole attack of materialism by declaring that, since all our experience is mental, mind must be foundational to the universe; and that therefore man's nature is guaranteed fulfilment. Or the movement of withdrawal from the conflict and from reality may take yet another form. The value-experience which is the core of romanticism may be mistaken for a unique mystical apprehension of the reality behind all phenomena; and in an age when phenomena are very perplexing and shocking this yearning for the hidden reality may be so powerful as to trick the mind with many curious illusions and sophistries. Thus attention may be turned from the precise but often tragic forms of Western thought to the confused vision of the East, whether by way of theosophy or by way of Spengler.

The second movement to be noted must also be derived from romanticism, but it is romance reformed, "modernised" and aggressive. And it has captured the hearts of many who were at first on the side of materialistic science, though distressed by its materialism. This is essentially a movement of loyalty or moral obligation towards something which may be very variously described, but is always thought of as striving against obstructions to achieve a great end, and an end moreover which is only to be conceived little by little in the course of mind's development. In this mood we feel the distinction between good and evil to be absolute, and we pledge ourselves to fight for the realisation of the good. Obviously this essentially moral experience derives in part from militant religion's loyalty to a God who strives within the universe against an equally real prince of darkness. Obviously also the chivalry of nineteenth-century romanticism contributes to this zeal. But the object on which it is directed is very different from the God of the churches. In a sense, indeed, it is worship of a tribal deity, though the tribe is in this case the whole race of man; but more strictly it is devotion not to an external power, but to the human race itself, or to that spirit which is thought to work in the human race for the achievement of a more glorious mentality.

Very diverse are the prophets of this militant faith, and often they reject one another. Their doctrines range from a modernised kind of

theism and vitalism to Marxian materialism and its consequent prole-
tarianism, and again from the crudest evolutionism to the most sophisticated humanism. Sometimes man is regarded as the blind instrument
through which a hidden creative energy progressively achieves a goal
not patent to men themselves. Thus the movement draws inspiration
from Samuel Butler, and later from Bergson and Driesch, and comes in
line with those modern champions of instinct and the unconscious
who follow Jung rather than Freud; while in literature the movement
contributes something to the inspiration of such writers as Mr. D. H.
Lawrence, with his cult of "the dark god." Sometimes, on the other
hand, it is claimed that man himself must take charge of his own
evolution, directing the "blind" biological forces towards whatever
end is progressively revealed as good to his own consciousness. Thus
contact is made with social meliorism, and even with Comte's essentially non-mystical religion of humanity, with its motto, "Love, order,
progress." Sometimes, with an optimism inherited from the churches,
it is claimed that in the long run life must of necessity triumph. Sometimes, however, in view of the spatial and temporal immensity of the
cosmos, and all the difficulties that confront man in his own planet
and in his own nature, it is recognised that the victory of mind is very
far from certain, that such success as has hitherto been won has been
mostly accidental, and that in the modern world new forces are coming
into play which may well result in the suicide of civilization, if not
actually in the destruction of mankind.

But though very diverse theories may be assumed by this mood
of moral zeal, one conviction is essential to it. Always it emphatically
declares life or mind or spirit to be good absolutely, and their negation
absolutely bad; always it renders whole-hearted allegiance to one side
in a universal conflict. Always it is blind to the possibility of any kind
of excellence other than the value of the fulfilment of vital teleology. It
would spurn a universe in which life were ultimately to fail.

One poet of the movement is Meredith, with his devotion to the
Spirit of Earth. And he also links it both with earlier romanticism
and with a later classicism. He admired nature less for her appearance,
as Wordsworth did, than for her vitality. And man he admired less
for his individuality, as Browning did, than for being Earth's self-
conscious intelligence. But Meredith is more than an apostle of the
faith in Earth and Man. His Comic Spirit gropes towards the mood of
detachment which I shall presently describe. Meanwhile we may note
in Bernard Shaw and H. G. Wells the same dualism of good and evil
grounded in the dynamic nature of life, the same fervent champion-
ship, the same sense that man's real importance lies not in his individuality but in his instrumentality to the achievement of a goal which he

himself has not yet clearly conceived. These writers have contributed to the faith which inspires militant "Labour" today, which distinguishes so sharply between the elect and the damned, which claims from the individual a puritanical loyalty to a certain social ideal or formula, which in fact is the modern, popular, and social-democratic form of Calvinism. Shaw, like Meredith, is saved by humour from rigid sectarianism, and gropes sometimes beyond the moral view; but Wells is more strictly confined within his faith. Bertrand Russell in his social writings, and in spite of his professed ethical scepticism, sometimes assumes the mood of righteous indignation; but though he renders allegiance to the ideal of cultural development he is also detached, and capable of dispassionate salutation.

The movement of moral zeal, then, which directs itself now in worship of a Life Force, now in loyalty to the awakening consciousness of man himself, has many sources and many expressions; and sometimes it has seemed to promise a widespread though new-fangled "religious revival." Indeed for many persons it is in fact to-day a living religion. But it is not distinctive of the modern spirit, and its original minds belong to yesterday rather than to-day. Not that it is outworn; on the contrary it should make an extremely important contribution to the culture of to-morrow. Shame to us if we evade that whole-hearted obligation to the advancement of mentality on this planet. But there is also another and more difficult lesson to learn, a lesson which in our day at least, it is seldom possible to grasp at all save through complete disillusion from all our most cherished ends.

And disillusion is the third of the four movements of thought which we have to record in our sequel to Professor Whitehead's study of the mental climate. It is a movement that is distinctively modern. Not only have we in these latter days doubted the existence of anything worthy to be called God, not only have we despaired of man's capacity to achieve his ends in an unfriendly universe, but also we have tasted complete cynicism with regard to those ends themselves, and about man's very nature. The virtues and the heaven of an earlier generation are now scribbled over with jibes; yet we have little to put in their place, little that can withstand any better the point of our own criticism. And so it comes that the modern young so often seem to belie the very nature of youth by their cynicism; for they can find nothing better to do than evade all serious activities and seek conventional pleasures, suppressing a yawn. Who can blame them? There *is* nothing better to do in a world of disillusion. But it is well known that a life of undirected "pleasure" leads nowhere but to nightmare, such as Mr. Noel Coward has epitomised in his sketch, "Dance Little Lady."

Few would deny that disillusion, sometimes rising to disgust and horror, is the dominant mood of our age. When the plain man has time to look up from his work he sees a world in disorder; society strained and rocking; authority concerned chiefly to keep its seat; nations devising slaughter while they chatter of peace; churches seemingly bankrupt of divinity, and forced desperately to speculate in pew-filling attractions; prophets on all sides trading in questionable doctrines; the live and intricate thought of our time soaring further and further beyond the comprehension of the unspecialised, and shedding abroad only vague and dismal rumours of man's insecurity, futility, and insincerity. Such is the panorama that confronts any unprejudiced and intelligent observer. It is a view so familiar that to state it is to speak platitudes.

No wonder the plain man turns from a prospect so dreary, and concentrates on his private problems; for these, however futile in the wider view, have their tentacles about his heart. Even while he yawns at them they constrain him. For he is breathlessly engaged in the current of his own career, and all the intricacies of his relations with his fellows. His days are a ceaseless tennis in which he is nearly always the weaker player; so that without respite he can but struggle to get the ball over the net somehow and be ready for the next stroke. To look around and ask himself seriously what it is all about is to risk losing his grip on the game. Now and then indeed he is inevitably disturbed by rumours of the great world, or by movements of the very ground on which he plays his little life. Political crises, strikes, mysterious changes of the market and a slump in his wares—all sorts of obscure and uncontrollable public events threaten him or actually embroil him. And always in our time there is the dread that there will be another war, that his whole life will be fused and cast into a new mould; and then perhaps destroyed. He can only hope that the bedrock of society will outlast his day, and even support his children. But his great-grandchildren? He shrugs his shoulders. They are beyond his ken. If ever they occur at all, of what kind will they be, and on what treadmill will they find themselves sweating? Will they remember him? Will his own children remember him only to condemn him for thoughtlessly procreating them in this squirrel-cage adrift in space?

For the modern man regards his own occurrence without enthusiasm. Reviewing his endless pursuit of a carrot that is ever removed, or which, being captured, is found to be plaster, he looks forward to death without revulsion; even perhaps with complacency, as when in a day of worries he looks forward to sleep. If only there were no old age, no rising tide of contemptible distresses; and at the end no pain. If only dying were as delicious as falling asleep.

Nothing but loyalty to some admired thing greater than oneself can render a life of drudgery tolerable; and today the old objects of loyalty are losing their power. The God whom our fathers served is now revealed to many as a tiresome old gentleman vacillating between brutality and sentimentality. Even the great phrase "God is Love" has lost much of its appeal. If it means that love is the fundamental principle of the cosmos, we doubt it. If it means that the sentiment of love is the highest of all values, we are in no mood to worship mere affection. Our allegiance is not for love but for that which is lovable. There was indeed a time, not long past, when it seemed that the greatest concrete object of love was one's nation; but the war has at least shown us that nations are but hordes of individuals behaving in the crude horde manner. And even internationalism, humanism, the religion of Life, are now suspected of being parochial fervours about matters of no real moment; for they all take for granted that man himself is a thing which ought to be preserved and can be improved; and this proposition is no longer self-evident.

Here lies the root of all modern disillusion. Having lost faith in everything that might be called God, we turned our admiration on man, and now man also is found to have feet of clay. We see him essentially a self-deceiver, a brute, pretending but never really striving to be an angel. His will we are told by the psychologists is at heart animal craving, though more cunning and less downright. Even his most generous impulses are said to draw their strength merely from the dynamics of the brute body, or at best from the itch of the brute mind. His love is mere greed; and his loyalty a response to no objective excellence but to the demands of his own tortuous nature. His intelligence, which was once thought capable of dispassionate knowledge of the thing that really is, is now said to be blinkered in the service of instincts. This view of human nature, which was so vigorously advertised by the psycho-analysts, is accepted by most psychologists, such as Professor McDougall, and many philosophers, such as Mr. Bertrand Russell, who reject other parts of the Freudian doctrine. And through their able advocacy it is likely to be incorporated in popular culture before the grain in it has been sorted from the chaff.

No wonder that we are disillusioned. All that was said to be noblest in man we suspect of being at heart motivated solely by a mere relic of the brute in him. The very distinction between noble and base fails now to ring true in our ears. Anything that anyone calls good or beautiful is suspect through the very fact that such radically insincere terms have been applied to them. Only the naive and the insincere, we feel, can use such words to-day without shame; and things which are applauded by the naive and the insincere are likely to be at heart other than they seem. And so in revulsion we affect to cherish things that no one could possibly call good or beautiful. And when it occurs to us that even this admiration is insincere, since it is the expression of a mere pose of sincerity in ourselves, we turn even from these idols and renounce admiration itself. Then our only solace lies in ridicule, and especially in jibing at whatever is commonly held sacred. Thus from disillusion we have at least distilled a refreshing draught of humour, wit and iconoclastic irony, which some would say is the best achievement of our age. But iconoclasm itself may become a cult, degenerating into a meaningless ritual of horse-play. Finally perhaps we are left with nothing but a bleak contempt for our own contemptuousness.

Modern literature of disillusion is of two kinds, which, though they are often difficult to distinguish and may be even blended in the same work, spring from very different motives. There is the literature which springs from disillusion solely. This is at bottom a mere gesture of disgust and revolt, a sort of spiritual vomiting-up of matter repugnant to our nature, of a whole universe, perhaps, apprehended as nauseating. This activity was wholesome at first, and was inevitably fostered by the war and its consequences. Thus in the war-verse of Siegfried Sassoon, though disgust is the dominant note, we feel it to be fired by loyalty to certain high values. But disgust itself may become a mere mannerism no less offensive than the gentility of the Victorians. In much contemporary work nausea seems an end in itself. And it is often difficult to say of any writer whether his vomiting is spontaneous or artificially induced for fashion's sake. Witness much that has appeared in certain "modernist" periodicals, often of transatlantic origin.

But there is another and more noteworthy literature of disillusion, whose motive is neither mere disgust nor mere protest against insincerity or prettiness. It is indeed concerned with disillusion, with all the defeat, pain, futility and insincerity of common life; but it is concerned with them not merely to vomit them up but to incorporate them in an organised and splendid texture. And further it is concerned, I should say, not merely to contrive aesthetic unities of light and shade, to fashion ideally formal tragedies out of the elements of a world that is merely chaotic and hideous; it is concerned with a strange and compelling attribute of the world itself. Such I take to be the spirit of the mature Shakespeare, for instance in *King Lear*, and again the spirit of Hardy at his best. The novels and poems of Thomas Hardy were once thought to be merely disillusioned. But does the memorable description of Egdon Heath express only the weariness of a mind trapped in a world of drab and futility; or does it symbolise the objective excellence (there is no other phrase for it) that is sometimes discovered *beyond disillusion?* And in Marty South and Giles Winterborne, and again in the Reddleman in *The Return of the Native*, do we not find a very different mood from mere world-weariness? These and others of the "strong" characters of Hardy's fiction preserve both in good times and in bad, and even during their most intense emotions, an unassailable peace of mind, such as is sometimes the expression of religious faith, but in these cases demands some other explanation. And surely this attitude of purged admiration is Hardy's own attitude, though he cannot justify it, and often adulterates it with his intellectual pessimism. Again, such tortured characters as Tess and Jude were thought once to signify nothing but futility; but surely the novels in which they are set are misread if they are regarded as protracted whimperings. More truly they are hymns of praise, spontaneous acts of adoration directed upon the world itself. *Two on a Tower,* even though it perhaps fails as a novel, expresses even more fervently and unambiguously that same disinterested salutation of the objective world for its own sake, quite apart from its friendliness or unfriendliness to man. Surely the whole work of Hardy is moved throughout by a spirit of admiration, even of worship, which is no less remarkable for having been perhaps unintelligible to Hardy himself.

Tennyson, harassed by the problems of his day, could but cling to the faith that somehow in the end the universe would fulfill our demands of it; but Hardy accepted the universe as it appeared to him to be, and was rewarded almost in spite of himself by a vision more splendid than Tennyson's. No doubt he was unduly influenced by a crude metaphysics; yet in spite of that he was the forerunner not merely of modern disillusion but also of modern worship. Meredith also, though chiefly humanist and optimist, could regard man with detachment. Thus, while in the myth of *Earth and Man* he symbolises truly the relation of the evolutionary process to human mentality, in "The Thrush in February," especially in the last two stanzas, he glimpses a value which is not dependent on the triumph of life's enterprise. In fact both Hardy and Meredith seem to have experienced, even though they failed to interpret, the second mood of the modern spirit, the fourth of those movements of thought which were started by the conflict of science and romance. Meredith dimly experienced a value other than victory, but could never distinguish it from his faith in the future. Hardy, on the other hand, saw the universe as a sorry muddle, yet worshipped it while he condemned it.

The attitude of disinterested admiration is, I suppose, an element in classicism. Certainly it derives in part from the Stoics; and again in part from the more objectivistic and classical moods of Christianity. But today it is less easily learned through classical study or devotional exercise than through such non-human interests as mathematics and physical science. Mr. Bertrand Russell has well expressed the fervour which may illuminate such activities; though sometimes, as in *A Free Man's Worship*, he adulterates this ecstatic detachment with an irrelevant and self-conscious romanticism over man's supposed tragic fate. This is a double error; for in the first place the mood is not focused on man at all; and secondly it does not necessarily involve a pessimistic view, though perhaps only through tragedy can it be attained to-day. In itself it is an interest, not in man for his own sake, but in the world within which man is a striving member. Consequently, it regards man neither with hopeful assertiveness nor with submissiveness or heroic resignation.

Yet, though it is in this sense a mood of complete detachment from all striving and all strivers, emphatically it is no mere apathy, nor does it consent to inactivity. But, while espousing earnestly all the values that emerge from the nature of life and mind, it yet maintains an inviolable peace; for whatever befalls, it has a vision of this actual world as excellent. Mr. George Santayana, in *Platonism and the Spiritual Life*, has given an account of this attitude more purified than Mr. Russell's because more dispassionate. But by describing it as a disintoxication from all values he has confused with mere apathy what is essentially a value-experience, though not merely an experience of biological fulfilment.

Indeed, this mood of ecstatic yet dispassionate admiration is akin to that "sporting" attitude which, prizing the game more than victory, yet strives in every fibre. It appreciates the universe as though it were art, perhaps tragic art. But let us repeat that it is not tragical in essence. Not only in defeat, but in victory also, we may enjoy the game for its own sake. Alike in victory and in defeat this ecstasy includes a hunger to play a part in the drama of existence with vigour and delicacy, yet it holds spiritually aloof from every cause which it champions. We give ear, so to speak, not merely to the theme of human striving, or life's evolution, but to that celestial music in which our planet's whole story is a passing melody serving an end beyond itself. We are tempted to say that our attention is directed on the form of the universe as a whole. But so bold a claim should be made only with qualification, since, after all, we experience the universe only as fragments, not as an aesthetic unity. Nevertheless it is essential to this mood that in it we do seem in some sense to glimpse a supreme form in which man is contributory, not final.

I would hazard the guess that the work of Mr. T. S. Eliot is inspired by this admiration of an objective world whose form involves both good and evil. Mr. I. A. Richards, I know, argues that such writing is concerned solely to make a "music of ideas"; but in this view he is perhaps prejudiced by his own theory of value and of the nature of art in general. It would seem more true to say that Mr. Eliot calls forth or indicates a music of objective characters. Or perhaps with more strictness we should say that he constructs symbols which are indeed themselves "music of ideas," but in their music they purport to symbolise or epitomise the music of the spheres. This is perhaps the nerve of the matter. In disillusion, we may sometimes discover, or seem to ourselves to discover, an unlooked-for music of facts. And whatever be the true epistemology of value it is very important to inspect clearly the deliverance of such experiences.

There are times in the lives of most men when they wake from the game of private living, and even from the more enthralling intricacy of public service, to see themselves and the whole race of men as dust in a far mightier sport. Some, perhaps, are wholly exempt from such moments; while others, when the blue or grey sky of their world is ripped away like a tent, bury their heads. But some, even while they resent and fear the star's sudden intrusion, are stung into a strange clarity of mind. Even while they see their comforts and defences scattered, and their most admired ends snuffed into irrelevance, even while perhaps they are dissolved in fright, they are thrust into a new and splendid view of things; so that if they were not all the while paralysed with terror they could shout in the zest of amazed admiration. Unlike hares, they crouch before the serpent of eternity not in horror merely, but in ecstasy. After cursing the universe for its seeming mental deficiency, suddenly they recognise that the gods are playing a game very different from man's game, and playing it brilliantly.

Not that they merely swing from pessimism to optimism about their private fortune or their nation's welfare or the future of man; for it must be insisted that this unique enlightenment may occur in the very agony of private defeat or public calamity, even in the terror of death, even in pain, even while they watch the sufferings of their beloveds, or the downfall of their society. Not that their agony is diminished or evaded, but rather that its very intensity wakens them to an aspect hitherto ignored. Not that with the mystics they pierce the veil of sorry phantoms and stand face to face with reality itself in all its reputed benignity. No, they see the very same world that they saw before, but they unexpectedly exult in it. They judge it to be, in some sense which cannot yet be defined, intrinsically excellent or "worthwhile." Having long lived in intimacy with the world, and having ever condemned it for not conforming to their ideal, they suddenly fall in love with it, fall into worship of it, admire in it a severity incomparably more desirable than the sweetness they had demanded of it. And as an actor may enter into the hopes and strivings of his part the more sympathetically just because he appreciates to the full the aesthetic character of the drama, so they now champion the more earnestly the very causes from which they now hold themselves spiritually aloof.

Indeed, so well schooled are they in detachment from all that they take most seriously, that their reaction even to the inhuman excellence of the cosmos is not incompatible with laughter. In mere disillusion we laugh at the hollowness of fallen idols; and our laughter is bitter. But in this other mood, so well have we learned the virtue of laughter, that humour is surprisingly infused throughout our admiration. Without bitterness, and with no need for shame, we can deride the thing we most adore.

Sometimes in this mood man is regarded as a mere irrelevance; but in a shrewder vision we seem to see that man, sensitive dust that he is, has also his part to play, though not the part he thought. For even the dust is in the picture. When the bright vision is past, and we try to think out its significance, it seems indeed that the office of the human mind must be to strive toward ever clearer percipience, and to master and enrich its own imperfect nature always for the end which our fathers called worship; so that we, tiny and ineffectual players in the gods' game, may at least enter intelligently into the spirit of the game, and admire it not merely so far as it favours the ends of man, but for its own character. But we must not claim that man's discerning admiration and participation is necessary to the full achievement of the cosmos; for man's part after all may be finally tragic, and he may never fulfill his supreme office of worship. But in such experiences of dispassionate appreciation as we already know it does seem to be implied that, if man has any cosmical function whatever, it is at least to strive towards ever finer knowledge and will, whether victoriously or toward the doomed failure which is tragedy. For in this mood, though certainly we have no evidence that man will thus flower, we have strange but sure conviction that, whatever the issue, it will be the right issue, in the eyes of the gods.

But what is this talk of "gods"? For good or ill the distinctively modern spirit finds deity both improbable and unattractive. The universe that it admires, even in spite of itself, is conceived as a godless universe. Then how can there be a game, since no one is playing it? Or art, though no one creates it? How can there be any virtue in the unwitting process of things, however vast and subtly systematic? If the excellence of the universe lies neither in its expression of God's idea nor in its conformity with man's own nature, in what sense can it be excellent at all? The claim is that in certain moments of unusually clear percipience, or even through long periods or a whole life-time of vision, a man may discover in the universe, or at least in his schematic view of it, an intrinsic good not commonly revealed, an excellence not in any way dependent on the fulfilment of our purposes, or Life's capacity, or even God's will. But surely this claim is meaningless; unless indeed the universe as a whole is itself alive, is an active and self-fulfilling organism. Perhaps it expresses its unconscious nature as a plant does, but with minds for flowers. Perhaps in these moments of vision we do indeed glimpse the form or the spirit of the cosmic tree which bears us. And perhaps the tragedy of our existence is but the tragedy of petals that wither when the fruit sets, not the tragedy of universal frustration. Perhaps the faith of the Romantics was right, though they could not justify it rationally and often interpreted it too simply and optimistically in the light of their romantic preconceptions. Perhaps the truth which they groped for and confused stands revealed at last in Swinburne's "Hertha."

Perhaps this, perhaps that. Only technical philosophy can ever judge the significance of that seeming insight which most of us probably experience at one time or another. But unfortunately the philosophers are still at loggerheads about it all. For it is not clear that there is any meaning whatever in saying that an object can have intrinsic value, or be intrinsically good, apart from any mind's appreciation or purpose. Yet only by such phrases can we do justice to the actual content of this ecstatic mood of appreciation. In this dilemma some incline to sacrifice logic, others to suspect the logic-defying experience. While Professor Whitehead applauds the vision of the Romantics, Mr. Bertrand Russell would probably remind us that our nervous systems are known to play strange tricks, that this judgment of the excellence of the universe may be but a projection of our own confused emotion upon a world which is itself alien to all value; or again that our admiration of an objective system which is careless of man is at heart merely enjoyment of our own supposed emancipation from prejudice, or our own skill of cognition.

The policy of explaining the more mature activities of mind in terms of the more primitive has certainly been fertile in psychology. But whenever it has definitely succeeded, the facts explained have been of the same order as the explanatory facts. In this case, however, the experience to be explained appears to be of a nature different in essence from the primitive impulses which are supposed to explain it. And the more closely it is observed, the more different it seems. For it appears to be in its very essence an interest in objectivity; and all attempts to explain it solely in terms of the enjoyment of subjective activities or of the activities of the individual organism, however complex and "sublimated," seem therefore beside the mark. Those who favour such explanations seem to their opponents unable to focus clearly the experience they would explain. They fail to distinguish in it a quality wholly absent from primitive experience, a disinterested admiration, implying detachment not merely from private desire but from the whole endeavour of humanity. This quality, so foreign to primitive mentality, and so unintelligible in terms of a psychology confined to the primitive, comes to us in the actual experience itself as the just, though scarcely rationable, response to the universe as it is revealed in our time.

There is then at least some reason to suppose that in this unique ecstasy of disinterested admiration something is apprehended which is only to be attained by an "emergent" activity of developed minds. But there remains the epistemological question about the status of value. Do such adjectives as "good" and "bad" apply in strictness only to subjective states, or do they name characters of objects? We cannot here enter into this technical discussion. But we may note that in one theory the essential meaning of the word "good" is the character of fulfilment of capacity or activity, and that this theory is borne out by the experience of disinterested admiration. For in this experience we seem to apprehend the world as fulfilling its own capacity or nature perfectly, though in a manner wholly distinct from the ordinary biological fulfilment. But if we are asked just how the world seems to fulfill itself, we cannot answer intelligibly, and can only plead that the experience is not necessarily deceptive because it cannot yet be rendered intelligible.

But whatever be the truth of these matters, this kind of experiencing, the deliverance of which certainly appears to many modern minds as the supreme good, calls for close attention to-day. For surely it is significant that though the dominant mood of our time is disillusion, our disillusion is strangely flecked with this other, seemingly contradictory, mood of admiration. In times of optimistic faith disinterested admiration is blended with, and indistinguishable from, gratitude toward a divine benefactor; but in times of disillusion it stands out sharply from its background. Thus we may conceive it not as doubtful evidence that "God is on our side," that the universe is after all kindly disposed to us, but as a spontaneous salutation. Our task, then, is to single it out from all that has hitherto confused it, and to recognise that, whatever its true intellectual significance, it is itself an intuition of a value which eclipses all other values. Certainly we must criticise it by bringing to bear on it all the material and instruments of modern knowledge. Certainly we must disentangle it from all the fair myths that have been woven round it. Certainly we must recognise that it offers no comfort, no hope, to our more primitive human longings. But also, in criticising it, we must develop the experience itself. For to-day there are many who, though they reject all the consolations of the churches as either unbelievable or trite, cannot but recognise in this unique act of the spirit the very essence of religion, and in the deliverance of this experience something indestructible and splendid, something in the light of which all other experience should be interpreted.

The Remaking of Man

On the evening of 2 April 1931, in the afterglow of the triumph of Last and First Men, *Stapledon made his first national broadcast. The speech illuminates some episodes in* Last and First Men *but also recapitulates his old interests in eugenics and biological engineering. On 8 April the speech was the featured text in* The Listener, *the official publication of the B.B.C., which hailed Stapledon's "prominence as a historian of the future." Paragraph divisions were altered and some colloquialisms were formalized for the print medium; more importantly, the text was also abridged. While limitations of space may have been a factor, censorship—to which Stapledon was no stranger in his career—may also be suspected. The talk was branded as blasphemy by some who tuned in their radios, and the editor at* The Listener *saved space by excising, among others, precisely those sentences that rejected the immortality of the soul and hypothesized a godless universe. The version in this* Reader, *taken from the script on deposit at the B.B.C. Archive, is the full text of the broadcast and preserves the texture of Stapledon's speaking voice.*

HUMAN NATURE is like our English climate. No one can be sure what it will do at a particular time and place, but we all know that it will be mostly dull or bad, and that it can't be altered.

That, at least, is the common view. Yet both the climate and human nature change. There have been ice-ages. There have been ape-men.

No doubt our own inborn nature is much like that of the earliest true men. But man has only been man for about a million years, and his future may be very much longer. The perfected men and women who are to come will probably regard us as quaint prehistoric monkeys, dignified by a mere spark of humanity. They will perhaps have changed so much that we shall scarcely recognise them as men and women at all. Possibly their bodies will have passed as far beyond the present human form as ours beyond the reptile. Even if they are still erect bipeds, their physiques will have been refashioned through and through by the aeons of natural events that are to come, and probably by artifice also. I should expect that if we could meet a man and woman of that race we should regard them as monstrously ugly. Yet, to one another, they would seem beautiful with a kind of beauty beyond our grasp. For those who had eyes to see, she, that woman of the future, would express in her strange body a far nobler and lovelier womanhood than is found in our world; and he a more virile, a more triumphantly human, manhood.

But let us think of things nearer home. There is one sense in which man is changing very quickly. The man-in-the-street today is mentally a very different being from his counterpart of even two hundred years ago. He may be born much the same, but he has been moulded by a very different world. It is a world which, in spite of all our disastrous muddles and quarrels, is coming more and more under our control. And clearly in so far as we control man's environment, we control human nature itself, at least in a superficial sense.

But further, we have our clever biologists and our bold eugenists. They want to control man's inborn nature, too. Already they have learnt a few surprising tricks, and probably within a century or two they will have learnt many more.

Almost certainly, then, attempts will be made sooner or later to remake man, not only superficially, by changing his circumstances, but radically, by selecting and influencing the germ cells of successive generations.

Now "remaking" man may very easily turn out to be mere monkeying with man. There are two kinds of monkeying. Either you may know what improvements you want, and not know how to produce them; or you may know the technique, without knowing what it is you really want to do. In the case of man, both these dangers are very great.

The problem of technique we must leave to the scientists, bearing in mind, however, the kind of alterations which may be possible, sooner or later. Tonight let us consider whether human nature ought to be changed at all, and if so, in what direction.

Well, I for one am sure that our present human nature needs altering. I can think of many ways in which I myself, for instance, might be better than I am. And my wife would probably welcome even more radical alterations in me.

The general direction of desirable changes I would summarise in this way. They should afford me a richer, wider, deeper, more subtle, more accurate experience of this amazing world. Further, they should help me to see more clearly what is really desirable. Finally, they should enable me, in every kind of situation, to take all relevant facts into account, and behave always with supreme tact, intelligence, insight, foresight, so that always the best possible results may follow.

That *I* should be remade, or you, is impossible. But do we not desire that a race of beings far happier and more vital than ourselves should some day occur? I for one hope that the creation of such a race will become in time the constant policy of all mankind. And though this radical remaking of man is not practical politics to-day, already some of the preliminary steps need no longer be dismissed as fantasy.

There is one obvious way in which either man himself or his world must be improved. Little by little the great diseases, such as cancer, tuberculosis, heart-disease, digestive disorders, nerve and brain disorders, must be abolished. So must all the special troubles of women. And maternity must cease to be a grievous burden. We must create a race gifted with the health and vitality, the beauty and perennial youth, of the mythical heroes.

This leads to the question of longevity. If only we could keep young, most of us would certainly desire to live much longer than the normal span. But from the point of view of the race, and of the far future, would it really be good that the lives of individuals should be longer? The brevity of human life certainly enables the species to keep on starting again with a clean slate. Think of whatever historical period you most despise. How lamentable if *that* generation had occupied the earth for ever! On the other hand, very much of our short life-time is spent in merely overtaking our seniors. And no sooner have we become properly equipped for carrying on the work of the world than our powers begin to fail.

From the racial point of view, then, two complementary improvements are needed. In the remote future, when the race has reached its prime, the individual must live much longer than is possible today, say a thousand times as long; but also his youthful suppleness and vigour must continue till death. In fact senility, not only extreme senility, but that blunting of percipience and slow dying of the mind, which with us begins before middle life, must be abolished.

It is not desirable that the individual should live for ever, since that would prevent any further improvement in the inborn nature of the species. It is natural that we, who are such self-centered beings, should want to live for ever, either here or in some heaven. It is natural that we should demand some kind of immortality for those whom we love and admire. But, as I see it, not only must these cravings remain unfulfilled, but also it is better so. I must learn to regard myself and every other individual, even my dearest, as having the kind of excellence that a theme or phrase of music has. The phrase must not go on all through the music. It has its proper place. It must come to an end, and make way for other musical forms. So also with the man and woman.

Even the lengthening of the life-span would raise a serious population problem. Obviously, if all men and women are to last for many thousands of years, reproduction must be greatly reduced. It must therefore be regarded as a very rare and noble privilege. And those to whom it is not permitted must turn their energies in other directions. We are sometimes told that parenthood is a function without which the human spirit cannot flourish. I do not believe it; but if so, then here is another respect in which we must change human nature. A function which was very important in early days may well have to be restricted before man can become mature.

What other alterations can we imagine?

Perhaps it will be possible some day to increase man's sensory powers. Sight, for instance, cries out for improvement. Future man might see ultra-violet and infra-red colours. And he might analyse our present primary colours into several new ones. Moreover, by equipping his eyes with many more of the microscopic units of sight, he might become capable of much more detailed seeing. Thus, to take an unimportant example, when flying at a great height over a city, he would be able to single out, from the crowd of upturned faces, the men and the women, the young and the old, the blue eyes and the brown, and his own particular acquaintances. Similar improvements might be devised for the other senses. Perhaps entirely new senses might be created, such as a direct awareness of minute electrical changes.

Memory, also, might be so perfected that the individual's whole past might be recalled at will in all its original detail and vividness.

There might also be great improvements in man's perception of time in two manners. In the first place, he may come to hold together a longer span of time in one "now." Thus he might perceive in one act of vision the longer rhythms of nature, such as day and night, or even the four seasons, as *we* perceive the movements of dancing or a stroke in tennis. Yet also, perhaps, his perception might be so refined that when a musical tune was sounded, he might at will either hear it as a single quality or sound, or distinguish its separate pulsations, as we do the ticks of a clock.

Great improvements will probably occur in man's intelligence. I myself, who am perhaps not much below average intelligence, find much difficulty in coping with my own unimposing income tax returns. Imagine a man of the far future entering our present world and discovering our social and economic confusion. He would see the solution of it all in a flash, just as we solve those little problems that small children bring us, with tears of despair. "Why," he would say, "*this* is what you must do, and *this*." And (still greater miracle) he would probably have such powers of persuasion that he would actually get us to *do* the sensible thing. Imagine him also talking to our scientists and philosophers. "My dear fellows," he would say, "your theories are unnecessarily cumbersome and fantastic. Try this new starting point, and all will be clear." And then (greatest miracle of all) he would get them to share some fraction of his own insight.

By far the most important improvements in man I have still to mention. Today incalculable misery and waste of life are due to sheer imprudence and selfishness. Most of us are for ever failing to resist momentary temptations, even when we know that our own lasting welfare is at stake. And as for loving our neighbours as ourselves, we seldom have enough imagination to realise them as human beings at all, and even when we do we almost never regard them without prejudice in favour of ourselves.

Now, as I see things, all this has to be altered, either by nature or by artifice. The man and woman of the far future will, of course, be each one of them a vivid personality; but also each one of them will imaginatively realise, not merely a few intimates, but the whole race, as a glorious community of fellow-workers. They will no more be tempted to put private interest before public interest than we are tempted to test out razors by cutting our own throats. In fact, as I see it, their neural organisation will be so perfect that they will always choose to do whatever is seen to be best in the light of all the circumstances.

Yet they will not be moral prigs. Probably they will not care anything for righteousness as an end in itself. They will just be *sane*, with an order of sanity quite impossible to us. Imprudence and selfishness they will regard as mere madness.

Some of you think, perhaps, that a race of such inordinately perfect beings would lack all the variety of character and caprice of conduct that make us so fascinating to the novelist and so unreliable in real life. Yes, and no. Reliable the remade men and women would certainly be; but they would not lack diversity. On the contrary, I should expect them to regard us as mere sheep, afflicted with a most wearisome sameness and poverty of character. For their own nature would have a far more complex gamut on which to play infinitely diverse themes of temperament.

Do not think, either, that they will be bloodless highbrows. Compared with us they will be both more spiritual and more animal. For in us, poor transitional creatures that we are, the fact that we have not courage or strength to be fully men troubles us with a morbid shame of being animal. But in them the spiritual and the animal would both be stronger, and each perfectly harmonious with the other. They will enjoy food and drink, and play, with the zest of children. They will delight in their variegated and colourful world with a barbarian fervour, yet also with piety. They will lover each other's exquisite bodies no less than their subtle minds. Their whole instinctive nature, no doubt, will have been remade and harmonised; but far from being subdued, it will be enriched and completely shameless. They will surely be devoid of those conflicts and obscene repressions which distort and cripple our minds so often without our knowing it. On the other hand, they will not make the modern mistake of supposing primitive instinctive fulfilment to be all that matters.

Then what, you ask, will these very far future and tiresomely perfect beings *do?* Well, their most serious racial enterprise will of course be concerned with matters as remote from us as ours from a rabbit. Perhaps they will once more be striving to remake man for some high destiny beyond our comprehension. Perhaps, since there is a limit to the weight of brain that a single organism can safely carry, they will need to put all brains into some kind of telepathic union with one another, so that, for certain purposes, all may function together as one brain, capable of some higher order of experience. Perhaps they will have discovered that man's true end is to contemplate and enjoy the whole world of space and time and living forms, with whatever insight he may, before the ultimate frost destroys him. But whatever man's final goal may be, for us the general direction is clear. Man in our day is faced with two problems. The first is one on which all will agree, namely, to make possible a full and happy life for whatever individuals that occur in this and succeeding generations. The second is to *begin* to learn to see man in his cosmic setting, and to discover how to make of him, in the fullness of time, the best that can possibly be made. For in our modern age the human race seems to be going through a crisis something like the passage of the individual from childhood to boyhood. In every child's life there comes a time when he begins to see himself as a personality, and to make plans, however fantastic, for a long future. He determines to be a pirate or an engine-driver. Similarly man is just beginning to be conscious of his racial past, and of his prospects, and to ask himself whether he has any part at all to play in relation to the stars. Perhaps he has none. On the other hand, perhaps he is not wholly unimportant. At present he cannot possibly tell. He is too ignorant and dull-witted. But clearly, whatever his cosmical function, the first thing for him to do is to fulfill those human capacities which are at present so feebly exercised in him, those capacities in virtue of which he justly considers himself the finest of terrestrial animals.

But very possibly, long before he can fulfill his capacities, long before he can even attain spiritual adolescence, let alone maturity, some accident may destroy him. Astronomical or terrestrial events beyond his control may easily disinfect the earth of the microbe, man. More likely still, he will commit some huge folly which will ruin him for ever.

Machinery and Labour

Late in 1934, at the depth of the worldwide economic Depression, Stapledon spoke in a B.B.C. series on the history and future of mechanization. By then he had earned a reputation for visionary prophecy and was a natural candidate for the broadcasts. He had also made clear his socialist politics, most recently in Waking World, *published earlier in 1934, and the subject of machines and workers could not elicit from him an uncritical technophilia. In his twenty-minute talk, Stapledon imagined a future in which all strata of society would benefit from technology, but he warned against taking such an outcome for granted. His utopianism often had a grim underside, and here his ambivalence is evident in the structure of the speech. The utopian vision is bracketed by an unforgiving analysis of how rapacious bosses might harness an advanced technology to tighten their grip on their employees. The fantastic tour of a city of the future in the broadcast has visual images similar to those in the final, utopian section of H. G. Wells's screenplay for* Things to Come, *which was not released until the following year. But the apocalyptic epilogue to the vision, a pure Stapledonian touch, prevents the speech from becoming a piece of Disneyfied world-of-tomorrow fantasy. Printed here for the first time, the text is from Stapledon's handwritten manuscript in the B.B.C. Archive; the profusion of underscored words suggests that he used this script to rehearse the emphases and inflections of his delivery.*

IF I WERE FEARING UNEMPLOYMENT, I should not be quite happy about this series of talks. I should say, "Here are these blighters, who *thrive* in a mechanized world, trying to persuade *us*, who have been knocked out by it, that what we want is more and more mechanization. For them it means life and comfort. For us it is a living death."

Now that's the plain truth. There's no getting over it. And before saying anything else I want to make it clear that *I* think mechanization has proved quite as much a curse as a blessing. It *might* be used to give everyone a full, interesting, happy life; but actually it has turned us *all* into slaves. Some of us are far more wretchedly enslaved than others, but in one way we are *all slaves.* Very many, of course, are forced to spend their lives grinding and sweating for others. They can't move about freely,—yet think of our cars and trains and planes. They have to live huddled together in shocking conditions,—yet a modern house *can* be a pocket palace. I don't know whether "all God's children have *wings*," but I'm sure they might fairly soon all have pocket palaces (or apartments in larger palaces), if we *really* set our minds to the job. And those palaces might be filled with articles of use and of luxury from every part of the earth. Yet actually in many cases people haven't enough blankets, and not even enough food.

Well, that's what we have done with machinery, for many people. But that's not all. Even those of us who are lucky, who are well fed and housed, are in a way enslaved to machinery. For we are *all* more or less machine-mad. Our minds *stink* with machinery, and the lust of mechanization. Our gods are speed, mechanical invention, and mass production. We are like children that are crazy over some new mechanical toy. We are becoming insensitive to all the really interesting things in the world. And we are going dead inside, dead in our essential selves. If you spend your time driving a car as fast as you can, or in running a factory or a business as fast as you can, you won't be troubled by uncomfortable thoughts. Mechanization is a dangerous drug that has got hold of us, and is eating into our minds.

Yet it *might* be a means for making such a world as has never existed before, a world of an entirely new kind, in which every man and woman would be developed in body and mind right up to the limit of his or her native capacity. As we were told last week, "We have all the resources and skill to give comfort and leisure to *all* men." And further, if *"we"* (which just means all of us working together), if we can secure for all men *much* leisure (voluntary leisure, not the forced and desolate leisure of the man out of a job), and if we can see that all children are helped to learn how to get the *best* out of their leisure, the world will—how shall I put it?—flower mentally. Men will cease to be the crippled, stunted minds that most of us are today. And then they will see *through* this obsession of machinery, and begin to use machinery purposefully, for sane ends. Instead of wanting to be speed hogs, they will want to be real persons, well-formed in body and mind. And they will want to make their world community into a fully awakened human community.

It would be dishonest and cowardly of me to paint a bright picture of the future of mechanization without first pointing out that everything depends on how we control the whole process, and *who* controls it. Whatever happens, mechanization will almost certainly increase (unless, indeed, civilization crashes, and science is lost). The machine age has only just *begun* to begin. Now hitherto the change over to mechanization has been managed by people whose *effective* motive has on the whole been private profit, and whose main interest has been— just mechanization. No thorough attempt has been made, save recently in Russia, to direct the whole process purposefully and strictly for the benefit of the community. And so things have gone in a haphazard, muddled way. The destiny of millions has been determined by massed, day-to-day private buyings and sellings, by the financial operations of private persons or groups of persons. Thus great power has come into the hands of a single section of the community.

Now these economic masters of society are mostly decent folks in private life; often kindly, self-sacrificing, and sincere. It's silly to think that all capitalists are knaves. According to their own lights they are often public spirited. Often too they are able. But the system that they work is uncoordinated, undirected to any clear social aim. Moreover, to the cobbler there's nothing like leather. And so with the economic masters, just because they have spent their whole lives in the atmo-sphere of individualistic commerce and industry and finance, they cannot help feeling "in their bones" that the great process of mechani-zation *must* be carried on by individuals seeking private profit, and that the dominance of their class is necessary to the community.

Well, I see no hope for the full and proper use of mechanization until the control passes from this one class that is pledged to economic individualism.

But let us suppose that mechanization *does* at last come to be directed purposefully and strictly toward the benefit of all ordinary human beings. Let me try to give a sketch of life as it may be in that sanely mechanized world.

Imagine that we find ourselves in a city of the future. We notice first that its great buildings are clean and bright in the clear air, for there is no smoke. The wide streets are thronged with pedestrians. Yet, surprisingly, there are few vehicles. This is because only *freight* goes by road. Passengers, when they are not walking, travel by air or under-ground. Small flying machines are seen streaming above the buildings, or entering great doors in the various stories, or hovering in the streets. But the *people* interest us more than their machines. They are a striking crowd, well-set-up, and as brown and healthy-looking as though they had just come back from a holiday. Dress, we note, is very varied. Most people seem to be wearing spick and span new clothes, except a few, who (we are told) seek distinction by looking a bit shabby. The streets are lined with shop-windows, in which are displayed all sorts of arti-cles, of use and luxury from every part of the world. Along with a great profusion of machine-made goods appear quantities of *hand-*made articles,—fabrics, crockery, metal work,—many of them obvi-ously the work of highly skilled craftsmen or artists. For, since *all* routine work is done by machinery, a vast amount of human energy and skill and interest is set free to express itself in handicrafts. And, since everyone is brought up to become a leisured citizen with developed taste, there is a great demand for this kind of thing. In the centre of the town, along with many great public buildings, such as municipal offices, libraries, galleries, news theatres, picture houses, and so on, there are many huge blocks of flats. But since everyone has his own flying machine, most people prefer to live outside the city.

On our way to one of these residential quarters we pass through a manufacturing district, a region of more great bright buildings, interspersed with green lawns and trees. One of these factories we enter. It turns out to be a clothes factory. The interior is clean, roomy, and in a severe business-like way beautiful. We find that a dozen persons are superintending the whole mechanical operation of the place. This is possible because the principle of automatic transport has been carried to its logical conclusion. To use the old gag, the pigs go in at one end and the sausages come out at the other. But here the *reality* far surpasses the fantasy. Cloth of many qualities is automatically fed into the building from the automatic goods train which brought it from the weaving factories many miles away. This system is controlled, we learn, by a handful of citizens who move switches far away in a great regional railway centre. Once the cloth has reached the clothes factory, it is automatically fed into cutting machines which turn it out in pieces of innumerable standardized shapes. These are automatically sewn together into a great diversity of suits and dresses; and the finished articles are again fed out of the factory automatically to find their way to the stores, where skilled *hand*-workers may sometimes alter them slightly to suit individual needs. This sort of thing, we are told, is typical of the whole industrial organization of the world.

We begin to watch the few *persons* in the place. One or two are in overalls, tinkering at the machinery. A few are holding telephone conversations with the Central Clothes Board, or the Railway Centre, or other factories, or with the Stores. One is sitting before a switch board, pressing switch after switch, and thereby arranging what *kinds* of cloth are to be worked up in what quantities and styles and sizes during the day. We note a certain peacefulness about these people, very different from the worried manner of our own industrial workers. This is evidently largely due to their extremely short hours, and the curious deliberateness of the whole process.

One girl does, indeed, seem worried. Yesterday (we are told) she pressed the wrong switches, and the unfortunate result was a thousand sports coats made of satin and a thousand evening dresses made of rough tweed. The factory manager seems much more amused than annoyed. "What does it really matter," he says. "There's plenty of everything, now that we have got the world organized properly. But in the old days, during the transition to the new order, it was very different. Still, that sort of thing *ought* not to happen. It's inartistic." We ask if the girl is a case of overstrain. He laughs. "Yes," he says, "she spends too much of her time chasing round the country from one play-acting competition to another."

We very soon learn that these people are not only leisured, but that they do *use* their leisure. This is because they are not too tired to use it, and because they are educated as much for leisure as for work. For in the fully mechanized world a *practical* education, an education suited to the *facts* of the ordinary man's life consists not merely of learning to be an efficient and docile industrial worker, but in learning how to make the best of himself as a *person*, how to be keenly and accurately aware of his world, how to think critically and fearlessly, how to play an intelligent and responsible part in the great common enterprise of maintaining a truly human and civilized world-society. Of course everyone has some profession or other. There are factory workers, agriculturalists, doctors, teachers, and so on. But a man's working hours are mostly *very* short, and his leisure occupations are often socially quite as important as his official work. Moreover, the authorities strongly disapprove of anyone who becomes so absorbed in his work that he begins to grow mentally blinkered. Everyone's *first* duty is to keep himself mentally wide-awake to the life of the world around him. Government is of course carried on by experts chosen for their skill in statecraft, but every grown person is liable to be called upon to vote on questions of general policy. This voting, we find, he does in a very novel way. When we have passed through the factory area, and are looking at the "pocket palaces" in a residential quarter (a country-side interspersed with private houses and great blocks of flats), we are of course surprised at many things in the interiors that we see, at the labour-saving devices that reduce household chores to a mere brief diversion, at the innumerable domestic uses of electric power, at the organization for communal cooking and cleaning, and so on. But *one* dodge is quite new. Everybody entitled to a vote can cast his vote in his own house, simply by turning an electric button, to register "yes" or "no," or one of a number of alternatives. Ingenious adding machines tot up the national poll, or the world poll, as the case may be, and issue the results on the very day of the question. This machinery, you can well imagine, is not *very* often used. Daily plebiscites would cripple any government. But the device is invaluable in times of crisis, when far-reaching decisions have to be made in a hurry. Moreover, it gives the private citizen a vivid sense of his responsibility.

The immense increase of travel, and the huge development of radio, we learn, have turned the world into something like an ancient Greek city state, in which everyone is everyone else's neighbour. Each person has his own aeroplane; and great air liners are at his service to take him in a few hours to any region of the planet. He can flit off for the day to a conference in Patagonia or a tennis tournament in Australia. Even when he is too busy to travel, he may hear and see in his own home every interesting event in any part of the world. Not only so but on the phone he can speedily call up his friends in every country.

Now in spite of all this vast development of mechanization, mechanism (we soon find) forms only the *background* of the mental life of these people. They are mildly interested in it, but on the whole they take it for granted. They are far *more* interested in one another, as personalities, and in all the really *human* activities of their world-society, and of course in the universe within which their planet is a mote. The more intelligent sort of ordinary citizen (we find) is really much concerned with world-politics, science, history, the arts, and even philosophy. Incredible, you say. But you see, he is not dogged by the need to earn wages. And he is not hypnotized by machinery.

I have tried to imagine the sort of life which the increase of mechanization *should* bring. Let me end by repeating that, in my view, this possibility depends on our controlling the whole process *purposefully* for the social end. If control remains in the hands of a class which is devoted to private enterprise, this dream will never be realised. Instead the future will be far blacker than the present. For as the existing economic system becomes more insecure (and it is daily doing so) those who believe in it will sincerely feel that *every* means must be used to preserve it. And in a not very remote future increased mechanization will give them immensely increased power to crush opposition. The plain man's freedom, such as it is, will vanish. He will become a helpless cog in a rickety machine. If he rebels or criticizes, all sorts of grim mechanical dodges will be used to suppress him. But indeed few persons will have the imagination to criticize authority, for by means of highly mechanized propaganda, the government will mould every man's mind to suit its own purposes. The press, the cinema, and above all the radio will be used in such a manner as to give voice only to officially approved ideas and moral principles. Ordinary human beings will become mere mindless robots. And sooner or later, slowly or swiftly, the whole system will break down, and civilization will be lost.

On Cultural Diversity

Published in the column "Personal View" in the Manchester Evening News *in the summer of 1937, this short, untitled journalistic essay is Stapledon's account of a holiday in the remote and isolated Shetland Islands. The title it is given here reflects concerns articulated also in "Literature and the Unity of Man" that the homogenization of culture threatens those unique local traditions and ways of life that enrich the global community.*

THE CROFTER-FISHERMEN of Shetland may sometimes be overawed by the superficial glamour of life on the largest of the British Isles, but they possess a treasure which we have lost—if, indeed, we ever really possessed it. Their country, whose very real beauty is too subtle to spring to the eye, is not likely to attract many tourists. It is remote, bleak, monotonous, and singularly devoid of amenities. But its inhabitants are human. In comparison with our specialised, robotised minds, they give an unexpected impression of vitality. This is the more surprising because inevitably it is from the larger island that they receive most of their intellectual food.

Many times during my short visit I asked myself how it was that these people, who were obviously much less "educated" than myself, impressed me as being in some important way more fully human.

I am not one of those who assume that the countryman is necessarily a nobler creature than the townsman. Indeed, I am inclined to regard the townsman as, on the whole, more sensitive and quicker-witted, and far more aware of the general pattern of the human world. In Shetland this impression had to be qualified.

In some respects, undoubtedly, the better type of townsman has the advantage over the countryman. But in certain less obvious yet in the long run perhaps more important ways the countryman really is the superior. Or rather the Shetland Islander is the superior. For I cannot help believing that a good deal of the excellence that impressed me did indeed spring from the special circumstances of this island population. Theirs is a distinctive native tradition and culture, compounded of British and Norse. Also the influences of land and sea have been intimately blended in the making of their lives.

Even in England one may meet occasional landworkers (and, of course, occasional town workers also) who seem in an obscure manner more "real" than the rest of us. In spite of their obvious ignorance, and even mental crudity, they convey an impression that within the sphere of their own direct contact with life they experience more precisely and feel more justly and sincerely than most men. It is as though they were exceptionally fine instruments that were being used for rather simple music, while the rest of us are rather poor, battered, and machine-made instruments from which very subtle music was being painfully and unsatisfyingly wrenched.

In England these less spiritually damaged people are rare, in every social class. Most of us are not only damaged but also mass-produced, turned out to pattern. And the pattern is mechanical. In Shetland, so far as I could judge, average human beings are of the finer type.

Perhaps I am exaggerating the virtue of the Shetland Islanders. I met them in particularly favourable circumstances, not as a tourist but approximately as the guest of a native. From the first hand-shake, reserved but friendly, to the rather warmer farewell the relationship was a natural human relationship, very different from the usual inter-course between tourist and natives. But I am convinced that this was not the whole explanation of my sense of the presence of remarkably aware and remarkably responsible and generous and "well-born" individuals. And this, let me repeat, although their opinions about such remote matters as the Royal Family and an after-life sometimes seemed pathetically naïve.

I suppose this exceptional human excellence should be attributed partly to the crofters' great variety of practical skills and partly to a remarkable absence of class distinctions, or at any rate of the snobbishness and servility that usually spring from class distinctions.

The diversity of the Shetlander's life is due mainly to its combination of fishing and agriculture. The coastline is so fantastically indented that every bit of land is within easy reach of salt water. The crofters are at once fishermen, agriculturists, and shepherds. They work long in their little patches of cornfield and kitchen garden. With the help of their amiable dogs they round up their sheep on hills where the grass is often scanty and the heather is so dwarfed as to be almost unrecognisable. The fine Shetland wool, famous throughout Britain, is still spun and knitted in the crofts, particularly in the long winter months. In the sheltered firths or voes and out on the ocean these descendants of the Vikings take whiting, haddock, mackerel, herring. Their boats, of strikingly Norse pattern, nose in and out among fantastic rocks where sea birds are constantly wheeling, crying, diving, and crowding the cliff ledges. At certain seasons they cut peat on remote hill sides, and carry it by boat to stack near the croft.

Such are some of their very diverse skills, easy to mention, difficult to acquire, as we found when we tried to lend a hand. The fish got away with our bait. Half a day's work on the peat stiffened our backs. Theirs is a hard life and often dangerous. But it is a life of skill and varied interest.

And it is a strikingly communal life. Neighbours are always helping one another with their peat-shifting or their sheep-dipping. Such co-operation is not necessarily an expression of special friendliness. It is the normal order of life. Both for work and pleasure the crofters living round a particular voe, or centred in a particular village, are in constant touch with one another. In summer there is a very extensive coming and going, for men of different districts meet at the regattas which are held at all the principal centres. There they display their seamanship in racing their own seaworthy and often home-built boats.

The seeming absence of class-distinction has its roots in the remote past when the free "odallers" held their crofts in their own right, though paying a tax to the crown. Subsequently, however, this system was broken down by Scottish feudalism, and in recent centuries the crofters were cruelly oppressed, almost enslaved. But lately they have recovered much of their old security of tenure and their old independent spirit. For practical purposes the crofter is his own master, arranging his work as he wills. The basic fact of his life is that with his own strength and varied skills he wins a scanty livelihood from the land and sea. Conscious of his security, his prowess, and his intrinsic worth, he bows to no man but is kindly disposed toward all. Such, at least, was my impression. Here, it seemed, was a real example of the true spirit of the classless society—or as nearly so as might be in a system which is after all fundamentally capitalistic.

Much rubbish has been talked about the dignity of manual toil. But where manual toil is an expression of fine maritime and agricultural lore it does indeed enrich and dignify the spirit. Judging from their behaviour I suspect that the crofters themselves, even while they consciously envy the opportunities and excitements of Britain, have an obscure but deep sense of their own human worth in comparison with us. It is true that the young are emigrating in increasing numbers to our cities. But this is not simply due to city's lure. Economic necessity compels them. The bleak islands can only support a small crofter-population. And Lerwick, the only considerable town, has suffered grievously from the decline of the herring industry. Political causes have deprived us for ever of the Russian and Italian markets. The huge fleets of drifters that formerly visited Lerwick have now sadly dwindled. But though these factors have increased emigration, some emigrants return, disappointed, home-sick for their native voes. They are lucky if they manage to gain a footing once more in some croft. A large proportion of Shetlanders joins the mercantile marine. A common plan is for a young man to spend some months of the year working on the family croft and the rest voyaging as a seaman or ship's carpenter to China or New Zealand.

Things are changing very rapidly in Shetland. The impact of the larger island and of the world is ever intensified. Though there are no railways the motor is affecting life in many ways. The marine oil engine facilitates communication with outlying islands, such as storm-bound Foula. In Lerwick the shops are crowded with the familiar machine-made products of Britain, America, Germany, and Japan. The cinema is beginning to have its usual effect. Radio is a commonplace in the crofts. Far to the south, the more fertile Orkneys have already been largely assimilated to Scotland. Shetland itself must soon succumb.

Sentimental considerations incline one to deplore this prospect. There is a romantic spell about remote islands with distinctive cultures and we readily protest when they become less remote and less distinctive. Our curiosity, our idle curiosity, is robbed of a possible titilation, our town-bred claustrophobia is deprived of a symbolic appeasement. Is this regret justifiable?

Obviously there must be no question of preserving the islands as a museum piece. If the islanders want our civilisation they must have it. But can we give them our best without our worst, stimulus without the subtle poison that has so lamentably depraved us? Some Shetlanders, I am convinced, prize their distinctive life highly, and recognise that modern conveniences cannot compensate for its loss. Having tasted city life, these struggle to return home. Others are less far-sighted.

What precisely is it that we should envy in them, and what that they may reasonably envy in us? It is very difficult to say. We should envy them, I think, their far richer, more varied and concrete practical life. They may reasonably envy our more voluminous social inter-course and contacts with the world at large. They attain a personal solidity and depth of root which we for the most part lack. But they attain it at the expense of isolation from the great world. We, on the other hand, have impoverished roots, and so we cannot properly uti-lise our greater opportunities.

If this analysis is true we must indeed regret the passing of the distinctive island life and culture. We should wish it not to be pre-served unchanged but to be fostered as a nursery of well-born and well-nurtured human beings. We should wish, that is, the preservation of its two main sources of strength, namely, the essential fisherman-crofter skills, and the spirit of "classlessness," of human dignity; but we should wish the islanders also to receive full benefit of all modern aids to their way of life, and of full cultural intercourse with the rest of the world. Perhaps this ideal is in its very nature unrealisable.

Those who, like myself, desire a unified world-wide culture should also desire all distinctive and valuable insularities of culture to be preserved, though for their own enrichment they must also be modified by contact with the rest of the world. What we desire is a true world-community; but a community in which there was no diversity would be barren. The greater the diversity of the components the richer their communal life, so long as diversity is based upon a deeper identity of character and will and interest. Without this, diversity must lead to misunderstanding and strife.

Mysticism
from *Philosophy and Living*

Philosophy and Living, *published in two volumes in 1939 and intended as a "plain man's" practical guide to the history and practice of philosophical inquiry, sold more copies during his lifetime than anything else Stapledon wrote. The book culminates in an analysis and cautious endorsement of mystical and intuitive vision as a counterbalance to rational and materialist ways of experiencing and interpreting the world. This is a case Stapledon often made, in both his philosophical and his literary works; indeed,* Philosophy and Living *treats dispassionately the problem of the morality of the cosmos that torments the narrators and dominates the concluding chapters of several of his philosophical romances, including* Last and First Men, Star Maker, *and* The Flames. *In discussing mysticism Stapledon also deploys his favorite portmanteau term, "personality-in-community," which he used to describe a twofold human ideal: spiritual self-cultivation united to an active social responsibility, inward- and outward-looking habits of mind and behavior.*

THROUGHOUT THIS SURVEY it has been borne in on us that intellectual knowledge, though reliable up to a point, is superficial, piecemeal, and sometimes treacherous; but hitherto we have barely noticed the claim that there is another kind of knowing which is penetrating, comprehensive, and infallible. I shall now briefly consider this claim as it is put forward by the mystics. European philosophy has been mainly intellectualistic in temper; Indian philosophy has been mainly mystical. The great European mystics have been moral leaders, but they have not been philosophers.

I shall consider mysticism only in the most general manner, and shall merely try to show what, in my view, is its relation to philosophy, which we have defined as the love and pursuit of wisdom.

The word "mystical" is used in two very different senses. In the more general sense it applies to any ideas which are not strictly rational but have an element of intuitive guesswork in them. In this sense "mystical" sometimes becomes synonymous with "superstitious." In the stricter sense the word "mystical" applies to a special kind of non-rational experience, in which, it is claimed, the individual attains some degree of illumination or insight into the essential and normally hidden nature of reality. This insight is reported to be not merely a kind of knowing; it is the supreme achievement of knowing-feeling-striving in one all-fulfilling act. The "knowing" aspect of it is said to be not abstract, like intellectual knowing, but concrete, like sense-experience. In fact, in so far as it is knowledge, it is an immediate acquaintance with the hidden essence of a "reality" which is said to lie behind all ordinary and illusory experience.

The reports of the mystics vary greatly, but in spite of their differences they show a remarkable agreement about the general character of the experience. I shall consider only the features which are most general.

The mystic's starting-point is often a condition of torturing self-contempt or of revulsion from the cruelty and injustice practised by his fellow men. It is important to recognise that his motives, like most human motives, are very complex. He certainly desires, amongst other things, personal salvation in some sense. Christians conceive this as eternal personal life, but some Indians reject this view. Another and a subtly entangled motive is spontaneous compassion and the desire for the spiritual fulfilment of others. Different from these motives is the self-oblivious admiration for virtue or for the spiritual way of living. In this mood the spiritual way of living is conceived not merely as a means to salvation but as an intrinsic good. Different again is the admiration or adoration or worship of a personal God, or of the universal Spirit, or of something quite indescribable save as the supremely holy object of worship. This may be conceived either in terms of love and tender intimacy or in terms of awe and even terror, or in both of these manners.

The aspirant to mystical experience is generally a highly self-conscious individual, and often highly other-conscious also. He seeks to escape from the bondage of the bodily hungers and of personal self-regard. And he seeks very often, but not always, to free others from this slavery. In Europe he is apt to say that he denies himself in order to save his soul, or find union with his God. In the East he generally longs to annihilate his separate self and lose himself in the universal spirit.

Two different impulses appear among the mystics, often in the same individual. The first is the tendency to withdraw from the world in order to concentrate on self-discipline for the sake of the desired self-mastery and self-transcendence. The other is the tendency to play an active part in the world, to find his self-discipline in heroic social service, to find self-transcendence through absorption in the lives of others. It is claimed that the greatest mystics, at any rate in the West, have been not world-forsakers but world-embracers. In the East too, I understand, it is recognised that the final and most lethal temptation, the final snare of self, which traps many noble spirits when they are well on their way, is the temptation to shun all mundane responsibilities and seek self-annihilation for purely selfish motives.

Mastery over the flesh and the self-regarding passions is sought by various kinds of self-discipline. It often begins with special exercises to acquire voluntary control of bodily functions, such as breathing and blood-circulation. It may include fasting and other forms of asceticism, or actual "mortification of the flesh" by self-torture. It generally involves the religious exercises and ritual characteristic of the individual's social environment. Good works among his fellow men may also play a large part in it. It may take the form of meditation, in which the individual tries to concentrate his attention upon, or to yield himself in utter passivity to, the spiritualising influence of God, or of the Whole. Or he may seek by introspective meditation to discover hidden imperfections in his own nature, so that he may eradicate them by spiritual discipline.

By such methods the mystics have sought their goal. Each method contains its own peculiar snares. Discipline of the flesh may turn into a perverse lust of self-torture or of spiteful cruelty to others. Every kind of self-denial may produce puritanical harshness. Good works may starve the inner life, and reduce the individual to a kind of charity-dealing robot. Meditation may lead to flight from social responsibility, and self-indulgence in a world of dreams; or to such a habit of self-analysis that the will is paralysed.

Amongst all these snares the traveller's progress is bound to be fluctuating and slow. Very different experiences are reported by different individuals, but the underlying identity is unmistakable. The story generally includes a phase, sometimes known as "the dark night of the soul," in which all contact with the universal seems to be lost, and the spirit sinks into despair. Subsequently the adventurer struggles out of this slough of despond to find himself nearer to his goal than he expected. Little by little he may gain complete detachment from all worldly desires and be able to meet every issue of fate not merely with stoical resignation but with joyful acceptance. For all things have now come to seem particular manifestations of the universal spirit in which he desires to lose himself.

The final illumination and self-transcendence are of course described very differently by mystics of Eastern and Western culture. All differences, it may be, are differences in the *interpretation* of experiences that are essentially identical and indescribable. Such, perhaps, is even the seemingly radical difference between those who claim union of the personal self with a personal deity and those who speak of the annihilation of the personal self in the impersonal Whole. We must bear in mind always that any experience that is beatific, and also too subtle for literal description, is likely to be interpreted in terms of the most cherished ideas of the individual's traditional culture. Consequently, in Christian lands and ages it is almost inevitable that interpretation should conform to the ideals of personal immortality and union with a personal God.

In general the ecstatic experience, which is the mystic's supreme reward, is said to give profound insight into the essential nature of reality, along with a stammering inability to describe *what* has been revealed, save in the most metaphorical and paradoxical terms. Sometimes the reality thus revealed is referred to in terms of dread, and even terror, as the divine and ruthless "Other," rightly careless of man and his petty desires. In some cultures, on the other hand, it is said to be the divine, personified Love, which embraces, or gathers up into itself, the spirit of the individual lover of this all-loving God. In other cultures it appears as the impersonal and wholly dispassionate universal spirit, or the underlying reality which constitutes the unity of all things. One point on which there is general agreement is that in the supreme experience time is in some sense transcended. What is discovered is a reality which is eternal.

The effect of mystical experience on the individual's ordinary life is claimed to be far-reaching. All his conduct is irradiated by memory of his vision. He is able to surmount all troubles with fortitude and joy. He behaves with increased wisdom, sincerity, courage, and devotion to whatever social ideal he has espoused. He is spurred by a new sense of the reality that informs all ordinary phenomenal things. Even sense-perception may reveal unexpected significance to him, significance of the essential nature of the universe. He has an immensely increased capacity for delighting in everything. In particular he may discover an intrinsic worth and lovableness in his fellow human beings, even in those who, in their blindness, pursue evil ends. In short, he becomes a much more sensitive, more practical, more alert, more integrated, more genuinely social personality. Such is the claim.

It is easy to dismiss these contentions as mere delusion. It is easy to point out that alcohol, nitrous oxide, opium and other drugs may induce ecstatic moods and beatific visions remarkably like some aspects of mystical experience. Simple starvation also may cause a striking mental lucidity and exaltation. Most remarkable is the well-attested fact that the onset of an epileptic attack may be accompanied by a conviction of profound insight and beatitude. Such evidence suggests that the mystic merely deludes himself into "projecting" upon the external universe a sense of extreme personal well-being which has been caused in him by nothing more exalted than glandular action in his own body.

Another argument against the objective validity of mystical experience may be derived from modern psychology. It is obvious that the language in which some mystics describe their experience is tinged with sexual metaphor. This vaunted union with the divine may after all be merely a hallucination bred of suppressed sexual craving. Or alternatively it may be a grandiose expression of primitive self-regard, or of the infantile longing for parental care, or for return to the womb, and annihilation.

The cogency of all such arguments is immensely enhanced by the contemporary disposition to regard explanations in terms of scientific concepts as more credible than any other. We have already noted that the supposed metaphysical implications of science are based on the hypostatisation of the physical categories and the dismissal of all others as unreal. But though we must discount this prejudice in favour of the physical, we must not rush to the other extreme of accepting the mystic's claims uncritically. We must consider whether they can in fact be properly accounted for in terms of familiar concepts. What then must our judgment be? What is the reasonable verdict from the point of view of the plain man who has not himself had any mystical experience?

The mystic can account for the physically-induced seemingly mystical experiences by arguing that *of course* there is a physical aspect to the process of mastering the flesh, and that some of the phenomena produced during self-discipline may also be produced by purely physical causes. He may go further, and say that these physically-induced experiences really are approximations to the authentic mystical experience, though so oddly caused. In fact, if he has already made up his mind about the validity of mystical experience, he need not be disturbed by the arguments derived from physiology, nor yet by those derived from psychology.

But *ought* he to have made up his mind? Or rather, ought we, who do not share his experience, to accept his verdict? The main facts to remember are: that a large number of persons in all countries and all ages have claimed mystical experience; that in spite of diversity their reports show on the whole a surprising agreement; that many of them, though certainly not all, have been persons well above the average of intelligence and integrity; that some of them are the world's greatest saints, moral teachers, religious and socially dynamic leaders; that among ordinary people in most phases of the world's history, though not in our own, the belief in, and the very fragmentary apprehension of, some kind of mystical reality has been a source of strength. It is true, of course, that, like other good things, mystical experience may become a snare. It may be used as an occasion for flight from the responsibilities of this life. Undoubtedly this has often happened. But such withdrawal is emphatically condemned by some of the greatest mystics. It is possible that it occurs only in individuals and in cultural phases of somewhat depressed spiritual vigour.

In view of all these considerations it seems rash to accept the simple materialistic theory that all mystical experience is merely an illusion. It seems on the whole probable that the mystics do have access of some kind to something which is missed in ordinary experience, and may have a supremely invigorating effect on the individual, and therefore on his behaviour.

On the other hand, all intellectual descriptions and interpretations of the mystical experience must be regarded with great suspicion. It is after all very unlikely that human thought and language, which are adapted to much simpler, more commonplace experience, should be able to cope with experience of a very different order. Descriptions and interpretations can be intelligible only to those who have at least some slight immediate acquaintance with the matters described.

The plain man may reasonably feel that this conclusion is both vague and unconvincing. He may say, "You *may* be right. But the whole thing *may* be moonshine. I have no personal knowledge of any such experience, and I shall continue to regard the mystic's claims with grave suspicion."

But *has* he no personal acquaintance with mystical experience of any kind? Have not very many fairly sensitive people some acquaintance at least with a mystical aspect of normal experience? In our materialistically-obsessed civilisation it is difficult for them to recognise the fact. Perhaps many who have it overlook it. There are many kinds of normal experience which to the sincerely observing mind do *seem* to reveal an aspect which deserves the name mystical. In these experiences some particular fact is strongly felt to be in some incomprehensible manner significant of the essential nature of the universe.

The most obvious example of this kind of experience is perhaps youthful falling in love. Sometimes, but not always, the lover feels very strongly that either love itself or the nature of the loved person gives him a new and penetrating insight. It is easy to dismiss this seemingly mystical aspect as merely a product of uncritical emotion. It is always fatally easy to dismiss unobtrusive facts that do not accord with our theories. Another kind of experience which may have a mystical flavour is the appreciation of "natural beauty," as Wordsworth knew. Less obviously, and less frequently, intellectual exploration may give the same impression, when matters which were obscure suddenly assume a far-reaching pattern. Artistic creation and appreciation are often felt to have a mystical aspect over and above their normal aesthetic character. Most strikingly this is revealed in tragic art. In watching a great play, in which the leading characters present themselves both as unique individuals and as symbols of humanity striving to mould its destiny, we are torn between human sympathy for the individual and acceptance of his tragic fate. The experience is not purely aesthetic; or if it is, then the aesthetic itself has a mystical aspect. We feel that in some obscure way the tissue of fictitious events symbolises a terrible and yet somehow a *right* characteristic of the universe. It is too easy (to repeat) to explain away this aspect of tragedy, in terms, let us say, of suppressed sadism or some other unwitting craving.

Perhaps the most impressive of all the ways in which the normal person may sometimes gain a hint of mystical experience is in grave personal danger or pain, or distress of any kind, and even in the agony of pity for one who is loved and is suffering. On such occasions one may find oneself strangely divided. The normal self is strained almost to breaking-point by unbearable terror or pain or compassion; and yet, even in the case of compassion, one sees the dread event as a revealing symbol of reality, and as such one accepts it, not merely with resignation but with a sense that even this is involved in the terrible but somehow *right* nature of the universe. And so, even while one is perhaps behaving with panic terror or horror, one is also, in some strange manner, fundamentally peaceful and glad.

I suggest the following tentative conclusion about this whole subject. In mystical experience, of all sorts from the humblest to the most exalted, the human mind gropingly reaches out to a mode of apprehension very different from all "normal" experience. This kind of apprehension is attained confusedly and precariously by quite a large number of people in the course of normal experiences, though it is seldom recognised as such. A very small number, whose mental development reaches to the extreme limit of human capacity, enjoy a much fuller measure of it, and can know it with much greater clarity and assurance. I suggest further that mystical experience is both one of the most dangerous moral snares and one of the most important sources of moral strength, not only for those who go far in it but also for all normally intelligent and sensitive persons.

But what of the philosophy of mystical experience? How are we to think of it? Is it really a kind of *knowledge,* a peculiar insight into hidden reality? We may perhaps more truly think of it in a somewhat different manner. In every kind of mystical experience, from that most closely associated with normal experience to that which is described by the great mystics, there occurs some kind of self-discipline and some kind of consequent vision. But the vision, I should say, is not most satisfactorily described as a discovery of hidden reality; it is rather a discovery of a new kind of value or worth or excellence or beauty in the normally experienced world. This *rightness* (we have no more satisfactory word) was formerly overlooked, and now suddenly confronts the mind. In fact, mystical experience constitutes essentially a new and more awakened way of *feeling about* the world. But "feeling about" must not be taken to mean a purely subjective attitude. It must mean a subjective attitude which is *appropriate,* objectively justified by, the real nature of the universe in relation to the real nature of the individual mind.

In this theory of mystical experience there is a very serious difficulty. How can the mystical attitude of delighted acceptance of the universe as perfect be reconciled with the moral attitude which distinguishes between good and bad, right and wrong, and recognises an obligation to struggle for the good against the bad, seeking thus to improve a universe which is regarded as very far from perfect? Plainly there is a logical conflict here, and it is useless to pretend that there is not.

I have argued that moral right and wrong depend on the intuited goodness of the free activity of conscious beings, and particularly on the fulfilling of personality-in-community. It almost seems as though the mystic, and the plain man in his rare half-mystical apprehension, had access to another kind of "good," independent of conscious beings, a "good" which somehow embraced ordinary good and evil, right and wrong. This view, it must be admitted, is both unintelligible and dangerous. It is dangerous because it may lead to a complacent acquiescence in the misfortunes of others, as being "all in the picture," all needed for the perfection of the universe.

On the other hand, it is undoubtedly a psychological fact that, in spite of the seeming logical inconsistency, mystical experience does very often clarify the moral consciousness and strengthen moral behaviour. Gautama Buddha, Socrates, Jesus Christ, Mohammed, and, I believe, Spinoza are outstanding examples. It is not impossible that Lenin, too, though he would have been indignant at the suggestion, owed his strength partly to unrecognised mystical experience.

It may be that at the human level of mental development a satisfactory intellectual solution of this conflict between moral protest and mystical acceptance is impossible. But we may grope toward a solution in the following manner. We may regard the human mind as having two aspects. In the one aspect a man is a finite individual; and his concern, his whole duty, is to champion the cause of personality-in-community in the human world. And this human enterprise is probably one minor theme in the universal enterprise of the advancement of the spirit through personality-in-community in a host of worlds. It may be that at some date in the history of the cosmos this enterprise will be fulfilled in the attainment of the perfection of knowing-feeling-striving through the experience of some cosmical society of worlds. Or perhaps this is too trite a way of conceiving the culmination of the cosmical process. Perhaps the spiritual perfection of the cosmos as a whole involves no such triumph of the enterprise of finite minds, but rather their partial defeat, much as the well-being of a living organism involves all sorts of internal, intra-organic conflicts, strains, and partial defeats. Of this we know nothing. But clearly the human individual in one of his aspects feels called to play a minute part in the great widespread struggle for personality-in-community.

Let us suppose, however, that he has also another aspect, in which he finds precarious contact with the eternal and perfected spirit of the cosmos, and in which his will tends to conform to that spirit, in the sense that he is no longer enslaved to the cravings of the separate self, or even to the service of the ideal of personality-in-community, but is able, so to speak, haltingly to feel all things from the universal point of view. In this mode of experience he recognises intuitively that the cosmos *is* an overwhelmingly glorious thing, and that all the struggle and defeat and agony of finite minds, no less than their partial triumph, are justified by the perfection of the whole. He realises that it is foolish and impious to demand that the universe shall be moral, or that the universal spirit shall be moral, or that "God" shall be good. These, he feels, do not exist for the sake of morality. On the contrary, morality exists for them.

In some such manner we may try to cope with the seeming logical conflict between the two fundamental religious experiences: between the moral protest, which seeks to alter the universe, and the ecstatic acceptance of the universe, with all its glory and its shame, its joy and its distress, its beauty, and all its squalor.

But if this intellectual reconciliation is unsound, which it may well be, let us never forget that these two experiences do in fact support one another, and that for the wise conduct of practical life both are needed.

Escapism in Literature

One of three articles Stapledon wrote for F. R. Leavis's Scrutiny *in 1939 and 1940, "Escapism in Literature" is his most extensive published discussion of the nature of literature and a useful compendium of the principles that underlie his own fiction.*

WE OFTEN HEAR IT SAID DISPARAGINGLY that some writer or other is a mere "escapist," or that a particular piece of writing is sheer "escapism." It is implied that the true function of literature is, not to offer escape from unpleasant facts, but to help the reader to face up to reality, and cope with it successfully. On the other hand we are told by many of those who are interested in the theory of art that the proper function of all art, and therefore of literature, is "cathartic," that it should purge the spirit of pent-up forces which cannot express themselves in actual life, that it should afford symbolic fulfilment to our starved needs. Through art these pent-up forces are said to obtain "release." Sometimes it is claimed that, by diverting attention from the sordid actuality, art constructs symbols of a deeper reality, more consonant with the spirit's real needs.

What degree of truth is there in these seemingly opposed views? It must, I think, be admitted that there is, indeed, a vice which may appropriately be called "escapism." Besides "release," literature has another function, which cannot be called release save in a very far-fetched manner. The charge of escapism, I shall argue, is justified only when this other function, though ostensibly fulfilled, is as a matter of fact evaded.

In order to defend this opinion I must say briefly what in my view literature is, and what its relation is to the rest of human life. One who is not a literary critic ought perhaps to refrain from discussing this subject, particularly in a literary journal. The expert may be able to show either that my categories are false or that my whole view has been stated long ago, and much more aptly. However, when fools rush in, they may with their mangled remains pave the way for angels.

Literature is the expression of thoughts and feelings in words; but obviously not all writing is literature in the strict sense. All writing takes effect by affording expression or fulfilment, direct or symbolical, to human needs. Every kind of need, simple or subtle, moral or immoral, may be grist to the mill of literature; but there is one kind of need, and one kind of satisfaction, which literature must to some extent fulfill. In order to be literature, a piece of writing, I should say, must satisfy the impulse for the clarification and development, and also, of course, the expression, of experience itself. For example, it must afford fulfilment not only to romantic love or the love of nature but also to the need to be more precisely and vividly aware of these experiences. Even if many of the needs which gain expression in writing are unconscious needs, the writing is not literature unless it affords something more than unconscious symbolical fulfilment of those needs. It must also satisfy the need for precise and vivid consciousness of all that is available to conscious inspection. If it can actually extend the frontiers of consciousness into the territory of the unconscious, so much the better.

This need to clarify and develop experience, then, seems to me the essential motive and the essential import of all that is genuine literature. By "clarification" I mean the detailed clarification of familiar modes of experience. By "development" I mean the development of new and more subtle modes. This distinction, though not absolute, is useful. Out of this need for clarification and development of experience springs the need for accuracy or efficiency of expression, and therefore for pregnancy and economy and coherence of expression. Efficiency of expression, though at first instrumental, comes to be valued intrinsically, and is, indeed, one of the main sources of literary delight. But to regard literature as solely concerned with efficiency of expression, no matter what experiences are expressed, is surely mistaken. The question as to what *kind* of experience is expressed is not irrelevant. The efficient expression of trivial experiences cannot fully satisfy the essential motive of literature, which is not only the clarification but the development of consciousness. There are then two criteria by which literature is to be judged, but one is primary and entails the other. The primary criterion is the significance of the subject-matter in relation to the demand for the intensifying, clarifying, broadening, deepening, and unifying of experience, and the development of new modes of experience. The other criterion is the efficiency of expression by which this end is pursued. This distinction, however, is to some extent misleading, since the effort for efficiency of expression does not merely convey experience to the reader, but actually creates, in some degree, new capacities for experience in the writer's own mind.

I am assuming that there is a real difference between the relatively superficial and the relatively penetrating kinds of experience, and again between the relatively narrow or dissociated and the relatively comprehensive or integrated kinds. This distinction seems to be implied in nearly all serious literary criticism, and indeed in nearly all educational theory. Also we constantly employ it in our judgments of the calibre of our acquaintances. In my view, it lies at the foundation of a sound social philosophy.

Of course in practice we often violently disagree as to what constitutes the more clarified or the more developed experience or behaviour. But in the abstract, the development of experience seems to involve progress in respect of more penetrating and comprehensive awareness of the self and the world (including other selves), and more appropriate and creative feeling and striving in relation to the character of self and world. This formula, no doubt, is very controversial, particularly in respect of the meaning of "appropriate." But both in literature and in our daily practical lives it is assumed that feelings and actions can, in some important sense, be appropriate or inappropriate to objective situations. The essential function of literature, then, is to render experience cognitively more true and affectively and conatively more appropriate.

One of its subsidiary functions is to afford symbolical satisfaction to extant conscious or unconscious needs which do not obtain adequate satisfaction in actual life. These needs may be of any degree of development, from simple animal functions, such as rest, muscular activity, and physical sex, to capacities which emerge only on the distinctively human level, or at the extreme upper reach of human nature. Somewhere in the human category we must include, for instance, capacities for self-conscious and other-conscious personal intercourse, for intellectual comprehension, for aesthetic appreciation, and for a religious "coming to terms with the universe." All these needs may demand "release" in literature.

Since all literature, to be literature at all, must in some manner clarify experience, we may say that all literature must be to some significant extent "creative." I say "significant" because obviously there is a trivial sense in which every fresh statement is "creative." It causes *something* to happen in the mind of the reader, and in the mind of the writer himself. In this sense even the extremely familiar proposition $2 + 2 = 4$ is "creative." But when Keats said, "Beauty is truth, truth beauty," he produced something creative in a more significant sense. Even though, as I believe, this famous pronouncement is more false than true, it came, presumably, as something of a revelation to the poet and to his readers. It was a growing point for far-reaching new experiences in men's minds.

For our present purpose we may distinguish between four types of literature. Any particular work is likely to have aspects or passages characteristic of all four types, but it may also be predominantly of one type rather than another. Though all literature is to some extent creative, I shall call the first of these types distinctively "creative literature." The others are "propaganda literature," "release literature" and "escape literature."

In "creative literature" the dominant motive and the main import are creative. In the writer's own mind the producing of the work is a creative experience; and in the reader's mind, the reading. "Release" and propaganda in creative literature may play subsidiary parts, but they are made to serve the essential literary function of clarifying and developing consciousness, of world or self. In so far as this process is cognitive, it will consist in an apprehending of fresh aspects of world or self, or of hitherto unnoticed relationships between things remote from one another. Or it may take the form of constructing universes of fiction which symbolize aspects of the actual universe. In so far as it is mainly affective and conative, it will consist in the evoking of new appreciations, and in the creation of new and more developed capacities for action.

"Propaganda literature" must be distinguished from mere propaganda, in which there is nothing significantly creative. The writer of mere propaganda is concerned simply to popularize facts, ideas, and emotions with which he is familiar. He uses *clichés* and slogans to produce the desired effect on the minds of his public. The cause which he is serving may happen to be good or bad, momentous or trivial. Of course efficient propaganda in a good cause does produce a development of experience in the public, and is therefore in a sense creative. But in the writer himself, it is not an expression of developing experience, and the activity of producing it does not further develop his experience. However well he does his job, he is merely using sound advertising technique. But in propaganda that is literature the idea to be propagated is still alive and growing in the writer's own mind. It is a creative influence irradiating and transforming his experience. He is dominated by it, possessed by it. It is a growing shoot which ramifies through his mind. And since he has also an aptitude for verbal expression, he is able to communicate to his public not merely certain ideas, dried and salted and conveniently packed, but a potion which may transform their whole attitude to life. In so far as he does his work efficiently, his efficiency is not that of the advertiser but that of the artist, whether he uses the direct method of expression and exhortation, as Ruskin did, or the indirect method of fiction, like Dickens. In either case, and whether the message is true or false, the whole texture of his work will be in the strict sense literature, although its dominant motive is not the developing of experience simply for its own sake.

By literature of release, or "release literature," I mean literature in which the dominant motive and main import are neither creation nor propaganda but simply the assuagement of starved needs, the release of pent-up forces in the personality. Now "creative literature" also affords release to pent-up forces, but it uses these "releases" in such ways as to serve its main purpose of clarifying and developing consciousness. Whereas "creative literature" may evoke, and also express and satisfy, new and more developed capacities, pure "release literature" does nothing of the sort. It merely assuages familiar needs. In this there is nothing creative. Writing which does no more than afford symbolical satisfaction to extant needs cannot be literature. But there is a kind of writing in which, though the main import is sheer "release," the manner in which the release is obtained is one which includes a great deal of genuine, though minor and incidental, creation. Thus there are romances, detective stories, thrillers, poems, *belles lettres*, which, though essentially concerned with "release," are written with such originality of perception and expression that they have a really quickening effect.

It may, I think, be truly said that, whereas literature of the predominantly creative type generally tends to undermine or transform the conventional system of ideas and values, "release literature" in the main accepts them, tacitly and inadvertently. It is creative only in its detailed illustration of the fashionable ideology. There is one purely "release" motive, however, which expresses itself in iconoclasm, and dominates a good deal of "release literature" in our day. Those who have been seriously irked by authority may develop a need for revolt for its own sake. Those who have suffered under an insincere puritanical morality may crave to deny morality altogether, or to transpose the old ideas of good and evil into their opposites.

A great deal of genuine literature is in the main "release literature." And of course an immense amount of writing which is not literature at all is mainly or wholly concerned with "release." Even in literature, "release" is a quite legitimate function. Incidentally release was probably literature's original office, or the office of that which was later to develop into literature. When wish-fulfilment was sought through magic incantation or bardic stories of the deeds of heroes, the seed of literature was sown. In modern times much poetry (not of the first rank) and many good novels have "release" as their main function, witting or unwitting. Rightly we go to literature for symbolical fulfilment of our thwarted capacities, for our craving for adventure, for triumph, for sexual romance, for peace and contemplation, and so on. Literature of the lighter sort, which is dominated by "release," may be wholesome both for the writer and the reader, provided that it does not purport to be more creative than it is. Purgation is a necessary function. Moreover the incidental and minor creative power of "release literature" may benefit a wider public than that which is capable of appreciating literature of a more far-reachingly creative type.

"Escape literature" is less easy to define. And since it is superficially very like "release literature," there may be great difficulty in deciding whether a particular piece of writing is essentially "release" or "escape." To say that anyone is an "escapist" is to charge him with shunning unpleasant reality. Instead of recognizing and grappling with the facts, he either withdraws into some safe corner, where he can live in peace and occupy himself with activities unrelated to the vital struggles of his contemporary world; or else, unable to find actual escape, he solaces himself by constructing a dream world wherein he can live "in imagination," a world after his own heart's desire. "Escape literature," then, should be literature the main import of which is to protect the mind from unpleasant reality. This essential notion needs qualifying so as to bring it in line with the central ideas of this essay.

In the first place, "escape literature," to be literature at all, must of course be in some way significantly creative. Even if its main import is escape from some intolerable aspect of reality, it must in some respect genuinely clarify experience. It may do this by the detailed texture of its thought and expression. It may do it even through its intention as a whole. For instance, even if it constitutes a symbol falsely claiming to be true of reality, the presentation of the symbol may constitute a genuinely creative experience by opening up vistas of possibility. Further, while all literature is to a greater or lesser extent concerned with "release," in "escape literature" release is used with the ulterior motive of escape. It is so employed as to make the fictitious world more attractive and more seeming-real.

From one point of view "escape literature" is a special kind of "propaganda literature," since its main import is to advocate certain ideas and values. There is, however, this difference. In "propaganda literature" the motive is conscious, whereas in "escape literature" it is mainly unconscious. The escape motive is generally an unrecognized fear, which causes an unwitting incapacity to face up to reality. A morbid blindness, a self-protective and perversely creative blindness, not only blots out the obnoxious aspect of reality but also reconstructs the remaining characters into a coherent and lying image. This is the essence of escapism. Even in escape fiction the fantasy, which is in fact a false fantasy, purports to be in some significant manner symbolically true of the real world of men and things.

"Escape literature" may include a great deal of genuine creation, but its main purport is the reverse of creative. It tends to prevent the development of experience, to prevent the mind from facing up to some unpleasant but important aspect of reality. The creative power of the writer is prostituted for an unnatural end, namely to frustrate creation, to distract attention from the way of development. Thus, quite apart from any question of morality, from the purely literary point of view "escape literature" is a debased kind of literature, since it involves a gross limitation of sensibility and an insincere use of creative power. And from the moral point of view "escape literature" is bad because it tends to prevent men from facing up to urgent moral problems.

Of the four kinds of literature, or the four kinds of import which any writing may have, I judge "creation" (as defined) wholly good and "escape" wholly bad. In the case of propaganda, moral judgment depends on the goodness of the end preached. Even from a literary point of view propaganda for a bad end, however well done, is to be condemned in so far as it involves a restriction of consciousness to prevent the badness of the bad end from being perceived.

"Release," as we have seen, is harmless or actually desirable. No doubt, to spend a life-time writing "release literature" is to deny one-self the greater experiences; but this is true of any respectable and absorbing work. No doubt the writing of "release literature" may be used to distract the mind from duties; but so may any pursuit. No doubt "release literature" may be handed out to the young or to the populace to divert them from discovering that society is heading for disaster. On the other hand, the more unsatisfactory a society, the more urgent is it that there should be effective means for "release," so that harassed individuals may so far as possible preserve their mental health. The condemnation of pure "release" is not to be justified except when release becomes an addiction or obsession, so that energy which might be used constructively is frittered away. The fact that such addiction to release does so often occur is no reason to censure release as such. In a society which is ripening for revolutionary change pure "release" is apt to be condemned by the revolutionaries, and regarded as escapism, because it distracts attention from social ills, and thus prevents the gathering of pent-up energy for the revolutionary explosion. But for the individual's mental health, "release" is necessary. And the more exacting a man's life, the more necessary is it that he should have some diversion. Further, the more specialized his work, the more is there in him that needs release. To deny him release is to turn him into a neurotic, a puritan or a fanatic.

So far I have merely discussed in the abstract four possible kinds of import in literature. Is this classification of any practical service? Does it refer to objective characters which literary works actually have? And if so, how are these characters to be detected?

I must leave to literary critics the task of finding out how to assess the creative function of literary works. The fact that the critics so often disagree among themselves does not disturb me. Anything so subtle as the quickening of human minds is bound to be excessively difficult to estimate. To deny that the clarification and development of consciousness is the main function of literature is, in my view, to make nonsense of literary criticism.

The assessing of the "escape" element in literature cannot be left wholly to the literary critics. The psychologists and sociologists ought to have something to say about it. I hazard a few remarks. The distressing situation which gives rise to escapist activity may be peculiar to the individual, or it may be something inherent in a group or in society as a whole. The extreme case of individual escapism is neurotic fantasy, such as the delusion of grandeur or of persecution, or the symbolical satisfaction of unconscious cravings for mother-love or for triumph over the father. No doubt neurosis in one form or another has often contributed to the creative power of literature. A hidden conflict may goad the mind into vigorous action. Frustration in actual life may strengthen the life of imagination. In spheres of experience that are not blacked out by the repression, neurosis may quicken sensibility and intelligence. And sometimes the result may be great literature; but only in so far as the main import of the work is *not* neurotic and *not* simply "escape."

For there seem to be two possible reactions to trouble in the unconscious. One course is to acquiesce in the repression, to avoid recognizing that *something* or other is amiss, and to allow the hidden conflict to work upon consciousness without criticism, in fact to give rein to fantasy and spin sweet dreams of wish-fulfilment. In literature this results in typical works of "release"; or, if the fantasy purports to be symbolically true of reality, the product is typical "escape literature." The other course is to try, however vainly, to probe the self so as to lay bare and solve the hidden conflict, and to see it in its true relation to the rest of the universe. The effort to do this, though it cannot fully succeed in its task, may well produce great creative literature. In "escape literature," on the other hand, there is no self-probing, save in safe regions, not inflamed by the hidden conflict; and no attempt to relate the self's torture to the rest of existence. The resulting work, even if it is executed with literary skill and with a blinkered kind of creative imagination, is in essence merely a protective fiction, falsely purporting to be a true symbol of reality.

The word "escapism" generally implies flight not from individual but from social troubles. In particular, those whose political opinions are well to the Left, use it to disparage all writing which might distract attention from the need for social change. I have already noted that much which is thus condemned is merely release literature. But undoubtedly there is a great deal of writing, and some of it is literature, which is indeed escapist in the social sense. The criterion of such writing is that its main import is to persuade the reader and the writer himself that after all there is not much wrong with the existing social order, or that God is backing it, and that certain conventional and outworn ideas and valuations, adequate in an earlier phase of society, are also adequate to-day. It was said above that "release literature" tacity and inadvertently accepts conventional ideas and values. "Escape literature" does more than this. It actively asserts them, and at least by implication denies the newer ideas which are appropriate to a changed social situation. I should expect the historian of literature to be able to point to typical "escape" works in all the periods of far-reaching social and cultural change.

Escapism of the Right is not the only kind of escapism. A great deal of ardent Left Wing writing is itself, I believe, inspired by the need for escape. Of course its import is to escape from a very different aspect of reality from that which is shunned by escapism of the Right. It affords cover not from the need for social revolution but from the need for a revolution in the mind of the writer himself. For revolutionary ardour, though it may and often does spring from genuine zeal to found a better world, sometimes has a very different root. There is a familiar psychological principle according to which unconscious guilt and unconscious inferiority may cause a conscious "projection" of guilt and inferiority upon some scape-goat. In a good deal of Left Wing writing the discerning critic may find evidence that the author uses the wicked capitalists or the bourgeois class or economic determinism or dialectical materialism as scape-goats to bear the burden of his own sin, or as excuses for his own mental and moral flabbiness. He has in fact constructed, though with an air of "stark realism," a fictitious world, which, superficially so like the reality, is false in the same way as the neurotic's delusion is false. It is a dream world. The main import of it is to afford him and his readers a sense that their personal flabbiness and ineffectiveness are the product of forces beyond their control. Whereas for the reactionary escapist true salvation lies in facing the fact that the existing social order and his own part in it are unhealthy and immoral, for the Left escapist it lies in recognizing that his motive for condemning the social order is not as disinterested as he believes. Both are seeking escape from a personal moral challenge; but whereas in the one case the moral imperative is, "Do something about the social order," in the other it may be metaphorically expressed as, "Do something about the state of your own soul."

Left escapism is but a special case of the escapism which characterizes so much of modern "scientific" culture. Accepting the temper of our age, we tend to withdraw attention from the inner life, and to seek escape from individual moral responsibility by constructing a fictitious world in which individuals are wholly the product of external forces, physical or social.

Literature and the Unity of Man

During the 1940s Stapledon was an active member, and elected to the executive committee of the British chapter, of P.E.N., the writers' association. He frequently addressed its international congresses, most of which were held in London during World War II. "Literature and the Unity of Man" was Stapledon's contribution to the 1941 P.E.N. Congress, whose theme was Writers in Freedom. Although usually associated with galactic immensities and a style of impersonal detachment from human affairs, Stapledon here draws attention to the writer as shaped by and speaking in the voice of his own regional and national identity.

IN WHAT WAY, if at all, can writers create mutual understanding and sympathy between peoples; or between social classes, or individuals of different vocation, or of different psychological type? Should writers even try to use their special powers deliberately for this end?

Some writers hold that, however urgent human unity is, literature has no direct concern with it. The writer, in this view, should simply develop as fully as possible the potentialities of his own peculiar experience, gained in personal intercourse, in practical life, in parochial lore, in his national culture, and so on. It is no more his business, we are told, to work deliberately for the harmony of the race than it is the business of the engineer or the agricultural labourer. Of course, in the nature of the case, some literature will, as a matter of fact, influence the race towards harmony, but more or less accidentally. The outstanding literary works of one people will be read by some of the educated among other peoples, for the sake of their common human value, or through the craving of intelligent minds to assimilate alien modes of experience. But very few men will ever attain more than a superficial insight into an alien literature, because literature is essentially an expression of a certain idiom, an idiom not merely of language but of thought and feeling; in fact an idiom of living. Consequently, in this view it is far better for writers to devote themselves single-mindedly to their special task than to impoverish their work by trying to make it intelligible to all men. Even when the aim of literature is to symbolize rather the universal fundamental human experiences, such as love and hate, it cannot do so save by drawing upon the minute particulars of the writer's own life. And his life is bound to be confined, in the main, to some small section of the life of the human race. A writer may be superficially a cosmopolitan. He may spend much of his time in travel, and in absorbing foreign cultures. He may have access to more than one social class. But unless he is firmly rooted in one particular national culture and the tradition of one social or vocational class, his experience will be superficial and his writing shallow. To attain insight into all the modes of human life and mentality is as impossible as to attain personal intimacy with all the individuals of a great society. Without personal intimacy, without prolonged intercourse with a few personal friends and fewer beloveds, a man's awareness of human nature must be shallow. Similarly without daily intimate contact with some particular social tradition he cannot write anything but banal generalities.

In this view James Joyce did well to load his work with subtle allusions to the life of a little western city that few Europeans ever visit. Dante did well to crowd the Divine Comedy with Florentine notables. For only in so doing could each give concrete and significant expression to such experience as he himself had gained.

I agree that literature of this kind is of great value to the race as a whole; is after all a contribution not merely to local or sectional but to human culture. I agree, too, that for those who have linguistic facility and a special bent for the study of foreign cultures it is abundantly worthwhile to spend much time and energy in gaining as deep an insight as possible into such topical and idiomatic great works. But not all of us have the aptitude or the opportunity. I speak with feeling, for I myself happen to be a very bad linguist and a very obtuse reader. In early days I struggled through the Divine Comedy, missing, I have no doubt, nine-tenths of its meaning. At a later stage I was told to read the French Imagists. I gained about as much understanding of Laforgue's subtle but alien world as an astronomer wins from the planet Mars by looking at it through a field-glass. My difficulty was not merely linguistic. For I read Joyce's *Ulysses*, delighting in the temper of it, but intelligently appreciating very little. I now read our contemporary English poets, again strangely enjoying the rhythm, the sensuous quality, and the mental mode of their works; but intelligently appreciating, alas, how little! For they, like the Surrealist painters, are apt to deal in odd personal associations or the jargon of a particular clique, or again in erudition in which I have no share. God forbid that, just because stupid people cannot follow them, they should cease to write their pregnant cross-word puzzles. For I recognize that pregnant their works often are. Sometimes I have been privileged to have a modern poem minutely explained to me by the author, and sometimes the result has been for me wonderfully illuminating; not, be it noted, when the elucidation has given me merely oddities of personal or parochial association, or cliquish jargon, but when the strange juxtaposition of words, and of images, has opened up for me fair new vistas of experience. To gain such experience is certainly worthwhile, for the individual seeking self-increase. And, of course, there is no way to reach facility in this appreciation save long practice in watching the poet's mind jump, so to speak, from image to image in unexpected, idiosyncratic directions.

But excellent as this kind of literature is in itself, valuable as it is for those who have the gifts and the opportunity to appreciate it, its direct contribution to human unity must at present be very slight. If I, a middle-class intellectual, who speak the same language as our modern English poets, cannot properly understand them without help, what hope has a French peasant, a German engineer, a Chinese soldier? Difficult modern poems may, no doubt, contribute to human unity indirectly. They may chance to influence Chinese students of English culture, and these in turn may influence the thought and feeling of the Chinese people.

But is there no more direct and effective way in which writers can work for human unity?

Some, who care more for human unity than for human diversity, and very little for literature, would like to sacrifice national idiosyncrasy and national literature entirely. They desire a single, universal language, perhaps an artificial one, and a world-literature written in that language. Probably there will, indeed, come a time when all men will speak one language and have one literature. But it is to be hoped that this will not happen till the diverse riches of the present national cultures have been absorbed and transmuted into the new world culture. For man can ill afford to lose any of his diversity. The uncompromising cosmopolitans, however, assure us that there will be ample diversity within the new world-culture, a diversity not of mere tribal customs but of temperamental and vocational points of view among men all of whom speak the same language and share the same basic thought-forms. True, indeed! But meanwhile? How can writers in the national tongues work for human unity?

Before facing this question I wish to form a more precise idea of the kind of unity that is desirable for man. What is *not* desirable is uniformity, whether within the individual mind or in a society. I assume that the goal for the individual mind should be the fuller development of his particular human powers, in fact his capacity for being an awakened and unified personality. He must avoid two opposite psychological dangers. One is disunity, the mental dissociation of experiences from one another in water-tight compartments; in fact, multiple personality. The other danger is the barren impoverished unity of the "one-track mind." In this state no experience can be assimilated which does not conform to the simple dominating pattern. The rest falls off like water off a duck's back. Clearly what is desirable for the individual is unity *in diversity*, the integration of as much diversity as possible. He should be capable of many *kinds* of experience, many moods, many activities. The more the better, so long as each is accessible to the others. For each should illuminate and enhance the others. This aim clearly demands that he should receive and assimilate impressions from other individuals, different in character from himself; and from other social traditions different from his own. And clearly literature should be a powerful agent for deepening, broadening, unifying his experience; at the very least within the limits set by his own language and national culture.

In the case of society also the goal is unity in diversity, as great a diversity as possible, so long as the individuals and groups within the society, whatever their differences and conflicts, can appreciate one another's common humanity and accept the basis of their society. It is a privilege of the human species to attain greater diversity than any other species; particularly, greater mental diversity. It is another privilege that men, when they are being truly human, can to some extent appreciate their differences; that instead of being thrown into conflict by them, they can, to some extent, not merely tolerate them but actually gain mutual enrichment from them. Mutual awareness, of the sort which breeds mutual respect, mutual responsibility and mutual enrichment, I take to be the distinctively human way of social behaviour. It is unfortunately rare; for man is at heart still largely sub-human. Only where there is personal contact of receptive outward-feeling minds, is it fairly easy to attain the human kind of social behaviour, at least in a moderate degree. Where there is little or no personal contact, for instance, between members of large groups, and between large groups themselves, whether nations, classes, vocations, the genuinely human social-relationship is rare.

It is natural to hope that literature should be an instrument for creating this desirable unity-in-diversity among men. But though literature can certainly bring men together if they are not very far apart, it cannot easily bridge very great mental differences. The problem is this. Literature must have its roots in concrete living, in minute particular experiences. To be vital, to be deeply significant, it must be very concrete and idiomatic. But the more idiomatic it is, the less intelligible it is to those who have not been shaped to that particular idiom of living. Every writer's work falls in this respect between two extremes, two ideal limits. On the one hand there is the writing in which the idiom of language and of experience is intelligible to no one at all but the author himself; on the other, that which sacrifices idiom and concreteness entirely to universal intelligibility. Near the one extreme lie some intensely national or provincial works, and those which are transfused with the idiom of some particular social class or section of society. This is essentially literature of the parish pump, significant for the parishioners, barren for the "foreigners" of the next village, or nation. Near the other extreme I should place the more banal kind of hymns and popular songs, but also those great, though almost universally intelligible writings, such as certain passages in the Bible, which have contributed to the mental texture of many millions. This is the true literature of our common humanity; though the scope even of this is limited by the fact that men speak different languages, and translation can never be fully adequate. These writings deal with experiences which are possible to all men, and in a manner intelligible to all men. Inevitably, therefore, they sacrifice the particular to the general, at least to some extent. Their greatness consists in their doing this without falling into vague generality, platitude, insipidity. Their success, I take it, depends partly on the sheer skill of the writer, partly on the *kind* of human needs or experiences which they express. If the matter itself is trivial, or if it has already been over-emphasized, so that its expression is inevitably hackneyed, then the result is failure. If, on the other hand, the subject-matter is of great human importance, particularly if the writing brings to light deep and obscure needs, it may have great effect. Indeed, if those needs are blindly striving for fulfilment in a world-situation which is unpropitious to all men, then, I take it, the gifted writer may express them in a form powerfully significant to multitudes.

The function of literature, I suppose, is to deepen and broaden, and to integrate human experience. It should make the reader, in one way or another, either more minutely or more comprehensively conscious of his world, or of himself, or of other selves. It should, of course, clarify not only understanding but also, and more particularly, feeling. It should fit the reader for more delicately graded and coherent action in the world. Pascal and Mr. Aldous Huxley insist that a man is many conflicting selves, and that he should not try to force them all into a single mould. No doubt there is truth in this view. Let no mood be simply repressed. Let each have its say. But surely dissociation, sheer multiple personality, is a pitiable condition. Let each mood, so far as possible, be sympathetically aware of, and integrated with, all the others, so that the result is a single many-faceted personality, unified under a coherent dominating sentiment or *Weltanschauung*. And similarly with society. Diversity of individual psychological types and of groups, such as social classes and nations, we emphatically need, if we are to avoid an impoverished, mass-produced uniformity; but our diversity must at all costs be unified under some great unifying idea. Otherwise we shall be for ever racked with irreconcilable conflicts. No doubt, conflicts of some kind are very necessary for the health of society. Only in conflict do we become fully alive, and wring the best out of ourselves. But it is important that conflict should be subordinate to an underlying unity of purpose.

Writers, I suggest, have a special responsibility in this connection, one which in the past they have, indeed, often fulfilled, though more or less carelessly. To-day some are realizing that in this time of desperate need the responsibility should be accepted very seriously and fulfilled with conscious purpose.

There seem to be two ways in which writers can fulfill this responsibility. One is by doing all in their power to help the various sections of mankind to know and respect one another. The other way is to think out and express with all the skill and passion at their command the great unifying idea which we now so urgently need.

To help the sections of mankind to know one another, some writers might sometimes write deliberately for a foreign public; in fact they might, and some already do to some extent, function as cultural *liaison officers* between their own culture and some particular foreign culture of which they have sufficient knowledge. The aim would be to transmit to their chosen foreign people or class as much as possible of the temper, values, ideals, thought-forms and mode of life of their own people or class. They would write, of course, in their own language, but with special care for lucidity. They would deal largely in turns of thought and expression common to the two peoples; but also they would be at pains to introduce the idiom of their own people in such a way that the sensitive foreign reader would be able to "jump to it" in the course of his reading. Their writing might sometimes take the form of fiction specially suited to their purpose. Sometimes they would produce essays and discussions on the history and prevailing temper of the two peoples. Sometimes there might be a correspondence of open letters between writers representative of the two peoples, or of several peoples. One can even imagine a series of symbolic love-letters exchanged between such national literary mouthpieces. One can imagine, too, in this present time of suffering, letters of mutual greeting and encouragement smuggled across the frontiers and circulated from hand to hand.

The other way in which writers can fulfill their responsibility is perhaps the more important. They can earnestly think out and compellingly express in every channel available to them that great unifying idea toward which already all thinking men and women are groping. This great new idea is at bottom a very ancient idea, but it needs new expression, couched in our modern idiom, significant to our modern minds; and purged of many ancient errors. It is the idea that the more sensitive, more awakened and lucid, more coherent and integrated way of living is intrinsically right and beautiful. This the writers know to be so. They know it in their hearts, if they are worth their salt. Some have already borne witness to this idea in glorious words and deeds. It is time for us all to escape from the chilly shadow of scepticism about this fundamental value, of scepticism born of a still only adolescent, though brilliant, natural science and of an already senile commercialism. Let us more purposefully, more uncompromisingly, more unashamedly than in recent times, proclaim not only the unity of man, but the absolute rightness and beauty of that way of experience and action which we all in our more lucid states and in our distinctive manners falteringly pursue. Let us, in fact, even we moderns, proclaim the spirit.

Some Thoughts on H. G. Wells's *You Can't Be Too Careful*

Throughout the 1930s and the early 1940s, when he and Wells were in frequent correspondence, Stapledon often reviewed Wells's new work or made reference to it in his own books—notably in Waking World *(1934). Stapledon was often referred to as a Wellsian, but both in private and in public he took pains to emphasize those issues on which they parted company. While he continued to admire Wells's utopianism and to envy his ability to influence a world-wide audience, Stapledon was uneasy with what he saw as Wells's rigid materialism and the cynicism that seeped into the books of his old age. The 1942 review of* You Can't Be Too Careful *in* Plan, *the journal of the*

Progressive League, marked the end of what had become an increasingly frayed relationship.

I AM NOT ATTEMPTING to review this book as a novel, but simply to consider it as an expression of Wells's attitude to mankind. The central idea is that we are a half-developed species, not a finished product of evolution. "We are a lowly and infantile breed. There is hardly a quadruped in the Zoo that is not more modified, evolved, distinguished and finished than ourselves." The primates branched early from the main mammalian stock, and they retain many primitive characters, for instance a relatively profound metamorphosis during adolescence, and the remains of a lunar sex cycle underlying the more developed solar one. More significant, I suggest, is that man's most distinctive character, his very complex and integrated brain, shows signs of imperfection and instability, and is comparable rather to the pterodactyl's wing than to the bird's perfected organ.

"The genus *Homo*," says Wells, has "blundered along dismally and dirtily" since its beginning. Man is today a "disagreeable and suicidally backward animal." But each generation is far worse than it might be if its circumstances were less frustrating. Has man got it in him to grapple with his environment resolutely and wisely enough to produce the conditions which could raise him to a higher level of development? Wells holds that man's nature is primarily self-seeking. He "has been forced into an uncongenial social life in the brief course of a million years or so. Yet still his fundamental nature remains. Still he wants to feel successful, masterful, lord and owner of all he surveys." Therefore, if men are to succeed in overthrowing their present damaging social system and the blind privileged class which controls it, they will do so "not in any mood of love or that sort of thing, but because they hate the pomp and glories of incapable authority." Not for love but for the satisfaction of getting their own back against tyrants men will combine for action, and if necessary sacrifice their lives. Resentment, Wells believes, has always been the effective source of revolutionary passion.

Jesus Christ was resentful. A more obvious case is Lenin. But Wells sees that if revolution springs from resentment, still a stable community needs "religion." By this word he means "the binding system of ideas and practices which holds a community together." And "the religion a world-community needs is a very simple one," namely, "a dogmatic assertion of the supreme duty of outspoken truth, of the common ownership of the earth and the equal rights of man."

Wells's view of man seems to me to need qualification. Social feeling, if we may believe the Sutties, is not simply derivative from self-feeling; and anyhow self-regard is not quite so exclusive as Wells believes. Our species is, indeed, half-developed; but the hero of this novel, E. A. Tewler, who is meant to be a symbol true essentially of the whole species in actual conditions, is a misleading though brilliant caricature. The book is a skilfully executed diagram of *one* immensely important aspect of human nature, but there is another aspect, equally important. Swarms of people are, indeed, predominantly Tewler, but my own experience of men and women forces me to recognise that very few are sheer Tewler. Wells allows that human beings have an innate *possibility* of being something more than Tewler, a possibility that has been completely frustrated by circumstances; but somehow he cannot see that they manifest in their actual behaviour something which, we are expressly told, Tewler never did manifest, and none of our species ever can manifest in existing conditions. Tewler "never in the whole course of his life really loved or felt honest, generous friendship for any human being such as the codes of our literary tradition require. That demands an amount of deliberate mental synthesis of which his early up-bringing and education had already rendered him incapable." In my experience this statement is simply not true of the ordinary people whom Tewler is meant to symbolise. We are of course very often wrong-headed, self-centred, mean, cruel and morally feeble; but in spite of shockingly unpropitious circumstances we do also occasionally, within our pathetically narrow limits, behave with real generosity and moral courage. Indeed in a small way, and if the strain is not too great, we frequently do so. Moreover even quite ordinary people in exceptional circumstances may rise far beyond this. To overlook this aspect of human nature is to misrepresent human nature just as seriously as the sentimentalists do.

This capacity for genuine respect for one another *as persons*, for comradeship, love or what you will, offers the only solid foundation for the religion which Wells himself postulates for the stable world-society. It must also play an important part in any desirable revolution. Jesus and his followers were not *merely* resentful. Lenin's fire was kindled, no doubt, by indignation against the power that killed his brother; but indignation in him and his followers sprang in turn from a passion of comradeship, which means respect for the individuality of the common man. And it is very unlikely that the desired revolution will be brought to fruition simply by resentment, because it will demand an amount of sustained self-abnegation which mere resentment can never produce. Wells's commendable determination to see man without rose-coloured spectacles has led him to adopt a jaundiced pair instead. The truth surely is that both personal resentment and a disinterested passion of comradeship, not only in a resolute minority but to some extent in the majority also, has an important part to play. Further, it is only under the pressure of changing circumstances that this change of heart will arise; but, on the other hand, only through the beginnings of a change of heart can a force be generated for the purposeful reshaping of the environment.

Social Implications of Atomic Power

Like many others in August 1945, Stapledon learned of the destruction of Hiroshima from a radio broadcast. He was horrified, although the news did not take him completely by surprise. He had imagined a first atomic test, the use of atomic weapons in war, and the destruction of human civilization by an accidental chain-reaction in his first work of fiction, Last and First Men. *In sketching a hopeful future for the social uses of the split atom, Stapledon drew on his long career, since 1912, of teaching the history of industrialism in courses given through the Workers' Educational Association. And in imagining how the quality of daily life might be ameliorated by atomic energy, he refurbished ideas advanced in his broadcasts of the 1930s, "The Remaking of Man" and "Machinery and Labour."*

DURING THE BATTLE OF BRITAIN, when it seemed likely that the Nazis would conquer this island, we used to wonder seriously whether our typical English society was really to cease for ever. And because of its new precariousness, we began to cherish it more poignantly, instead of taking it for granted. That dangerous corner was turned. And later, when the German war was obviously won, we realised with thankfulness that, after all, things would go on. Later still came the dropping of the first atomic bomb. When I heard the announcement on the radio, I was flung back into that sense of the precariousness of all good things. This time the prospect was not simply the ending of the English way of life but the ending of civilisation, perhaps the final ruin of mankind. Surely this discovery of titanic might had come too soon. Man was not yet fit to be trusted with it. Moreover, the manner in which the bombs were used seemed to me shocking and irresponsible. No doubt, by hastening the end of the war, they probably reduced the total number of Allied and Enemy casualties; but how easily a demonstration of their power could have been given without dropping the very first one on a city.

J. B. S. Haldane recently made an interesting suggestion. There might, he said, be a general law of nature that any intelligent species which learned to use atomic power before it had unified its world must destroy itself. I should put the matter rather differently. To avoid self-destruction, I should say, any species that wins atomic power must have a firmer grasp of true values and, therefore, a stronger will for world-community, than mankind has to-day. Our only hope is that, just as the Battle of Britain wakened the inhabitants of this island to a more vivid communal feeling, so the hideous danger of the prostitution of atomic power may force mankind to will world-community more earnestly than before. The hope may be slender, but one thing encourages it. Never before has so grim a danger threatened the human race as a whole. We are all in the same boat together, and we all know it. In an atomic war the victors, if there are any, will suffer almost as much as the vanquished. In face of this unique common danger perhaps the peoples of the world will at last be forced to co-operate.

At the moment the prospects are not bright. The American policy of clinging jealously to the secret is short-sighted. What on earth is the good of holding a secret when we all know that within five years it will be open to everyone? By doing so the Americans merely encourage the suspicion that they intend to *use* their secret before it is too late. Secrecy foments mutual distrust. Had the Americans and British agreed to hand over the precious technical knowledge to an international organisation, including the Russians, the gesture would at least have done something to allay the present increasing fever of distrust.

The only sane course is to set up a special world authority to control the new power. This body should supervise research in every country. It should have the right to inspect every undertaking connected with atomic power. It should itself have exclusive control of all atomic weapons, and it should organise the distribution of atomic power throughout the world for industrial purposes.

I understand that the scientists who have protested against the policy of secrecy are alarmed not only by the prospect of atomic warfare, but also by the danger that irresponsible and hasty research, in countries impatient to discover the processes for themselves, may cause titanic accidents. Already we hear of research by a German in the Argentine and by a Japanese professor. And though we are told nothing of Russia's attack on the problem, we can be quite sure that Russian scientists are hard at work. Let us always remember that the use of atomic power is in its infancy. We are promised bombs two million times more powerful than the old block-busters. Moreover, though at present only certain radio-active atoms can be disintegrated, a successful attack will surely be made on stable ones. If ever men start disintegrating these, the possibility of wrecking the whole surface of the globe, or actually blowing up the planet, will no longer seem fantastic. The Asteroids, between Mars and Jupiter, are the remains of a shattered world. How did it come to grief?

Science is like Aladdin's lamp. The genie gives whatever is demanded, whether good or bad. Thus far science has given us a strange mixture of both. Is atomic power to be used so as to bring final disaster, or to create a new *kind* of world-society, in which every individual will have the best possible conditions for developing his human powers in co-operation with his fellows in the great common enterprise of human life on this planet?

We may be sure that, if the present dangerous corner is turned, and the threatened atomic war is avoided, there will be plenty of other problems to solve. We shall be plunged into a Second Industrial Revolution. All our familiar methods of transport and production will sooner or later be abandoned in favour of methods based on atomic power. This will cause immense social changes; and, unless these changes are very strictly planned, there will be chaos. Vast unemployment, class-conflicts, national conflicts, will only be avoided by means of planning on the world-wide scale.

If men succeed in coping with the Second Industrial Revolution more intelligently than with the first one, atomic power will indeed open up new horizons of experience and action. As power increases, the possibilities alike of evil and of good are increased. How desperately important, then, to form a precise idea of the goal to which the new power should be directed! Up to a point there is already general agreement about the aim of true progress. Every child must be afforded the chance to develop into a splendid man or woman. Every adult must have the means of using his powers for his own delight and the profit of the community. To-day it is a mere platitude to say that, equally for all human beings, there must be the best possible food, medical service, education, and general living conditions; and that for all there must be suitable work and plenty of leisure.

Of course, we might use atomic power to abolish work altogether, but this would be a mistake. Men need work as much as leisure; but the right sort of work, and not too much of it. They need, for their own personal fulfilment, to be called on to play a part in the great common venture. But each must have work suited to his particular capacity, and it must be neither too boring nor too exacting. Moreover, each must be able to take pride in his contribution to the general good. Atomic power affords the opportunity of transforming the whole work of the world to suit the needs of the worker. Hitherto there was always an excuse for planning jobs solely for the maximum output in relation to the power used; but when power becomes almost as plentiful as water, nothing should stand in the way of planning jobs primarily for the welfare of the worker. And since our aim must be to turn all workers into aristocrats, jobs must be planned for the needs of aristocrats. All work unsuited to aristocrats must be done by the universal slave, atomic power. The whole population of the world-wide aristocratic democracy will be engaged on innumerable forms of skilled work, manual, intellectual, artistic, social, and so on. The first impact of machinery was to destroy the old crafts, and increase the demand for unskilled workers. Atomic power, if it is wisely used, will gradually abolish all soul-destroying labour, and create a vast number of new skills and crafts. Very soon the problem will be to find enough skill.

Though man needs work, he also needs leisure, and a great deal of it. He needs it both for resting such powers as have been overexercised and for affording expression to such powers as find no outlet in worktime. But if he is to make good use of his leisure, he must from childhood be helped to learn what to do with it. True democracy is impossible unless the citizens have plenty of leisure and the ability to use their leisure well. The social function of leisure is to allow the democratic citizens ample opportunity for free and humanly developed personal intercourse, and for keeping themselves informed about the life of their society as a whole. It should also give them the chance of voluntary cultural and social service in some of the innumerable ways which are bound to occur in any vigorous democracy. Atomic power, by greatly reducing normal work hours, should greatly increase leisure and the ability to use it.

It should also have an immense effect on education. In the first place, the appalling danger of the wrong use of atomic power may force us at last to ensure that all men shall be educated to distinguish between true and false social values. And secondly, when power is almost limitless, we shall at last be able to allow to every individual the chance of a leisurely and liberal education. But let us always remember that, unless education is backed by a favourable social environment, it must remain impotent. Atomic power makes it possible to do away with all serious frustration, and, therefore, to abolish the kind of environment which disposes the masses to such perverse faiths as Fascism.

What kind of practical changes might result from the wise use of atomic power? Probably domestic work will be transformed by labour-saving devices. Transport by atomic ships, atomic cars, atomic planes, will vastly increase communications. There will be a constant interchange of visitors between even the most distant lands. Cities will be rebuilt to ampler and (one hopes) nobler plans. Mountains, when inconvenient, will be removed, coastlines changed to suit man's needs, deserts irrigated, the arctic and antarctic lands warmed for habitation. But probably it will always be desirable to keep large tracts of the earth in a natural state for man's recreation. For fundamentally man is a wild animal, and he needs to keep in touch with the primitive environment.

Equipped with atomic power, scientific research will leap forward. In time disease will be abolished, maturity prolonged, maternity relieved of its excessive burden. Interplanetary travel will soon become possible. If we see fit, we may breed special types of human beings to live in the extremely alien conditions of Mars, Venus and perhaps Jupiter. But first we should have to equip Venus with vegetation, so as to stock its atmosphere with breathable oxygen.

What would be the use, it may be asked, of these wild ventures? Are we not better off as we are? The only right answer is a religious answer, though not one that is religious in the orthodox sense. Little by little, more and more of us are realising that the true way of life, for the individual and for the race as a whole, is to live for something other than the individual, and, in a sense, even other than the race. Only if we regard ourselves and our human species as instruments for the fulfilling of the spiritual potentiality of this planet, can we find real peace. We have to develop our capacity, but not *simply* for our own satisfaction. Always we must keep that sense of instrumentality which used to be expressed in the old phrase "for the glory of God." Since the word "God" is so ambiguous, I should prefer to say "for the glory of the spirit" which is experienced as the very essence of each of us, and yet so much more than all of us together.

If this is so, then the true function of atomic power is that it should be used as a means for the further development of man's spiritual capacity. This means, in the last analysis, the development of man's capacity for sensitivity, intelligence, love and creative action. It is our nature that we are all members of one another, each contributing in some degree to the mental and spiritual life of all. The way of life for all self-conscious and other-conscious beings demands the greatest possible diversity of individuals, of groups, of peoples, and perhaps of worlds. The greater our differences the better, so long as we can be sufficiently sensitive and imaginative to recognise beneath all our differences our underlying kinship as personal beings. The final justification of atomic power is that it may immensely increase the possibility of development in these two fundamental respects, namely our diversity and our mutual insight.

Finally, lest these considerations should seem to point to a complacent humanism, let us remember the littleness of man, and the immensity and mystery of the physical and the spiritual reality that lies beyond him.

Mankind at the Crossroads

In 1947 Stapledon made a three-week lecture tour of France under the sponsorship of a French educational organization devoted to international understanding. For some of his presentations Stapledon drew on notes for lectures he had often given in England, but the centerpiece of the tour was a talk specially written for the occasion and delivered in French. Never published, "Mankind at the Crossroads" is a plea for Europeanism, a celebration of the mature European values Stapledon believed might provide an antidote to the aggressive and dangerous posturings of the Soviet Union and the United States in the emerging cold war. While the talk was motivated by the political anxieties of the moment, it also is full of favorite themes from Stapledon's whole body of published work. The final two paragraphs, in particular, which relocate the European crossroads to an intersection somewhere among the stars, recall the strategies and perspectives of his great cosmic romances of the 1930s. The text given here is an abridgment of Stapledon's corrected English typescript in the Sydney Jones Library, University of Liverpool; the omitted sections are an opening salutation and a long discussion of Stapledon's ideas about religion, adequately presented elsewhere in this Reader.

THE FRENCH HAVE PLAYED a glorious part in creating European culture; and without their continued and vigorous participation in the New Europe that culture cannot flower again. This revival of Europe I believe to be of immense importance not only for Europeans but for the human race.

Today the human world is distracted by two world-wide conflicting impulses, each of which dominates one of the two mightiest peoples, the Americans and the Russians. Both these two formidable peoples have very important contributions to make to the life of mankind. But each of them is in a sense still adolescent. Though culturally both derive from Europe, each has also developed its own characteristic and vigorous genius. In neither case is that genius yet freed from the extravagance and insensitivity of youth.

Each of these two peoples, let us admit, is the custodian of a very important truth, or rather half-truth; but neither is at present capable of appreciating the equally important half-truth of the other.

America, as we all know, stands mainly for individual freedom and individual responsibility, both moral and intellectual; and fundamentally for the importance of individuality. This principle, the importance of human individuality, was discovered intuitively nearly two thousand years earlier, and was one aspect of the great twofold truth on which Christianity was founded. The fact that the realization of the importance of individuality, so cherished in America, has also, in America and in Western Europe, been grossly perverted into licentious commercialism must not blind us to the truth itself, that individuality matters.

Russia, on the other hand, stands for the necessity of social planning and discipline, and individual loyalty to the approved group organization and culture. Fundamentally what the Russian Revolution championed was not simply the triumph of the workers but a social order based on the relationship of true community or comradeship in a common cause. And this principle, the importance of human brotherhood and love, was the other aspect of the great truth that inspired Christianity. In the Christian tradition this relationship of community is expressed in the saying that we are all "members one of another." Let us realize that, even if in some respects the present Russian regime has betrayed that truth by ruthless treatment of its opponents, yet the emotional drive and passion of the Revolution itself sprang from the essentially religious conviction of human solidarity, mutual involvement, mutual responsibility, in fact the sanctity of comradeship. The Scottish philosopher John Macmurray was perhaps justified in saying that the Russian Revolution was the greatest *religious* event of modern times. In theory anti-religious, because it was in revolt against a corrupt Church, the Russian Revolution was at first nonetheless essentially religious in feeling, and (up to a point) in practice also. The fact that Christianity deified this religious spirit of love, whereas the Russian Revolution rejected all religious doctrine, must not blind us to the underlying identity of motive.

Each of these half-truths, of individuality and community, if championed fanatically without care for the other, inevitably leads to extravagance; in America to cutthroat commercialism, in Russia to ruthless discipline of all individuals who do not accept the "party-line."

It is easy to see why each of the two great peoples is fanatical about its own half-truth. The Americans rose to their present power by the exercise of unrestrained private enterprise and by the practice of individual self-reliance. The Russians, on the other hand, broke the Tsarist tyranny and created the new and mightier Russia by corporate action and severe social discipline. In a secure society, individual liberty seems all that matters; in a society where danger constantly threatens from within and without, liberty (as we of the West understand it) is less prized than the social discipline without which no grave danger can be effectively resisted.

We may hope that both the dominant peoples will in time learn to appreciate the other's half-truth. Economic difficulties will perhaps force the Americans not only to learn the need for discipline and corporate action but also to rediscover that comradeship is more worthwhile than individual triumph. On the other hand, if Russia enters on a phase of security, the Russian people may in time come to feel that social discipline is not enough, and that personality deserves respect and forbearance even in eccentric individuals and tiresome minorities.

But these desirable changes will take time, and may be forestalled by world-wide disaster. Until America and Russia learn from each other, only Western Europe is in a position to appreciate properly both the half-truths. In the past, Western Europe, like America, achieved prosperity by private enterprise, and thus learned to cherish individuality. But today, like Russia, Western Europe has discovered in blood and tears the necessity of social planning and discipline, and also the importance, the sanctity, of human solidarity, of comradely mutual responsibility. We, with our more complex social and political experience and our recent internecine conflicts over these very half-truths, may perhaps achieve the synthesis which mankind so desperately needs. We may give the world the example of a society in which, though unimportant liberties are sacrificed for social discipline, the liberties that are necessary for healthy personal and social development are jealously preserved.

Unless we can begin to achieve some such synthesis quite soon, the clash of those two great adolescent peoples, and the conflict of their half-truths throughout the world, may overwhelm us all in the Third World War, the first atomic war, and the ruin of civilization, if not the end of Man. The danger has been much increased by Europe's downfall. For this has produced a void into which the two great antagonists fatally rush to grapple with each other. Thus, even from the point of view of power politics, the rebirth of Europe is urgently needed. For Europe, I mean Western Europe, could hold the balance. In the present tragic state of the world, power politics cannot be ignored. One cause of Russia's uncompromising policy is surely the fear that, as the second greatest power, she will find herself at grips with a combination of the first and the third, America and Britain. For my part, much as I cherish our British kinship with the Americans, I deeply regret that we are becoming so inextricably involved with them, instead of maintaining our independence and throwing in our lot with Europe.

However this may be, power politics do not go to the root of the matter. The important point is that culturally only Europe can work out the real synthesis of the conflicting ideals of Russia and America.

It is perhaps not an exaggeration to say that we are now living through the most momentous decades in the whole career of Man. For the first time in the history of our species men face the possibility either of annihilation or of the founding of a new *kind* of world society, in which all individuals will at least have the opportunity to develop their human capacity to an extent which was hitherto possible only for a small minority.

I like to think of the career of our species by means of the image of a river. The obscure source from which the river sprang, the biological mutations from which *homo sapiens* originated, lies perhaps as much as half a million years away in the past. From that point it wanders slowly over a vast plain. Change in human affairs is incredibly slow. Tribes rise and fall. Crude techniques are discovered, forgotten, and discovered again, only to be lost once more. Conditions in a man's childhood are generally much as they will be in his old age. For hundreds of thousands of years the river wanders sluggishly hither and thither.

But some mere six thousand years ago the river of human life reaches a somewhat steeper place. The waters hurry forward as rapids. Owing to improvements in the methods of production, there is time and energy to spare for new kinds of activity. No doubt the majority still spend their years in crippling toil. Indeed their servitude becomes even more oppressive. But civilization has begun. For the few, at least, there is more comfort; for very few, the new ease and leisure opens up the possibility of the life of the mind.

The hurrying river still accelerates, with the ever-increasing improvement in the means of production. The world of a man's old age becomes appreciably different from the world of his youth. At last, only two or three centuries ago, comes modern science. The advent of science, seen in the perspective of man's whole career, is sudden, almost instantaneous, and catastrophic. The river of human history is in the very act of plunging over a precipice as a cataract. Change is immensely accelerated. Today, the world of a man's maturity is bewilderingly different in kind from the world of his youth. We live in that moment of history when the turbulent waters slip over the cliff's edge for perpendicular descent, no man knows whither.

It is a commonplace that science has given man power without wisdom. The application of science has already led to a fantastic increase in the means of production; and with the harnessing of atomic power it now promises an increase of an entirely different order of magnitude. Yet wisdom remains no greater than it was. Indeed, in some respects, much of the ancient wisdom has been lost or discredited. And, as yet, nothing new has come to take its place. But the dictum that science has given power without wisdom is only a half-truth; for, after all, science has at least led to the outgrowing of many superstitions and cherished illusions. And it has surely opened up the possibility of greater wisdom in the future, a wisdom in which the ancient and forgotten truths may be rediscovered and synthesized with a more mature science.

Meanwhile the gift of crude power is indeed terrifying. Like the djinn of Aladdin's lamp, science is a slave which serves its master faithfully and mightily, whether the orders given to it are wise or foolish. At the moment, three main practical results have followed from the application of science: an increase of industrial power; an increase of military power; and an increase of the power of governments to discipline the bodies and minds of their subjects, by means of the whole diabolically efficient machinery of the modern police state, and by the great mechanical instruments of mass propaganda, such as the press, the cinema and the radio. Of these three results of science, it may be said that military power and disciplinary power have done far more evil than good. Military power, in the form of atomic bombs and bacterial warfare, now threatens to destroy the race, and to render much of the planet's surface lethal to all the more developed forms of life. The disciplinary power of governments enables the state to reduce all men to slavery, physical and mental. And since, as Lord Acton said, power corrupts, and absolute power corrupts absolutely, governments tend more and more to ruthlessness. Industrial power, on the other hand, is good or bad according to the measure of wisdom that directs it. Wisely used, it might create a new and glorious world-society, a society of "aristocrats," in the best sense, with the machines as slaves and no longer as masters. But actually, through the operation of uncontrolled private enterprise, its effect has been, I should say, on the whole more bad than good. It has indeed given us increased health and comfort, but these benefits have been very unevenly distributed. Unfortunately it seems also to have impoverished the quality of average minds, both by imposing on most individuals stereotyped forms of work, which permit far less expression of individuality than the old handicrafts and agriculture; and also by enervating them with the seductive, trivial and mainly passive kinds of mass-produced pleasure, such as the cinema and the radio. Thus, both in play and in work, average minds in our time are on the whole more impoverished than average minds before the industrial revolution. . . .

The issue that confronts mankind today is simply this. Having gained prodigious power, shall we also gain wisdom? And shall we do so quickly enough to forestall the apocalyptic disaster that threatens us? We can save ourselves only by solving the two great dialectical conflicts that now torment us. Socially, we must conceive a "liberal communism" which will combine the essential liberties with planning and discipline. While resolutely planning the transition to the new age, and accepting the high degree of social discipline which is inevitable in our complex world society in its period of supreme crisis, we must plan for the full expression of personality in all men; or rather, since personality and community involve each other, for "personality-in-community." And since a high degree of freedom of expression, of freedom of association, of freedom from economic servitude, and so on, is essential to the health of personality and the health of society, we must plan to secure to every individual these essential liberties in as high degree as possible. Many liberties may have to be sacrificed, for instance the liberty to buy and sell as we please; but the essential liberties, without which we cannot be fully human, must be secured. Without them men are inevitably warped, either by slave-mindedness or rebel-mindedness. But alas no high degree of the essential liberties is possible save in a stable society, acceptable to the great majority of citizens. In our present world-crisis, therefore, *some* curtailment even of the essential liberties is inevitable. We must see to it that governments do not use this need for discipline as an excuse for tyranny.

This "liberal communism" is impossible unless we solve our religious conflict. For no society can be wholesome unless it is orientated to something more than man, or something in addition to the greatest happiness of the greatest number of existing human individuals. This goal, the greatest happiness of the greatest number, we must of course seek; but in the last resort the greatest happiness is to be found only in service of the spirit. Christians might say that no society can be healthy that is not theocratic. Metaphorically, but not literally, this is true. The "God" to whom we give allegiance must be no universal power or person, about whom we know nothing, but the spirit that invades and conquers our own hearts. It comes we know not whence; but it comes with manifest right, to possess us.

Is there any hope that a sufficient number of human beings will awake once more to the pure religious experience sufficiently clearly to solve the great dialectical conflict between faith and scepticism? I can only speak for my own country. There at least there does seem to me to be a very widespread but a bewildered and rather painful waking. During the recent war it was my privilege to discuss these matters with many audiences of average men and women in the British armed forces. Though of course the majority were still insensitive, or else hopelessly entangled either in the old religious doctrines or in the newer doctrines of materialism, I found a surprising number who were already groping. The ideas which I have been haltingly putting before you are in a way an expression of their perplexity, reflected in my own mind.

If Man does successfully come through his present crisis, what kind of future will be possible for him? Certainly no dull and enervating utopia of physical luxury. Rather we must expect that when man's present troubles are overcome, he will rise to a new stage of social and cultural growth, and find himself confronted with new problems and troubles at present inconceivable. Having passed through the growing-pains of infancy, he may begin at last to attain something like spiritual adolescence.

Lest some should feel that this view is but a re-statement of the cult of human progress, let me add this. It may well be that from the cosmical point of view it matters little whether Man prospers or fails, whether he fulfills his spiritual potentiality or damns himself. Cabbages in a garden labour to produce flowers and seeds, but from the gardener's point of view their function is not fruition but merely to be eaten. Perhaps the spiritual fruition that man is now obscurely beginning to desire is not, after all, his true function in the cosmos. Perhaps his part is merely to strive half-heartedly, to betray the spirit, and to destroy himself. Perhaps other races in other worlds are destined to triumph, but not man. Biologically man is an unfinished creature. He is not like the bird, which is perfected for life in its appropriate environment. Man, in his more subtle medium, is more like some clumsy flying lizard which can only flap and flounder, and is destined for extinction. But indeed, perhaps nowhere in the whole universe is triumph required. Perhaps the divine purpose is wholly other than any purpose that we can conceive or dare applaud. Or perhaps, quite simply, there is no divine purpose at all. Or again, and more probably, there neither is or is not; and the truth is wholly beyond the reach of our understanding. No matter! In our own hearts the spirit claims us. When we are most conscious, most clearly aware of ourselves and of one another and of the world, we cannot but will to conceive and to express the spirit as best we may in our individual lives and in the whole common life of our species.

At night we may sometimes raise our eyes to the stars, and imagine also, far beyond the limits of unaided vision, hosts of other stellar systems. Who knows what worlds, what intelligent races live out their lives around us in the depths of space! Whether they be few or many, we may, I think, be sure that they too, like us, must be concerned fundamentally with the spirit. Hail! Oh unseen, inaccessible, unimaginable comrades! But beyond those flashing suns, those distant galaxies, what is there? There, or rather no-where and no-when, or everywhere and all-when, we are confronted by the unspeakable, the inconceivable, to which we have no clue at all; unless perhaps, after all, the one clue may be the spirit that so imperiously in our own hearts demands allegiance. Perhaps! But perhaps this too is no clue at all to ultimate truth about the universe. Well, what matter? The spirit itself alone, whatever its cosmical status, gives meaning to our lives.

Interplanetary Man?

Stapledon's 1948 address to the British Interplanetary Society, invited by its secretary, Arthur C. Clarke, is his most famous essay. It combines extraterrestrial fantasy with ethical inquiry in a familiar Stapledonian recipe, but his audience in this instance was unfamiliar to him. The Society, comprising mostly engineers, aerospace technicians, and industrial scientists, turned to Stapledon as an imaginative pioneer of a subject — space travel — that they confidently and correctly expected would soon leave the realm of fantasy. "Interplanetary Man?" is a profoundly utopian essay, even though it was written under threat of atomic apocalypse in the midst of the emerging cold war. Stapledon worked on this speech while deeply engaged in the political activities of a new peace movement, and it is a sign of the pressures of time he was under that he lifted or reshaped some passages from the address "Mankind at the Crossroads" he had delivered in France eight months earlier. The text of the speech was printed in the Society's Journal *in November 1948.*

I. Introduction

IT IS WITH SOME HESITATION that I address this very expert Society. I feel much as a man might feel who, merely because he once wrote a children's story about a magic carpet, has undertaken to discourse to a society of aeroplane designers about the future of aviation. Contributors to the *Journal* of this truly epoch-making Society overawe me with their scientific knowledge and their wealth of mathematical formulae! Let me at once put my cards on the table by confessing that my training in science ended when I failed to pass the "London Matric" in what used to be called "organic chemistry," and that my knowledge of mathematics is far more sketchy even than my knowledge of the sciences. I am a dabbler in many subjects, an expert in none. As such, my only function to-night must be to bring to bear on interplanetary travel light from other fields of knowledge.

Modern civilization cannot get along without experts of many kinds. In most fields the day of the amateur is past. But just because this is pre-eminently an age of experts, we have to face the serious danger that the human race may come to consist wholly of experts none of whom understands what his fellows are doing, or why they are doing it, and all of whom are ignorant of the pattern of human life as a whole. Knowledge has become so vast that no single mind can speak with authority save in relation to his own particular corner of it. But such is the prestige of scientific expertism that scientists are apt to make far-reaching pronouncements about matters lying beond their special competence, for instance about politics, ethics, religion and philosophy. One of the most serious problems of our day is to work out an educational technique which, while producing real experts in each field, will ensure that each one of them will also be a reasonably well informed and responsible democratic citizen. Even when this end has been achieved, it will still be necessary for some people to tackle the work of correlating the various growing points of thought. This is supposed to be the task of philosophers, or of one particular sort of philosophers. They have to learn something from all the main kinds of experts, and to relate the findings in each field to the findings in others. This is indeed a formidable task; and unless these universal intruders combine intelligence with humility, they are likely to make a mess of it, and to be reviled by the experts in every field.

It is therefore with a combination of humility and the hardihood that leads fools to rush in where angels fear to tread that I venture to talk to you at all. The only useful thing I can do is to try to show you how, as it seems to me, your bold and highly specialized venture of interplanetary travel fits into the total venture of man in this formidable universe.

I start with an assumption amply justified by the Society's work. I assume that, if all goes well with man, men will, in fact, be able to reach the other planets within a few decades, and able to effect landings on them. This assumption may, of course, turn out to be unjustified. Unexpected difficulties may arise. Or, on the other hand, all may *not* go well with man. His folly may quite well lead to the destruction of civilization, to the extermination of his species, and even to the extinction of all terrestrial life. It is not entirely fantastic to surmise that he may even blow up his planet, and reduce it to a new swarm of asteroids. In gaining control of atomic energy, man clumsily grasps an instrument of incalculable potency, both for good and for evil. J. B. S. Haldane has suggested that it may be a law of nature that any species that gains atomic power before unifying its world-society must destroy itself. I should myself say, not merely "before it unifies its world-society," but "before it disciplines itself to the true values."

Probably there has never before, in the whole career of our species, been so momentous a crisis as that of our day. Our own human species is said to have begun about a quarter to half a million years ago. For most of this period the river of human life has wandered sluggishly through the plains of time. If we consider the average length of a human generation over this period to be about twenty-five years, then some twenty thousand generations have passed since *Homo sapiens* began. During almost the whole of that vast period (perhaps a four-thousandth part of the aeon that has passed since the earth's formation) men had little power, and change in human affairs was very slight. Tribes, no doubt, rose and fell. Improvements in technique were rarely discovered; and discovered only to be lost again, and rediscovered ages afterwards. Conditions in a man's childhood were generally much the same as conditions in his old age. But at last this slow and tortuous advance in the techniques of production achieved agriculture, and later the building of cities, the founding of civilization. This seems to have occurred some six thousand years ago, or a little over two hundred and forty generations. The river of human life accelerated somewhat, tumbling forward in rapids. Power and leisure and comfort increased; but almost always only for the few. The masses seem to have been more and more deeply enslaved. Not till almost the end of this six thousand years, say three hundred years ago or about twelve generations, did modern science begin to take effect on human life. Thus man has used science only during the last thousandth part of his whole career, and his career is the last four-thousandth of the period since the earth was formed. In our own day, man is snatching at atomic power. We are the first generation of the atomic age. Change is already far more rapid than ever before, and will soon become catastrophic, for good or ill. The river of human life has reached a precipice. The cataract plunges—whither? It is quite possible that we may be the last of all human generations. Yet, barring accidents, the earth should be habitable for a period as long as it has yet existed, say two thousand million years, or some eighty million of our present human generations.

There seem to be three possible futures for man: (1) actual and speedy annihilation; (2) the creation of a world-wide totalitarian ant-state, based on atomic power and the reduction of all human individuals to robots; (3) the founding of a new kind of human world, in which the Aladdin's lamp of science will be used wisely, instead of being abandoned to that blend of short-sighted stupidity and downright power-lust that has played so tragic a part in the application of science thus far. It is a platitude that man has gained power without wisdom. If he does not at the eleventh hour, or half a minute before zero hour, become just a little less silly, his doom is sealed. On the other hand, given a modicum of wisdom, we shall be able greatly to raise the conditions of life for all human beings, no matter what their colour, and to afford to every one of them the chance to develop and express such capacity as he has for truly human living and truly human work in the great common enterprise of man. What that enterprise is or should be, I shall consider later.

This possibility of affording to all men full opportunity is now no merely Utopian dream. Its progressive attainment is at last physically possible. Nothing now stands in the way but the ignorance, the stupidity and the evil will of men. And let me say at once, though I shall later enlarge on this point, that the promise is not simply one of increased luxury and hoggish ease. Rather it is a promise of a deepening and enriching of human experience. Man's present condition of constant frustration and torment and fear makes most men to-day think only in terms of the hope of luxury and security. But if ever we do successfully turn our present dangerous corner, and a generation appears that is freed from crippling conditions, then men's minds will at last be able effectively to desire something more than mere luxury and security. Be sure, also, that in the promised world there will be no lack of challenge and danger and even tragedy. The novelty will be rather that man will have outgrown at last the diseases of mere infancy, and will be able to enter for the first time into the more dangerous, more troubled, but ampler and richer and more conscious life of adolescence.

II. If the Planets Are Inhabited

At this most critical moment of human history man finds himself on the very threshold of a new freedom, the freedom to travel beyond the terrestrial atmosphere and explore the whole solar system. What should he do with this new power?

Much depends on the conditions of the planets that he visits. Two possibilities must be noted. Either man will find elsewhere in the solar system other intelligences, or he will not. If he does, then again there are two possibilities. One is the possibility of wars between the worlds. This situation might perhaps cause at least a temporary unification of mankind in face of the common danger, much as Russia and the West united against Hitler. The War of Worlds would be followed either by man's defeat and ruin or by his victory, and then by exploitation of the conquered races for man's advancement. The other possibility is interplanetary co-operation. But in view of our sad inability even to unite mankind, it seems extremely unlikely that man in his present state would succeed in co-operating with alien races on other planets. Far more likely is it that the rival imperialisms and ideologies of this planet would be extended to struggle against each other in other worlds, tyrannizing over and ultimately destroying the native peoples. If, on the other hand, man does soon succeed in unifying his world-society, then it is at least conceivable that some kind of mutually profitable symbiosis with intelligent races on other planets might be established.

On the whole, however, it seems unlikely that any of the other worlds within the solar system is inhabited by any race even approaching man in intelligence. Bear with me while I summarize the data, and correct me later if I am mistaken. Let us begin with our nearest neighbour, the moon. I am told that it is almost wholly without atmosphere and water. There seems to be no reason at all for supposing that it has, or ever did have, intelligent inhabitants. Of the planets themselves, Mercury is far too hot on one side and far too cold on the other. Venus is more temperate, and has a copious atmosphere; but apparently it lacks oxygen, and would not support life such as we know on our own planet. Water also may be lacking. Mars, owing to its feeble gravitation, has already lost most of its atmosphere and most of its water. Indeed, its polar caps may turn out to be composed of carbon dioxide snow, or something worse. However, there is considerable evidence that vegetation of some sort does exist on Mars; but certainly no convincing evidence of the artifacts of an intelligent race. Probably the process of biological evolution on the planet was less rapid than that of the earth, since on the whole, the larger the geographical field, the greater the chance of the occurrence of a wealth of varieties on which natural selection could work. Further, the evolutionary process was probably cut short or greatly retarded by the rapid deterioration of conditions. On the whole, then, it seems unlikely that on Mars life (such as we know) has evolved to the human level. The asteroids are of course much too small. On the other hand, Jupiter and Saturn, and probably all the outer planets, are too big, and have apparently quite the wrong kind of atmosphere for life of the terrestrial type.

Of course, we cannot entirely reject the possibility that on some of the planets life has evolved on a different chemical basis, and that atmospheres lethal to us may be hospitable to biochemical processes alien to ours. But I understand that terrestrial life depends on the unique diversity of the carbon compounds, and that, though a biochemical system based on some element other than carbon is not impossible, it would have a far smaller range of compounds, and so the scope of its biological evolution would be very restricted. However, we should not dismiss the possibility that Jupiter or some other great planet is inhabited by minute intelligent creatures whose constitution is quite unknown to us. The evidence is opposed to this view, but not overwhelmingly.

At this point I cannot resist a digression, and indulgence in the wildest fantasy. Fundamentally life seems to consist of a utilizing of some particular form of the general process of the increase of entropy so as to gather power for the maintenance of vital activities. Life taps and canalizes part of the vast spate of energy, thus forming a "mill-stream" by which its own little "water-wheel" may be worked. Well, might there not be living creatures based not on chemical action but on the energy released by the disintegration of atoms? Might there not be, not on any planet but in the sun's turbulent outer layers or in its middle depths, flame-like organisms of this type, and might not some species of them equal or excel man in intelligence? This is indeed a flagrant digression from the purpose of this paper, for it seems quite impossible that man should ever in his space-ships invade the sun and make contact with such incandescent beings.

To return to our subject, it seems very unlikely that there is any intelligent race anywhere in the solar system, except mankind. Mars is the only planet that should make us hesitate to accept this conclusion, but in this case too the betting is heavily against any highly developed life.

III. If the Planets Are Uninhabited

If man finds the planets uninhabited, what should he do with them? If mankind is still disunited, no doubt there will be a race between rival imperialisms to annex those vast virgin territories. The coming struggle between America and Asia, with Europe as a battlefield, might well spread to Mars. Already one of our vigorous but still culturally adolescent cousins across the Atlantic is reported to have suggested that the moon should be annexed as soon as possible as an industrial field for American exploitation. Alas! Must the first flag to be planted beyond the earth's confines be the Stars and Stripes, and not the banner of a united Humanity?

In passing, let us remind ourselves that merely to circumnavigate a planet does not necessarily imply the possibility of landing on it and walking about, let alone staying there and undertaking any sort of survey or industrial operation. Clearly the pioneers would have to be equipped not only with food and water and air for their journey but with pressure-suits, oxygen and an ample water supply for their stay on the planet. And as things stand, they might also need weapons to defend themselves from attack by emissaries from rival terrestrial states.

But let us suppose that mankind has at last become effectively united, both politically and socially. Then what should a united mankind do with the planets?

Obviously, the first thing to do would be to explore them. Sheer scientific curiosity would certainly insist on thoroughly surveying them. They would offer the kind of lure that was offered in the nineteenth century by Darkest Africa, the north and south poles and the unclimbed Himalayas. Bold young people would be very ready to give their services for planetary exploration. Their effective motive would probably be sheer adventure, though the rational justification of such costly and dangerous undertakings would of course be the advance of science. It is conceivable, however, that everything really significant about those desert worlds might be learned by merely circumnavigating them without landing on them. Perhaps men will be so absorbed in the general advance of science and in the exciting task of creating a really adult human society on earth, that they will simply never bother to take the necessary trouble to set foot on another planet. No doubt this is unlikely, because the irrational, romantic glamour of opening up unexplored worlds will be too strong, even if those worlds turn out to be inhospitable and dreary wastes.

Apart from the motives of sheer curiosity and sheer adventure, the obvious motive for exploring the planets is the hope of discovering immense fields of natural resources, and exploiting them for human welfare. They might, for instance, yield valuable stores of uranium or other sources of atomic power, or any of the rarer elements or minerals needed by man. I am quite incompetent in this field, and must merely note that the motive of economic gain may play a leading part in man's dealings with the planets.

Let us admit, however, that it would be far best for man to postpone his exploitation of alien planets until he had concentrated seriously on improving terrestrial conditions. Equipped with highly developed scientific knowledge and atomic power, he should first undertake the comparatively easy task of turning his native planet into a more convenient and more delectable home. Climates might be improved, coastlines modified, deserts irrigated, jungles tamed, mountains (where they happened to be obstructive) blasted out of the way. Mineral wealth might be brought up from the depths of the terrestrial globe, Antarctica and the great Arctic Islands might be warmed and colonized. And so on. But let us hope that none of these vast enterprises will be attempted till mankind has attained a rather high level of wisdom, and has a clear knowledge of the kind of world that would really favour human development. For my part, since I am by nature something of a savage, I cannot help hoping also that many regions will be preserved in their wild state for the recreation and refreshment of a species which, after all, is biologically adapted to a primitive environment.

But however desirable this reconstruction of the earth's surface, sooner or later for good or ill, a united mankind, equipped with science and power, will probably turn its attention to the other planets, not only for economic exploitation, but also as possible homes for man. Perhaps the most promising is Mars. If the venture seemed really worthwhile, that small, cold, arid world might be rendered at least habitable, if not a paradise for man. All the necessary materials would be present in the crust of the planet itself. Human ingenuity, with atomic power, should be able to increase the atmosphere and the water supply, irrigate the desert surface, produce a suitable vegetation, and even raise the surface temperature. Whether this huge undertaking would be in fact worthwhile or not, is a question which I shall consider later. At present I suggest merely that it probably could be accomplished. In frivolous moments one feels that Mars might be used as an extra-terrestrial "Siberia" in which to exile all our really tiresome people. But I fear that the little planet would soon be overcrowded, and Earth depopulated.

Like Mars, the moon could perhaps be rendered distressfully habitable by terrestrial man; though in this case, presumably, the artificial atmosphere would escape far more rapidly, and would need to be constantly replenished. Incidentally, much of it would be drawn off by the Earth, thus complicating our terrestrial problems by increasing our atmospheric pressure.

What of Venus? The task would probably be much more formidable. From the little that we know of Venerian conditions, it would seem that the first problem would be to alter the composition of the already existing atmosphere, which, so far as is now known, is quite unsuited to terrestrial life. And water, if indeed it is absent, would have to be created in bulk. Then we should have to produce a vegetation for the maintenance of a supply of free oxygen. But on the whole, though Venus offers a more difficult problem than Mars, it might in the long run become a more satisfactory home for man. It is much larger, and of course far warmer. Instead of affording the human colonists a distressful and precarious existence, it might in time rival and surpass the Earth as a home for intelligent beings.

The greater planets would seem to offer no possibility of human colonization, owing to unfavourable atmosphere, chilly remoteness from the sun, and such gravitational pressure that a man's body would be an insupportable burden.

IV. Adapting Man to the Planets

It is time to approach the whole matter from another angle. If the mountain will not come to Mohamet, Mohamet must go to the mountain. If the planets are unadaptable to man in his present form, perhaps man might adapt himself to the alien environments of those strange worlds. Or rather, perhaps a combination of the two processes might enable man to make the best possible use of those worlds. In fact, given sufficient biological knowledge and eugenical technique, it might be possible to breed new human types of men to people the planets.

Once more, Mars seems to offer the best opportunity. It should be fairly easy to produce a variety of *Homo sapiens* capable of surviving the rigours of an improved Martian environment. Perhaps the best human stock from which to start would be the Tibetans, who are used to a cold, arid climate and a rarefied atmosphere. But unless the Martian atmosphere could be augmented quite a lot, and the surface temperature greatly raised, the specialized human Martians would probably lack the vital energy for any kind of highly developed civilization. Only where nature blossoms with a certain luxuriance can the human spirit itself blossom. However, by a combination of environmental and eugenical alteration, it might perhaps be possible in the long run to establish a vigorous population on Mars.

On Venus, given oxygen and water, man's biochemical and eugenical technique might perhaps produce a well-adapted human variety or a new human species. Since Venerian man would have to stand great heat, the work might start with experiments on some Equatorial varieties of our species. Presumably in that hot world a dark skin would be useful; unless, indeed, permanent shade was maintained by a cloud-blanket over the whole planet. There would certainly be a tendency for a large proportion of the planet's water to remain permanently suspended in the atmosphere.

On the outer planets, eugenics would have to play a major part. Even if the problems of the atmosphere and the extreme cold could be solved, there would be very great difficulties to face. It would be necessary to create a specially adapted human species of very small stature to cope with the excess of gravitation. This might well involve a serious reduction in the size of the cerebral cortices, with a consequent reduction of intelligence. For intelligence seems to depend on the actual number of top-level cells in the nervous system; or, as it were, on the complexity of the telephone exchange. Thus the attainment of human intelligence in a very small mammal would be impossible, unless some way could be found for greatly reducing the size of the individual cells and the thickness of the fibres without impairing efficiency. There is one other conceivable way out of the difficulty. By very drastic eugenical operation on the existing human form, it might be possible to enable the present human brain to be supported, in spite of excess gravitation, by throwing man into the quadruped position, greatly strengthening the four legs, and at the same time pushing the head far backwards so as to distribute its weight evenly between the fore and hind legs. But what of the problem of providing hands? The fore-limbs would be fully occupied and unavailable for manipulation. My only suggestion is that the nose might be greatly elongated into a trunk, equipped with delicate grasping instruments like fingers. It would probably be desirable to have two trunks, if not three. The eyes, by the way, would have to be projected well forward from the thrown-back brain-pan, otherwise *Homo Jovianus* would not be able to see where he was stepping.

Enough has been said to suggest that the colonization of some of the planets may in time become practicable, if terrestrial man continues to develop his control of the physical environment through atomic power, and if he attains sufficient biological knowledge and eugenical art to breed, or otherwise construct, human or quasi-human races adapted to strange environments.

But a word of caution is necessary. It is extremely important that none of these eugenical ventures should be attempted without thorough knowledge of the probable indirect results of each proposed change. For instance, it would be disastrous to aim at very small stature without doing something to avoid reduction in intelligence. Further, it is necessary to have very clear ideas as to which human characteristics are unimportant and might be safely sacrificed, and which are indispensable and should never be endangered. Thus good vision, high intelligence, co-operativeness and manual dexterity are indispensable and should if possible be increased; while teeth and cranial hair could if necessary be sacrificed. The result of thoughtless "messing about" with human nature might be the psychological and spiritual ruin of man.

V. What Is It All For?

This brings me at last to the real crux of my subject. Would there be any point in colonizing the planets? What are we getting at? What is it all for? Why not just stay put on our native planet and muck along as before?

Broadly, there seem to be three possible motives that might control man's dealings with the planets. (I exclude scientific curiosity, which, though it might be an important motive with some individuals, is not likely to be the determining factor.)

First, the physical resources of those worlds might be exploited simply in order to increase the luxury of human beings on earth. This aim might involve the creation of industrial settlements on the planets, but it might not involve large-scale colonization. The policy would be simply to use the planets to afford to human beings as much pleasure as possible, to give to all of them the greatest possible affluence; in fact, to create a society in which every individual would have the privileges that only millionaires have to-day. Drudgery would be completely abolished. All manner of superfine food and drink, and all manner of ingenious amusements would be constantly available at the cost of merely pressing buttons or switches. Not only the "movies" but also the "feelies" and "smellies" and "sexies" would provide unending beatitude, in the manner foreseen by Aldous Huxley and others. Any subsequent boredom or lassitude would be at once corrected by means of fresh interests or appropriate drugs. No-one would ever do anything unpleasant or uninteresting. Machines of all sorts would be the tireless and obedient slaves of every man. All men would be aristocrats in the worse sense of the word, not the better. All would be pleasure-addicts, accustomed to every luxury; spoilt children who, through being shielded from the sterner possibilities of life, would simply never grow up. Of course, *before* the attainment of this strictly hedonistic Utopia, many men would have had to live laboriously and dangerously and devotedly, in the cause of science and exploration and invention, in order to make such a luxury-world possible. But once the new order had been thoroughly established, it might maintain itself perpetually with a minimum of direction of human action.

Most of us, I think, would agree that, though a certain amount of luxury is a harmless and even civilizing thing, there is a point beyond which the increase of luxury leads to spiritual degradation. Man has risen by versatility and intelligence. If he were to enter at last upon a stable condition of perfect adaptation to an unchanging environment, he would gradually lose his distinctive powers. Intelligence would atrophy. The world-society might perhaps survive unchanged for millions of years; but sooner or later man would be confronted with some new challenge from the environment, and would have lost the wit to cope with it. I conclude that if the fruit of all the devotion of the British Interplanetary Society is to be merely the debauching of mankind with the riches of other worlds, you had better all stop paying your subscriptions.

The second possible aim in relation to the planets is simply to increase man's power over the environment, and to extend that power so as to tackle fresh environments.

In the heyday of the industrialization of Europe and America, power did seem to many people an end in itself. The craving to leave one's mark on the environment, any sort of mark, so long as it is *my* mark, made actually by me, is very strong in a certain type of uncultured mind. Human animals carve their initials on trees, rocks, school desks and public monuments. They deface beautiful objects simply for the lust of power. They satisfy their primitive impulses for construction thoughtlessly, without regard to the remoter consequences; sometimes harmlessly, but sometimes disastrously in ways that are less *constructive* than *de*structive. Children harmlessly make mud pies or play with meccano sets. Adults less innocently build empires or great commercial ventures. Generally some fairly plausible excuse is found for all this feverish activity. The mud pies are magic castles; the empires, instruments of civilization; the commercial ventures, purveyors of comfort or luxury. But at bottom the motive is often simply the insatiable itch to make a mark on the environment, any old mark, but the bigger the better. In itself, the impulse is harmless, even worthy; but we have to learn to make our mark in inoffensive and if possible actually useful ways.

More precisely, the itch to leave a mark is quite wholesome, on condition that, even if it does not serve some higher aim, at least it does not positively hinder proper development. It must not be allowed to degenerate into mere obsessive doodling or meddling on however vast a scale. The danger for mankind as a whole is that, having solved its present urgent problems, it will slip into the assumption that the goal of all its corporate action is simply to make a bigger and bigger mark on a bigger and bigger environment. Power is all too apt to become an end in itself. In the old days self-assertive individuals aimed at local tyranny or world empire. Henceforth they will be more likely to dominate either through money power or through fulfilling important functions domineeringly in a highly organized state, perhaps a world-state of totalitarian type. It has been said that power corrupts, and absolute power corrupts absolutely. Those who control the world-state, whether it is capitalist or communist or social-democratic, will be in danger of grave corruption unless they are imperturbably orientated to the true values. They will readily idealize their own power lust, and persuade mankind that the right goal for man is simply dominance over the environment. And so in time the planet may approximate to Aldous Huxley's *Brave New World*, in which society is organized to the extreme pitch of efficiency with the aim simply of producing as much as possible. In that horrid world the workers are given unlimited easy pleasure, while the élite, the bureaucrats and technicians, have the satisfaction of directing the whole life of society.

If the future terrestrial society is organized on these principles, then the other planets will be used for the same end. Ostensibly the aim will be to use them as sources of raw material for man's comfort and luxury, on this planet or others; but behind this orthodox economic motive will lie the unacknowledged motive of sheer power. And if individuals can be corrupted by power, so can a whole species. Man may become obsessed with a passion merely to make a big mark on the solar system. In principle there is no difference between this aim and that of the urchin who sets fire to the heath or throws stones at windows.

The third possible motive for gaining control of the planets is that of using them to make the "most" of man, or the "best" of him; in fact, for the full expression of the most developed capacities of the human species. Here we have a goal which, though extremely vague, is more promising. What does it really imply? Broadly, it may be interpreted in two different ways, one purely humanistic, the other involving a reference to something over and above man, though it is known to us mainly through its imperfect manifestation in man himself. The question to be faced is this. Are we justified in regarding man *simply* as an end in himself? Is "good" *simply* whatever man wills? Is a thing to be called "good" merely *because* or *in that* man wills it? Or, on the other hand, is man to be regarded rather as a means to an end, an instrument for the fulfilling of an end that is in some sense independent of his actual nature in its present stage of development? These questions cannot be even clearly stated, let alone answered, without raising very difficult philosophical problems. They cannot be truly answered with a plain "yes" or "no." Rather the answer must be of the type, "In one sense man is an end, in another sense not an end but an instrument." In the same manner the physicists may justifiably say that in one sense an electron is a particle, and in another sense not a particle but a train of waves.

VI. Fundamental Values

Perhaps we shall be able to form more precise ideas on this subject (which really does concern an interplanetary society) if we try to answer the question, "What is man?"

Clearly, whatever else he is, he certainly is (or has) a body, which is a physical or electromagnetic system of protons, electrons, etc. J. B. S. Haldane (I think) remarks somewhere that the human body contains some millions of millions of millions of millions of hydrogen atoms, and corresponding amounts of other elements. Julian Huxley (I think) has pointed out that man's body is approximately half-way in size between an electron and the whole universe. Astronomically, man is very small, an inconceivably minute parasite on a minute planetary grain floating in an immense void that is extremely sparsely sprinkled with great suns. Size is in itself of no importance; but if in the minute human body the physical can be the vehicle of some degree of mind or spirit, how great may be the mental and spiritual capacity of the whole cosmos of star-systems!

Biologically, man (as we have already noted), or rather our own species of man, which we have ludicrously called *Homo sapiens,* is of very recent growth. But he is the most developed of terrestrial organisms. That is, he is objectively the most complex, integrated, versatile. He has specialized in being unspecialized. Hence his remarkable adaptability, and his dominance over all other species. He has indeed made a bigger mark on this planet than any other species, and a much more complex and purposeful and organized mark. Basically he remains just a mammal, a primate. His unique gift is his relatively high intelligence, which has depended on the unique development of hands and eyes and cerebral cortices. There is good reason to believe, however, that man is a very imperfect species. The bird is just about perfected for its appropriate life, for flight in the terrestrial atmosphere; but man, though he has powers far beyond the range of the bird, has not perfected those powers. In his appropriate medium of intelligent purposive action, abstract thought, personal sensibility and artistic creation, he is little better than a clumsy flying lizard.

Psychologically, what is it that distinguishes man from the sub-human creatures, even from his nearest relatives, the apes? He has the same ground plan of organs, reflexes, innate behaviour and emotional reaction. He shows fear, aggression, self-regard, sexuality, gregariousness, curiosity, manipulative meddlesomeness, and so on. What is distinctive in him is his superior power of discrimination, of attending to likenesses and differences. Hence his native intelligence, by which I mean the power of solving *novel* problems, not to be solved by instinct or by established habit. This unique aptitude for discrimination and intelligence has opened up for him vast new universes of experience, impossible to any other terrestrial creature. All intelligence involves the power of attending to the relevant while ignoring the irrelevant. Hence, in man, comes the power of abstraction, of attending to a particular character and relating it to other instances of the same character, and giving the identity a name, such as "red," "two," "pleasant." Hence language and all the worlds of abstract thought and of concrete poetry.

Man's great power of concentration of attention has been applied not only to the environment but also to his own nature. Thus he has developed the possibility of a unique kind of self-awareness and awareness of other selves. In fact, he has become capable of personality, and of genuinely personal relationships, including all the forms of developed loving and hating. From this has arisen a distinctively human or personal kind of sociality. In sub-human animals, sociality is no more than a combination of the impulse of gregariousness (including self-abasement to the herd) and the impulse of self-assertion, rising to dominance over the herd. Of course, human beings themselves often behave in this sub-human way, but the distinctively human or personal way is something of a different kind, in that it involves respect for the other as a conscious person. The distinctively human society is best understood by considering the nature of genuine human love, which again is beyond the range of sub-human consciousness.

When John *really loves* Jane, he does what no beast can do. He does not *merely* have a pleasant glow of feeling about her. Of course he has this, but something more also. He is aware of her as a conscious being, distinct from himself, and different in character and needs and capacities. He accepts her as she is, without wishing to impose his will on her. He respects her as a person, takes responsibility for her, cherishes her, depends on her, is mentally enriched by knowing her and loving her, and is profoundly moulded by her. The two together form a little society of distinct beings united in mutual love, and cherishing not only each other but also the "we" that they together form. No doubt they also remain self-regarding individualists, and their self-interests often conflict. All love is complicated by hate. But in genuine love the conflict is largely transcended in the will for mutual adjustment and mutual dependence.

Perhaps I ought to apologize for wandering so far from the planets. But, believe me, this digression is very relevant to my theme. If one undertakes to discuss what man ought to do with the planets, one must first say what one thinks man ought to do with himself. And that is what I am trying to do. It cannot be done without a certain amount of fundamental thinking, not in the way of theorizing about the universe, but through trying to get a clear view of human experience itself.

Well, to continue this venture, from the experience of love or friendship or some form of genuine community in the field of personal contacts, the human individual may rise to the will for genuine community in *all* his dealings with his fellow human beings, no matter how slight his contact with them. Thus arises the ideal of universal Christian love, or the brotherhood of man. This ideal has haunted man for thousands of years. In one form or another, it has played an important part in all the great religions of the world. In Christianity, love is deified. God, we are told, actually is, in some obscure way, Love. The Holy Spirit is Love. And love is believed by Christians to be the fundamental power which created the universe. To believe such a proposition seems to me to go far beyond the legitimate scope of human thinking; but the fact that in the past many of the best minds *have* believed this has to be taken into account.

Why is it that love, kindness, fellowship, genuine community between persons, in fact, the distinctively human or rather personal kind of sociality, has been so greatly praised? Obviously it has survival value. And if you are determined to explain the most developed kinds of human experience and behaviour, *simply* in terms of the social conditioning of primitive impulses, quite a plausible explanation can be given. But this explanation does not go to the root of the matter. It is sheer dogma that the most developed and conscious human experience and behaviour can be fully explained simply in terms of its primitive sources. To do so is to leave out the most distinctive thing about man, namely his power of standing outside himself, to some extent, and being interested in things other than himself for their own sake. Anyone who has really been in love should understand this. Anyone who has had any genuine religious feelings should know it even better. The great Saints, Western and Eastern, were concerned (I should say) with experiences at the highest reach of human capacity, experiences which cannot be adequately described in terms of merely primitive impulses. I would add that neither should we accept uncritically the saints' own interpretations of their experiences, stated in terms of their own contemporary ideas about the fundamental nature of the universe. Human language and human thought itself were not then, and are not even now, sufficiently developed to make reliable statements about those most fully "awakened" experiences. Nevertheless, the experiences themselves, I suggest, are extremely important for anyone concerned with the proper ordering of human life. Someone may protest that, however important those experiences were to the saints, they are of no importance to us, because we do not share in them. The objection is worth answering. No doubt the saints had religious experience in a peculiarly vivid and compelling form which most of us cannot attain. But even ordinary men and women, or at any rate the more sensitive of them, if they take the trouble to discipline themselves a little, and concentrate their attention on their felt relation with each other and with the universe, can quite well discover in their own experience the *kind* of thing that the great mystics were trying to describe.

For lack of a better term, I shall call this most significant kind of experience "spiritual experience" or "experience of spirit." But I hasten to add that the word "spirit" need not be taken to mean some *thing* or *substance* other than matter, which is conceived as another thing or substance. Still less must spirit mean a divine person or God. I mean by "spirit" simply a particular way of experiencing and behaving. In fact, it is that kind of life which Christians sometimes call "the life of the spirit" or the "Way" of the Spirit, and Chinese sages have called simply "Tao," the "Way." What kind of a life the spiritual life is, I shall consider presently, trying to describe it in modern language and in relation to modern experience.

Meanwhile, I suggest that whatever *theories* men invent to justify the goodness or rightness of that way of life, what actually confronts them in their direct experience is simply a vision of the Way itself as supremely right. Whatever the status of spirit in the universe, what matters is simply spirit. The saints and sages yearned for the full expression of spirit in their own lives and the lives of others. They yearned to outgrow, or wake up from, the life of mere self-interest. They sought the ampler view. They sought, through self-denial, a real self-detachment for the sake of the ampler view, the deeper, more penetrating view. Through the discipline of the ordinary self-interested worldly self, they sought to "wake up," and adopt the point of view of a supposed universal self. Sometimes they persuaded themselves that they were actually gathered up into that supreme self in mystical communion; but even if one feels very sceptical about this, and about the existence of such a universal self, one must recognize that what they strove for was a transcendence of the limitations of mere *self*-concern, a self-forgetting through concern for other individuals and for the whole universe. In fact, a vision of the spirit as an ideal way of living, and as in some sense what we are *for*, intruded into their ordinary experience and claimed their allegiance.

But what *sort* of a way of life is the spiritual life? Leaving out the intellectual trappings of religious and metaphysical doctrine about the universe and fundamental reality, and bearing in mind aspects of knowledge that were not available to the ancients, I think we can express the essence of the matter in modern language. The very brief account that I shall give would not satisfy the ancient teachers or their modern followers, just because it leaves out the metaphysical doctrines; yet it does seem to me to describe the essence of their experience, in so far as it can have any meaning at all for ordinary human beings.

I must begin with a few words about the nature of personality, for the spiritual way is essentially a way for personal beings. Something is aware of something. "I," whatever that is, am aware of my body in its physical environment, and also of my "self" or psychological personality (as a creature with a certain character, needs and capacities), also of other persons, of societies of persons, of abstractions such as physical laws and moral principles, and (in a very sketchy way) of a whole objective universe *in* which I am. No doubt my awareness of these things is very confused and erroneous, but we all assume that there is *something* to be aware of, something which is independent of our experiencing it. In fact, there *is* an objective universe.

Now the innermost ring of objectivity, so to speak, is my own body in its relation with a physical environment. My body is experienced as a going concern, as dynamic, as tending toward certain actions and needing certain things of the environment. I consciously "espouse" my body's needs. I desire their fulfilment. For instance, when my body needs food, I desire the activity of eating. Similarly with the needs for sleep, sexual activity, and so on. In infancy this innermost ring of objectivity is all that is experienced. But gradually the growing child becomes aware of another ring of objectivity, namely that of conscious persons. He begins to be self-conscious and other-conscious. He "espouses" the needs of his own psychological person, and (less constantly) of a few other persons, such as his mother. In genuine love we "espouse" another person, forming a psychological symbiosis with him or her. The important point is that both the other person and my own self, with its particular character and needs and powers, are facts objective to my awareness of them. Of course, my awareness of them may be largely erroneous, I may make mistakes about them, as about any other objective facts. But they are not just fancy. They are what they are.

Beyond the sphere of the persons with whom I have personal contact, we may place another ring of objectivity, namely that on which occur all societies of persons, and the incipient society of mankind as a whole. Beyond again, comes the ring of abstract ideas, true and false, both kinds being objective to the experiencing "I." True ideas, in the final analysis, are simply objective characters apprehended by minds, and abstracted from their particular settings. The idea "dog" is the common character distinctive of all dogs. Of course, all ideas are partly false, some more so, some less. But even the false elements in ideas are rooted in objectivity. So to speak, they result from "squinting" objective characters together in wrong patterns, much as the drunkard may see two moons instead of one. He sees one moon twice, or in two places. Consider the idea of a "centaur," half horse, half man. There's no such beast; but the idea "centaur" is the product of "squinting" half a man and most of a horse together, and so forming a new abstract idea.

Now the overwhelmingly most important abstraction is the spirit, the ideal way of life. It is an ideal which is implied in, and emerges from, the actual experienced nature of personal beings, much as the law of gravity is implied in and emerges from the actual experienced nature of the behaviour of falling objects and the movements of planets and stars.

In the same way the ideas of good and evil and all possible kinds of values arise out of the impact of some region of objectivity on the conscious individual. Mere abstract subjectivity is no more than a featureless possibility of being aware of something, including values. All values arise from the conscious "espousal" of objective needs. Some are needs of one's own body, some are the more subtle needs of persons, myself and other selves.

Note further that personality *involves* community. There cannot be true personality save in true community with other persons. By community I mean not simply a relationship in which each individual strives to use others for his own advancement but the distinctively human social relationship, in which individuals are united in mutual respect for each other *as persons*. The spiritual way is essentially a way for persons in community with other persons. As Christians might put it, it is the way for a "Church," not simply for the individual, seeking individualistic salvation. As Communists might put it, it is the way for comrades working devotedly in a common cause.

Now I suggest that the spirit is essentially the way of life in which we strive towards full, comprehensive and true awareness of the objective universe, and toward appropriate feeling and appropriate creative action in relation to it. The universe, of course, includes oneself as an object, a self among other selves. In the spiritual life one strives for sensitive and intelligent awareness of things *in* the universe (including persons), and of the universe *as a whole*. One strives also for appropriate feeling about things and people and the universe as whole, without prejudice in favour of oneself as an individual or one's own family or nation, or even the human species. Finally one strives for appropriate and creative action in relation to all this.

The experience of the spirit, as the supreme good and as in some sense what we are "for," needs no support from metaphysical argument or religious doctrine. It is simply "given," as a datum, to the relatively awake mind, or rather to the awake mind that has not been perverted by obsession with some minor good, such as power, or bemused by some particular theory, such as materialism or theism. Let us never forget that, if theism is a frail invention of the human intellect, so is materialism. All such ambitious theories are almost certainly more false than true. All such metaphysical speculation, though interesting and educatively valuable, is quite unreliable, whether as support or denial of the experience of spirit, which needs no support other than its own overwhelming authority for the awakened mind. We all know the difference between being less awake and more awake, less responsive to the objective environment and more so. And we all trust our relatively more awake states more than our relatively somnolent states, for the very good reason that, the more comprehensively and accurately we are aware of the objective environment, the more our enterprises are likely to succeed. The kind of experience that I have called "spiritual" comes with an undeniable sense of "being very much awake," in the sense that it presents a vision or revelation of aspects of the objective reality that are *not* revealed in the self-absorbed kind of experience.

Incidentally, the more awake kinds of experience are also the more developed biologically and psychologically, and have had survival value in the long run. But in the sphere of spirit, survival value is not itself the test. The criterion must be simply the verdict of the most lucid consciousness itself, which emphatically declares the way of life called spiritual to be the highest good.

VII. A Commonwealth of Worlds

In the light of this all too superficial discussion of the spirit, I can now say what, in my view, is the right use of the planets.

If any of them is inhabited by intelligent beings, then clearly man should do his utmost to adopt a relationship of genuine community with those non-human intelligences, seeking earnestly to enter into their point of view, and to co-operate with them for mutual enrichment, both economic and spiritual.

But since it is unlikely that any other planet is in fact inhabited by intelligent beings, then the question that we must answer is, what should man do with those virgin worlds? And the answer is that he should deal with them precisely as with his native world. He should use them neither for the sole purpose of increasing his luxury, nor simply as a means to power for mere power's sake. He should use them for the spirit. He should avail himself of their resources in such ways as to advance the expression of the spirit in the life of mankind.

He should use them so as to afford to every human being the greatest possible opportunity for developing and expressing his distinctively human capacity as an instrument of the spirit, as a centre of sensitive and intelligent awareness of the objective universe, as a centre of love of all lovely things, and of creative action for the spirit. He should strive to make of the human race a glorious example of personality-in-community, a society of very diverse individuals united in mutual insight, understanding and sympathy, and in co-operative expression of the spirit. And for the full expression of the spirit in any community, the greater the diversity of individuals the better, provided that they all have sufficient imagination to enter into each other's points of view.

It is in this connection that the planets open up new possibilities. If man can establish in some of those other worlds new and specially adapted human or quasi-human races, then those races, living in their appropriate ways, should develop new expressions of the spirit at present inconceivable to terrestrial man. And through the intercourse of these diverse worlds, provided that each species has sufficient imaginative power, all should be spiritually enriched. Thus the goal for the solar system would seem to be that it should become an interplanetary community of very diverse worlds each inhabited by its appropriate race of intelligent beings, its characteristic "humanity," and each contributing to the common experience its characteristic view of the universe. Through the pooling of this wealth of experience, through this "commonwealth of worlds," new levels of mental and spiritual development should become possible, levels at present quite inconceivable to man.

A homely analogy may be hazarded. The really satisfactory marriage is not one in which husband and wife have identical character and interests, but one in which each is as different as possible from the other, though each has enough imagination to enter into the other and share the other's interests. In fact, the satisfactory marriage is a unity in diversity and a spiritual symbiosis.

Another analogy may help. Mankind to-day is deeply divided between two profoundly different systems of thought and value, two ideologies. Roughly, these ideologies centre upon America and Russia respectively. Each, I believe, contains very important truth which the other ignores. If war is avoided, and if in due season each side can learn from the other, the result may be a far more adult and spiritually enriched humanity than could ever have occurred without this cultural clash of mighty opposites. Incidentally, I cannot help hoping that Western Europe, and particularly Britain, may play an important part in the unifying of the two half-truths. For Europe is in a position to sympathize with both the half-truths. Formerly champions of individual liberty, we are now being forced by dire circumstances to plan our own society and discipline our individualistic impulses. Perhaps we shall be able to give the world an object lesson in planning for liberty. Add to this the fact that after all, with due respect to those vigorous adolescents, the Americans and the Russians, Europe, with all its faults, is relatively adult; and moreover is the custodian of a great tradition of civilization and spiritual life which has still an important function in this largely barbarian world. America and Russia, yes, and India and China, have doubtless momentous parts to play in the future; but to-day it is the European temper, yes, and particularly the temper of this island people, that is needed to restore unity to a divided mankind, and save our species from destroying itself. It is a solemn thought that perhaps our actions here and now, in this island, in this great city, may determine whether that dream of a commonwealth of worlds is to be made real or made for ever impossible.

VIII. Man and the Cosmos

I shall now add a postscript on a larger theme. Thus far we have been considering only the solar system. What of the stars? What of the galaxies of stars? And the cosmos as a whole? Interstellar travel seems to us the wildest fantasy. However, we should not entirely rule out the possibility that a human race far more advanced than ourselves might some day travel far beyond the limits of the solar system. It might for instance be possible, through skilled use of atomic power, to propel a planet on an interstellar voyage. The substance of the planet itself would have to be used up for the initial propulsion of the planet beyond the range of solar gravitation, also for subsequent steering, also to provide its inhabitants with heat and light and food on the longest of all voyages. For the shortest of interstellar voyages would certainly take a very long time, in fact, thousands or millions of years. But if the task was considered worthwhile, it might perhaps be undertaken. And, who knows? It might conceivably be worthwhile to explore in this way some of the nearest planetary systems. But the method would obviously be extremely cumbersome. It is not quite inconceivable that a far better method may some day be developed. In view of recent spectacular but still very fragmentary discoveries in the field of paranormal psychology, it is just possible that communication with intelligent races in even the remotest planetary systems may be effected by a highly developed technique of telepathy. This, of course, is a surmise of the wildest sort; but to-day, when the very foundations of our knowledge are being transformed, it should not be ignored.

One thing we can say with confidence. *If,* by one means or another, man does succeed in communicating with intelligent races in remote worlds, then the right aim will be to enter into mutual understanding and appreciation with them, for mutual enrichment and the further expression of the spirit. One can imagine some sort of cosmical community of worlds.

Further, we may, I think, be certain that, wherever, in any age or any galaxy, beings exist who are developed up to or beyond the level of awareness precariously attained by man at his best, there the imperious claim of the spirit, and therefore the ideal of personality-in-community, will surely be recognized. For this ideal and this claim are implied in the very nature of the awakened consciousness. It is nonsense to suppose that any humanly or superhumanly developed beings might permanently seek quite different values. The ideal of the spiritual life is involved in the very nature of personality. Apart from special cases of perversion or obsession by minor ends, the supreme end, which is the fulfilling of the spirit, cannot but be acceptable to the awakened consciousness. The ultimate goal of all awakened beings must inevitably be (how can one least misleadingly put it?) the expression of the objective cosmos in subjective experience and creative action, the fulfilment of the cosmos in cosmical awareness.

The more obvious way in which this goal is to be approached is through a cosmical community of worlds. But such a community may be nothing but the most fantastic of human dreams. Far more probably, the intelligent races within the cosmos may be for ever isolated from each other by the spatial immensities. In this case we are faced with two alternatives. We may suppose that God himself (or the supratemporal mind of the cosmos) embraces in a single cosmical experience, all the worlds and all their age-long lives; or we may declare simply that the goal of cosmical awareness is not attained, and is only a crazy human fantasy. In this case we may suppose either that there is no general purpose at all behind the cosmos (which may very well be the case), or else that the purpose is something wholly unintelligible to human minds, and indifferent to the expression of the spirit in any world. Or we may suppose that it is equally false to say either that there is or that there is not a cosmical purpose, since the truth is utterly beyond our comprehension. The cabbages in a garden are grown not that they may fulfill themselves in flower and fruit but simply that, before reaching maturity, they may be eaten. Similarly, it may be that the intelligent worlds of the cosmos are required merely to reach a certain low stage of spiritual growth before being destroyed. Let us remember, too, that if modern physics is correct, there awaits all worlds the cosmical night promised by the increase of entropy. Thus there is a race between cosmical fulfilment and cosmical death, between the complete awakening of consciousness in the cosmos, and eternal sleep.

But probably these wild speculations are all entirely beside the mark, because conceived in terms of ideas wholly inadequate to the actual conditions of the cosmos. For instance, our conception of the time itself is now turning out to be very incoherent and superficial. Perhaps (who can say) from the point of view of eternity the end of the cosmos is also its source and its temporal beginning. Perhaps the ultimate flower is also the primal seed from which all sprang. Perhaps the final result of the cosmical process is the attainment of full cosmical consciousness, and yet (in some very queer way) what is attained in the end is also, from another point of view, the origin of all things. So to speak, God, who created all things in the beginning, is himself created by all things in the end.

Such fantasies may have some kind of symbolic truth, just as the Bible story has symbolic truth. Anyhow, whether true or false, they may at least help us to feel something of the mystery and immensity that surrounds our little human life.

To-day there are hints that the immensity may be far greater than is supposed even in modern astronomy. Paranormal investigations obscurely suggest that the whole spatio-temporal physical universe may be but one very limited and easily misinterpreted aspect of an underlying reality which transcends space and time and the whole seeming-solid world of common sense and science. This is not the place to open up so vast a subject; but I should like to make one comment. Even if in the end these uncertain hints are justified, we shall not have to suppose that therefore the familiar universe is unreal, or sheer illusion. Rather it will have to be regarded as real but not the whole truth; and as "false" merely if we take it to be the whole truth. Further, it seems clear that, whatever the immensities beyond our familiar sphere, for us, who are so deeply implicated in this sphere, the supreme concern must continue to be life here and now. What we have to do is to make the best of this planet of ours, and perhaps of other worlds also.

Memoirs and Meditations

The Reflections of an Ambulance Orderly

Written in Belgium in 1916 after the passage in England of the Military Service Act, this short article appeared in the Quaker newspaper, The Friend, *on 14 April. At the time Stapledon, who was not a member of the Society of Friends, was a driver for the Friends' Ambulance Unit, and the Unit was torn over the question of whether to withdraw its pacifist volunteers to face imprisonment in England as absolute conscientious objectors or to continue the "compromise" of working alongside the battlefields, tending and transporting the wounded and evacuating both civilians and soldiers during poison gas attacks. In April Stapledon's convoy was based in the towns of Crombeke and Woesten (identified only as "W" in the article because of military censorship rules) near the Franco-Belgian border, and everyone was nervously anticipating an apocalyptic "big battle," which finally erupted on the Somme in early July. As both on-the-spot war journalism and as an anti-absolutist argument for continuing to serve in the ambulance unit, the article is interesting in its own right. It also stands as an early statement of some of Stapledon's characteristic philosophical and literary themes.*

CERTAIN YOUNG AMBULANCE DRIVERS sat together drinking cocoa and smoking. They talked of motors, guns, the condition of England, and finally of conscription. That was the burning subject. Some were determined to claim total exemption; some would be content with compulsory alternative service. All sighed for peace as the only satisfactory solution.

The door was opened by a Frenchman, who gave the order. "A gas attack has begun. You must send five cars to help your friends at W. Take helmets and respirators. Everyone else must be ready for work here."

Outside, in front of the old grey church, engines were soon started. The sun had set. Venus and Jupiter shone close together in the twilight. It seemed that those bright spheres could never be theatres of war. Yet what if this earth should after all be the first world to throw off this primeval strife?

From the east came a roar of guns, continuous, like the noise of a waterfall. At that distance the cannonade sounded not savage, but methodical, deliberate. It seemed not the cry of nations madly fighting, but the roar of machinery, the final expression of Western civilisation. Was this the great battle at last, or only another little experiment, resulting in pain, death and the conquest of a few ditches?

A group of drivers stood before the cars awaiting orders. "It's come at last," said one of them, "what we have been waiting for." "No, too soon," said another. A staunch pacifist cried, "Go it our guns," and checked himself in shame with the apology, "It's nicer to hear ours than theirs, somehow"; but another broke in, "It's awful, it's ghastly, no matter whose guns. It's just a huge hideous dog fight." After a pause he said, "Think of the pluck, though! And a fellow can't go into that fire without some ideal."

All stood impatiently quiet, awaiting further orders. Some perhaps had need to screw up their courage in preparation for expected shell-haunted runs, and all were humbled by the thought of the incomparable devotion of the fighting men. Helpless anger at the war fought against a longing to share fully the great burden of danger.

The old grey church stood quiet as ever. Its spire dimly soared into grey sky. Its clock tolled the hour deliberately, ringing through the noise of war. The aloofness of the church seemed a symbol of that consciousness of all humanity which sometimes flashes on the mind to make war ridiculous. The quiet church declared peace ultimate, war merely a stage.

Another order came, and cars dispersed to evacuate the sick and wounded from the hospitals. Men and baggage were safely stowed, stretchers strapped into place; rugs and hot bottles comforted the lying. One driver, who was without a car, helped his friends to load, and chatted with the patients in his best French. So sudden an evacuation must needs perturb weak men recovering from wounds. To chat with them is to cheer.

The moon rose red from the enemies' lines, and climbed among tall trees. She seemed indeed a hostile moon, lighting the attack. She might end the lull that had come with the darkness. Someone seeing her murmured with quaint urgency, "Couchez-toi, la lune." He added, "Our people at W. will be busy to-night. Helmets and respirators are no farce there. Some of those roads will be hot enough if this is really the battle. And one is always short of sleep at W."

Gradually the hospitals were emptied. The last man, with a bad foot, had to go sitting, for lack of space. There were still cars in reserve and others expected from headquarters. What would be the next order? Must all move forward to a rendezvous arranged in case of heavy fighting? Some hoped for that and "a good dose of the real thing till we are done up and have to rest."

"But why, why, why," cried one, "why must there be any attack? Think of the live men to be snuffed out! Think of the smashed bones and torn-up bodies! Think of the blood! Plenty of soaking stretchers for us for a while. Surely it's better to help clear up the mess than to go home and talk peace."

The great battle did not begin. This was merely a feint, costing some ammunition and life, but seriously harming neither side. One by one these young men of compromise returned and supped with thankfulness. Their share of work had been done without a hitch, and there was prospect of a night's sleep after all. They duly went to their straw beds, and puzzled drowsily awhile over those gallant but mistaken multitudes ranged against each other across Europe.

Some say that peace can be established only by a passion of goodwill. But may it not be that some are called to that work here and some there? While there is the chance of serving those who nobly suffer through humanity's error we cannot stay at home. Toward these patient, courageous, cheerful, and no doubt misguided fellow-men we extend our "passion of goodwill." Because of our oneness with humanity we dare not hold ourselves apart from the calamity. War is indeed strife of the right hand with the left; it is heart-splitting discord; yet under the shadow of our old grey church, and under the light of the stars, war itself may help a man to a new knowledge of the communion of all men.

The spirit that is mankind is mad to-day perhaps; but out of the madness she will come purified wondrously. We, her tiny members, need to be purified with her. That is why we are here.

Paul's Changing World
from *Last Men in London*

Some of Stapledon's best published autobiographical writing appeared under the guise of fiction in Last Men in London *(1932). Although he invented almost as much as he remembered in constructing the early life of his protagonist, the section of* Last Men in London *that describes the scientific education Paul received from his father is very closely modeled on the relationship of Olaf and his father William Stapledon. Paul's lessons in physics and astron-*

omy are essentially the lessons the author received from William Stapledon at the lakes of North Wales and on the rooftops of Port Said, Egypt, in the 1890s.

PAUL'S SENSE OF THE AUSTERITY of the physical universe awoke early. Even in the nursery he had conceived an uncomprehending respect for the mechanism of natural events. This spontaneous movement of piety toward "nature" developed not only into a strong scientific interest, but also into a strangely exultant awe, for which there seemed to be no rational justification.

It was his father who first pointed out to him the crossing wave-trains of a mountain tarn, and by eloquent description made him feel that the whole physical world was in some manner a lake rippled by myriads of such crossing waves, great and small, swift and slow. This little significant experience took place during a holiday spent on the Welsh moors. They were standing on a crag overlooking the grey "llyn." They counted five distinct systems of waves, some small and sharp, some broad and faint. There were also occasional brief "cat's paws" complicating the pattern. Father and son went down to the sheltered side of the lake and contemplated its more peaceful undulations. With a sense almost of sacrilege, Paul stirred the water with his stick, and sent ripple after ripple in widening circles. The father said, "That is what you are yourself, a stirring up of the water, so that waves spread across the world. When the stirring stops, there will be no more ripples." As they walked away, they discussed light and sound and the rippled sky, and the sun, great source of ripples. Thus did an imaginative amateur anticipate in a happy guess the "wave mechanics" which was to prove the crowning achievement of the physics of the First Men. Paul was given to understand that even his own body, whatever else it was, was certainly a turmoil of waves, inconceivably complex but no less orderly than the waves on the tarn. His apprehension of this novel information was confused but dramatic. It gave him a sense of the extreme subtlety and inevitability of existence. That even his own body should be of this nature seemed to him very strange but also very beautiful. Almost at the outset, however, he said, "If my body is all waves, where do *I* come in? Do I make the waves, or do the waves make me?" To this the father answered, with more confidence than lucidity, "You are the waves. What stirs is God."

This experience stayed with Paul for ever. It became for him the paradigm of all physical sciences, and at the same time an epitome of the mystery of life. In his maturity he would often, when he came upon still water, pause to disturb its serenity. The little act would seem to him darkly impious yet also creative. He would mutter to himself, "God stirs the waters." Sometimes he would take a handful of little stones and throw them into the pond, one after the other in different directions. Then he would stand motionless, watching the intersecting circles spread and fade and die, till at last peace was wholly restored.

Paul's first view of the moon through his father's modest telescope was another memorable experience. He had already seen a ship disappearing below the horizon, and had been told that the earth and the moon were round. But actually to see the rotund moon, no longer as a flat white shilling, but as a distant world covered with mountains, was an experience whose fascination he never outgrew. Throughout his life he was ready to gaze for ten minutes at a time through telescope or field-glass at the bright summits and black valleys along the line between lunar night and day. This vision had a startling power over him which he himself could not rationally justify. It would flash mysteriously upon him with bewildering and even devastating effect in the midst of some schoolboy activity, in the midst of a Latin lesson, or morning prayers, or a game of cricket, or a smutty story. Under the influence of this experience he began to devour popular astronomy books. He looked with new eyes at the first page of the school atlas, which had hitherto meant nothing to him. Rapidly the schoolboy universe ceased to be the whole real universe, and was reduced to a very faulty picture of a tiny corner of a universe which teemed with suns and inhabited worlds. For at this stage he imagined that every star was attended by a dozen or so populous planets.

He was perplexed to find that most adults, though many of them fully believed in some such universe, did nothing with the knowledge. That which to him was so significant was to them either tiresome or terrifying. Even his father, who had helped him to discover the new world, did not seem to appreciate it as it deserved. To the father it did indeed seem wonderful. He called it "sublime." But for him it remained merely a sublime irrelevance. It compelled his attention, and in a manner his admiration also; but the tone of his voice, when he was talking of it, suggested a veiled reluctance, almost resentment. He seemed, in spite of all his scientific interest, to be happier and more at home in the world of the Iliad or of the "Faerie Queene." The son, on the other hand, though he did his best to appreciate these dream worlds, was never moved by them. But the stars gave him an intense exhilaration, which, when he tried to justify it to his father, turned out to be, or to seem, wholly irrational.

Fields Within Fields

The multiple manuscripts for this unfinished book—a forerunner of Youth
and Tomorrow *(1945)—are complex, and it is difficult to know the author's
final thoughts before he abandoned the project, or why he abandoned it. Written after Olaf and Agnes Stapledon moved from the seaside town of West
Kirby into a new house near the village of Caldy in Spring 1940, the most
complete version of "Fields Within Fields" breaks off with a brief telling of
the family incident that opens* Youth and Tomorrow, *when young Olaf is
caught between competing views of knowledge held by his parents. That
manuscript lacks the second and third paragraphs printed below (in brackets),
but an addendum starts the whole narrative again with the bracketed sentences. The two drafts are not consistent with one another: the bracketed
paragraphs observe Simon's Field in late spring but the next sentences describe the earlier time of planting. Both are included here as striking examples
of Stapledon's twin gifts for visionary speculation and simple naturalistic
description. The second and third paragraphs recall the panoramic sweeps of
time in* Last and First Men, *and they amount to a distinctively modern
revision of a moment in Stapledon's favorite Shakespearean play. Hamlet in
the graveyard, holding the skull of Yorick and brooding on the relationship of
mortal human flesh to dirt, is cousin to the figure of Stapledon ruminating
on the history of the clods of earth in Simon's Field. But the natural cycles of
decay and transformation that Hamlet finds depressing, Stapledon celebrates
as evidence of the astonishing energy and economy of the cosmos. The entire
excursion into memory takes place under the shadow of the German bombardment of Merseyside which began in 1941.*

THERE IS A FIELD called Simon's Field. Who Simon was, and why the
field was his, nobody knows. His life is now only a fibre indistinguishable in the matted felt of the past. All that is left of him is this field's
name in a few local minds; and on our letter paper, for with money-
power we seized an acre in the middle of the field and built our house
on it. And now the name of the field is the name of the house.

[Young wheat plants now occupy the rest of the field. They stand
in ranks, swaying, whispering, an assembled youth-movement twenty
million strong. Among their feet a few lesser plants struggle for light
and air. Thistles irrepressibly crane their stiff necks up to the ever-

rising surface of this green sea. Overhead larks sing; but their music is buried deep under the oppressive singing of the planes, daily preparing for battle. The bombers, with heavy wombs, move slowly. The fighters, those speeding three-dimensional skaters, stoop to the chimney-tops, then climb into the clouds, filling the sky with their warsong. Over these again, the unseen stars, the unheard music of the spheres.

Unheard? The field itself echoes with spheral music. Its own history is woven into the cosmical counterpoint. Take a clod in your hand, and your fingers and eyes resound with cosmical and hypercosmical themes. Brick-hard at this season, dusty, very recalcitrant to the hoe, this clod has been trampled by generations of farm workers, following the plough and the harrow, in reveries of lust and love and rest. Hobnailed boots and thonged sandals and the horny feet of ancient Britons and palaeolithic hunters have pressed this very earth. The other day on a neighbouring hill a girl picked up one of their flint arrow-heads, neatly faceted as a jewel, the pride of some prehistoric craftsman, the treasure of some bowman. This very clod, how many times, I wonder, has it been actually held in a hand? Or is this, improbably, the first time it has made contact with human flesh? But how many feet of toiling horses and of sheep and cattle have again and again crushed it, so that the rain and the sun had once more to coagulate it and bake it? And how many deer and boar? Wolves have sniffed at it, hurrying on the trail. Plants have penetratingly searched it with their rootlets. Worms have nosed through it. And before ever they began, the crude clay, deposited by some archaic river, was pioneered and broken up and sifted and chemically transformed by some archaic vegetation, until this very soil, this very clod was made. But from what vanished rock in what corroded mountain were its granules first washed? And where were they in the days when the giant reptiles cooled their bellies in a still more ancient mud? And the primaeval atoms of this clod, how many have actually passed through what living bodies of men and beasts? How many have been within the dung collected from ancient privies and scattered for manure, how many have been dropped by cattle, or by deer or tiger or mastodon? How many million times have they passed through the bodies of worms, modern worms and the many ancestral types before the familiar worms appeared? What part have they played in the lives of primitive one-celled creatures in the warm primaeval soup where life began? Earlier these very atoms, these nuclear protons and electrons which now form fertile soil, were molten lava, were part of that drop of liquid fire which was the embryo earth. Earlier still they were in the sun. And long before the sun had condensed out of diffuse haze of matter they drifted like solitary motes. And earlier, earlier still, before the initial cosmos-creating explosion, the initial crashing chord of spheral music, what artist conceived the form? Or was there no artist, and no earlier time?]

At this time of year the field is bare earth. Recently an old man and a young man, each with a horse and plough, passed hundreds of times from side to side of the field. The plough-shares nosed into the soil. The lifted clods tumbled in a steady wave. Along each of the two furrows, along the wakes of these two earth-faring ships, gulls clamoured, searching for worms. Settling a few paces behind the men's heels, they clambered over the clods, pecking; then rose to follow the plough or wheel overhead on their keen sails, so different from the ancestral reptile's limbs, so much more functional and lovely than the wings of pterodactyl and bat. On some days the ploughmen were accompanied by a black dog, hearty in voice and tail. Then the gulls avoided the plough, returning to the mud-flats or the tide. But the dog would trot importantly around, laughing. His subhuman mind, half humanized by contact with farmers and labourers, zestfully though blindly participated in man's daily work.

When the ploughing was done the old man and his horse went over the field with a harrow, and then with a more cunning implement which sowed the seed through little funnels and covered it with soil. Then they rolled the field with a ribbed and clanking roller. Then they left it alone. So now for a while the field is brown bare earth, and no green is in it. But under the surface the population of the wheat is already waking. As a sleeping child is wakened by a cool hand on its brow, moisture rouses the seeds. Already innumerable root-tips are thrusting down and tight-folded cotyledons are shouldering upward toward the light.

Simon's Field is broad and long. Our acre is only a minor part of it. To the ploughman it is a great plain confronting him with the necessity of work. Yet on the Earth's round breast this field is an insignificant skin-cell. And of course our planet herself, gyrating round the sun, is a midge beside a great fire. And the sun, as we very well know, is a spark among other sparks. They are far more numerous than all the sand-grains on all the beaches; yet they are isolated by the unimaginable fields of space. Proportionately they are more remote from one another than a candle at Land's End from a candle at John o'Groat's. Unforgettable commonplaces! Far from belittling the field, somehow they discover its depth. For the field is integral to the farthest galaxies. Moreover, each buried grain in the soil is inwardly a universe. Each cell in each germ is a microcosm too subtle for clear comprehension. The atoms in each cell's nucleus are as many as the stars.

But what is there of significance in mere hugeness and littleness and in mere complexity? Nothing, nothing! Yet in the complexity of the cosmos may we not at least surmise an unfathomable depth of life, an immeasurable potentiality of spirit? True, very true, provided that we know already, from living adequately here on the earth, what life is and what spirit might be. And Simon's Field is a focus within the great field of mankind's existence. It is shot through and through by influences from every mode of existence on the planet, as though by rays of every colour in the spectrum of the spirit. It is warm, too, with its own intrinsic and by no means undiversified life.

Simon's Field's eastern boundary is a lane. In winter time a great winding snow-drift sometimes lies along it, a white and serpentine monster, with here and there its young hanging on its flanks. But today the ruts and the grass are once more uncovered, and in the hedges the blackbirds and thrushes, for so long intent wholly on the fight with frost and snow, are occasionally noticing one another as possible mates or rivals. Beyond the lane lie more fields, and little woods, and ponds for water-rats. In amongst all these the houses have year by year encroached, the homes of citizens who have profited by modern industrialism, through ability or luck. Beyond all this again lies Thurstaston, a low brown hill, play-ground for town workers. On the hill there is a rock, Thor's Stone, where long ago, they say, men spilt sacrificial blood. But now the sugary pink sandstone is everywhere foot-worn, and scratched over with the initials of self-advertisers. From Thurstaston you can see, across more fields and woods and beyond a far suburban hill, the smoke-haze of Merseyside, sprinkled with balloons, the droppings of flies on yellowing paper. A few of the tallest of Liverpool's buildings peer over the hill. With a field glass one can see on the twin pinnacles of the Liver Building twin bronze birds looking down on the gravely wounded city and on the wrecks in the Mersey. To the right the tower of the well-bred modern cathedral impotently recalls an age when religion was a power, and is in the main unresponsive to the new stirrings of religion in men's hearts. To the left lies the Mersey's mouth, where formerly the liners headed confidently for the open sea, but now convoys of freighters and tankers creep out under escort.

On the west the field is bounded by a railway, a single track in a shallow cutting. When trains pass, almost sunk out of sight, they appear from the field to be swimming through the ground. Hourly these giant reptiles, survivors from a vanishing world, slide, grunting, to and fro. They are friendly beasts. At night, sometimes, when the air is crackling with the clatter of war, one of these Victorian creatures, passing calmly on its way, seems to snort assurance that, after all, Britain is unconquerable, that the Empress Queen (do not whisper that she is dead) is not amused, and that she insists on speedy victory. But overhead reptiles more modern and winged cruise with murderous intent.

Beyond the railway lies pasture. We reach it by an old bridge, overgrown with hawthorn, brambles, nettles. Long ago this region was the field's own western half, but now, as though by fissiparous reproduction, it has become a separate organism, the Links. There sheep and golfers perform their several but symbiotic activities, regardless of one another. Westward again, the land breaks off in clay cliffs, overlooking the Dee Estuary, and toppling into it, a yard a year. Along the beach a line of disordered but shaped sandstone blocks, the remains of a sea-wall, marks the land's surrendered frontier. Along the beach, too, innumerable pebbles, of every size from pea to football, are currants and raisins in the sand. Scores of the pebble clans are here represented. Granites, both the reds and the grays, black-green basalts, schists and shales and mill-stone grits, jostle one another, assembled here aeons ago by the great Manx Glacier before there was an Irish Sea. So at least I was told by an old geologist with a hammer, prospecting among them.

The Estuary! Twice daily the tide transforms it. An even beauty of broad water, with here and there a fishing boat or a distant coaster, alternates with a more varied beauty of mud-flats, sand-banks, and channels. Never, surely, would Socrates have denied to mud an ideal form if the Grecian inlets had been tidal. Today a line of bomb-craters pocks our mud, surviving many tides. Across the estuary lies Wales, a long hill-side, mottled with fields, woods, villages, but the shore bristles with factory chimneys, like stiff, plumed grasses. On still days faint sounds reach us from that foreign country, the murmur of trains, and muffled, inexplicable eructations, perhaps from the furnaces. With luck and a good field-glass you may sometimes see a puffing engine with a truck creep along a jetty of slag and suddenly vomit down the slope a bright flood of lava. Plunging into the water this raises a tree of steam that overtops the hills. With a glass you may pick out many other signs of life on that distant world. You may see cows, dotting the fields like granules in the Welsh skin-cells. On a clear day sheep may be detected. A man is a minute erect bacillus.

To the south of Simon's Field one looks across hedges to a hill-shoulder, sloping to the estuary. From behind the hill a townlet, once a fishing village, now mainly a citizens' dormitory, extends into view a front of brickwork. High on the hill a ferroconcrete ship with masts and funnel marks the training school for difficult boys whom society will send to sea to keep them out of mischief. Meanwhile, now and again, they escape in twos and threes over the countryside and raid the larders, carrying off the week's unreplaceable ration of butter and jam. Nearer, two fields away and at the cliff's edge, is a collection of huts. Thence a bugle punctuates the day.

North of Simon's Field a large townlet advances southward, and the Estuary opens northward into the sea. Two low islands and a rock form a little convoy off the point. In that townlet, in a suburban avenue, we two settled after the first war; and when the second war had already begun, we came to Simon's Field.

Within the boundaries of the field our acre, a field within a field, is an unfulfilled garden, occupied mostly by the original grass; for at the time of our coming the whole field was pasture. Today our infant hedges divide the brown field from the green acre with its incipient brown vegetable plots. For slowly, foot by foot, our bright spades are biting into the sod and turning the acre into garden, to produce food, we say, for this beleaguered island of Britain.

How well this sounds, as though we were pioneers at grips with the jungle! But in fact our power lies not in stout hearts and iron sinews. Our power is money. Money-power, passively acquired, won this acre for us, built this house, and has persuaded a gardener to work on our behalf. Without him our own spare-time spades would be defeated. Digging our way too slowly through the acre, we should see the hard-won tilth steadily re-conquered by the wild. But money has secured extra muscle and much-needed skill.

I must here at the outset face up to this matter of our money-power. I have money. I have, that is, the legal right to direct the labour of others for my own advantage. This right I mainly inherited from my father, who bequeathed me stocks and shares, mostly in shipping. This means that to give me money-power men have toiled and sweated long hours in stokeholds in the Red Sea. Some have been so driven to distraction that they have jumped overboard. It means, too, that men have shivered in crow's-nests in the Pacific when deep valances of ice hung from the rigging. All this they did for a wage that I would scorn, having no need of it. And by doing all this they gave me the legal and the moral right to say to other men, "In exchange for a fraction of my money-power, make me a coat, or bread, or a house; or educate my children in the best way yet devised; or take me and my family for a holiday beside the Lake of Annecy, where we can climb the alpine pastures and crags and hear the cow-bells, or sit in the open-air cafés watching the people and trying to follow their French talk; or take us through Sweden in an electric train, northward, till we pass the line of white stones labeled 'Polarcirkel,' and on beyond the iron mountains and mines of Kiruna to the great cold lake of Torna-träsk, to see the Lapp camps, and the lemmings that swarm in the tundra, and to follow the reindeer over the bleak mountains called Tsasinaskatchoko and Nissanjaro, that are piebald with snow." Those who won for me this power were travellers themselves, but how differently they fared in their stoke-holds and crows'-nests. This flagrant discrepancy has produced in me a boringly familiar guilt and shame, like an old corn. But I have taken no serious measures to remove it.

By what right could I do this? There was a time when I determined to have no truck whatever with inherited money-power. I would be a coal-miner or an ordinary seaman and so earn my living, and use whatever energy and time was to spare for exercising the superior talents which I wishfully believed were mine. But having those talents, it seemed a sin to waste them burrowing underground or freezing in crows'-nests. And so little by little I persuaded myself that I must use the God-sent gift of money-power to enable me to pursue my true work fully and freely. And so, after many strange antics, here I am in Simon's Field, with more than half a century behind me. And what *really* is there to show for it all?

My father bought those stocks and shares. He won the power to buy them by hard work, intelligence and responsibility in service of his shipping company. He was nothing of a drone. He was a worker, but a human worker, not a worker-ant; for he knew what he was working *for*, however indirectly, namely for the well-being of human individuals and the clarification of human culture. He knew about ships and he cared painstakingly for the men in them. And they loved him, because he understood them and respected them, and because he did not spare himself. But the seamen and stokers worked in their manner no less hard than he worked. Their homes, which they so seldom visited, were cramped and mean, and not at all like his home. Their children were taught in over-crowded schools, and not in the best way yet devised. And while they were still children they were cast into the economic cauldron, not sent to the university to be assiduously tended. My father was a good man in a bad system. He had ability, and he was loyal, but also he had luck. The system, through the person of his father, gave him a good start, which it denied to others no less able. And I was given an even better start; unless, indeed, in all this careful cultivation of the young there is some hidden error, some emasculating poison.

This book is not to be about me. It is about the world seen through these eyes and this brain, and seen from the focus that is Simon's Field. But its purpose requires me to dwell for a while on the sequence of three lives, my grandfather's, my father's, and my own; for both their contrast and their similarity yield striking information about the world, and about these eyes and this brain and these hands of mine, by means of which I see the world and react upon it by reporting its revealed character. Trying to know my grandfather I shall the better know myself. By knowing my grandfather's world I shall the better perceive the contrasting temper of my own world. History, after all, is made up of the over-lapping fibres of human biographies. You cannot catch its spirit by taking merely a cross section of it, like the translucent section of a rock, prepared for the microscope. You must observe the interlocked fibres. The interlocking from a grandfather through son-father to grandson should prove significant of history's movement throughout a century.

My father's father was a sea-captain in the days when sea-captains were little kings. He went to sea at sixteen. At twenty-one he took command of a ship. On one of his early voyages he wrote a journal, now at Simon's Field. When I first came into possession of this heirloom I regarded it only with superficial curiosity. It was not quite old enough, I said, to be really interesting. But since then I have wandered to and fro among its pages with increasing fascination. There is nothing outstandingly remarkable in it, but it has come alive in my hands, as though, after long hibernation, the warmth of human contact had awakened it. Somehow, I feel, it has a special message for me, as though my young grandfather had written it with a deep unconscious purpose of communicating something to his aging grandson in another world. I cannot clearly understand what that something is, yet I can feel it. Perhaps it is just the temper of his life on little sailing-ships, beating about the oceans in constant discomfort and frequent danger during that age when the red ensign carried most of the world's trade, and the white ensign kept the world's peace; when danger lay only in storms, diseases, famines, and men could not yet fly; when righteousness was everywhere respected, and its reward hereafter confidently expected.

My grandfather wrote his journal when he was master of the barque "John Patchet." He sailed from Glasgow in the autumn of 1852, aged twenty-three. After trading to Australia and the East Indies he returned to Liverpool in the spring of 1854. His careful copper-plate handwriting fills two foolscap volumes. The covers are now stained and worn and spotted with white paint, but the pages are in good order. Some are written over twice, the two scripts running at right angles to one another. My grandfather's style is in the main "correct," though grammatical errors are occasionally imported from his sea-faring speech. The spelling is erratic, as is usual in my family. He shows a great liking for capital letters, sprinkling them freely along every sentence for no discoverable reason. The word "has" nearly always appear without the "h" and with a capital "A."

The frontispiece of the journal is a pencil drawing of his barque. He used a ruler for the masts and rigging and the lines of gunwale and deck. The whole picture is shaded with smeared pencil, faintly lined to give the form of sails and waves. A number of little wiggly strokes represent gulls. Later on he probably taught his young son to draw ships, for the much stylized art was handed down by my father to me. But my father drew for me mainly steamers, in that transitional stage when yards were still carried on the masts, and sailors in steam were still apologetic about their vocation. Throughout my youth I was addicted to drawing ships, for as a child in Port Saïd I was constantly along-side or on board all kinds of vessels. But my drawings, though they involved far more technical skill than my grandfather's, seem to me now far less vital; which is not surprising, since for me ships had never more than a romantic fascination. My sailor-grandfather knew these almost organic, almost living human artifacts far more intimately and objectively, since all his active life was spent in servitude to them. My grandfather's journal contains also a spirited drawing of three water-spouts, and others of a small island. There are also several ornate maps on which the ship's course is marked. The conscious motive of all these rare artistic ventures was doubtless to record facts or to kill time. But there is evident in them a certain love of drawing for its own sake, and a remarkable though untrained vitality. Like the palaeolithic hunters, he drew the things he lived by, with little technique but with insight into the spirit of the object.

The bulk of the journal is a record of daily events. There are pages of navigational calculations. The winds and currents are carefully noted, and every alteration to the sails. There are discussions about the ship's exact position, particularly when the chronometer is suspected of inaccuracy. All kinds of work on the ship are reported, painting the long-boat, repairing the sails, shifting heavy cables to adjust the vessel's weight and put her on an even keel.

But my grandfather's journal is far more than an official log. Interspersed between notes on the weather and jobs allotted to the carpenter or the sail-maker are descriptions of sunsets and storms, meditations on human life, yearnings for home, and particularly for a beloved sister and an adored young woman whom I take to be his future wife and my grandmother. He worshipped "female beauty" all the more because he was so seldom in its presence. His ideal for the sex was a combination of classic grace, Christian charity and Victorian chastity. Among the temptations of Sydney, that sink of iniquity, temptations to which he was by no means unsusceptible, he preserved his virtue by remembering his own beloved women at home, and by social intercourse with the virtuous and accomplished ladies whom he encountered not in the city but in homesteads in the surrounding country-side. For during the month of his enforced stay in Sydney he was invited to the houses of planters and merchants, and was delighted by the piety and culture of "the natives," meaning not the blacks but the native white population, who were at the time destroying the blacks like vermin. In his journal he frequently parades his own culture. It contains many quotations from the poets, from Wordsworth, Cowper, Moore, and several long ones from Montgomery. What, I wonder, would my grandfather have thought of Macaulay's diatribe on that once popular poet? Montgomery's influence is detectable in Captain Stapledon's own verse, which he has rather frequently inscribed in his journal. And though both these poets, both Montgomery and the master of the "John Patchet," plainly lack the gift of novel and accurate vision without which no verse can be poetry, their empty and hackneyed phrases acquire in the setting of this journal a surprising significance. Though he is no poet for the public, my grandfather's verse compels a certain respect. This young seaman, struggling with an overloaded ship and a crew discontented to the point of mutiny on account of drenched bunks and spoilt food, was something else besides a man of action. Bringing the vessel successfully through great storms, dangerous channels, and inexplicably tumultuous places where he suspected submarine eruption, haggling with shippers in Sydney about freight, touting for a crew for the return voyage, he kept one side of his mind intent on matters which to the ordinary sea-faring man were an unknown world, an unsuspected ocean, so to speak, beyond the barrier of an impassable isthmus. A ship-master in those days had great responsibility, and spells of continuous activity, but also immense tracts of leisure. He was not only a navigator, a magistrate, a housekeeper, a doctor, a priest to perform the last rites over the dead, but also a recluse with ample time for meditation. My young grandfather had to keep the peace between the quarreling members of his crew, to cope with a rebellious chief officer, to deal as best he could with diseases, with no aid but a medical book and a medicine chest. One of his men, whom he had regarded as merely lazy and had treated with appropriate sternness, became at last so weak that he was useless. Presently, in spite of the master's medical treatment, he died. My grandfather buried him at sea, retiring afterwards to his cabin to record the event and his meditations on death.

This habit of recording his meditations probably afforded the young man several kinds of satisfaction. It relieved his feelings about the difficulties and disappointments of the voyage. It gave expression to his longing for home and to sexual hunger. It gave him self-respect and moral strength. The unsympathetic reader might judge that the real function of my grandfather's literary efforts was to prove that he was a cut above other men; in fact the motive, it might be suspected, was sheer snobbery. His diction is stilted and conventional. The thoughts and feelings which he records show no originality. But this is only half the truth. To the more sympathetic reader it is evident that for the young sailor himself these meditations and their recording were a genuine means of expression for the more sensitive side of his nature, the side which a ship-master's life might well have starved. These high-sounding platitudes were not platitudes to him. They were truths, discovered in his own experience of life, and expressed in the kind of language which he believed to be appropriate to such august truths. For a seaman, my grandfather was evidently remarkably well-read; but not so well-read as to be clearly conscious of the true canons of literary art. Obviously he enjoyed the craft of writing. Within his knowledge of it, he worked conscientiously and skilfully, and for the love of expression.

His verse, in particular, though it contains errors of grammar and spelling, shows a genuine aesthetic feeling and is metrically correct. Like his drawing of the "John Patchet," it is "done with a ruler," but done also with a real love of craftsmanship. His pen goes deeper than his pencil in expression of his thoughts and feelings. Though the sophisticated reader cannot but see that his imagery is banal and second- or even tenth-hand, nevertheless his writing is sincere with a kind of naive sincerity, which the sophisticated cannot easily detect. For the sophisticated are apt to suppose that what would be insincere in them must be insincere in others. In three stanzas on the theme, "Time speeds away—away—away" it is not only their setting in the journal of a young sea-captain that compels the reader to recognize a sincerely felt and universal experience. These verses were written about three weeks from the end of the voyage, when my grandfather was longing most impatiently for home. He consoles himself with the thought that "the wings of time are swift," but the poem which follows is concerned wholly with the tragic aspect of their swiftness. In their classical mode they record the very same experience as that of the early Englishman who likened the life of man to the passage of a bird through a lighted room and out again into the dark. My grandfather was a pious Victorian, but his final attitude to time is this:

> Like fiery steed—from stage to stage
> He bears us on—from youth to age:
> Then plunges in the fearful sea
> Of fathomless Eternity.

These verses are inscribed with more than his usual care and signed "Wm. Stapledon" with a generous flourish sweeping to and fro across the lettering.

My grandfather in his time commanded many ships, both sailing ships and steamers. At last in virtue of proved intelligence and responsibility he came in for a good shore-job as a shipping agent in Port Saïd. He trained his sons to the business, and in due season retired to enjoy his prosperity. As a small boy I could confidently look forward to a half-sovereign whenever I met him. His house in Devon overawed me with its in fact not very flagrant luxury and its accent of gentility. He drove about in a carriage and pair. He travelled first class on the railways, and preferred to smoke his cigar in a non-smoking carriage, since the smell of stale smoke offended him. My last memories of him are of a wildly muttering old man who had had a stroke, was bed-ridden, and could not recognize me. He remained in that living death for many months before plunging into "the fearful sea of fathomless Eternity."

What kind of a man, I ask myself, was my grandfather, really? At least he was a real man. He made good, not through luck but personal character. His rebellious chief officer reviled him as a "bull-dog"; and possibly he was too masterful, for he certainly had difficulties with his crew. When he was desperately trying to engage new hands in Sydney he was outraged by one possible employee who asked for a written testimonial of the master's good behaviour, signed by the departing crew. Perhaps one ought not to expect a Victorian sea-captain to regard this demand as anything but gross "impertinence." After all, he knew himself to be a capable and righteous man in a responsible position which he had won by his own ability. What right had any riffraff seamen to question him? The truth is, though he would not have put it in this way, that he was a member of a class which was justifying its privileges by its success in advancing British commercial imperialism and carrying forward the industrialization of the world. And this process, horrible as its immediate results have often been, was probably necessary. Without it the species would never be able to attain that greater power and greater mental lucidity and richer individual life which is the proper goal of all its striving.

We have a portrait of my grandfather in the prime of life, painted, I suspect, in China, for he made many voyages to the Far East. He appears in evening dress, with a large gold stud in his shirt-front. That stud is now at Simon's Field. His face is clean-shaven but fringed with a dark and sturdy Krüger beard. The mouth is firmly compressed, but with a readiness to smile. There is humour in the eyes, but also complacency. Comparing that face with my memory of my father's face in his prime and with my own in the shaving mirror, I see the unmistakable but subtle family likeness behind the idiosyncrasies. All have the same strong hair, though the colour is different, and my grandfather's is oiled and waved, my father's close-cropped, and mine like grass that has been badly scythed. Our noses are similar, but mine the most uptilted. And so on. My father's prevailing expression I remember as definitely different from that of my grandfather in the portrait and in his photographs. My father's is gentler, kindlier, more humorous, but also sadder. There is more humility in it, and perhaps a deeper-flowing consciousness. I wonder how far this difference was due to differences of individual temperament and individual experience and how far to prevision of the great change from Victorian optimism to latter-day self-doubt and disillusionment.

My grandfather's portrait used to dominate the dining room at Port Saïd. After his retirement my father used to sit at the head of the table beneath it. I seem to remember (or is it fancy?) the pictured face looking down with grim humour on a terrible incident in my childhood. My father, who began my scientific education very early, was illustrating the effects of suction by holding a plate of porridge upside-down over my head. The experiment had worked several times before, but this time it didn't. And the porridge was hot.

My father's interest in science was very strong. My grandfather, though he was capable of careful descriptions of natural events, gives no hint of that intense intellectual curiosity which led my father, throughout his busy life, to do his utmost to "keep abreast of science." When I was a child popular science was beginning to flourish. Such names as Darwin, Huxley, Tyndal, Lockyer were constantly in use. Science primers competed with volumes of English poetry for dominance of my early home. At Simon's Field we have a bundle of letters from my father to his newly married wife in England entirely devoted to her scientific education. They form a series of lectures, and they include problems which she dutifully solved in her answers. We have note-books, too, written with extreme minuteness and neatness consisting entirely of long quotations from scientific works. As soon as I was old enough to respond, my father undertook my scientific education also. The formulae, the diagrams, the experiments! How I remember them! Once he put too big a lump of sodium in a basin of water. The molten metallic sphere fizzed hither and thither, then exploded. A bit of it found my eye. My father collected birds' eggs with me, and blew them. On one occasion the embryo was beginning to form. A leg and bits of guts came through into the saucer. My mother was outraged that her innocent child should see such things, but my father was glad that I should learn.

Time and Eternity
from *Death into Life*

The seven meditative interludes in the 1946 Death into Life *are the most impressive parts of an otherwise plodding narrative. The fourth, "Time and Eternity," blends autobiography with poetic reverie in a version of a recurrent motif in Stapledon's writing: his visionary encounter in 1903 with his visiting nine-year-old Australian cousin and future wife, Agnes Miller. He always spoke of this moment, so like Dante's first glimpse of Beatrice at age nine in the* Vita Nuova, *as the wellspring of his creative life.*

TODAY! TOMORROW!

Today comprises the whole present universe of infinite detail and inconceivable extent. Today is fields and houses and the huge sky. Today human creatures are being conceived, are born, are loving, hating, dying. Electrons and protons in their myriads are everywhere busily performing their unimaginable antics. Planets attend their suns. Galaxies drift and whirl.

All this today comprises, and with all this the whole past is pastly present in today: Queen Victoria, Babylon, the ice ages, the condensing of the stars in the primeval nebula, and the initial inconceivable explosion of creativity.

But tomorrow? It is a wall of impenetrable fog, out of which anything may come.

When we remember or discover the past, we confront something that is what it is, eternally though pastly. It is such and such, and not otherwise. Our view of it may indeed be false; but it, in itself, is what in fact it was, however darkly it is now veiled. No fiat, not even an Almighty's, can make the past be other than in fact it was, and eternally is. God himself, if such there be, cannot expunge for me the deeds I now regret.

But the future? It is not veiled, it is nothing. It has still to be created. We ourselves, choosing this course rather than that, must play a part in creating it. Even though we ourselves, perhaps, are but expressions of the whole living past at work within us, yet we, such as we are, are makers of future events that today are not. Today the future actuality is nothing whatever but one or other of the infinite host of possibilities now latent in the present. Or perhaps (for how can we know?) not even latent in the present, but utterly unique and indeterminate.

Yesterday is palpably there, there, just behind me; but receding deeper and deeper into the past, as I live onward along the sequence of the new todays.

But tomorrow?

Yesterday I had porridge and toast for breakfast, as on the day before, and the day before that. Yesterday, according to instruction I caught a train to Preston. I had set my plans so as to reach the station in good time. And because a thousand other strands of planning had been minutely co-ordinated, at the appointed minute the engine driver, who had been waiting in readiness for the guard's whistle and his waving flag, moved levers. The train crept forward. In that train I found myself sitting opposite a lovely stranger, not according to instruction, nor as the result of any plan. Soon we were talking, looking into one another's eyes; talking not of love but of nursing and hospitals and the wished-for planned society, and of her Christian God, and of a future life, and of eternity. Before we met, before our two minds struck light from each other, our conversation had no existence anywhere. But then in a fleeting present we began creating it. And now the universe is eternally the richer because of it, since irrevocably the past now holds it, now preserves in a receding yesterday that unexpected, that brief and never-to-be-repeated, warmth and brightness.

With her I have no past but yesterday, and no future; but with you, my best known and loved, I have deep roots in the past, and flowers too, and the future.

Some fifteen thousand yesterdays ago there lies a day when you were a little girl with arms like sticks and a bright cascade of hair. In a green silk frock you came through a door, warmed your hands at the fire, and looked at me for a moment. And now, so real that moment seems, that it might be yesterday! For that particular fraction of the eternal reality is always queerly accessible to me, though fifteen thousand yesterdays ago.

But tomorrow?

Tomorrow, shall I, as it has been planned, catch the bus for Chester? Or shall I miss it? Or will it refuse me, or never start on its journey? Or having absorbed me will it collide with a hearse or a menagerie van? Will the freed lions and tigers chase people along the street? Shall I feel their huge claws in my flesh and smell their breath, and know that for me at least there is no tomorrow? Or perhaps some hidden disease is ready to spring on me tonight? Or a bomb? Or will the laws of nature suddenly change, so that stones leap from the earth, houses become soaring pillars of rubble and dust, and the sea rush into the sky? Or will the sky itself be drawn aside like a curtain, revealing God on his throne, his accusing finger pointing precisely at abject me? Or at a certain moment of tomorrow will everything simply end? Will there be just nothing any more, no future at all?

I cannot answer these questions with certainty. No man can answer them with certainty. And yet if I were to bet a million pounds to a penny that things will go on, and half a million that they will go on fundamentally much as before, few would call me rash.

Yesterday the events which are now so vividly present and actual were in the main inscrutable and not yet determined. And therefore yesterday they had, we say, no being. And yet, and yet—there are moments when we vaguely sense that, just as the past is eternally real, though pastly, so the future also is eternally what in fact it will be, though for a while futurely to the ever-advancing present. We move forward, and the fog recedes before us, revealing a universe continuous with the present universe, and one which, we irresistibly feel, was there all the while, awaiting us. Could we but by some magic or infra-red illumination pierce the fog-wall, we should see the future universe as in fact it is. So at least we sometimes irresistibly feel. My conversation with that lovely and serious travelling companion—was it not always there, awaiting me, knit irrevocably into the future as it is now irrevocably knit into the past? When I was born, was not that journey awaiting me? Through the interplay of external causation and my own freely choosing nature, was not that happy encounter already a feature of the eternal fact, though futurely? Was it not equally so when the Saxons first landed on this island, and when the island itself took shape, and when the sun gave birth?

And fifteen thousand yesterdays ago, when you and I first looked at each other, was not our future even then just what in fact it has been? It was of course related to us futurely, and was therefore inaccessible; but was it not all the while there, lying in wait for us? One does not suppose that the centre of the earth, because it is inaccessible, is therefore blankly nothing, until someone shall burrow down to it.

And indeed I cannot even be sure that in that moment of our first meeting the future was, in very truth, wholly inaccessible. For in looking into your eyes I did (how I remember it!) have a strange, a startling experience, long since dismissed as fantasy, yet unforgettable. It was as though your eyes were for me windows, and as though curtains were drawn aside, revealing momentarily a wide, an unexpected and unexplored prospect, a view obscure with distance, but none the less an unmistakable prevision of our common destiny. I could not, of course, see it clearly; for it was fleeting, and I was a boy and simple. But I saw, or I seemed to see, what now I recognize as the very thing that has befallen us, the thing that has taken so long to grow, and is only now in these last years flowering. Today our hair is greying, our faces show the years. We can no longer do as once we did. But the flower has opened. And strangely it is the very flower that once I glimpsed even before the seed was sown.

Fantasy, sheer fantasy? Perhaps! But when we think of time and of eternity, intelligence reels. The shrewdest questions that we can ask about them are perhaps falsely shaped, being but flutterings of the still unfledged human mentality.

The initial creative act that blasted this cosmos into being may, or may not (or neither), be in eternity co-real with today, and with the last faint warmth of the last dying star.

The Core

One of Stapledon's most lyrical essays in autobiography fuses memory and anticipation in an alternately philosophical and passionate fantasia on identity, time, love, and destiny. Written as Stapledon neared his sixtieth birthday, "The Core" articulates a fear of old age and senility, but retreats from the intellectually unacceptable embrace of a wishful personal immortality. In a desperate struggle for integrity and in deep self-doubt, the author echoes the appeal of Shakespeare's King Lear: "Who is it that can tell me who I am?" In celebrating the differences between himself and his wife (the "you" of the second half of "The Core") Stapledon pursues in the microcosm of his own marriage his favorite theme of "personality-in-community" and one of his favorite metaphors: symbiosis. A slightly revised portion of "The Core," originally published in 1945 in an obscure journal, was assigned a year later to one of the "interludes" in Death Into Life.

I! I! I!

But what is it that I truly am?

In the flying moment things happen to me, then vanish. To me, me, me! But what am I? My fingers are playing with a pencil. I have caught them at it. Now they have stopped, like guilty schoolboys. Was it I that was playing, or just my fingers? At the moment I have a headache, my very own, for no one can share it with me. At the moment I want to go off into the hills, but instead I must go to the town. I want this and that, and I do this and that, but what am I?

Some tell me that I am just the life-long sequence of all the things that happen to me, and that I do; the sequence of moving images on the cinema screen, each one made up of a thousand static pictures, yet by the slow eye of the spectator all blurred together into movement and life. But I, for whom this blurring and this movement happen? Am I just the screen, just this particular human body, with a scrubby head of hair and a turned-up nose? Strange that a body should span the instant, and perceive the bird flying, the flag waving, the bursting bomb!

Some assure me that I am an enduring, and indeed an eternal, spirit, resident in this body. Just because I am a spirit, they say, only because I am no creature of time, can I hold past and present together, perceiving movement and change, preserving within my vanishing "now" all my past "nows," for ever pastly present. The smoke from my cigarette streams smoothly, waveringly upward, then blossoms into wreathing filaments of cloud. All this I hold magically within my "now."

But I, my very self? Is it at all sure that I am anything more than a little fume of sentience trailed by a smouldering body? When the fire goes out, will not that be the end of me?

But how I span the days, the years! Yesterday's voices, yesterday's greetings and disputations, echo now in my memory. Far behind these, and behind the bomb-blasts of our present warfare, I remember the shell-bursts of another war, now laid up in history. And farther still, I remember being a schoolboy with an ink-splashed Eton collar and a passion for model boats. Did I, the very I of to-day, wear that collar, feel that passion? Surely that was a very different being, whose experience I have somehow inherited, like an old photograph album full of impossible uncles and aunts, grandparents and great-grandparents, all seemingly in fancy dress. I of to-day nurse no passion for model boats; I am for philosophy and for mankind and all high questions. And yet, and yet even now, with my hair grey, when boys sail their trim or their dowdy craft on the park lake, I linger to watch them. That child lives in me still; I was and am that child. Yes, and a still earlier child. I, and no other, as a very little child, left a wet patch on the knee of a doting visitor in a Victorian drawing-room. Oh yes, it was I, for I remember it.

Very soon, unless something happens by accident or design to cut my life short, I, who am interested most in man and the cosmos, shall lose my grip on the adult mentality, and lapse into the second childhood. The high themes will be too much for me. I shall finger my memories in public, and repeat my anecdotes. My feeble passion will be only for warmth and sleep and such food as I can digest. How can such a poor creature be I? But indeed, I he will surely be; for this body, formerly addicted to sucking, and now beyond its prime, and breaking up in little ways, retains its past in its ever-vanishing present. And I am that identity, of body and of experience.

Identity? What identity is there in me even within a single moment, let alone in a lifetime? I am always at loggerheads with myself. I long to dare, but I cling to safety. I will to concentrate all my energies on a great task, yet in each moment I want to fritter. I am determined to be a responsible citizen, but equally determined to avoid all responsibility. I long to be gathered up into the life of a close-knit community, but I jealously protect my individuality, and play a lone hand. I am unwaveringly consecrated to spiritual discipline and high religion, but also I am intransigently sceptical; yes, and I take cover under cynicism, I avoid awkward challenges, I have a good time.

It seems that I am just a trampled arena where hundreds of gladiators and wild beasts have been fighting day and night for more than half a century, and none ever conquers. At one moment sheer hunger bids fair to possess me wholly, at another fear, at another intellect, or inarticulate worship, or frank bawdiness. Not one of these pretenders is more I than any other. Even that mighty war-lord, my self-love, with his turbulent band of brigands, even he is not really I.

Indeed, he is not I, for now I wake. I, I, the true and essential I, stir and wake. And how I laugh at all this nonsense! For now I know certainly that there is something over and above the arena and the gladiators, something more truly I than any of these. And they themselves, even in the very act of rebellion, may sometimes be forced to admit, though grudgingly, that I, I, am their rightful sovereign. For I am they more fully awakened, more clear-sighted. I will constantly and singly, and in its totality, the very thing that they, cribbed within their particular blinkers, seek so hypnotically, so partially, so conflictingly.

Then what is it that I truly am? Surely I am the constant will to be fully spirit, the will to be aware, to love, to make; the will to do these with complete integrity. When appetite runs riot, I, the essential I, will unattachment, philosophic aloofness. In the very crisis and tumult of love-making let me quietly watch the event! But equally when great abstractions and universal principles obsess me, I, the true I, will to be fully sensitive to the flying moment in its revelation of the near or the far actuality. Let me in all circumstances be fully aware of each variegated event as it flows over me. Let me savour tones of voice and all the delicacies of their significance. Let me not miss the rainbow in a fly's wing, nor the dark under-currents of my own desires, nor the lightning illumination that reveals the fateful pattern of history or the horror of the distant battle-field. Even if the event hurts me, let me not miss its essence. Let me be strong enough to bear it and scrutinize it. Even if it kills me, let me to the end see it clearly and dispassionately. For I, the true I, will constantly (but how ineffectively) to perceive the real as it really is, both in its whole cosmical form and in the heart of the electron, both in the tissue of human society and in the heart of man, both in Jesus Christ and in strange, torturing, tortured Hitler.

But to be coldly aware is not in itself enough. I will also right appraisement: to loathe where loathing is indeed due, to love where love is due, to worship where it is right to worship. I loathe the urchin's cruelty to the cat, but I will not loathe the urchin. I loathe Hitler's mass-torturing, but not Hitler; and the money-man's heartlessness, but not the man. I love the swallow's flight, and I love the swallow; the urchin's gleam of tenderness, and the urchin. And I, the true I, will constantly to worship what for short I call the Spirit, fountain of all clear awareness, all love, and all brave creating. But also I will, I must, salute without rebelliousness the dread Other who seemingly is behind the hugeness and the intricacy of the cosmos, behind the star-streams and the facets of a bee's eye, behind the vast finitude of space and the mystery of the electron's leap; that most alien Other, who seemingly has spawned both light and darkness, both the Spirit and its enemy.

Yet even with this perplexed salutation in my heart I will to strike for the Spirit only, and with all my strength, however feebly.

The great reality that confronts me is formidable and veiled. Its heart is not laid bare in the electron, nor is its form displayed in the huge dance of the galaxies. But there is one experience which seems, oh seems, to bring me near to it, and give insight into it. In love I seem, I seem, to touch it; and to have assurance that even the dark, the alien Other is at heart spirit. Telescopes and microscopes and tomes of sociology tell much, but superficially. Only in community with another living individual do I make an inner contact. For our relatedness is internal. Each is to the other an envoy from remote reality welcomed within the citadel of the self. Each is to the other the perceived angel of an ever inaccessible God. Or so it seems, it seems. I must not positively believe it, for to do so would be to betray intellect's integrity; but equally I must be true to the sharp, the insistent feeling that in loving I come near to the heart of things.

Of the two thousand million human beings, most are beyond the reach of my imagination. They are mere specks or portents on my horizon; or at most they are useful or harmful things, within my grasp but impervious to my imagination. Some few do indeed become fragmentarily alive to me, do confront me as living presences. These are my acquaintances, and among them those whom I feel as enemies, because they oppose my cherished desires, or because they are harsh to my mind's antennae, or because they cling. But some few, you my real friends, live more roundly in my imagination, and I in yours. In spite of our differences and roughnesses we feel ourselves more deeply at one, either in our hidden roots or in our flowers, or both; either in our unconscious needs or our most considered purposes, or both. Our differences are forgiven, are indeed prized, so long as we are in harmony in our roots or our flowers.

And you, you most single and singular, whom I love best? Even you are in fact immensely remote from me, you dear centre of an alien universe. Though you are the most near of all things, you are also sometimes perplexingly remote. Over how many decades have we been growing together in a joyful, a life-giving, an indissoluble symbiosis! Yet even now sometimes I have no idea what you are feeling or thinking. You are apt for action, I for contemplation; you for responding to the minute particular that claims your service, I (oh fatally) for the universal and the far-flung. Although our minds do indeed most often move in a common rhythm, like a close-dancing couple, yet sometimes we are at arm's length, or we break step, or we fly apart, cleft by some sudden discord. How many times have I said to you, "Quick, there is a train to catch," and you have answered, "There is plenty of time"; or I, "Now we are too late," and you, "The train may be later." (Even in Hell you would be an optimist.) But in the end, of course, through some black magic which you are forced to use on such occasions, the train is caught, and we sit together silent, waiting for it to start. Again and again our diversity hurts, it even infuriates; but it does not really matter. Indeed in the end it is an enrichment, a painful but in the end a welcome participation of each in the uniqueness of the other.

Even in that most sharp discordancy of all, when I hurt you so much, did we not become more real to one another? In the end we had grown together more closely. We know one another the better for it; we love one another the better. We are more intimately and indissolubly "we."

Of course each of us is still "I," and the other is "you," the far centre of an alien universe; but increasingly, and now indestructibly, the two of us together are also "we," the single though twi-minded centre of a universe common to both of us. We see the world together. No longer does each of us look at it merely in solitariness, with single vision, merely as a flat picture. We see it now in depth, stereoscopically. With our common binocular vision each regards all things from our two alien view-points.

Our distinctness is as precious as our unity, and our unity as our distinctness. Without deep harmony, in our roots and our flowers, how could we hold together? But without our difference, how kindle each other?

Nothing in my world is identical with anything in yours. Not a flower, not a poem, not a person. Is redness, even, to me just what it is to you? Probably it is much the same, for we are similar organisms; but perhaps (who knows?) your "red" is what I call "green." What matter? That difference would be eternally insignificant for us, since it would be for ever indiscernible. But justice, beauty, truth and a good joke have meanings that we can share with one another, and are discovered to be never identical for the two of us. And though we have friends in common, they are never quite the same persons. Though the friends of each are the friends of both, yet also and inevitably the friend, the lover, of one is the other's possible antagonist. These our differences, that haunt us elusively at every turn, or step suddenly forward and bar the way with fire, cannot without disaster be ignored. Blind love is no love at all.

We are indeed for ever separate, for ever different, for ever in some measure discordant; but with a discordancy ever more harmonized in the "we" that is for each of us so much more than "I," yes, and perhaps even than "you." As centres of awareness we remain eternally distinct; but in participation in our "we," each "I" wakens to be an ampler, richer "I," whose treasure is not "myself" but "we." And so "I" without "you" am a mere torn-off ragged thing, a half-blind crippled thing, a mere phantom whose embodiment is only in "us."

This precious "we" that we have conceived together, this close-knit unity in difference, this cohabitation and communion of two spirits, will not for ever exfoliate on this planet. Soon or late, one or other of us will die. Then "we," no doubt, will live on for a while in the survivor, as a cherished but a growthless thing. When both are dead, it will vanish from this world.

Some assure us that we shall meet again in a bright heaven to live joyfully onward for ever. It may be, may be. In some strange subtle way, too deep for telling, that affirmation may indeed be true; but only as a parable is true, not, surely, in the familiar mundane way of catching trains, and gathering drift-wood for the fire, and cooking, and washing up, which is the only plane of living that has kindly significance for little me and little you. No! Let us not cling to immortality, not pledge our hearts to it. We have been given so much, let us not be greedy for more. Let us not insist on believing for mere longing's sake. Let us rather surmise that if death is indeed the end, it is better so. Let us be prepared for the link's sudden breaking in the death of one of us, or its slow crumbling in the senescence of both. Let us look forward to eternal sleep. When we are tired, sleep is the final bliss. Asleep, we are in the same bed together; and when we are dead, we shall still and eternally be in the same little universe together, though perhaps fast asleep. But perhaps, after all, what dies is only the dear trivial familiar self of each, and in our annihilation some vital and eternal thing does break wing, does fly free. Then indeed our love will have its fulfilment.

But even if death is the absolute end of us, yet our loving has not been in vain; for it has left some small bright mark on the living world, in our children, our friends, and the causes that we have unheroically served. Moreover, even if it is ephemeral it is in a manner also eternal. It is at least eternally a fact in the universe. When all the stars are cold balls of rock, this "we," this little flower, so bright, so short-lived among the stars, will always have been, will indeed eternally be, though pastly. So in some way we have, after all, our inalienable share in eternity.

But that great word, "eternity"? Is it after all a false symbol with no significance in reality, but with treacherous power over our hearts; a mere amulet to which the doomed and frightened cling, faced by the firing squad? Or is it a true, though a vague, sign for that reality which man's mind, straining a-tiptoe, can barely touch? Is time's passage an incomplete, a self-contradictory and illusive, appearance of that eternal actuality which man can never grasp? Who knows? Not we!

But this at least we know. Our loving has high significance. For "I," discovering with "you," a fuller life as "we," discover also that for every awakened "I" throughout the galaxies and the aeons such is the way of life, to be transmuted into "we," whether with a single beloved, or with a few close friends, or in a close-knit group of work-mates, or a harmonious world, or (who knows?) in an all-embracing cosmical republic. Or perhaps (who knows, who knows?) in mystic union of the lowly individual with some ulterior, some all-pervading Thou. Such, surely, is the goal, in little or in great, in the home, the crew, the gang, the city, the universal brotherhood; or perhaps, if the saints are not deceived, in the individual spirit's death into some God's great life.

But how many, how many millions in all the lands, in all the worlds, are without that consummation! Not only the mystic's high beatitude they lack, but even friendly love. Whether inwardly, through their own twisted nature, or through crippling circumstance, they are doomed to desolation. And because of their inner desert, or the misery that a barbarian world inflicts on them, they trample one another like cattle stampeding before a forest fire.

Dread, and to us unintelligible are the dark ways of the dark Other.

The Heavens Declare—Nothing
from *The Opening of the Eyes*

At his death in 1950 Stapledon left a nearly complete text of fifty-four inter-laced meditations addressed to an unnamed "you" — deity or, to use his term, "daimon." The manuscript was edited by his wife Agnes and published in 1954 as The Opening of the Eyes. *As in much of his fiction, Stapledon was searching for a spiritual language adequate to the modern world, one that could encompass the newest understandings of physics: the big bang, the expanding universe, entropy. Meditation 32, "The Heavens declare — Noth-ing," is a response to Psalm 19, which opens: "The heavens declare the glory of God, and the firmament showeth his handiwork." It is one of the most concise statements of Stapledon's agnostic piety, his earnest attempt to yoke science and theology, to reconcile spiritual longing with intellectual skepti-cism. For Stapledon the night sky replete with countless stars was at once a scene of never-failing beauty and a profound dilemma. It is viewed in this meditation from the prospect of Caldy Hill on the Wirral peninsula, overlook-ing the town of West Kirby and the Irish Sea. His parents' house stood on Caldy Hill, and he evoked this landscape in his first published book* Latter-Day Psalms *and most memorably in his greatest,* Star Maker. *Indeed,* The Opening of the Eyes *is in many respects similar in mood to* Star Maker, *though here the dark night of a soul struggling to understand a remote and disturbing spiritual entity is portrayed with greater intimacy and simplicity.*

ON THIS MOONLESS and star-brilliant night, I have come out on to the hill yearning to find you, if not in my heart, then in the heavens. But in my heart and mind you are silent, and the constellations are not your features. The heavens declare nothing. The human lights of the town beneath me tell me nothing. Beyond the houses the sea is nothing but a flat darkness.

Overhead a flight of geese, unseen but vocal, momentarily eclipse one star.

To the eye of imagination, the great earth has become visibly a sphere; now great, but now a granule in the huge void. Bright Jupiter lies far afield. The vault of the sky, no longer a pricked black tent, is expanded to be depth beyond depth of empty darkness, with here and there a sun, reduced by distance to a mere punctual star. The Milky

Way, that vague over-arching stain, is seen now as a tenuous dust of suns, extending outwards disc-wise, far afield beyond the constellations. The blackness around the pole is deep beyond all sounding, is space boundless; wherein the immense galaxy itself is but a mote, a minute wisp of stars. Within that darkness, for imagination's eye, the swarming galaxies drift like snowflakes; each flake a host of suns, numerous as the sand; each flake the matrix of a million earth-like worlds. The whole unnumbered multitude of the galaxies, so some astronomers say, bursts ever apart, the more remote of them racing away faster than light's own speed; inaccessible, therefore, to vision.

Some surmise that the boundless throng of many million galaxies is finite. Space itself, though boundless, they say, is finite, and mysteriously re-entrant upon itself. Imagination, they say, cannot picture this truth, which mathematics alone, with its exact symbols, can precisely figure. In this view, the galaxies, stars, worlds, and even the very electrons, are numerable. There are just so many of them and no more. Long ago there was a single creative and explosive act, first cause of this expanding universe. Long hence, all the energies of that creation will be dissipated, and death will be universal. By then, perhaps the purpose of the cosmos (if purpose there be, which seems unlikely) will have been achieved; and with the ceasing of all change, time itself will cease.

But others, rejecting this strange boundless finitude, prefer another fantasy, no less unimaginable to man. They declare that between the ever-separating, ever-dying galaxies, a new sparse dust of matter is ever being created, here and there a lonely atom; and that the new matter gathers slowly into nebulae, which mature into galaxies, each with its million earth-like worlds where man-like beings may emerge from brutishness. Thus in the infinite host of the galaxies the worlds are infinitely many. Imagination overstrains and collapses. And for ever, within the interstices and ever-wider-yawning chasms of the ever-dying, ever-infinitely-expanding universe, an infinite sequence of fresh universes is for ever being created, in turn to mature and die. If purpose has indeed determined this strange, this seemingly crazy scheme, it must surely be a purpose infinitely alien to man's desires.

Whichever of the two modern cosmical pictures is the less false to the facts, man's understanding is defeated. Truth slips between the fingers of the exploring mind.

Yet some such picture we must accept. Gone for ever is the East's great elephant that supports the world and is supported by a greater tortoise. Gone for ever are the celestial spheres, that box of boxes, which Dante described, Hell-centred, God-surrounded. Gone too the sun-centred universe within the sphere of the fixed stars. Gone the uniquenes of the sun's system, the uniqueness of our earth, the uniqueness of man.

Instead, we must conceive, as best we may, at least a host, perhaps an infinity of habitable earth-like worlds, each housing its own human or parahuman race.

Yet well it may be, it must be, that both the new pictures of the cosmos, these latest, proudest feats of terrestrial observation and intelligence, are but a very little nearer to the truth than the East's elephant and tortoise.

Yes, but for us today they have authority. Some such explosion of ever-receding galaxies, each with its scattered population of earths, is now the background of all human life.

Letters

Two Letters to H. G. Wells

Stapledon and H. G. Wells had an intermittent correspondence from 1931 to 1942, exchanging books and ideas about politics and art. In the first of the two letters printed here Stapledon introduced himself to Wells and explained with modest gestures of respect his debt to Wellsian thinking. By the time of the second letter, written at the beginning of World War II and just after the publication of Well's The Fate of Homo Sapiens, *Stapledon was on more familiar terms with his correspondent. He made a spirited defense of himself against Wells's dismissive critique of* Saints and Revolutionaries *and took some trouble to emphasize the ways in which he was* not *a Wellsian.*

16 OCTOBER 1931

Dear Sir,

A book of mine, *Last and First Men*, has received a certain amount of attention, and nearly every review has contained some reference to yourself. Recently I have come to feel that if you happened to notice the book, a copy of which the publishers must have sent you, you might wonder why I had not the grace to make some acknowledgment of your influence. Of course it cannot matter to you whether a new writer admits his debt or not; and anyhow you may not have seen the book or the reviews. All the same I should like to explain. Your works have certainly influenced me very greatly, perhaps even more than I supposed when I was writing my own book. But curiously enough I have only read two of your scientific romances, *The War of the Worlds* and *The Star*. If I seem to have plagiarized from any others, it was in ignorance. Your later works I greatly admire. There would be something very wrong with me if I did not. They have helped very many of us to see things more clearly. Then why, I wonder, did I not acknowledge my huge debt? Probably because it was so huge and obvious that I was not properly aware of it. A man does not record his debt to the air he breathes in common with everyone else.

Yours very truly
W. Olaf Stapledon

16 November 1939

Dear H. G.

Thank you for your very interesting comments on my "Saints and Revolutionaries".... I am *not* a materialist, unless it be in something like the Marxian sense, which is not really it at all. Certainly I am not a dualist but a monist of some sort. As for "belief" and "faith," it all depends on the meaning one gives them. *Of course* I can do without "believing," if you mean believing in metaphysical doctrines. I like to think of myself as following in your footsteps, as you suggest, but as a matter of fact I don't think I am quite on the same track, and recently I have in some ways been going badly astray, from your point of view. I have even at times been called a Christian, which is a bit disturbing, I confess. But at least I have come to realise that, silly as the Christians are, in their way, the pucker scientists are quite as silly in theirs, with their inordinate confidence in their neat little concepts, which mostly turn out to be meaningless when used outside their natural universe of discourse. However, it is easy to see that both lots are silly, and not so easy to escape being silly oneself, and very likely I've been it in appearing to side with the clerics.... But I don't really side with anybody, even with you. I have thankfully followed you a long way, but with occasional excursions hither and thither beside the track which you have made and so many have since pursued. And by now I seem to be mostly on a more or less parallel way on the other side of the valley, so to speak. But the metaphor is getting in a muddle.

In moments of confidence I might claim that though you have incomparably greater power and skill than I have, and a far more encyclopaedic mind, or encyclopaedic range of knowledge, yet in a horribly sketchy sort of way I do take into account aspects of experience which you are inclined to underestimate, mainly because in your early days it was *necessary* to underestimate them, whereas in my early days it became necessary to recover the essence of them without the silly wrappings. After all, great innovators like you are almost bound to do less than justice to the traditional culture. For the rest, well, I wish I had the prospect of making a small fraction of the contribution that you have made, to modern culture. But it is not possible for me, being what I am.

And now, belatedly, I will settle down to read you on Homo Sapiens. I hope your verdict on the poor creature will turn out after all to have been too pessimistic. But he is certainly in a horrid fix.

Good luck in this miserable war.

Olaf Stapledon

Two Letters to Naomi Mitchison

The Scottish novelist, poet, and social activist Naomi Mitchison introduced herself to Stapledon in 1931 shortly after the publication of Last and First Men *and became one of his strongest supporters, gathering him into her small literary circle at London's Café Royal. At the outbreak of World War II she retired with her husband and children to her farm at Carradale near Campbeltown, Scotland but continued to discuss politics, literature, and family life with Stapledon by letter. In 1940, when Stapledon was working as an air raid warden (A.R.P., as opposed to the civil defense unit, L.V.D.), doing volunteer work for the new Common Wealth Party of Richard Acland, and resettling at his new house at Simon's Field, Mitchison suffered the loss of her last child, a day after her birth. This was a slack period in Stapledon's literary career when he felt depressed by the war and adrift imaginatively. A few years later, though he was weary and approaching sixty, his fortunes seemed considerably brighter with publication of one of his greatest achievements,* Sirius.

10 JULY 1940

Dear Naomi,

It was terribly bad luck about the baby. You must be feeling wretched. Anyhow I hope you are yourself recovering from it all, and that you will soon be fit again. It must be frightfully depressing to spend so many months preparing for a birth, and then to find it wasted. I hope you will find consolation in your surroundings in Carradale, where you seem to have a good community. Thank you for your letter of ten days ago. You sounded pretty fed up. And indeed things are in a hideous mess, but not hopeless. People really do seem to be waking up a bit at last. And Churchill with all his faults is better stuff than Chamberlain. And if we can get through to the winter without being conquered, there's a chance the waking up may go further. I have been doing a bit of work here for Acland's movement. Yesterday I handed out immense quantities of leaflets in Liverpool streets, and incidentally got marvelously wet. It seemed to go rather well at first, but people are too much wrapped up in war work now. We had a meeting for Acland to address and it was a huge success. He's not a great leader, but I think he struck the right note for the moment. How I hate all political work however. And if you hate a job

you can't do it well. Now-a-days I feel horribly useless, and am reduced to doing local A.R.P. and cultivating my acre. We have a new
house, by the Dee estuary, and we hope to produce quite a lot of food.
I am spending half my time breaking up our brick-hard field with a
spade. It makes one sleep well. I am writing occasional articles (e.g. in
Scrutiny) and a book, but it's all futile now. We must concentrate on
keeping Hitler out, surely, bad as our present regime is. I think the
country is learning its lesson fairly rapidly, and there *may* really be a
chance of something better after the war, if we are not wiped out. I
offered to join the L.D.V but was turned down because I am on A.R.P.
The LDV seem to have more people than can be dealt with. My (qualified) pacifism has been put in cold storage. But how loathsome it all
is! And of course I remain fundamentally just as much pacifist as
before. But at present pacifism simply won't work. I note in Gandhi's
autobiography that his non-violence movement's success depended on
the fact that some officials were decent folk. It would not have worked
against a Nazi regime. But though so far as I can see we must keep the
Nazis out, we must also keep our heads; and at present many people
are losing them, particularly over refugees. Our Austrian student
whom we had for 15 months has been taken away, and was very
miserable about it. And our German domestic had to leave this district
because it is a protected area. We have no domestic now, except a daily.
Mary is at home from Oxford and gives a hand. We are expecting
David from school in due course, unless things get much worse here,
in which case he will stay at school.

Good luck! I often see things of yours in the journals. Somehow I
just can't do that sort of thing. Too lazy, or something.

Yours with love,
Olaf

10 JUNE 1944

Dear Naomi,

Thank you very much for your letter, and I am so glad you
like *Sirius*. Yes, I know I alternate between cold intellectualism and
more emotional patches. I always do. I just don't know how to
integrate them, and both moods are necessary in the sort of stuff I
write. Methuen turned the book down as obscene, so I am a bit
anxious about people's reaction to it. All is well so far. I sheared about
half a sheep once, but no more. Yes they are stupid. I was brought
up with a rather intelligent fox-terrier in Egypt, and this book
profited by that quite a lot. In fact it now seems to me a sort of
distorted act of piety toward that former but never quite forgotten
beloved.

Your present life sounds good, the real thing, to judge by an article of yours in the *Manchester Guardian* some time ago. You said you were writing a book for your local people; when is it to appear? I am very glad to hear that your children are all safe, and flourishing. So are our two. (How I wish we had more than two!) David still in a destroyer in the Med, Mary in the Board of Trade in London, *and* starting a medical course. She has a flat which we find very useful, as we both go up rather often. We are both very busy, Agnes with the Land Army etc etc, and I with talks to troops & others and odds & ends of writing. Also we have our acre, which takes up far too much time and is the hell of a worry, what with rats, rabbits, blights, cows, sheep, horses and other pests, and weeds, my God you should just see them! And the wind that blasts the young potatoes, kills off all the trees, or ruins them, withers even the hawthorn, and has blown windows off their hinges. The place does produce a bit of food—we reckon on about 6 × our own needs—but it all seems nothing in proportion to the labour we put in. Our spirits are now just about broken, and we shall probably have to call in help.

Thanks for the manifesto on Scotland, with which I wholly agree.

Well, good luck! And may this frightful struggle in France speed up the war to successful conclusion! But afterwards? The prospects are bad. I am all for Common Wealth, by the way.

Yours,
Olaf

Letter to Virginia Woolf

Woolf had written to express her admiration for Star Maker *shortly after its publication, including the unexpected compliment that Stapledon's fiction embodied goals she had aspired to but never attained. The letter was forwarded to Stapledon while he was on holiday, and he responded at once.*

SHETLAND ISLES
15 JULY 1937

Dear Mrs. Woolf,

It gives me great pleasure to know that you liked my book, and that some of the ideas in it fall in line with your own thought. The book falls very far short of my hopes for it, both in plan and expression, but I suppose that is almost inevitable. I have recently read "The Years" with delight, and also with despair at the thought of the contrast between your art and my own pedestrian method.

A wet and friendly sheep dog that has been swimming in the "voe" has sprayed this paper with her tail-wagging.

Yours sincerely
Olaf Stapledon

Letter to C. E. M. Joad

The popular philosopher and broadcaster C. E. M. Joad often reviewed Stapledon's fiction, and Stapledon in turn wrote reviews of Joad's philosophical works. They met frequently in London, where both were members of the Progressive League and of the Aristotelian Society. Here Stapledon takes up Joad's query whether his passionate political speeches during the war and his commitment to postwar social reconstruction are at odds with the philosophical detachment of his fiction. The letter also offers a concise statement of Stapledon's notions of the relationship between philosophy and religious faith. The full presentation of his stance of "agnostic piety," which he likened to "the Way" of Taoism, was published as "Morality, Scepticism and Theism" in Volume 44 of the Proceedings of the Aristotelian Society.

27 MARCH 1944

Dear Cyril,

I have been intending for some days to answer one of the points you made at the Aristotelian meeting the other day, a point I forgot to deal with at the time. (Incidentally I am afraid I missed a lot of the criticisms that ought to have been replied to, because I got my notes in a muddle. I am more used to taking each point as soon as it has been made.)

You said that in taking the present tellurian situation so seriously I was in conflict with my own earlier attitude in imaginative books. But no! As I conceive it, every "minded world" must take its crises very seriously, and in particular any crisis in which the issue is whether it will get stuck in a primitive stage of growth or break through into a new range of experience and action. This is the sort of crisis that faces man today. I think of each world as, so to speak, a vessel of the waking spirit. (Meaning by "spirit" not a substance but a form of living, cp. music.) For its individuals the supreme obligation is to be instrumental to that waking. I don't see any inconsistency between my earlier attitude and my present one in this respect.

Another point which I should have made clearer. I am not at all opposed to intellectual speculation about ultimate reality. I think it is very important, educatively. By all means go on speculating as you did in *God and Evil*. But I regard all such speculation as far too precarious as a foundation either for morality or for religious belief. (And since belief can have no other foundation, it must be abandoned.) In that book you seem to me (a) to *want* to believe in God for quite the wrong reasons, and (b) to *believe* in God for quite inadequate reasons. Your arguments against God are so much more effective than your arguments for him! From my point of view what you have done (like so many others) is (1) to discover that scientific materialism is inadequate, intellectually and emotionally, and then (2) to move back into an equally inadequate position, namely theism. I should say the present movement of thought is dialectical: Thesis, theism; antithesis, materialism; synthesis, still to be discovered. My paper was a groping attempt at the synthesis. So far as I personally am concerned it is adequate. It gives me a sense of an opened window, or new horizons etc, and an emotional satisfaction which neither of the other two positions ever gave.

Oh yes, and another point. I don't think my position is really mystical (in this matter of *ethics*, I mean). My intuition of the rightness of "the Way" is not a mystical intuition of the nature of the universe. It is merely a factual apprehension of the nature of self-conscious and other-conscious mentality, namely that it cannot but will the Way (when it is sufficiently developed, and unperverted.) True, I have *in addition* to this an intuitive sense of the instrumentality of individuals and societies. But this is not the sanction of my ethics. This intuition, I admit, is of practical importance to me in daily life; but I don't pretend to understand its real significance, and so I do not use it as a foundation for morality. To infer from it that "therefore God exists" would seem to me a betrayal of intellectual integrity. But I bet my boots it has *some* high significance, probably quite beyond my comprehension; probably beyond human comprehension, at present.

Damn it, though I think I put up a rather feeble defence the other day, I feel increasingly that my position does open up new possibilities for future clarification, while yours simply looks back.

It was a pleasure to have you taking the chair for me. Since you kindly asked me to dine with you some time, what about 3rd May, or 4th? I can't yet be absolutely sure of being in London then, but I think I shall, and anyhow I could let you know definitely some time before hand.

Yours
Olaf Stapledon

Three Letters to Aage Marcus

The Danish art historian Aage Marcus kept up a lively correspondence with Stapledon throughout the 1930s. For over five years they were not in communication during the war, and when they resumed writing letters in 1946 the two most frequent topics were Stapledon's fiction and paranormal phenomena, in which they both had become interested. Stapledon, intrigued but skeptical, had joined the Society for Psychical Research and had made extrasensory experiences increasingly central to some of his final experiments in fiction.

21 AUGUST 1947

Dear Marcus,

Thank you for your letter of the 12th, which was very welcome. Agnes and I were both delighted to hear from you again, and to know that you continue to be well and busy, and that you have at last moved into your new house. Congratulations on completing the building before it was too late! Congratulations also on beating me so handsomely in the race for grandparenthood! I hope all goes well with the expected new additions to the family. Our grandchild is a grandson, and a very fine specimen. He has now reached the stage of attempting the most primitive form of locomotion.

Lawrence Hyde's "Spirit and Society" has not, so far as I know, been published yet. I met him at a conference recently. He is an amiable and intelligent person, but (from my point of view) rather uncritical. He claims to have some special sort of esoteric knowledge. I should be more ready to believe him if I did not on other counts suspect him of being too ready a believer. The conference, by the way, was the Present Question Conference, at Birmingham, run mainly by Graham Howe, a rather wild sort of psychotherapist.

I was very interested in your experiences in psychical research. They seem to have been indeed sensational. I look forward keenly to seeing the full report which you say you may be able to send me. I have begun reading Tyrrell's new Pelican, and have read a number of interesting things in the current literature of the Society for Psychical Research. My own feeling about Tyrrell is that, admirable as his work is in many ways, he is rather too ready to explain strange phenomena in terms of familiar concepts. The first chapter of his Pelican, for instance, over-simplifies the issue. However, he has done a lot of fine work. There cannot be much doubt that paranormal psychology is the growing point of thought in our day. But for my part I feel it in my bones that "half the battle" is to work out the necessary new concepts to fit the new data. Of course the idea of the extra-temporal common ground as the medium of telepathy is a case in point; but I think we must expect the same *sort* of mental revolution as occurred as a result of the physical theory of relativity, and probably a far more radical revolution even than that. People like Broad and H. H. Price are likely to play a big part in this side of the work.

I am very pleased that you bothered to re-read my "Death into Life," and found it worth while. Like all that I have done, it is a mixture of good and bad, but I think it is one of my best efforts. I shall very soon be sending you a copy of my very short new fantasy called "The Flames," which is just out. It is very fantastic, but I think you will find it interesting. I have also finished another, longer, book, which is more or less a novel, about a divided personality [*A Man Divided*]. It has still to be typed and revised; and at the present rate of publishing perhaps it will appear in a couple of years. I have also another thing on the stocks, a series of reported conversations with "a mystic," "a scientist," "a Christian," and so on. A new line for me.

I hope you will be coming to England soon, as it would be very nice to discuss the subjects that interest us both, particularly psychical research. Agnes and I should be delighted to have you in our "new" home. In spite of our increased household, we can quite well accommodate you. But I am afraid that England is not much of a country to visit in this period of deepening crisis. Let us know as long as possible beforehand if you do come, as we are both very apt to be away from home.

David goes off to work every day on a local market garden, for training, under the Home Office. Mary is still doing her medical course, and has just had a good holiday on the south coast of France. Agnes is very busy being a grandmother, and at the same time a public woman, with innumerable committees.

I hope you all continue to flourish. Please give our best wishes to your wife and to Harriet and Benedicte. To yourself also, best wishes from us all.

Yours
Olaf Stapledon

26 DECEMBER 1947

Dear Marcus,

We thank you for your Christmas & New Year greetings, and the picture of your attractive new house. I wish I could drop in and see you there.

We thought of you on Christmas Day, but alas I procrastinated over my Christmas mail so badly that it became useless to send our greetings! But we do wish you all a Happy New Year, including health, success and a good measure of sheer joy. It would be nice if you could come over to England some time in 1948. We should like to have you in our formerly-new house.

I am ashamed that I never answered your letter of September. Life has been very crowded lately, and I seem to be months behind with everything. I am now looking forward with great interest to the long letter you promise about your levitation experiments. I am perpetrating two articles in Enquiry, the second of which tries to deal with the significance of the paranormal, and also makes some comments on the question of survival. I feel rather anxious about my intrusion into these fields, as I have no experience. But the editor asked for something.

I am so glad you liked *The Flames*. But I think you have too high an opinion of it, for it is really a bit of a muddle. We all enjoyed very much the pictures in the children's book you sent, and wished we could understand the Danish. However, the pictures spoke for themselves. Later, they will speak to our little grandson, but he is too young yet.

I look forward with keen interest to your anthology of Christian Mysticism—but of course, I was forgetting, it will be in Danish.

Our Christmas gathering includes our whole family and our more-or-less adopted member, the Austrian Wolfi, and also a young Indian man, Mary's friend. So we are quite an international party. We have had the usual good cheer. This is *not* a starving country yet. Also we have spent much energy carrying up drift wood for fuel, after a NW gale and spring tide.

I am at last finishing my novel about a divided personality, have recently contributed an article on Scepticism to World Review (February number), am busy preparing a lecture to give in France, after translation, and have recently become notorious in the worst section of the British press for some rash remarks about marriage. A Stockholm paper has telegraphed for an article. All this arose out of a casual lunch hour talk in Liverpool, summarizing a lecture I used to give to Army audiences.

As a very small token of belated good will I am sending you separately a King Penguin on English Book Illustration. If you have already seen it, hand it on to someone else. The pictures are rather nice, don't you think?

I expect your letter on levitation etc. will force me to revise one statement that I have made in my 2nd "Enquiry" article, namely that the evidence for telepathy and pre- and post-cognition is stronger than the evidence for other kind of paranormal phenomena. Anything that you can tell me about all these matters will be extremely helpful. I am thoroughly bewildered about the whole affair. Agnes & I are always intending to do some private experiments in telepathy, because she does sometimes seem to be a bit "spooky." But we are both so busy that our research never even begins. It is obvious that very important discoveries and new ideas are in the offing now. One possibility is that the whole of our ordinary experience is permeated by paranormal factors. For instance hypnagogic imagery. Where do those extraordinarily vivid and inconsequent things come from? It is sheer dogma to say that the sources are simply normal random associations, or Freudian influences. I have extraordinarily precise imagery when I am on the point of sleep, mostly of faces, never seen before, so far as I know; also voices. Possibly even ordinary uncontrolled reverie is also largely an expression of the paranormal. But this is sheer guess work, and quite impossible to verify.

Well, good wishes to you all from all four of us.

Yours
Olaf Stapledon

6 FEBRUARY 1948

Dear Marcus,

It was very good of you to send me Mr. Türck's extraordinarily interesting photographs. Thank you so much, and for your long and interesting letter. A few days after their arrival E. M. Forster was in this district, and we met him at the house of L. C. Martin, whom you used to know in Copenhagen. I took the opportunity of showing him and others the photos. E. M. Forster made a careful study of them, and was very interested. He formerly had some slight experience of mediumistic phenomena with G. Lowes Dickinson, author of "The Meaning of Good", etc.

Your experiences at the séances must indeed have been impressive. I wish it were possible to see the moving pictures as well as the stills, but the stills themselves are very striking. If, as you say, the possibility of any sort of trickery is completely ruled out the implication of the whole affair is quite revolutionary. Most striking is the incident of the clothes descending from the ceiling within a fortieth of a second of being on the medium. This does indeed seem to be making nonsense of time. The technique of taking the photos seems to have been very ingenious and efficient. I feel impatient to see the whole thing reported in Mr. Türck's forthcoming book. Also I am very anxious to hear the final reactions of the (British) Society for Psychical Research. They have by now become exceedingly clever at studying psychical phenomena. The current number of their Journal includes the annual report which records a depressingly large number of negative investigations. The more rigorous the research, the more impressive the cases which they finally pass as veridical. Türck's data certainly seem to the layman quite convincing, but in spite of that I feel that one should not pledge oneself absolutely to belief in them as wholly valid until they have stood the fire of public criticism, after publication of the projected book. The trouble is that those who were not themselves present at the séances cannot feel the full conviction which would be irresistible to those who were present. However, the cumulative effect of the photos and your letter is that I move at a bound from grave scepticism about "physical" paranormal phenomena to a state of cautious acceptance, coupled with bewilderment and excitement.

I will gladly send you a copy of my two articles in "Enquiry," when they appear. (They have both been sent off to the Editor.) Or perhaps I will send you a typescript, but I am afraid my carbon copy is in rather a mess. The second article deals with the paranormal; and I now feel that I have been too cautious about telekinesis. But really those two articles are written from the mere layman's point [of] view, and I doubt if you will find them at all impressive. I will also send you a copy of my "World Review" article, which is due to appear any day now. It was delayed so as to come after another man's article which it partially answers. I will also send you a typescript of my novel, "A Man Divided," since you ask for it. But I warn you, it is not anything but a rather fantastic psychological study. The book about a Christian, a Scientist, and so on is still only in its early stages. The novel, too, is not yet quite finished.

I hope that Harriet's baby is putting on weight now, and is quite strong. It is very worrying when babies don't do as expected. Our small grandson is very vigorous always, and often very amusing. We are all well, and at present Agnes and I are much occupied with arrangements for going to France in a little over a week. The currency regulations are causing all sorts of unexpected troubles. You, by the way, seem to have outclassed me completely as a grandparent. Congratulations both to Benedicte and to Harriet!

I am very much hoping that you will find time and energy to get on with your book on mysticism. You must not let your many other activities prevent you from doing that. Original and balanced work on that subject is so important.

Best wishes to you all!

Yours ever
Olaf Stapledon

Letter to Fay Pomerance

During the last four years of his life Stapledon maintained a correspondence with the visionary painter Fay Pomerance of Sheffield. He saw an exhibit of her cycle of Lucifer paintings at the Present Question conference at Exeter University in the summer of 1946. His first letter to her compared her visual with his verbal art and led him to reflect on the nature and limitations of his own imagination.

23 DECEMBER 1946

Dear Fay Pomerance,

Your very interesting letter has been waiting a long time to be answered, and you must be wondering whether it ever reached me. Letters like that deserve more than a tossed-off answer, and I have been too busy lately to write serious letters. But at last I have a chance of thanking you for writing it, and of making a few comments.

First let me say that since Exeter I have often thought of your pictures and your poetic description of them, and it was a great pleasure to hear from you, and to be told that you liked my "Death into Life." I wonder what you mean exactly by saying that your absorption in it "had been swept through by a feeling of personally experiencing and responding to it outside the limits of my personal self." Does this mean simply that the impact of the universe on you is in some ways similar to the impact of the universe on me, as I symbolize it in my book? Or does it mean something more?

I think your Lucifer myth is a magnificent theme, and your pictures express it with power. It seemed queer to me that such formidable things should come from so charming an artist. I look forward to seeing them again, together with the three that you have done since Exeter. Sometime I shall probably have an engagement in your district, and then I shall write and ask you if I may come and see them.

You say, "Unless I am willing to die for my creations, they are not going to live for me." True, indeed. It is necessary to add that one may be consciously and superficially willing and yet not deeply and whole-heartedly willing; and also, that even if one *is* deeply willing, even so the creations may not live. One may not, after all, have the power. That is the tragedy of the sincere artist who nevertheless fails. Sometimes, looking back on my own work, I feel I had the power of conception but not adequately the power of execution.

It is wonderful that you can live your domestic and your artistic lives both so fully. Of course some such two-sidedness is absolutely necessary in some degree. Art (of any sort) must feed through its roots in concrete life. And the more cosmical or universal its theme, the more of that concrete food it needs if it is to avoid being lost in abstraction. In my book [*Death into Life*] the Interludes symbolize the roots.

Your visions, described in your letter, are very striking, and they should give you much rich material for artistic creation. The one that you had before D-Day is particularly interesting, and I hope you will make some pictures of it. Visions, in your sense, do not come to me. I have to imagine everything laboriously, and criticize it step by step. These two powers, creative imagination and critical intelligence, are always opposed to one another; and yet it is only in their clash that great art or great intellectual achievement can occur, and only when they are well balanced. And in religion the same is true. There must be the felt creative vision of the spirit, and also a rigorous critical pruning away of all that is inessential or unsure. And what is left (*I* think) is a passionate and unshakable conviction about the excellence of the spirit, as we experience it in our concrete dealings with each other; and strict agnosticism about the underlying nature of the cosmos.

You are certainly not being presumptuous in feeling that your feeling for my creative themes is "not without a finger-touching, at least, of feeling and purpose." All the same, I am not quite sure what you mean. Do you mean that in our different ways we are trying to do much the same thing? If so, I agree. Our ways are very different, but the aim is in some ways much the same.

I should like you to read my "Last and First Men." If I had a copy to spare I would give you one, but all I can do is to lend you one, if you have not already secured one from elsewhere. Let me know. I think my "Star Maker" is a deeper but also a heavier book. You might like to read that some time. Of course it is out of print now, like most books. Again, I could lend you a copy some time.

I find that this game of creating myths and symbols, in whatever medium, is in a way rather frightening. One gets completely absorbed, and rides triumphantly on the irresistible wave of imagination; and then when the thing is finished one wonders whether one was at all inspired or merely rather mad; and again, whether, although to oneself it may seem magnificent, to others it may seem just silly. And sometimes one looks back on things done years earlier and sees so clearly the difference between the parts that are "inspired" and those that are not. I hope that when you look back, in years to come, you will see that mostly you really were inspired.

Hoping to see you again, and your pictures, and meanwhile wishing you all that is best for Christmas and the New Year,

Yours sincerely,
Olaf Stapledon

Letter to Gwyneth Alban-Davis

Stapledon had met Gwyneth Alban-Davis, a young painter, at Langdale in the Lake District where he often lectured. They had a short correspondence in 1950, focused largely on religious questions, interrupted by his lecture-tour to France. This was the last letter Stapledon wrote, the day before his death.

5 SEPTEMBER 1950

Dear Gwyneth,

Thank you for your letter written on 20th August, which was waiting for me when I got back from France. I agree with most of it, particularly what you said about art and the "bright dark." But there is one point that I feel I want to comment on, namely your remarks about the need for some sort of organized religion. Organized Christianity was formerly very much of a force for good in the world, and even today it probably helps a lot of people. But on the whole it seems to me to be much more dead than alive today, and to be doing on the whole more harm than good. It does harm in two ways, (1) by being generally a reactionary force in politics, specially in the case of Roman Catholicism, and (2) by giving people the illusion that what matters in religion is belief and ritual worship rather than a certain kind of awareness of reality, and a certain kind of response to it in action. (Oh dear! That is practically unintelligible. Sorry!) Anyhow, in my view, even if some sort of organized religion *is* needed, the existing organizations are mainly useless. Incidentally, the Communist Party is probably the nearest approach to a live organized religion today, but it too is rapidly losing the real (though topsy-turvy) religious drive that it once had.

But granted that some people do greatly need an organized religion, and that we should all be much better if there was an adequate one that we could sincerely join, it still remains a fact that real live religion is much more fundamental than any organized system of doctrines and institutions. And the most genuinely religious people at any time are very apt to be either simply not members of any contemporary Church, or members with their tongues perpetually in their cheeks, or interpreting the doctrines poetically instead of literally. These are the people who may become founders of new religious orders or sects or Churches. But very soon after the new organization has found its feet it loses its soul. That, surely, is what has happened to the whole lot of new religious movements, including even the Quakers, who in their prime really were a religious body with a live "soul."

I conclude that if one feels a real need for a religious organization, there's nothing for it but to use an existing one, unsatisfactory as they all are; but that some of us find it much better to keep out. I don't deny for a moment that religion is essentially *communal*. "Salvation" and "worship" are not really for the lone individual but for the group. And so, of course some minimum of organization is desirable. But it is desperately dangerous. And in a transitional time like ours, people who are really sensitive to the need for religion simply won't find a group anywhere. The real religious community today is not any Church but a widespread "peppering" of bewildered groping people in all sorts of odd places, inside & outside the existing religious groups, and inside or outside all sorts of other groups, political, cultural, vocational.

You challenge me to say what I mean by "real religion." The nearest I can get to it in a few words is this. It is an attitude of the *whole* person to the *whole* of the universe in so far as he experiences it; and it is a consequent pattern of behaviour which he feels bound to *try* to put in practice in relation to his universe. Or perhaps it is a vague but deep sense of unity with the whole of things, on the deepest (or highest) level of one's being; and a consequent line of action always in support of the forces making for more and more unity, hence the importance of love, human brotherhood, and again of the unified and sane mind.

Oh how badly put!

Little did I suppose, before I went to Langdale last time, that I should be carrying on a correspondence with Gwyneth on religion! You certainly brought it on yourself by being a stimulating person.

In France we had a week of hard work and a week of holiday, seeing the sights, talking French, eating French fare, and drinking French wine. Very pleasant. We did not go to Jugoslavia.

Love, in which Agnes joins,
Olaf

P.S. In the West we are all too apt to assume that Christianity is the only real religion, or is the best of the religions. A French friend gave me a book based on Eastern ideas. Some of them make our ideas of religion seem rather crude.

Poems

The Builder

Printed in The Old Abbotsholmian *in 1912, this was Stapledon's first published poem, probably based on his fantasies about the architect who designed either the Sphinx or Cheops's pyramid, both of which he visited in the Spring of 1912.*

Slowly he came to the iron door,
  And there laid down
  His hard-won crown,
His knowledge, and all his worldly store.

Then, with his hand on the bolt he turned,
  And saw far back
  His crooked, strange track,
And multitude eyes that against him burned.

'Twas but his people, his tool outworn,
  And gaunt all round
  The grey stone frowned,
The great world wonder his brain had born.

Firm was his hand as the bolt he drew,
  But what blank fright,
  At what fell sight,
Leapt in his face as he staggered through?

Poems from *Latter-Day Psalms*

Appearing just before Christmas, 1914, Latter-Day Psalms *was Stapledon's first book. The poems combined theological inquiry with commentary on working-class Liverpool, which the author had observed at first hand as a resident social worker at Liverpool University Settlement. The book was not a success, although it included some of the earliest formulations of characteristically Stapledonian motifs: the stellar vision; human and planetary mortality; the indifference of the cosmos (and of the Christian God) to human suffering. In the 1920s, when Stapledon wanted to collect all his poems he thought worth saving, he kept only a few from* Latter-Day Psalms; *most of those he also revised to make their diction less musty. The first three poems from* Latter-Day Psalms *that appear in this* Reader *are printed as they appeared in 1914. The last two are printed with the 1914 version from* Latter-Day Psalms *first and the unpublished 1924 revision (from the manuscript* Verse by WOS *in the Stapledon Archive) following.*

Men

Behold the sons of men, who sin, whose hearts are divine!
In selfishness they heap up misery upon one another; yet for love
    they die.
They are blown hither and thither like the dead leaves; yet for love
    they are steadfast.
They trample on their kindred for a little bread; yet for a vision they
    forget themselves.
Scatter gold among them, and they fall upon one another in lust.
Show them God, and behold them sons of God.
I went into the city to be with men, and to learn their hearts.
I met them in the streets and in the public places, and the Spirit
    greeted me through their eyes, even from behind their hardness of
    heart.
I was with them in their homes, and their hearts opened to me like
    roses, so that I am filled with the fragrance that is in men's hearts.

Time

Wherefore hast thou made the world that it shall die, and the heavens
    that they shall burn out like a flame?
What wilt thou do when the stars are all extinguished, and there is no
    place for life?

The sons of men have builded for themselves a house of beauty. It is
continually embellished.

The last of the generations shall dwell therein and die; and the beauty
that was builded shall be no more.

A lover and his beloved have met together in the evening. Evening
shall return, but they return not.

The home that seemed eternal is broken up and scattered. The
children remember it; they die; it is no more.

I am heavy of heart because of fleeting time, and because all things
come to nought.

Spirit

But behold, the heavens around me were very beautiful. The
multitude of stars smiled upon me.

The lights of the city trembled beneath me as it were in sorrow; and
her murmur was music.

Peace came upon me, and exaltation; and I marvelled that I should be
exalted.

I was as though some spirit within me had certain knowledge of God,
declaring, "He is gentle. He is merciful."

But I looked upon the city, and rejected comfort, saying, "Nay, thou
foolish imagination."

But the spirit would not be put down. It gloried within me.

And I saw that the spirit was excellent beyond all that I called good,
and merciful beyond my mercy.

And I was amazed, and said, "Surely thou only art God who dwellest
in my heart. And thou rulest the stars."

Omnipotence [1914]

I went into an open place under the stars. The city lay beneath me,
and her sound was subdued.
I saw that the hosts of heaven perform that which was ordained in
the beginning. The city was ordained in the beginning also.
I looked into the far place beyond the stars. I hearkened to a little
wind of the earth whispering among the grasses.
And a great fear fell upon me out of the heavens, because of the
majesty of God.
I said, "How shall I call thee just or unjust? Thou art mighty, and I
am very small.
I am weary of myself because I am so small. I am contemptible in my
own eyes because thou hast ordained what I must will.
Wherefore has thou sickened this thy little earth with a fever of life?
Wherefore hast thou made the swarms of men to fret upon her?
Thou hast made the heavens for thy plaything. Thou breakest the
heart of man like a toy."
My spirit was dried up within me. I sat without meditation.

Omnipotence [1924]

I went into an open place under the stars.
The city lay beneath me, asleep.
I saw the hosts of heaven perform the thing they must;
the city also lived as was ordained.
I looked out beyond the stars;
I listened to the airs whispering among the grasses.
Fear fell on me out of heaven,
and hate of the Tyrant.
How shall I call him just or unjust?
He is great; I am small.
I am tired of myself because I am so weak, because he
has fixed what I must will.
Wherefore has he sickened this little earth
with life?
Wherefore has he made the swarms of men
fret upon her?
The heavens are his plaything,
and the heart of man he breaks like a toy.

The Rebel [1914]

Thus spake the oppressed:
What have I to do with God? What has God done for me?
He thrust me into the world hungry, and I could get no food.
He made others to surfeit, that my mouth might water.
He made me to desire pleasure and shun pain, and overwhelmed me
    with heavy toil and grief.
He made me to love, and to hunger for love; but what home for love
    have I?
He made me to guess that there is beauty, and set his favoured ones
    to proclaim beauty lest I should forget.
But the door of his heaven he fixed ajar, that I might hear and not
    enter.
And ye speak to me of worship and the joy of sacrifice! Wherefore
    should I sacrifice to you and to your tyrant God?
Mighty is your God, for he made the stars and enslaved the peoples.
    Loving he is not, for he made me.

The Rebel [1924]

What have I to do with God?
What has God done for me?
He made me hungry,
and gave me no food.
He made me desire pleasure and shun pain;
pain I have,
pleasure I dream only.
He made me hungry for love;
but what home for love have I?
He made me guess that there is beauty;
and his favourites talk to me about it
But the door of this heaven he has fixed ajar,
that I may hear and not enter.
Do you speak to me of worship and of service?
Why should I serve you and your God?
Strong your God is,
for he made the stars, and men his slaves.
Loving he is not:
he made me.

Resignation

In his handwritten manuscript Verse by WOS *Stapledon dated this poem to 1924, a year when his wife Agnes had surgery for painful complications following the birth of their son. Reflecting on the cosmic purpose of human suffering became a hallmark of his mature philosophical writing and fiction, most famously in a question posed when humanity is extinguished at the end of* Last and First Men: *"Is the beauty of the Whole really enhanced by our agony?" Many of Stapledon's works refer explicitly to his marriage. Here the poet's acceptance of pain as inseparable from the beauty of the stars — the absorption of Agnes Stapledon's cry into the music of the spheres — is particularly chilling.*

> Even in my love's agony
> let me not forget
> how fairly to the horizon go
> stars on a cold night.
>
> For even my love's cry of pain,—
> that gash in heaven's face,—
> I must salute as a true tone
> in the music of the spheres.
>
> God! But this cannot be.
> And yet it must;
> for the world where beauty is
> cannot be accurst.

Our Shame

Also found in Verse by WOS *and dated 1 January 1925, this poem takes up the fear of aging and senility. Stapledon was nearly forty years old, and the poem can be compared with the account of the cult of the Divine Boy in "The Fall of the First Men," a chapter in* Last and First Men.

Old age!
Inevitable, yet unforgivable sin,
more treasonous than any other
addiction to poison.
That we should let our bodies wither
may well be pardoned,
since flesh was ever intractable to spirit.
But that we should tolerate the desiccation of our minds!
That we should cowardly lose touch with this young universe,
and cozen ourselves with shadows!
Terrifying is the first gray hair
encountered on the morning after love's night;
but more shocking, because reproachful,
is the first withered thought,
when, in the very act of adventuring youngly,
we bleakly discover, to our shame,
that the thought which we were tricking out with laughters,
and with youth's weapons and fanfares,
was inwardly an old, rheumatic, and rest-seeking thought,
flushed not with life,
but with the reflection of our life's sunset.
Then, by the dumb scream of our dying youth,
we know that we are old,
that we shall permit this treason increasingly,
and unwittingly,
till the whole army of our ideas
(which we must command but as lieutenants
of the eternally young
Boy-conqueror)
becomes an army of ghosts,
a draft of chivvied winter leaves,
a whispering hindrance
blown blindingly in the faces of the advancing host,
then trampled.

Poems from *Metaphysical Posters*

Until he was past the age of forty Stapledon's literary goal was to be a poet. His last major effort to satisfy that ambition was a sequence of philosophical and scientific poems written in the mid-1920s and titled, first, Astronomical Posters. *He completed twenty-three poems, mainly about the human relation to the galactic immensities, and had them typed while he began a "second volley," focused largely on submicroscopic reality. At that point he altered the title of the entire body of poems to* Metaphysical Posters *in two parts: the First Volley, Astronomical and The Nether World. But the second volley was never completed or typed; although the project contained Stapledon's most interesting experiments in poetic form he concluded that the entire enterprise was "a failure." These poems also provide the clearest forecast among his early work of the fantastic imagination for which he finally found an appropriate literary form in* Last and First Men *and* Star Maker. *He recycled a few of the poems, lightly revised, from the First Volley into his 1932 novel* Last Men in London, *but with a few isolated exceptions his career as a poet came to an end with the abandonment of* Metaphysical Posters. *Naomi Mitchison, who read through his poems in the early 1930s and unsuccessfully encouraged him to continue to search for an authentic poetic voice, considered Poem 15 his best work.*

Poem 2 from *First Volley: Astronomical*

Children suppose that chairs and tables
are an audience to their play;
and we, children always,
must still pretend
that the stars
care.
And yet we know them globes of gas,
immense and fervid,
but vapid.

We call them fixed,
and ancient.
And yet they fly like dust on the wind;
and each in its phases
is a cloud changing,

and like a man must end.
Not always was the heaven this wide
fire-pricked void.
Once was a closer, glimmering darkness,
whence the stars
crystallised.
In that beginning the sun was not,
life was not spawned,
nor anywhere
looked mind.

Nor Russell, Wells, nor Freud, nor Bernard Shaw
gospelled as yet through dark suburbia.

Poem 15 from *First Volley, Astronomical*

If man encounter
on his proud adventure
other intelligence?

If mind more able,
ranging among the galaxies,
noose this colt and break him
to be a beast of draught and burden
for ends beyond him?
If man's aim and his passion be ludicrous,
and the flight of Pegasus
but a mulish caper?

Dobbin! Pull your weight!
Better be the donkey of the Lord,
whacked on beauty's errand,
than the wild ass of the desert
without destination.

Vision! From star to star the human donkey
transports God's old street organ and his monkey.

Poem 17 from *First Volley, Astronomical*

If God has not noticed us?
He is so occupied
with the crowded cycle of nature.

The sea's breath,
by drenching the hills
and descending along the meadow brooklets
(whose backwaters
are playgrounds of busy insect populations),
returns seaward
to rise again.

Water beetles
skating on the stagnant skin of a backwater,
we get rumour of Oceanus,
of storm-driven worlds and island universes.
And we would annex them!
We would dignify the fiery currents of the Cosmos
by spawning in them!
But the minnow, death, he snaps us;
and presently some inconsiderable spate
will scour the cranny clean of us.

And long after man the stars
will continually evaporate in radiant energy
to recondense as nebulae
and again stars,
till here and there some new planet
will harbour again insect populations.

Poem 1 from *The Nether Worlds*

The world of breakfast, sixpences, and artificial silk,
of plans, and itch, and daily kindness and duty,
seems vast and safe,
seems all.

But minds are fledglings in a cliff-ledge nest,
Peering at last from our little circle of security,
we glimpse vertiginously, below us and above,
the steep drop and leap of the rock,—
down,
up,
to foreign worlds;
down, even to the mindless and dangerous turmoil of matter
(oceanic breakers thundering at the base),
up, even to the clifftop,
and to the wide, blank
heaven,
whence the rain comes,
and the sun,
and the raiding
hawk.

From spying over the nest's rim,
the nestling (deserted?),
sun-stricken, wind-ridden, bewildered,
by nether worlds visually wounded,
cowers back within the twittering circle
of things human.
Outraged by uncouth contacts,
the snail mind, with eyes retracting,
subsides within his brittle whorl.

Paradox

The last poem Stapledon ever published appeared in 1940 in John Middleton Murry's journal Adelphi. *It is a more sophisticated exercise in the "agnostic piety" that characterized his poetry from* Latter-Day Psalms *forward, and anticipates the difficult spiritual meditations of his final, posthumous book* The Opening of the Eyes.

> In despair I cry out for you,
> but there is no answer.
> My voice moves only the molecules of the air,
> and is lost.
>
> Nowhere among all the atoms of the universe
> is there anywhere that you might be.
> You are impossible: we have disproved you.
> You are the faded memory of a delusion:
> a projection, we say, of filial obeisance,
> or of tribal solidarity.
>
> Yet when I am in action, when choices are to be made,
> suddenly you confront me:
> you point the way.
>
> The theories that shielded my sight from you
> are torn off.
> You stand before me,
> pointing the way.
> There is no escape.

Recommended Reading

Selected Primary Bibliography

THIS IS A REPRESENTATIVE, but not complete, list of Stapledon's published work. Classification of Stapledon's work is not always easy or obvious, since many of his writings blur the boundaries between genres. In this list works have been sorted into the categories used in the *Reader*, with writings primarily political and philosophical included under the heading *Essays and Talks*. Texts that appear in whole or in part in this *Reader* are preceded by an asterisk (*). For a very full record of Stapledon's publications, including translations and posthumous editions, see Harvey J. Satty and Curtis C. Smith, *Olaf Stapledon: A Bibliography* (Westport, Conn.: Greenwood, 1984). A few published works, discovered since the Satty-Smith bibliography appeared, are designated with a plus sign (+) in the following list.

Fiction

+ "The Seed and the Flower." *Friends' Quarterly Examiner* 50 (October 1916): 464–75.
**Last and First Men: A Story of the Near and Far Future.* London: Methuen, 1930.
**Last Men in London.* London: Methuen, 1932.
Odd John: A Story Between Jest and Earnest. London: Methuen, 1935.
"A World of Sound." In *Hotch-Potch,* edited by John Brophy, 243–51. Liverpool: Council of the Royal Liverpool Children's Hospital, 1936.
**Star Maker.* London: Methuen, 1937.
**Darkness and the Light.* London: Methuen, 1942.
**Old Man in New World.* London: Allen and Unwin [P.E.N. Books], 1944.
**Sirius: A Fantasy of Love and Discord.* London: Secker and Warburg, 1944.
**Death into Life.* London: Methuen, 1946.
**The Flames: A Fantasy.* London: Secker and Warburg, 1947.
A Man Divided. London: Methuen, 1950.
**Far Future Calling: Uncollected Science Fiction and Fantasies of Olaf Stapledon.* Edited by Sam Moskowitz. Philadelphia: Oswald Train, 1979. [Fiction includes "The Man Who Became a Tree," "A Modern Magician," "East Is West," "Arms Out of Hand," "A World of Sound." Also Stapledon's

unproduced radio script "Far Future Calling," based on *Last and First Men*.]

Nebula Maker & *Four Encounters*, introductions by Arthur C. Clarke and Brian W. Aldiss. New York: Dodd, Mead, 1983.

*"The Peak and the Town." In *Olaf Stapledon: A Bibliography*, edited by Harvey J. Satty and Curtis C. Smith, xxvii-xxxviii. Westport, Conn.: Greenwood, 1984.

Essays and Talks

*"The Splendid Race." *The Old Abbotsholmian* 2, no. 8 (1908): 212–16.

"The People, Self Educator." *The Old Abbotsholmian* 3, no. 1 (1913): 203–7.

+"Poetry and the Worker." *The Highway* 6 (Oct. 1913): 4–6.

+"Poetry and the Worker: Wordsworth." *The Highway* 6 (Dec. 1913): 51–53.

+"Poetry and the Worker—Tennyson." *The Highway* 6 (Feb. 1914): 87–89.

+"Poetry and the Worker—Browning." *The Highway* 6 (Apr. 1914): 125–27.

+"Poetry and the Worker—Shakespeare." *The Highway* 7 (Jan. 1915): 56–58.

"Problem of Universals." *Monist* 34 (Oct. 1924): 574–98.

"Mr. Bertrand Russell's Ethical Beliefs." *International Journal of Ethics* 37 (July 1927): 390–402.

"The Location of Physical Objects." *Journal of Philosophical Studies* 4 (Jan. 1929): 64–75.

A Modern Theory of Ethics: A Study of the Relations of Ethics and Psychology. London: Methuen, 1929.

*"The Remaking of Man." *The Listener*, 8 April 1931, 575–76.

"Problems and Solutions, or the Future." In *An Outline for Boys and Girls and Their Parents*, edited by Naomi Mitchison, 691–749. London: Gollancz, 1932.

Waking World. London: Methuen, 1934.

"Education and World Citizenship." In *Manifesto: Being the Book of the Federation of Progressive Societies and Individuals*, edited by C.E.M. Joad, 142–63. London: Allen and Unwin, 1934.

"Mr. Wells Calls in the Martians" [review of *Star-Begotten*]. *London Mercury* 36 (July 1937): 295–96.

*Untitled ["On Cultural Diversity"], Personal View column. *Manchester Evening News*, 20 August 1937, 8.

"Science, Art and Society." *London Mercury* 38 (Oct. 1938): 521–28.

"But To-Day the Struggle." Review of *Studies in a Dying Culture*, by Christopher Caudwell. *London Mercury* 39 (Jan. 1939): 348–49.

Philosophy and Living. 2 vols. Harmondsworth, Eng.: Penguin, 1939.

Saints and Revolutionaries [*I Believe*, No. 10]. London: Heinemann, 1939.

New Hope for Britain. London: Methuen, 1939.

"Writers and Politics." *Scrutiny* 8 (Sept. 1939): 151–56.

*"Escapism in Literature." *Scrutiny* 8 (Dec. 1939): 298–308.

"Federalism and Socialism." In *Federal Union: A Symposium*, edited by M. Chaning-Pearce, 115–29. London: Jonathan Cape, 1940.

"Tradition and Innovation To-Day." *Scrutiny* 9 (June 1940), 33–45.

Beyond the "Isms" [Searchlight Books No. 16]. London: Secker and Warburg, 1942.
*"Literature and the Unity of Man." In *Writers in Freedom: A Symposium*, edited by Hermon Ould, 113–19. London: Hutchinson, 1942.
"Sketch-Map of Human Nature." *Philosophy* 17 (July 1942): 210–30.
*"Some Thoughts on H. G. Wells's 'You Can't Be Too Careful.' " *Plan* 9 (Aug. 1942): 1–2.
"Morality, Scepticism and Theism." *Proceedings of the Aristotelian Society*, new series, 44 (1943–44): 15–42.
"The Great Certainty." In *In Search of Faith: A Symposium*, edited by Ernest W. Martin, 37–59. London: Lindsay Drummond, 1944.
Seven Pillars of Peace. London: Common Wealth, 1944.
"What Are 'Spiritual' Values?" In *Freedom of Expression: A Symposium*, edited by Hermon Ould, 16–26. London: Hutchinson, 1945.
*"Social Implications of Atomic Power." *The Norseman* 3 (Nov.-Dec. 1945): 390–93.
"Education for Personality-in-Community." *New Era in Home and School* 27 (Mar. 1946): 63–67.
"Liberty and Discipline." *Modern Education* 1 (Apr. 1947): 109–11.
"Data for a World View: 1. The Human Situation and Natural Science." *Enquiry* 1 (Apr. 1948): 13–18.
"Data for a World View: 2. Paranormal Experiences." *Enquiry* 1 (July 1948): 13–18.
*"Interplanetary Man?" *Journal of the British Interplanetary Society* 7 (Nov. 1948): 212–33.
"Ethical Values Common to East and West" and "From England." In *Speaking of Peace*, edited by Daniel Gillmor, 119–21; 130–31. New York: National Council of the Arts, Sciences and Professions, 1949.
"The Meaning of 'Spirit.' " In *Here and Now: Miscellany No. 5*, edited by Peter Albery and Sylvia Read. 72–82. London: Falcon Press, 1950.
"A Plain Man Talks About Values." *Rider's Review* 76 (Spring 1950): 22–28.

Memoirs and Meditations

"The Novice Schoolmaster." *The Old Abbotsholmian* 3, no. 1 (1910), 14–18.
+*"The Reflections of an Ambulance Orderly." *The Friend*, 14 April 1916, 246.
"Experiences in the Friends' Ambulance Unit." In *We Did Not Fight: 1914–1918 Experiences of War Resisters*, edited by Julian Bell, 359–74. London: Cobden-Sanderson, 1935.
*"The Core." *The Windmill* 1 (July 1945): 112–17.
Youth and Tomorrow. London: St. Botolph, 1946.
The Opening of the Eyes. Edited by Agnes Z. Stapledon. London: Methuen, 1954.

Letters

*"The Letters of Olaf Stapledon and H. G. Wells, 1931–1942," edited by Robert Crossley. In *Science Fiction Dialogues*, edited by Gary Wolfe, 27–57. Chicago: Academy Chicago, 1982.

Talking Across the World: The Love Letters of Olaf Stapledon and Agnes Miller, 1913–1919. Edited by Robert Crossley. Hanover: Univ. Press of New England, 1987.

"Letters to the Future," edited by Robert Crossley. In *The Legacy of Olaf Stapledon: Critical Essays and an Unpublished Manuscript*, edited by Patrick A. McCarthy, Charles Elkins, and Martin Harry Greenberg, 99–120. New York: Greenwood, 1989.

Poems

*"The Builder." *The Old Abbotsholmian* 3, no. 11 (1912): 169.

Latter-Day Psalms. Liverpool: Henry Young, 1914.

Poets of Merseyside: An Anthology of Present-Day Liverpool Poetry. Edited by S. Fowler Wright. London: Merton Press, 1923. [Eight poems by Stapledon: "God the Artist," "Creator Creatus," "A Prophet's Tragedy," "The Good," "Revolt Against Death," "The Unknown," "Futility," "The Relativity of Beauty," 93–100.]

Voices on the Wind, Second Series. Edited by S. Fowler Wright. London: Merton Press, 1924. [Five poems by Stapledon: "Pain," "Swallows at Maffrécourt," "Moriturus," "A Prophet's Tragedy," "God the Artist," 165–67].

"Two Chinese Poems." *Poetry of To-Day: A Quarterly Extra of the Poetry Review*, no. 3 (Winter 1925): 18.

"Star Worship." *Poetry and the Play* 9 (July-Sept. 1926): 527.

"Be Absolute." *Adelphi* 15 (Sept. 1939): 571.

*"Paradox." *Adelphi* 16 (Mar. 1940): 247.

Selected Secondary Bibliography

AMONG THE CRITICAL STUDIES of Stapledon of the last twenty-five years, the following are particularly useful:

Aldiss, Brian W. "The Immanent Will Returns—2." In *The Detached Retina: Aspects of SF and Fantasy*, 37–43. Liverpool: Liverpool Univ. Press; Syracuse: Syracuse Univ. Press, 1995.

Aldiss, Brian W. with David Wingrove. *Trillion Year Spree: The History of Science Fiction*, 194–99. New York: Atheneum, 1986.

Bailey, K. V. "A Prized Harmony: Myth, Symbol and Dialectic in the Novels of Olaf Stapledon." *Foundation* 15 (Jan. 1979): 53–66.

———. "Time Scales and Culture Cycles in Olaf Stapledon." *Foundation* 46 (Autumn 1989): 27–39.

Clark, Stephen R. L. "Olaf Stapledon (1886–1950)." *Interdisciplinary Science Reviews* 18 (Spring 1993): 112–19.

Crossley, Robert. "Censorship, Disguise, and Transfiguration: The Making and Revising of Stapledon's *Sirius*." *Science-Fiction Studies* 20 (Mar. 1993): 1–14.

———. "Famous Mythical Beasts: Olaf Stapledon and H. G. Wells." *The Georgia Review* 36 (Fall 1982): 619–35.

———. *Olaf Stapledon: Speaking for the Future*. Syracuse: Syracuse Univ. Press; Liverpool: Liverpool Univ. Press, 1994.

———. "Olaf Stapledon and the Idea of Science Fiction." *Modern Fiction Studies* 32 (Spring 1986): 21–42.

Elkins, Charles. "The Worlds of Olaf Stapledon: Myth or Fiction?" *Mosaic* 13 (Spring/Summer 1980): 145–52.

Fiedler, Leslie A. *Olaf Stapledon: A Man Divided*. New York: Oxford Univ. Press, 1983.

Glicksohn, Susan. "A City of Which the Stars Are Suburbs." In *SF: The Other Side of Realism*, edited by Thomas D. Clareson, 334–47. Bowling Green, Ohio: Bowling Green Univ. Popular Press, 1971.

Goodheart, Eugene. "Olaf Stapledon's *Last and First Men*." In *No Place Else: Explorations in Utopian and Dystopian Fiction*, edited by Eric S. Rabkin, Martin H. Greenberg, and Joseph D. Olander, 78–93. Carbondale: Southern Illinois Univ. Press, 1983.

Huntington, John. "Olaf Stapledon and the Novel about the Future." *Contemporary Literature* 22 (Summer 1981): 349–65.

Kinnaird, John. *Olaf Stapledon*. Mercer Island, Wash.: Starmont House, 1986.

Lem, Stanislaw. "On Stapledon's *Last and First Men*." Trans. Istvan Csicsery-Ronay. *Science-Fiction Studies* 13 (Nov. 1986): 272–91.

———. "On Stapledon's *Star Maker*." Trans. Istvan Csicsery-Ronay. *Science-Fiction Studies* 14 (Mar. 1987): 1–8.

Lessing, Doris. Afterword to *Last and First Men*, 305–7. Los Angeles: Tarcher, 1988.

McCarthy, Patrick A. "*Last and First Men* as Miltonic Epic." *Science-Fiction Studies* 11 (Nov. 1984): 244–52.

———. *Olaf Stapledon*. Boston: Twayne, 1982.

McCarthy, Patrick A., Charles Elkins, and Martin H. Greenberg, eds. *The Legacy of Olaf Stapledon: Critical Essays and an Unpublished Manuscript*. New York: Greenwood, 1989.

Mills, Peter. "Between Jest and Earnest: Representations of Superhumanism in Olaf Stapledon's *Odd John* and *Sirius*." *Social Biology and Human Affairs* 59 (1994): 63–81.

Mitchison, Naomi. *You May Well Ask: A Memoir 1920–1940*, 138–42. London: Gollancz, 1979.

Scholes, Robert. *Structural Fabulation: An Essay on Fiction of the Future*. Notre Dame, Ind.: Notre Dame Univ. Press, 1975.

Science-Fiction Studies 9 (Nov. 1982). Special issue; eight essays on Stapledon.

Shelton, Robert. "The Mars-Begotten Men of Olaf Stapledon and H. G. Wells." *Science-Fiction Studies* 11 (Mar. 1984): 1–14.

Smith, Curtis C. "Olaf Stapledon: Saint and Revolutionary." *Extrapolation* 13 (Dec. 1971): 5–15.

————. "Olaf Stapledon's Dispassionate Objectivity." In *Voices for the Future*, edited by Thomas D. Clareson, 44–63. Bowling Green, Ohio: Bowling Green Univ. Popular Press, 1976.

Stableford, Brian. *Scientific Romance in Britain, 1890–1950;* 198–216, 277–81. London: Fourth Estate, 1985.

Tremaine, Louis. "Historical Consciousness in Stapledon and Malraux." *Science-Fiction Studies* 11 (July 1984): 130–38.

————. "Olaf Stapledon's Note on Magnitude." *Extrapolation* 23 (Nov. 1982): 284–93.